MOIRAI DEFINITION

MOIRAI; /Moy-rī/ n.– Destiny

ATLANTIS MOIRAI

GOLDEN AGE SERIES; BOOK 3

DD ADAIR

Spiral Path
PRESS

Copyright © 2018 by Spiral Path Press

First Edition

Published by Spiral Path Press PO Box 1183 Divide, CO 80814.

Cover design by Susan Krupp at yuneekpix.com

Maps drawn by Dr. Jason Grundhauser.

For information about special pricing for bulk sales, please contact Spiral Path Press at ddadair2@gmail.com

ISBN: 978-1-7328055-4-5 (paperback)

ISBN: 978-1-7328055-3-8 (ebook)

ISBN: 978-1-7328055-5-2 (audiobook)

Library of Congress Control Number:

Please visit the author's website at www.ddadair.com

To Those Who Remember;

the magic we made, the sins we embraced,
the flying, the falling, the limits we pushed

Those dances of Love are calling us from
ancient glories and darkness.

It's time to come home.

⊙⊙

Bourne of lightning and fire,
One shows the way. Mark
the hour of early birth with
crimson flower.
Darkness flayed in breast of men,
given now the way to mend.
Heed the two, follow one and
light prevails before
end.

One to come and turn
the tides, clear destruction
of evil minds.
Change the course and move
our race to fearless ground
on higher plane.
Be it so on mountains high
midst scouring wind and clouds
that fly.

Courses etched among the stars,
mirrored on earth in blood and flowers.
Salvation wove as dark and light
work together, ignite

a spark of endings to begin.
Birth causes death
and in between,
triumphs of time and sadness wing
to end unholy reign.

-Atlantis Book of Prophecies: Vol. Six

FESTIVAL OF THE SUN

9,970 BCE HIGH CITY, ATLANTIS

"I worship at the temple of the skies."

— ALBERT EINSTEIN

AIELA

"*MAMA! WHY DO WE CELEBRATE THE SUN?" Aiela's six-year-old shout rang through the little cottage overlooking the sea.*

"COME HERE AND I'LL TELL YOU", Mama bellowed back. She was dusting spiced sugar on top of tiny millet cakes riddled with dried cherries.

Tomorrow's sunrise began Festival of the Sun. Papa was due home anytime and Mama was determined to present his favorite cakes to welcome him—never mind she'd already burnt one batch and the second refused to rise. "Third time's a charm!" She'd said, treating the chickens and birds to their second feast of the day.

"You don't KNOW ANYTHING!" Ahna was red-faced as she pushed past Aiela to get to Mama first.

"I do TOO!" Aiela shrieked, bare feet slapped against stone floors, determined to beat Ahna for the answer.

But they were both too eager and plowed into Mama at high speed from behind.

Smacked against the counter, Mama dropped the bowl and spoon, spilling spiced sugar across the countertop in a fragrant cloud, crushing several dainty cakes into crumbs.

Aiela's brindle dog Charl, and Ahna's wild cat Yowl, joined in the spat, fighting over the cakes that had landed on the floor, further crowding the kitchen, one hissing and swatting, the other growling and snapping.

"YOU PUSHED ME!" Ahna swung at her sister.

"YOU PUSHED ME FIRST!" Aiela smacked her hand away.

"GIRLS!" Mama scolded, separating them. "Stop it! If I hear one more word there'll be NO CAKES!" She glared fiercely at her tousled daughters, still in their night clothes though it was almost noon. "You caused me to spill the spice and smash..." she turned to check, "five of Papa's cakes!"

Aiela opened her mouth but then closed it again. She knew Mama would follow through on her threat.

"Yowl, Charl, outside!" Mama ordered, swatting away her own pet, Sila, a lavender colored snake who was dangling from the rafters flicking her tongue at the cakes that weren't ruined.

Ahna glowered with all her might, small stiff tongue poking out.

Aiela stuck hers out right back.

"Alright, stop with the tongues. Ahna first. What's the argument?"

"Aiela says the sun is a big gold eye that watches everything we do and we have to make it happy so we do celebrations for it. An' that's not true!"

"Well, why do you think we do celebrations for the sun?"

Ahna shrugged. "I d'know. But I know it's not a EYE!" She sniffed disdainfully at her sister.

"Aiela? What makes you think it's a big eye?" Mama was trying not to smile.

Aiela with her long dark hair was already a bit taller than her golden-haired sister. Her friends loved the fantastical stories she made up, and even repeated them to other people. Only Ahna ever braved arguing with her, or pointing out things that weren't true.

"What else would it be?" Aiela replied breezily. "It's round and it blinks sometimes."

"It blinks? Uh, when does it blink?"

"When there's clouds. It doesn't want us to know it blinks, probably it's scary, so it waits until there's clouds and then the sun blinks 'cuz the sunshine goes away."

"And whose eye is it exactly?"

"It's the sky's eye." Her sticky hands spread out and she shrugged as if everyone should know this already. "Also, it cries sometimes."

"The eye does?"

"Yep. When it rains. The eye cries 'cuz it's sad it can't play and all it's friends had to go to bed for a long long time and there's no other suns to play with cuz—"

"Aiela." Mama interrupted, "That's a lovely fun story and you could draw it all in pictures if you want but the sun is not actually an eye—"

"Told you!" Ahna whispered loudly.

"Ahna, be kind. The sun is a planet like this one we live on, only much much bigger. What we see and feel from here is a processing of gases in its atmosphere. These gases produce energy that warms our planet and gives off light to grow our plants."

"Do fire people live there? And dragons?" Aiela breathed in awe, imagination already headed in a new direction.

"Not that we know of..."

"Why do we celebrate it then?" Ahna returned to the original question.

Mama pushed Sila aside again and scooped spiced sugar back into the bowl, brushing smashed cakes into a pile on a plate. "We celebrate things we're very very grateful for. Things that mean a great deal to us. Like your birth day for instance. Papa and I are very grateful for you so we have a special celebration for you." She handed the plate to Ahna. "Sit at the table and lean over the plate so you don't get crumbs everywhere. Because sunlight grows and heals, we are grateful for it. Some of the Beings who helped create earth and all it's processes live there, so we're honoring them too when we celebrate the sun."

"There ARE fire people! I knew it!" Aiela spewed cake crumbs as she spoke.

"Actually, they live underneath the atmosphere that we see. It's similar to our world. They've been around way longer than us and—"

"What do they look like?" Aiela interrupted.

"Some are like us, others very different. It's an advanced society that multiple species coexist in. I expect there's everything from purple-skinned beings with lots of arms to little green beings with big eyes and antennae." She bugged out her eyes and wiggled sugar-caked pointer fingers from the top of her head. Both girls giggled at the imitation.

"We celebrate the sun people... or the sun?" Ahna liked specifics.

"Both. We're remembering who designed and cultivated our biosphere and we're grateful for everything the sun makes possible. Sun and moon celebrations also help us track our seasons—"

"Where's my three rare beauties?" A masculine voice sang out.

Both girls squealed, launching from chairs, racing to find him. Papa was home!

AIELA SWAYED in a sea of thousands to hypnotic chanting, coaxing a new day's sunrise. Standing beside Ahna, as she'd done for nineteen years, she let her mind rest in memories of this day past, and in the present glory of this moment.

> *Come children come, raise the radiant sun.*
> *Up from the dawn, drawn by our song.*

This whisper from the lips of the entire nation, joined with the swish and pull of ocean waves, turning night into day.

I miss Turner. She conjured a favorite image of him; naked on his back staring up at her. She loved how his muscles formed wings behind his ribs and his brown eyes laughed under tight, fire-sparked curls when he looked at her. His expression always held wonder, as if she had bestowed a fairytale kingdom upon him.

Ahna stopped murmuring the chant to cast her a sideways look with raised eyebrows. Her dainty, blonde twin shared such a mind-bond she sometimes saw what Aiela did. Rolling her green eyes at the distraction, she went back to watching brilliant melon colors begin to peek over the horizon.

She's right. I should be grateful to be in such majesty. Grateful for those I do have.

Festival of the Sun had begun. Celebrated at Spring Equinox, holy and revered since the birth of Lemuria, this longest-held human tradition would rolick for seven days.

Behind her, the entire grounds of Poseidon's Palace were lustrous and festive, adorned with tiny orb lights outlining each corner, curve and cleft of architecture. Solar fabric shrouded windows and doorways, still glowing golden from yesterday's charge.

Eggs of all sizes, along with the exotic seeds of many plants, were combined into a dazzling array of artistic creations. From sculptures to paintings and even furniture. A nod to the origins of springtime festivals when they paid homage to the art of sexuality, and the magic of procreation.

Far-off clouds colored the eastern sky in vivid swatches, morphing as they moved and drank up the sacred newborn sun rays. This sunrise, on Spring Equinox morn, was considered the most holy of holi-days because it honored their physical source of life.

> *Here stand stones and people together*
> *Honoring light, bridging forever.*
> *For stars we were and stars we will be.*
> *Circling through eternity.*

I miss Mama and Papa.

Ahna stopped whisper-chanting again and squeezed her hand. Bubbles of sadness rose between them, glistening as tears when they shared a sad smile.

> *Return to us now, thou most cherished orb,*
> *We reflect your great light. For by you we're reborn.*
> *Rise this new day, never the same.*
> *Nourish us well as we walk on Earth's plane.*

All who could, travelled to High City for the celebration. Every guesthouse and inn overflowed. Every home hosted relatives and friends, whether hexagonal farm houses dotting fields, orchards and vineyards far outside High City's wall, or neat, closely spaced "outer city" row houses, or elaborate tree houses in OldForest, or high rise apartment buildings in High City proper. Elaborate linen tents erected in parks, gardens, and open spaces, housed the rest. It was estimated a full third of Atlantis' population packed into High City for part, or all of Festival of the Sun.

Come children come, raise the radiant sun.
Up from the dawn, drawn by our song.

The whispered chant grew collectively louder while the sky lightened, until the air itself hummed.

From their spot at the back of the Palace courtyard, Aiela watched performers onstage prepare in a buzz of positioning. Jam-packed with string musicians and vocalists, the eastern Palace stage would lead the hymns. Elevated here, at the foot of Holy Mountain, sunrise would light them first, sweeping across Atlantis' capital, borne on tunes of eloquent praise.

Sure enough, before the last refrains of the chant ended, a blinding shaft of sunlight reached over the horizon and the stage came alive with song. It was sweet and rhythmic music, rich with harmonies. The choir onstage sang softly, so as not to drown out the delicate stringed instruments. Everyone swayed to this new beat, a sea of faces tipped skyward.

Concertos would follow sunbeams as they spread over the city, washing across all the stages, concert halls and bands of musicians in the streets, until reaching the Temple of the Sun where trumpets, flutes, saxophones and tubas would greet it with blasts of joyous symphonies.

Feasts would be served after the sunrise ceremony to break the night's fast. Each day of the week would be filled with classes and lectures, presented by the best High City had to offer—scientists, oracles, healers, artists and priests at the forefront of their respective fields. People came to learn of the newest discoveries, to take home updated tools, skills and ideas.

Aiela's stomach grumbled. She'd usually have broken her fast and had two meetings by this time.

"Back to work. We've only a few hours." Ahna left her side, edging out of the singing crowd. Aiela followed her to a deserted small kitchen inside Poseidon's Palace, where they filled a basket with winter citrus fruits, soft-boiled duck eggs and buttered millet muffins.

"To my room?"

Ahna nodded and led the way.

Aiela grabbed a bottle of cream for the rich coffee she favored these days, and followed. "You brought the books?"

"Ugh. No, I forgot." Ahna frowned. "I'll go get them. Here." She handed the food basket to Aiela and veered off towards her own room. She seemed a tad grumpy this morning.

Aiela's mind turned to preparations. Ziel would be giving talks twice a day during Festival, about the possibility that Atlantis was facing disaster. He'd tell the packed-in crowds about Oracle visions and prophecies, then ask for volunteers who wanted to colonize other continents—just like he'd been doing for several weeks, only now the audience was a hundred times broader.

It was the twins job to organize these volunteers, assign them destinations, and advise on supplies and travel. They had whole teams of people helping them to carry out these plans, but Aiela was exhausted from trying to keep up with it all.

They'd spent the entire last week researching three new areas where they could send volunteers. Browsing through anything the archives held on the land, the climate, the culture or peoples who inhabited those lands, they'd pinpointed places on maps.

Already, expeditions had left to Egypt and Scotland. Families or groups would settle into these areas and send word back on the conditions, their needs, and how many more could be accommodated. Some were going to distant kin in Greece, taking small libraries with them. An entire abbey of priests and priestesses had sent word they were relocating to the mountains of Tibet. They had their own portents and prophecies about what was coming, and intimated they would establish a spiritual school in their new lands.

Aiela would meet with representatives of other like-minded groups this afternoon, to hear and record their plans and provide any needed resources.

Ahna returned, inhaling appreciatively the scent of coffee and warm muffins. "We still don't have many architects or builders. Experienced builders, healers and farmers should be our focus this week. Let's ask Ziel to specifically mention we're in need of those."

Aiela nodded, kicking strewn clothing into a pile. "We've an abundance of educators and scientists though, and those willing to do mundane work—which is good—they'll just need a few leaders."

They worked together, folding Aiela's bed up against the wall, pulling the largest nesting table out and unfolding matching bamboo chairs to sit on either side of it, continuing to talk all the while.

"We need more translators too—human ones." Ahna said. Those were the hardest to find. Not many Atlanteans had bothered to learn other languages because they'd always had technology that did it for them. "The groups can't depend on tech to build relationships with the local inhabitants."

Stacking four muffins on a plate beside the fruit, Aiela sweetened coffee for herself, tea for Ahna. "I keep thinking... what if we're wrong? What if a disaster isn't coming for hundreds of years yet? Or never comes? We're sending all these people away from their homes—from everything they know... it could be for nothing."

Ahna had slumped on a chair, silvery blonde head resting on crossed arms. She raised her head, rubbing at her face wearily. "They're choosing it. Nobody's forcing them. What if we're right and we're not doing enough?" Her tone was rote. They'd said all this before. Both of them worried endlessly. There seemed so much to worry about.

Aiela could feel her twin's disquiet as she set steaming mugs beside the stack of ledgers and notebooks containing their notes, records and plans. "The dreams again?"

"Yes." Ahna took a deep gulp of green tea, wincing when it burned.

"They're stronger than ever. Cycling now, trading details—nothing new."

"Which one... or ones?"

"The earthquake where the ground is falling away and I'm here in the Palace and can't find you. You're just... gone—which is the worst part, because of course I won't leave without you."

"You feel like it's prophetic they've started again or—?"

Ahna was shaking her head. "Probably just an outlet for all this worry and busyness. Maybe my fears are bigger than I realize. Maybe the crystals are trying to add urgency." She shrugged. "I suppose I should go down to them. See if there's more they want to show us. It's been awhile... "

"Your colors are off. You should go to the Healing Temple, get help balancing. You've been working too much." Aiela touched her sister's wrist, feeling immediately the exhaustion, and behind that, latent fear.

"You're working just as much! We should *both* go." Ahna reached for a muffin, biting into the comforting warmth.

"It *is* fear, here, I'll—"

"No." Ahna pulled her arm away. "You're doing enough without spending more energy on me. Let's to the Temple, alright? We could skip supper tonight. It won't be as busy then."

Aiela nodded slowly, understanding the wisdom behind the rejection. "Fine. And you know what else would help?" She let her lips curve in a sly smile, not waiting for an answer. "Sex. You need to find someone. Indulge in a little healthy recreation with him." She wiggled her eyebrows. "It really does raise my energy levels... and lowers stress."

Ahna rolled her eyes but she was smiling. They'd talked about this before too. "When have I had time to get to know anyone that well?"

"It's a vital connection. What about Jai? He adores you."

"Yes, and he's sexually attracted to *men*." Ahna spread jellied rhubarb on her millet cake. "I just—"

"—still miss Carver." Aiela finished, exasperation coloring her tone. "For the sake of every goddess Ahna! You can't go on forever 'saving yourself' for him!" She got up to splash more cream in her mug.

"I'm not saving myself. I've *had* sex since Carver."

"When? With who?" Aiela stopped, turning to stare at her, disbelief plain on her face.

"The night of Winter Solstice. With the Phoenix."

"What? That doesn't make any sense. And why haven't you told me?! Are you making this up so I stop bugging you?"

"It wasn't important... and we've been a little *preoccupied* wouldn't you say?"

Aiela put a hand on her hip, continuing to glare.

Ahna sighed, but a mischievous glint crept into her eyes. "He was some friend—or relation maybe—of Jai's lover. I don't remember the exact connection... I'd had a lot of wine. He danced the Phoenix on one of the stages and when we got on a boat after midnight it just... happened." She shrugged.

Aiela waited, knowing she'd fill in more blanks.

"He was lovely—so utterly... graceful. I remember that much. I've no idea who he was really... "

"We'll ask Jai. Maybe you can find this Phoenix again." As if it was settled, Aiela got down to the business of eating, digging out pens for their planning session.

"No! I don't *want* to find him. I don't want random sex with strangers, I want—"

"—love." Aiela finished through a full mouth.

"Yes. I want love. Like you have with Turner."

ꙮ

"LOOK AT YOU THREE!" Aiela hugged Nanat and the tiny sleeping baby she cradled, then big handsome Nirka. "So much has changed... it's SO good to see you again!"

"You're like a family of golden gods." Ahna took her turn with embraces.

They were on the way into a reunion of those who'd traveled to Ireland together. Because of the festival, most of the students would be here, and many of the teachers too. It would be the first time they had seen each other since, and excitement ran high. Aiela wished again that Turner wasn't gone, sailing to pick up another crystal cargo. He would have enjoyed seeing everyone.

"What's his... or her... name?" Ahna touched the dainty hand poking out of blankets.

"Nirka, like his daddy." Nanat had matured, but she still looked at her mate the same way she had aboard the sea cruiser bound for Ireland, when she hadn't even known his name yet.

Nirka's smile was proud as he took the baby from Nanat and held him up. "He looks just like me. See?"

The tiny bald head lolled next to Nirka's blonde one. There wasn't much resemblance yet but Aiela still nodded. "He does! He's got a nose, mouth, two eyes even." When Nirka looked disappointed at her humor, she added quickly. "You're both enjoying parenthood?"

They gushed, telling every detail of the birth, how much the baby slept, ate and voided, clearly fulfilled with having a new little family.

Inside a meeting room on the Palace's public level, they all greeted Felicia and then Jai. Spotting Helena and Healer Lira across the way, Aiela made her way over, stopping as other friends and acquaintances called to her. She wondered if she'd changed as much as some of them. No longer seeming new adults, many were mated now. All of them were ensconced in apprenticeships across Atlantis.

Finally, after midday meal was served, Aiela found time to speak with Healer Lira. "You've heard of the colonization movement?"

"Only a little. I did hear you and Ahna are organizing it. You girls have come a long way in a short time! I am not surprised. " Lira's reddish brown skin was lighter after the winter moons. Her long black hair hung loose and luxurious, unlike when they were traveling and she'd always kept it bound. The rosy glow of contentment surrounded her.

"Yes well, it's been a humbling task. I remember our conversations about teaching healing in other places and wondered if you'd be interested in going?"

Lira nodded slowly. "I might be. Tell me what you have in mind."

"We don't have many Healing Teachers yet. You could of course go anywhere you're interested, but there's a place—part of the western continent Merika—that offers what we're looking for. They call is Mayra (current day area of Nevada and Colorado). Sparsely populated with first and second epoch Lemurian, and even Atlantean descendants. Our own people really, just a couple epochs apart.

"Ahna and I both thought of you for leading the expedition there. If you lead it, you'd pick and oversee your team or new community, so to speak. We can supply you with people, but ultimately they follow you. We put you in contact with the transportation team, the supplies and resources people. The leader determines the timeline, though we do encourage haste for two reasons: we don't know how soon disaster might strike, and we're finding it's better to leave little time for people changing their mind."

Lira's brown eyes lit with interest. "I'll start researching Mayra. I am drawn, still, to establishing a school or schools on other continents, but I don't know that I'm interested in *leading* a group. I'm more comfortable focusing on healing and teaching. My mate is a weapons specialist in the military, so I'll need to have some conversations with him."

They talked until the others had moved on to other Festival activities. Ahna joined them, and Lira agreed to meet them at Temple later that evening. "I will give you both a healing session. It should be pretty empty during supper. We can talk more then."

BY SUPPERTIME THE NEXT EVENING, Aiela and Ahna had recorded triple the number of people willing to leave Atlantis. Ahna yawned, pouring a light soup into mugs on the table, while Aiela gathered dirty clothing out of the way.

"Ziel's only held three lectures so far! At this rate, we'll have a tenth of the population involved by Festival end!" The enthusiasm of so many volunteers had breathed new life into their project. She'd hardly thought of Turner at all.

"I'm shocked how many people have received their own warnings." Ahna said, pulling ledgers and knowledge crystals from her pack so they could compare and compile. "Did you notice they're using the word 'evacuation'? It seems surreal. But that *is* what we're doing. Evacuating."

Aiela nodded. "I notice quite a few of those going, have ties to Lemuria. It's almost like their beliefs are stronger that Atlantis really is facing a crisis." She paused to dig out her own record books. "Does it seem like we've become recorders and advisors more than organizers? Everybody I've talked to already has a plan and is putting together their own communities."

Ahna smiled. "Picking their own places too! No more spending weeks researching and trying to guess where might be best. They've thought of things we haven't." She looked like a burden had been lifted. "This morning I met with a group leader planning relocation to the Yucatan. He's taking almost his entire village, and their conrectus to help with building and farming. Even some warriors for protection. I'd just assumed our people will be welcomed because they bring methods and tools and healing to improve the lives of those they encounter, but this man explained that our people could easily be enslaved."

"How quickly we've forgotten the lesson of the islanders in Ireland." Aiela said wryly. "You'll never guess who I talked to today!"

Ahna was busy eating her soup, and shrugged.

"Zan! From home! My old 'still-life tutor'—except now I realize he isn't really that old... "

"You saw Zan? How is he?"

"He caught me up on happenings at home. Auntie Sage sends her love and will come visit once all this 'festival hubbub' is over." They both giggled. Auntie Sage avoided hordes of people if she could. "He's going with a group to the Pyrenees. They have plans to build a temple and educate people on spirituality, the beginnings of humanity, Source and all that. I guess it's an especially wild and ignorant place. They feel called to bring light there—had already planned a long-term mission. It's just amazing isn't it? We had no idea so many were already feeling the need to move out for different reasons! Zan's taking builders and tools and books of sacred teachings. They leave in two days!"

"Huh. Is anyone else we know going?"

"Nate and his whole family, Mira, a few growers and weavers." Aiela named several of their childhood friends, growing nostalgic as she and Ahna shared memories. "Most of the mission group is from the temple where Zan trained—"

"Oh!" Ahna interrupted her, " Before I forget... Ziel wants us to spend tomorrow morning at the Hall of Records. The Alexandria ship sails with the next tide, so they need to load the crates."

They'd spent two days with the Keepers of the Records, selecting precious items and complete histories to contribute to the world Library in Alexandria.

"He wants us to do a sweep of the restricted sections. He's made a list—things he thinks should go just for the sake of preservation—and look," she dangled a ring of keys encoded with crystals, "he gave me his *most secret* keys!"

Aiela's eyebrows shot up. Forgetting her protests, or that she'd already scheduled a morning of meetings, she reached for the keys. "He *would* give these to us when there isn't time to properly snoop!"

"We could skip the evening service tonight..." Ahna lowered her voice conspiratorially and raised an eyebrow.

Sunset services, held every evening during Festival, were as beautiful and varied as the sunsets themselves. Storytellers held the crowds spellbound, making them laugh and cry in turn. Of course there was music and dancing too.

In no way would it compare to this chance to delve into the underground chambers of the Hall of Records where so few were admitted.

"I'm just not sure the Keepers will let us in."

"We have the *most secret* keys..." Aiela replied, with growing excitement, "...and direct orders from Ruler Ziel! What else do we need?"

2

CAPTURED

9,970 BCE SOUTH AMERICAN COASTLINE

"Insight is not a lightbulb that goes off inside our heads.
It is a flickering candle that can easily be snuffed out."

— MALCOLM GLADWELL, BLINK: THE POWER OF
THINKING WITHOUT THINKING

TURNER

"**B**ut it's the dark o' the moon t'night... " Turner's self-doubt bothered him. He was supposed to be confident in making decisions. Yet he trusted the experienced crew more, men who'd sailed their entire lives.

"Aye." His first mate frowned. "Tis oon'y auld wives tales, that. We're needin' fresh water worse'n g'luck."

Turner squinted into a setting sun, not yet dropped behind the land they approached. It was true. They were out of fresh water and it was his fault. He'd neglected to appoint sailors to the refilling. Everybody thought somebody else was attending to it. Still, they could anchor somewhere up or down this coast, find fresh water and fill the barrels before meeting the Belials. It would delay them a day or two, just until moonrise began.

Aiela's voice played over and over in his head.

"OF COURSE *we're staying in tonight. It's a new moon silly."*

"What exactly does that mean t' ya?" He'd inquired.

Her look indicated he'd asked a toddler question like "Why do we need to bathe?" or "What direction does the sun rise in?" He disliked when she looked at him like that. "Yer doin' it again." He'd reminded. "The look..."

She immediately rearranged her face. "Sorry. Umm, let's see... we don't buy or sell, make decisions, work with anything potentially dangerous, have performances or spend time in groups when the nightside of life is strongest... during new moon."

"The nightside o' life...?"

At his blank look she fumbled to explain further. "Dark things. Spirits and thought forms and wandering evils looking for ways to gain power."

"Ah sure..." He was still confused. He didn't think Atlantis believed in these sort of things. "An' where do these wanderin' evils come from?"

She smiled. "Humans mostly. Our thoughtforms. Extreme fear or rage or unjust violence. Addictions for instance; they create an opening and pretty soon the addiction itself becomes... an entity. Pretty much any prolonged, low, or negative energy outputs can take on a life of their own. Of course there's the spirits of dead people that sometimes get stuck here. There are also entities intentionally created or summoned by those of the nightside. Really, it's all balance of course. Nothing to be scared of. We have light, we have darkness—and the ability to create more of either." She shrugged. "Better to not tempt the darkness. It only affects us when we act in negative ways... when we join it. Otherwise, we're not subject to its power."

"Sure an' the darkness has free-er reign during the dark o' the moon. Huh." He'd thought those who believed such things back home in Ireland were just superstitious. Maybe there was basis for their beliefs after all.

"Don't your farmers plant, prune and harvest according to the moon phases?" Aiela asked in mild surprise.

He'd shrugged. "I don't know. Now that I think o' it, fishermen bring in

greater hauls—most oft' shellfish—on black nights, other sorts during waxin'
moons."

"See?" She leaned in to nuzzle his ear. "Everyone lives by the moon phases
one way or another."

He caught her face and stared solemnly into her eyes. "I live by the phases
o' the Moon Goddess. What phase is she in t'night?"

"Oh very dark." Aiela intoned. "Very dark and very passionate..."

"THE CREWS WON' like waitin' another night fer fresh water." His first
mate's mild voice yanked Turner back to the moment, and the decision he had to make.

They'd been to this continent before. It wasn't new territory or a
new deal, Turner reasoned internally. With this wind at their backs,
they could anchor at the usual spot and fill the barrels before
midnight. *Probably just my own guilt, what I've done to the Belial's Mutazio*
that's eatin' at me. Making me wary of things that don't exist. They've no
idea I was involved, and this isn't even Belial. Just a far-off Mine their slaves
work.

He nodded at his first mate. "Take us on in."

"Aye Cap'n Turner." The man's face relaxed as he hurried off,
shouting orders. Turner wished he could shake the feeling that no
matter what decision he made, it'd be the wrong one.

By nightfall, they'd arrived at the mouth of the river where they'd
eventually meet Belial barges, floating low in the water with their
loads of crystals.

Anchored in a calm sea, Turner sent some of the crew from each of
his three cargo ships upriver with the water barrels. "No bathing in
the river t'night—or anything else ya'd normally do. Joost fill the
barrels an' return straight off. Supper'll be waitin' an' extra rations o'
rum fer yer patience wi' me." A hearty cheer went up. "Mabbe we'll get
lucky an' have a day or two o' rest before the cargo arrives."

It spoke volumes that none of the men seemed put out with him
for the simple, but potentially costly, mistake he'd made.

But supper waited and waited.

Long past when the men should have returned, Turner ordered

extra lanterns lit on every ship, lest they'd got lost in the dark. Starlight shone its ghostly promise, but the night was uncommonly still. Ominous worries clutched at his mind, breeding and circling.

"Should we be sendin' men ta look fer them?" He asked his first mate.

The man considered before answering. "Could be they ran into a problem requiring light, figurin' ta wait there till morning." But his tone was doubtful.

Then the slap of oars sent Turner peering across the water and he saw them. The small boats were well within the glow of ship lanterns before he noticed there were less men aboard them. "Ya migh' be right." He muttered to the first mate. "Somethin's amiss."

Four men boarded and approached, faces shadowed by the moonless night and small light wavering from the lanterns. They stood before him. Strangers. In their hands were light guns, strange as the ones Aiela taught him to use.

"Who are ya and where are my men?" His mind raced. These were Belials, with advanced weapons like the Atlanteans.

The man who stepped close with a menacing stare looked somewhat familiar. "I am Sarim, son of Dominus Mardu. Order your men to submit to us and no one will be harmed."

"What's the problem? Why are ya doin' this? Where're the men I sent fer water?" Turner asked again. Slowly his hands reached for his weapons. If he could just—

The blinding beam of light from Sarim's gun sounded like the sizzle of water droplets hitting hot oil.

Turner's first mate crumpled to the deck, body splaying, nearly knocking Turner down. Even in the dim, he saw the huge hole in the sailor's chest. No—*through* his chest, Turner realized, as horror rocked him.

Flashes came from the ships on both sides, two, three, four before he shouted, "STOP! I will, I'll give the order…"

Sarim shouted something and the flashes ceased.

"Go with them." Turner gave the order and it was echoed to the other ships.

"Tie him." Sarim snapped and his men bound Turner's hands and

loaded him roughly onto the small boat. Rocking in the water, he tried to think while the rest of his crew was rounded up, cuffed and loaded. Surely there would be a way to sort this. His ships were needed for their crystal delivery. This must be only a misunderstanding.

But they'd killed several of his men... "What is it yer wantin'? Where are ya takin' us? "Sure an' whatever the problem, I can fix it, if ya will joost talk wi' me."

No matter what he asked or how often, no answers were given.

BY MORNING, they'd rowed a fair distance upriver, marched through black jungle—tripping, stumbling, half-eaten by bugs, and thirsty—then herded into a cave. Its entrance was barred with a gate.

At least they found the missing water crews. Six had been killed before the rest submitted to cuffing and imprisonment. Eight more moaned with the pain of wounds that left parts of their body disintegrated. All eight eventually bled out, despite everything the healer tried.

"I'll fix this." Turner assured the crews over and over. "Whatever it takes, I'll make it right. We've still our weapons on us."

But nobody came that they could fight. No one came to explain. No one came at all for two days.

Their own full barrels of water had been rolled in and Turner organized drinking rations, glad they wouldn't die of dehydration at least. Wood piles loomed near the entrance but he made them wait to light a fire, until it was really needed. They used their blades to dig holes as far back as they could go for latrines. Judging by the supply of water and wood given, they might be here awhile.

The third day, a young giant came stalking out of the jungle, with long black hair streaming down one side of his head, the other side bald as a baby. Slung over each shoulder were deer carcasses, which he carried as though they were light as rabbits. The graceful deer necks had been snapped and the sleek bodies bled. Dumping the carcasses just inside the gate, the giant stared towards the men grouped in back of the cave. They stared back at this huge oddity, neither man nor child.

After a while of insistent questioning from Turner—unanswered—the young giant finally turned and left.

"Let's make a fire." Turner finally said with resignation as they stood round the deer carcasses. "Who knows how to skin and butcher?" The men who came forward were given the best blades, while Turner set others to building fire rings, whittling spits and arranging kindling. At least they ate well that night, and slept a little warmer.

For a full week they lived like this. Rough, but adequate. From the fourth day onward, there were always guards present. Some of Sarim's men.

Each time the gate was opened, they were instructed to gather at the back. If they got too close, a guard would simply shoot somebody with the horrific light beam.

Every day ,Turner respectfully approached the gate and asked for Sarim or Carver or even Mardu. "If I could just speak wi' them...my men don' deserve this. We've done noothin' ta provoke bein' prisonered."

It gave him hope that they were fed. Whatever this was, it wasn't about killing them all.

3

RESTRICTED ARCHIVES

9,970 BCE HIGH CITY, ATLANTIS

"There is a charm about the forbidden that makes it unspeakably desirable."

— MARK TWAIN

AIELA

*G*leeful anticipation danced inside, but Aiela managed to appear solemn and mature while the Record Keeper stared at them doubtfully.

"Ruler Ziel has sent you… Both?"

"We're loading the ship to Alexandria first thing in the morning." Aiela explained, again. "We're to gather his *list…*" She tapped a paper the thin, ghost-like woman was holding " …tonight. There won't be time in the morning."

"I can gather these things. I'm here half the night anyway. It'll take me less time." Even seated, the bony, faded guard was imposing. Aiela took half a step back when the big woman unfolded to stand. She wore the armor of a Knight of Atlantis.

They were inside the Hall of Records, a five-story, stepped, oval

Temple topped with scroll worked spires. Columns of lapis lazuli surrounded each level, supporting covered verandas, one recessed atop the other. Like drawing boards for those who studied here, the columns themselves were carved with stories and symbols in bas relief; a great amalgamation of the timeless histories stored within. So vast was this repository of life records, knowledge accumulated, and never-ending discoveries, guides were required if one had any hope of finding what was sought.

Those apprenticing as Keepers of the Records received daily additions to the archives, contributed by those with tales to tell, or perhaps diaries found after a loved one passed on. Initiates, Teachers and Master Keepers compiled these contributions both new and ancient, cataloguing and cross-referencing by subject matter, names, places and time lines. Historians studied these archives, attempting to produce accurate histories from multiple viewpoints.

All the Houses of Government came here to study what had been learned, or attempted in their particular field or niche of interest.

In the center of the ground level was a wide staircase that spiraled down to the nethers, where a vaulted entrance was barred by metal gates. The restricted archives weren't even a tenth as large as the annals stored above them, but what they contained was guarded day and night. An official letter bestowing admittance from a House Master or Ruler had to be presented before one gained entry here.

"Ruler Ziel requested we gather the items." Ahna spoke softly, gazing evenly up at the wan guard who'd come around her desk to tower above them. "He requires an Oracle who can foresee additional items that should be sent for preservation. That can only happen if *we're* in there gathering. You haven't been trained as an Oracle... have you?"

It wasn't an outright lie, but not exactly truth either. Ziel had mentioned they should send other items from the regular sections if they had a strong sign about it going. He hadn't told them they *couldn't* do the same for the restricted archives.

The guard wore several weapons, Aiela noted, secured by a double pointed belt circling a gaunt waist. Her ash-colored hair was cut short, further washing out an already grey complexion. Her hands were bigger than most men's.

She frowned at Ahna and commenced reading Ziel's list.

"Look, he even gave us his keys." Aiela jingled them up at the guard. "Because I'm on Ruler Kenna's small council, we've both been tasked with organizing the colonizations—more accurately, evacuations." The crystal-embedded keys tinkled against each other, drawing the guard's frown away from the list—which wasn't clear on who should do the gathering.

"We're missing evening service to do this for him." Ahna managed to sound disappointed.

But no pity came from the big woman barring their way. She merely blinked a few times, considering.

Finally she moved aside, returning the list with a dismissive shrug. "You have the keys. If your motives aren't pure our guardians will know. Thankfully, it is not only for me to judge."

"Guardians?" They chorused.

"What... uh... exactly, are the guardians?" Ahna asked.

"How would they know our motives?" Aiela added.

"Machines guard our archives better than any human could. They read frequencies of those entering. Those of ill motives have a low frequency in general and the machines catch them". The woman settled her considerable length back into her cushioned chair with a satisfied sigh. Her eyes strayed to a stack of books and knowledge crystals she appeared to be working her way through.

Aiela and Ahna glanced at each other. "And... what happens if someone gets 'caught'?"

The guard's eyes took on a knowing glint. "They're magnetized to the machine. Held there until someone, such as myself, comes to release them."

Aiela bit her lip. *Would the machines judge our intentions unworthy?* A sudden spark of idea interrupted her worry. "Do you have more of these machines? Some that aren't in use?"

The guard thought a moment. "I'm sure we do..."

"Because we should send some with the things being evacuated don't you think? I mean, if we protect the knowledge here, we should certainly protect it in other places. These machines sound like the perfect way to do that."

The guard managed a new look, something close to respect. "I'll inquire. Of course I'd need a letter of permission from a Ruler. How many do you need?"

Aiela shrugged. "How ever many we've got. There's going to be quite a few places we could use them."

Nodding curtly, the guard pressed a button and spiraling steel gates swung open soundlessly.

The room beyond was a perfect circle with three sets of double doors. Lit countertops of glossy, light-grained woods, provided space for examination or reading. Tall stools of matching wood were tucked beneath. Beaming from a marble pedestal in the room's center, one enormous light sphere illuminated shiny black walls sparkling with mica.

The three sets of double doors were carved blonde wood, ornamented with pale gold, and bearing the name of the archive they enclosed. But it was the matte black figures beside those doors that drew Aiela's attention.

Hollow clanks announced the gates closing behind them. The statues of dull black stone stood taller than even the guard woman. A sitting cat, complete with whiskers and a tail curled around its feet. A serpent, hooded head rearing from a pile of coils bigger around than her waist. An armored warrior with blades in it's belt and a spiked helmet topping it's head. The eyes of all three glowed green as they scanned her and Ahna.

"Motion activated... fascinating." She mused, approaching the cat. The light beam from the eyes followed her movement.

Ahna went to examine the warrior. "Hope our motives are pure... enough." Her voice was higher than normal, and Aiela couldn't tell which of them the nervousness came from.

"It feels like soapstone, or something similar."

"Magnetized. It pulls a person to it and they can't get away?"

"I guess so." Aiela shrugged, already losing interest since nothing had happened. "Where shall we go first?"

"Any. Pick one." Ahna lifted her hand from the warrior's chest and waved the list. "There's items from all three chambers on here."

"Let's start with 'Ancient' then." Aiela tried a key in the gilded lock plate. Nothing. The next key turned smoothly, and they heard the mechanical sound of systems giving way, then the doors clicked softly, opening a crack. "We're in." She grinned broadly, sobering as the warrior statue beside them soundlessly turned its head to fix them with glowing eyes, turned yellow. They froze for a moment, and when nothing more happened, pushed the doors open and hurried inside.

Orb sconces lit up along both sides of glossy walls, where polished pink sandstone created breathtaking designs that lined the cone-shaped room. "Well this is underwhelming." Aiela's glee vanished. Nothing but rows of utility shelving fitted with boxes, spread away into cool dim and then darkness.

"Not what I expected either." Ahna rubbed the chill out of her bare arms. "I thought there'd be things to look at—exotic stuff on display... I guess that wouldn't make sense for a vault."

"How exactly are we supposed to find anything?"

"There must be a catalogue of some sort."

Seeing nothing that resembled a system of organization, not even a knowledge crystal, they studied the nearest shelving unit. The boxes were gray, marked only with plain white numbers.

Aiela pulled a small one from it's shelf. "Hard composite... light, not stone or metal or clay." She tugged at the lid but it didn't open. "Aaurgh! They're locked!" Pushing it back into it's slot, she pulled out the next one and tried it. "Surely they're not *all* locked." But every single one she tried was. Frustration mounted as she shoved a box back into place.

"Maybe I should go back out and ask the Guard." Ahna suggested.

"What if she uses that as an excuse to gather the items herself? 'If we don't know how to use the system, we shouldn't be in here' type of mindset."

Ahna was already by the doors. " Hey I think I found something. Look at this."

Three spirals were etched to the left of the doors. She tapped them, pushed on them. Nothing.

Aiela crossed the aisle to examine it, but before she could touch it, the spirals slid open to reveal a slanted shelf hidden in the wall. At the bottom of the shelf was a rectangular box with a display glass. The glass lit up with words. "What item do you seek?"

"Yes!" they breathed in unison, while Ahna consulted the list, reading off the first item. "Sacred Naacal Scrolls." A beam of light shone words from the front of the box onto the slant of the shelf above it. Ahna read aloud,

"Item 777: The Sacred Naacal Scrolls were relocated from Crystal City to High City's Restricted Archives in early Epoch 2. Exact year unknown. The Naacal Priesthood brought a total of 13 scrolls from Lemuria when founding the Naacal College of Souls, from which they taught the Atlantean people. The information contained herein has served the spiritual edification of Atlantis and kept the people's spiritual understandings pure. These scrolls have been copied numerous times in their entirety, both translated to Atlantean and copied in the original Lemurian language. They are widely available in the unrestricted archives for reference.

These scrolls are (claimed by the Naacal Priesthood to be) exact copies of Lemuria's sacred spiritual teachings concerning the souls that incarnate humanity, and the Source of all things.

****Due to the extreme age of these items, their container should not be opened unless in a protected environment by a trained document preservationist.*

"Now to find container 777... " Aiela's voice faded as a light caught her eye off to the left of the wedge shaped space. One of the upright ends of the shelving was illuminated, glowing from within.

Almost running, they followed a horizontal shelf support, three tiers up, also lit, nearly all the way to the back of the room. A gray container's white numerals were glowing; 777.

Aiela lifted the long narrow box. "Doesn't weigh much." She crouched, setting it on the textured stone floor. Sure enough, it's lid was unlocked. Inside, thirteen tubes of transparent aluminum protected the scrolls. "Maybe it'll all be stored in clear containers." Her excitement was back.

"That would be nice. I wonder why the outside boxes aren't clear?"

Aiela shrugged and closed the box, carrying it to the front of the room. "I guess we'll just start a pile huh?"

Ahna was already calling up another item from the hi-tech catalogue. "The Iaspis Tablets".

"Item 1248: The Iaspis Tablets were relocated to High City (then known as Golden Gate City) Hall of Records in Epoch 2; year 42,449. Members of the Lemurian Elders brought a total of 33 engraved tablets from Lemuria for safekeeping, suspecting their continent would perish imminently. The information contained herein covers basic alchemy, and explanation as to Terra's most common organic substances, along with methods to manipulate or transform them. These tablets have been copied in their entirety, translated to Atlantean, and copied in the original Lemurian language. They are available in the unrestricted archives for reference.
These original tablets are (claimed by the Lemurian Elders to be) exact copies of Lemuria's sacred alchemical teachings concerning the laws of physicality and periodic properties of elements.
***Tablets 6 and 15 had been cracked before being preserved.
Consider the fragility of the aged stone when handling.

Ahna finished reading the lighted words aloud before following Aiela along another section of illuminated shelving. Container 1248 was heavy, and thankfully on ground level. It took both of them to carry it.

"Why does Ziel want to send this away?" Aiela panted under the weight. "Why not send one of the thousand books we have on alchemy?"

Setting it carefully by the doors, they straightened, and Ahna replied. "By request of High Priest Thoth'... remember?"

Thoth was their most learned alchemist. He'd written most of the procedures alchemists currently used, and had developed courses widely taught across Atlantis—although he'd long ago quit teaching.

He currently was the ambassador between Atlantis and Earth's underground Amenti civilization.

"I would like to have met him. They say he's ancient as days." He'd sent a representative to request these tablets along with several other items, while informing Ruler Ziel he was evacuating his entire family to Egypt. He planned to start a college there to teach writing, reading, healing and culture to the primitive peoples settled along the Nile floodplains.

"Next listed is a Sword of Light." Ahna located it in the catalogue, and read fragments aloud. "... 'made from metal alloys of unknown origin which glow when a 'worthy person' wields it. Suspected to have come from another world... stored with Atlantis' 'Ancient' artifacts because it was long used during previous epochs to select regionary Rulers after Poseidon's descendants died out."

"Let's find out if we're 'worthy'." Aiela grinned, opening the long, clear, inner case which revealed only a crimson silk-like fabric. Using both arms to lift the cloth-shrouded bundle, they unwrapped it together. It's blade was triple-edged and rose-colored like orichalcum, only quite pale. No hilt except a fancy guard, shaped like a dragon, completely encircled the handle.

"You go first". She prodded Ahna.

Ahna's eyes gleamed delight as she grasped it. "Feels harder than it looks." The handle looked to be reptile skin of a faded turquoise green. Using both hands, she lifted the sword and it began to glow in sunset colors of fiery coals. They both exclaimed at its exotic beauty.

"You better glow for me too!" Aiela threatened, gingerly taking the sword from her sister. It did—much to her relief. "Guess we're worthy of ruling after all."

"More accurately, we're of high frequency." Ahna was running fingertips along the blade closest to the handle, where markings they couldn't decipher were etched. "At least a third or more of High City would qualify as Queens and Kings according to this."

"It's so pretty."

"We better keep moving. Lots more to go." They bundled the still glowing sword away, and added it to their growing stack.

By far, the largest item was a perpetual motion solar system, disassembled into fifteen containers. A picture with assembly instructions showed it to be the size of a small room with all ten planets, sun, and moons. Once assembled and properly set in motion, it would continue indefinitely to emulate the movements of the Sol system.

Waiting to fetch the last item on the list from this chamber, Aiela complained, "Without knowing the names of things—and what all's in here—we can't locate anything."

"Now we know why Ziel was so free with his keys." Ahna smiled wryly, acknowledging his wisdom over theirs yet again. "Last is Poseidon's Pyramid... 'a large, pyramid-shaped knowledge crystal holding detailed accounts of the building of Atlantis during Poseidon's reign.'"

"Sounds heavy."

Aiela followed the lights.

PASSING the swiveling head of the snake guardian, eyes also glowing yellow once they were at the door, they fitted the correct key, and found that the middle archive, marked simply "Worlds", was smaller. The same cone-shape, its walls were polished turquoise, turned into art by breathtaking natural patterns and variations of color.

This time, Ahna held the key ring when they located the wall stone marked with three pyramids. "It's the nearness of the chamber key—most likely the tiny embedded crystal—that prompts the shelf to slide out!"

"Oh good." Aiela commented, scanning the listed items they were to find. "They all sound smallish." Everything in this chamber had come from other planets, either gifts from off-planet visitors, or artifacts brought by immigrants who'd settled here from other worlds.

There was an enchanted Mirror of Time, which showed scenes future or past. "It doesn't actually seem that useful." Aiela remarked, as they watched images fade slowly, one into another. Right now it showed a grey, barren landscape with dust clouds swirling by, before changing to a scene with human-shaped figures moving around in a dim purple light.

"The catalogue said it shows various dimensions, planes and

worlds at will, with no known way to control or direct it." Ahna turned back to the catalogue.

A Ring of Disappearance, made of black bone and gold filigree, bore a strict warning both in the catalogue and inside the ring's container that to wear and operate it, a person must prepare adequately or it would make them dangerously sick from a disrupted equilibrium, even unto death. They didn't take it from the box, merely studied it through its transparent casing.

Gravity reduction boots made of grainy, taupe colored stone from a high gravity planet were large and clunky, but provided great laughs as they took turns racing up and down the aisles, seeing how far they could jump.

"Crystal skulls, from the Arcturians, Sirians and Pleiadians'... " Ahna read, "... carries Terra's creation stories through many phases of trial and error to perfect the environment, introduce plants, animals and then five models of human bodies to house highly developed souls... blah blah blah, we know all that. Let's just get them." Clear as glass, except for two which had an octahedron-shaped emerald and a dodecahedron shaped sapphire where the pineal gland would be, the skulls varied in size and shape.

FINALLY IT WAS time for the third chamber, where items of great or dangerous power were housed.

The cat guardian's eyes flickered orange, and sent their hearts racing when they felt a gentle tug before the slanted eyes turned back to sunlight yellow, and released the slight drag on their bodies.

Entering under the carved word "Powers", Aiela consulted their list, as Ahna opened the catalogue. This one simply had three equidistant crosses.

"What's first?"

"Rams horn trumpets." Aiela replied, curious what the catalogue told of them.

"...capable of crumbling stone." Ahna read aloud from the projected description. "Huh. Basically like our sound weapons except these displace stone based materials and ours displace softer, organic material."

They shrugged, and went to find the case. Large and unwieldy, it was actually quite light.

"If these were actual ram's horns, those were some enormous rams!"

"Next is The Trance Crystal."

"Wonder how big that is?"

"...raises the bearers frequency so as to control the reality of others, including animals, causing them to see, hear, feel or think whatever the bearer tells them to..."

The container fit into the palm of Aiela's hand. Inside, the crystal looked like raw topaz, dark amber in color, and revealing no hint of what the description said it was capable of.

"Great goddess. Belial has an entire *section* back here!" Aiela exclaimed, when she went to find the next to last item on the list. At least a third of the shelving held containers all marked 'Belial'. "As if they might come and claim these someday?" She said sarcastically.

"Or maybe they're marked to be destroyed at some point." Ahna countered, as they wandered among the shelves towards the lighted box.

"The Belial Stones... I wonder why Ziel wants these moved? They'll be out in the open—less protected."

"Yes, but Belial probably knows they're here. Once we ship them away, they won't know where to find them anymore."

"Wish we could see these—but I'm not about to open this case." It was said to contain five marbled stones, egg-shaped, each the size of a hand. The catalogue had provided actual size, three-dimensional pictures for each, and gone to great lengths to warn against opening the specially lined and shielded case. Each stone amplified whatever energies was near it. Only those of very high spirituality and mental clarity could handle them unshielded. They'd driven people insane when placed out in the open, amplifying the energies of everything and everyone nearby.

"This I kind of want to see." Aiela declared, reaching from her tiptoes for the last item on their list. It was only a small box. Ahna made a face, but leaned in as Aiela tipped back the clear, hinged lid. "It's rather ghastly." It was as monstrous as it sounded. The man's screaming golden head looked too lifelike to be a piece of jewelry, with black diamond horns jutting from his temples and clear diamond fangs from his wide open mouth. The fangs held a tiny clear sphere filled with dark red drops of blood. Here was the original Ring of Belial—said to contain the blood of Onus Belial, from which he'd intended to be cloned, should he die before discovering immortality. According to the catalogue, this ring was programmed with a way to contact or communicate directly with him. Sharing Ahna's look of revulsion, Aiela closed the case. "Let's get out of here. I'm tired."

"Wasn't as fun as it all sounded in the beginning." Ahna agreed.

4

SET IN MOTION

9,970 BCE ANUBIS TERRITORY, EGYPT

"To be born is to come into the world weighed down with strange gifts of the soul, with enigmas and an inextinguishable sense of exile. So it was with me."

— BEN OKRI IN THE FAMISHED ROAD

CARVER

To Carver's annoyance, Balek watched him closely, bloodshot eyes squinting between strands of hair he rarely bothered to wash. It was hell, being in the psychotic presence of this cruelest of his brothers.

Being eldest had only made Balek bitter, as each ensuing brother usurped their father's attention. Not that any of them got much. When they did, it usually hurt. Balek's voice never progressed past the squeaky stage, but that didn't stop him from mocking, threatening and insulting constantly, to ease his permanent insecurity.

Carver suspected Balek had been ordered to monitor him. Which was worrisome.

Thankfully, Balek soon found distractions: staged hunts with the

Anubis, consuming their tongue-numbing drink that altered reality, using their harem of human girls.

Carver finished stuffing clothes, stiff with dried sweat, into his pack, just as the Anubis General arrived. How quickly he'd adjusted to the odd shapes of the half-canid, half-human race. With more body hair than human men, their heads remained oddly hair-free, sometimes with skin pink as a newborn, sometimes black, and very creased. Ears and snouts ranged from very human like, to very dog-like.

"Tails ends of troops loading in now minute, Dominus Carver." The Anubis General bowed, then stood at stiff attention. A full head taller than Carver, he spoke in Atlantean, though badly bastardized over the centuries since the Anubis were expelled from Belial.

"It's—I'm not a Dominus. That's a title, like King or Emperor—like your Vizier. There is only one. Mardu would be furious if he heard you address anyone else with his title."

The General bowed his head in deference, or maybe apology, and Carver was glad Balek hadn't overheard this exchange. The Anubis had favored Carver since they arrived, not trying to hide their preference for him, or their disdain for Balek. It only made Balek meaner—both to Carver and to the Anubis.

"Where's Balek?" At the averting of the General's eyes, Carver shook his head. "Disregard. I'll get him and we'll be on our way. Your people here will be well until you return?" Most of the tribe were coming to fight for Mardu. Only those with disabilities would stay behind.

The General nodded again. "People will be well, yes. Humans caring for them."

"Good. I'll be along shortly." Carver shouldered his pack, and glanced one last time around the dim, low-ceilinged space he'd headquartered in for a week. Balek's stuff was still discarded, flung about—but that was his problem. Carver'd be happy to leave him behind if he insisted on gathering it now.

He banged three times with the flat of his hand before entering the women's hut. A long, low rectangle of baked bricks, it was a cool haven in the tropical heat, and plenty large enough to house fifty human women. Women Mardu had gifted to the Anubis.

Carver still hadn't figured out if they were considered servants, or a beloved harem of lovers—and mothers. Apparently, the Anubis females were mostly sterile. When he delivered these girls, Mardu unknowingly brought the tribe a way to reproduce. Of course they all revered him even more for it. Having deified him already as Onus Belial returned, they thought he'd intentionally bestowed the great gift of progeny on them.

There'd only been three births so far, and a high rate of miscarriage, but most of the girls were in various stages of pregnancy. The three babies looked human except for a fine down of hair over much of their bodies, and the eerie blue-grey eyes of a wolf. It was said they stayed awake all night during a full moon. The tribe was collectively holding their breath, waiting to see what their offspring might become.

The human girls lived well here in their own quarters, and didn't seem to work any harder than the rest of the tribe.

"Balek!" He hollered peering through the dim. "We're loaded. Time to go."

"Stop shouting, fool!" Balek's high snarl came from his left. A naked girl with a relatively small stomach bump was helping him dress. Judging from his familiar, pained movements, he must have a splitting hangover headache. The rest of the hut was empty, all the others no doubt at the aeros seeing off their... whatever the Anubis were to them.

"Get my stuff." Balek habitually ordered Carver around still. Childhood habits had yet to die.

"No. We lift off in five with or without you." Carver stalked out, not waiting for a reply.

"You can't do tha—" Balek's sullen whine followed him out the door.

Mardu's swiftest sea cruisers were already en route, loaded with

Anubis warriors. They'd sailed two days ago from these lush, over-heated lands, headed downriver to the sea. Sailing round the southern end of Atlantis, they would rendezvous at the crystal mines.

Ten aero carriers lifted off to meet them. It wasn't a large army. Eighteen hundred and eighty-one to be exact, but armed with Belial weapons and facing a sick population, with the element of surprise, they should be able to punch a big hole in High City. Cripple—or at least distract—them enough for the Belial army to invade.

Balek had come running, much to Carver's satisfaction, screeching commands to wait for him. Now he slouched behind the aero pilot, nursing his head—and his right knuckles as well.

Carver allowed himself a smug smile. Balek had swept onboard the aero, stomped straight to Carver and took a swing, aiming for his stomach. But Carver wore armor under his tunics and had barely felt any impact. Balek had almost squashed the scream of pain. Almost.

Content to finally settle in and think, Carver let his mind go in directions he'd been avoiding since Mardu had abruptly shipped him off.

How do I warn her?

After thinking on it, several moons ago he'd decided to simply murder Mardu—stop the whole thing before it started. *I live with him. How hard can it be?*

But his father had guards with him every moment, though Carver could not recall when that began. Even while sleeping, eating, or ordering his sons and Generals about, there was never less than half a dozen armed men like a shield around Mardu—many more when he left home. And what, Carver wondered, if by succeeding, he just created space for someone even worse to take Mardu's place... Balek or one of Mardu's power grasping elite.

He had no illusions of getting away with it. There would be no second chances. Whether or not he actually killed Mardu, his own life would be forfeit just for trying. He'd certainly not be around anymore to protect Ahna from within. Which closed this circle of thinking every time.

Wishing fervently that he'd thought to set up a few spies for his own use, he sorted through everyone he knew. If there was even one person he could trust to deliver a message to High City, to become a link of information however tenuous, they might have a chance. Thinking of Drommen and Lister, he wished he knew if they were actually friends, or still being paid to spy on him. Orja was the only person he really trusted. But would she knowingly participate in a plot against Mardu—and all his brothers? Doubtful. And anyway, it'd be easier to get away himself, than to send her.

If he disappeared, went to warn Ahna and Aiela himself, Mardu would just change plans and they'd be blind again. Atlantis could at least prepare though—if they knew Mardu was plotting to finally overtake them.

Carver considered this awhile. The odds of getting away in one of his hidden aeros was good. Would High City believe him? Would it be better than staying at Mardu's side and feeding information to Atlantis any way he could? Surely so. He wanted to believe leaving was the better way—but he also wondered if the thought of being with Ahna tainted his logic. She would accept him, forgive him for who he was, if he saved them... wouldn't she?

When he woke, the Anubis were eating, and Balek was pacing in the aero bay, lecturing them on how best to plan their invasion. Carver shook his head. Balek had no idea what a squeaky-voiced fool he sounded, talking endlessly about things he knew so little of.

Moving up beside the pilot, Carver offered him the last of the food from his own pack. "How much further?"

"Two hours if we can get above these storms" the pilot replied, tapping blue masses on the top edge of the radar screen.

Two hours until I see what's been done with Turner. Carver's stomach already churned at the thought. Not knowing what he'd face was always the worst part.

IRISHMEN WERE BEING BUTCHERED ALIVE outside the cave, three at a time, when Carver arrived.

Mardu orchestrated the grisly scene, gripping the curls of a bound and bloodied Turner, forcing him to watch. "You'll watch every last one of your men die screaming for what you've done. After that I'll keep you alive until we have your family, your friends, each and every person you've thought to care about. You'll watch them suffer too... "

"Dominus Mardu." Carver had to shout over the screams and sobs of the men whose limbs were being severed one by one—but not cleanly—hacked at, until the bone was chopped through. He struggled to keep his horror at bay, while distracting this monster who had fathered him.

Turner's eyes kept rolling back. He was coughing and choking, his face swollen all colors of bruised, half a dozen splits oozing. More of his once-white tunic was covered in blood than not.

Mardu let go of Turner's hair abruptly and he swayed forward, toppling face first towards the ground. "You've the Anubis with you?" Mardu's eyes travelled beyond Carver to where Balek stood gaping at the loud, bloody scene.

"Sea Cruisers and aeros wait in the bay. The Anubis General is moving his troops onto the Irish ships." Carver affirmed, focusing on his words, trying not to look at his friend unmoving on the ground. "They await your orders and battle plan. Perhaps you'd want me to take over here while you and Balek see to them?" He inclined his head in deference, hoping against hope Mardu would go along. Mardu would have to dictate his invasion plan to the Anubis because he was the only one who knew it—but he had no need of Balek.

Mardu waited until each of the three Irishmen being butchered lost consciousness or died. The silence was deafening after such tortuous din. "Three more!" He barked at the young Mutazio.

These remnants of his Mutazio army were only children. They stood panting after their exertions. Machetes in their hands dripped clots of flesh, mixed with body fluids and bone shards onto the ground. Several thousand Mutazio children, too young to go to war were all that were left of the once unbeatable army. They were being used to carry on at the mine. Mardu still hadn't decided whether to bother rebuilding the muta population or just use what was left as slaves and forget the whole idea.

"The Anubis have no idea how to sail the Irish fleet." Carver inserted quickly as a reminder. Mardu seemed to have forgotten they actually needed these Irish sailors.

Growling in frustration, Mardu barked the contrary order at the Mutazio who were already wrestling three more wildly combative sailors from the cave. "Stop. No more kills. Put them back."

Mardu stripped off his sweaty blood-spattered tunic and the armored vest underneath, pointing at one of his personal guards, lined up behind them. "I need a clean shirt and armor."

The guard took off at a lope towards the nearest aero.

Carver hadn't seen his father's body in years. Despite a healthy paunch covered in black hair, his chest and arms remained bulky with muscle. His shoulders hunched forward slightly but not in a stoop, more as if constantly reaching forward to overtake anything or anyone who got in his way. His thick black hair was cropped shorter than usual.

"This vermin confessed to conspiring with High City in killing our *army*." He aimed a kick at Turner's inert body. "Fits the description. I knew soon as I saw him... maintains he acted alone... carried out Ziel's plot. For *gold*." Mardu spat out the word as if he'd never done anything for personal gain. "I don't believe he's told me everything yet. I mean to keep him alive and close until I've exacted revenge. That's going to take a fucking long and painful time." Mardu turned to where a guard offered a skin of water, drinking, then washing his face and torso. "Have them clean up this mess before it attracts beasts. Then ready the sailors."

The guard returned with fresh clothing.

Balek was sneering through the bars covering the cave's entrance, at the Irish sailors cowering as far back as they could get. At his father's summons, he joined Mardu and Carver.

"Tomorrow night we drop the Chimera on High City." Mardu announced abruptly.

Carver's insides jellied. *So soon? No time to warn them...*

"It'll be Festival of the Sun—the final day, when the highest numbers are gathered. They'll carry infection back to their towns and villages without even knowing. There're extra vaccination doses on my aero. You'll both want to use one. All of Belial has been dosed via the food and water supply this past week."

"How will we infect High City without them knowing?" Balek asked. Carver wondered too.

"Simple." Mardu shrugged a heavy shoulder. "Two of our aeros flying high above their air space will drop a thousand carriers, too small to register on their radars. Chimera will be airborne, with no way to stop, or contain it."

Carver swallowed. "How long till the sickness activates?"

"Mid-quarter moon. Now... " Mardu had finished cleaning himself up. " ...I'm going to tell the Anubis what's expected of them, ensure they have everything they need. You two use Sarim's men, and ferry the prisoners back to their fleet. You'll come home with me when it's done. We've much to prepare."

"DRINK THIS. IT'LL PROTECT YOU." Carver poured the tiny tube of vaccine down Turner's throat. He was barely hanging onto consciousness, struggling to speak. "Shhh. Don't worry, your men are safe for now. I'll do everything I can for them... swallow my friend."

He saw the wild look even through the caked blood and eyelids swollen half-shut. "Sorry mate but you're just going to have to trust me... I am still on your side. You just concentrate on staying alive so I can prove it to you."

They were riding on the large, raft-like barges that usually floated crystal cargo to the Irish fleet for transport to High City. Balek was on the other raft, but some of Sarim's men were on this one, keeping the Irish sailors corralled in a tight bunch until they could be chained into service on the ships.

"We haven't much time. These are two more vaccines." He stuffed them in Turner's hip pocket, guilt flaring again, and then anger, as Turner winced even at that light touch. Mardu must've worked him over plenty before Carver arrived. "Just in case you catch a break and can get them to High City somehow for them to duplicate." Carver figured it wouldn't hurt.

If everything went according to Mardu's plan, Turner would remain locked up, deep in the hull of one of his own ships until they reached High City. Then the Anubis would invade. It'd be too late for vaccines by then. Still, you never know what might happen during the voyage, and he was getting desperate for ways to help.

Carver spoke to the Irish sailors in their language as Sarim's men looked on, confused. "Take care of your Captain. Make sure you clean him up and supply him with plenty of water and food. Medicine if you have any. He means a great deal to me. I'll reward you well when I come for him in High City."

The sailors eyed him warily, not understanding why he was part of the enemy, yet acting as if he cared.

Once the sailors and Turner had been transferred to the ships, Carver found a chance to repeat the order to the Anubis General. "Do what you can to mend that one. Decent accommodations, plenty of food and water..."

"Dominus Mardu tell me that is most gold prisoner." The Anubis General replied, making it clear he'd follow the Dominus' orders over Carver's.

"Exactly." Carver nodded agreement. "Very valuable and we want him in excellent shape."

5

READY OR NOT

12,516 BCE HIGH CITY, ATLANTIS

"The supreme art of war is to subdue the enemy without fighting."

— SUN TZU, THE ART OF WAR

ZIEL

Sipping a springtime tea of jasmine green, flavored with strawberry, I gazed over our sumptuous Capitol coming awake below my window alcove. The sky had not yet begun to lighten, but people were already rising to assemble at temples, halls and stages for the final sunrise service of Festival week.

I planned to skip it myself, opting instead for a lengthy meditation, in hopes I'd find balance after seven days of teaching, ceremony, and advising.

Some weight dragged at me, growing more unbearable every day. I'd slept little and poorly all week. Mostly, I attributed this to the unrest of too many energies present in our uncomfortably overstuffed City. Or perhaps just being out of my routine.

So many had responded to my lectures on the possible calamities foreseen for Atlantis, Ahna and Aiela were overwhelmed with meetings, trying to support a high number of evacuation expeditions. The fact that they hadn't had time to enjoy the festivities, brought a spasm of regret. I wondered, not for the first time, if I asked too much of them. At any rate, today was the final day of Festival of the Sun, and we could soon return to some semblance of peace and quiet.

I startled out of my introspections at a frantic tapping on the door. It was Maya.

"Something's very wrong." She slumped into one of my high-backed floor cushions, surrounding the rosewood table. Still in her nightclothes, short kinky hair wild on one side and smashed on the other, she looked haunted. I stood speechless for a moment. I'd never actually seen her not polished and groomed. She'd been the senior female on my small council for decades, and seeing her this disturbed felt like a leg abruptly kicked out from under me.

"Wh—what do you mean? *What* is wrong?" Blinking rapidly to regain equilibrium, I poured her a cup of tea and sat.

Shaking her head, then scrubbing at puffy eyes (the first time I'd seen them not heavily lined with her usual intricate designs) she pushed the tea away. "I don't know. Every time I fell asleep a thick grey cloud descended on the city and people began dropping dead all around me. I'd wake—from the fright—and calm myself. 'Only a dream, only a dream, only a dream'...but as soon as I fell asleep it happened all over again."

"A thick cloud of grey? Like air? Did it have substance?" My questions didn't have purpose, I was just saying something until I knew what to do.

"I don't know... air... maybe." She looked exhausted.

"Perhaps you've been working too much." It was a lame suggestion but I was at a loss. Maya didn't *see* things. She was claircognizant—she *knew* things—but even that ability was sporadic. She didn't work as an oracle. I kept her busy carrying out the duties of my office and organizing the House of Oracles. She functioned as my right hand and at least half of my brain.

She stared at me with desperate eyes. "Yes. Perhaps. How do I make it stop?"

It was the desperation that jolted me, screamed at me to sit up and take notice. Maya was *never* desperate. "I want you to eat something and then—"

"I'm not hungry."

"Follow my instructions Maya. If you want it to stop, do what I tell you." I was using the tone I might with a frightened child.

"Yes. Alright. It's just the thought of food makes me ill."

I reached across the table to touch her hand. It felt like ice. "Start with the tea. Drink all of it while I order up some food. Then I will summon Pawn's group and I want you to commune with them. You'll need to replay the dreams, enter back into them fully, and let Pawn's circle in with you. They'll be able to explore what you're seeing."

"But it was *awful*. Everyone was sick with no help. *Dying...*"

"I know." I patted her hand, larger and darker than mine, reassuringly. "We'll figure this out."

I called to the kitchens for food, then set about tracking down Pawn. He would do the rest. His circle of nine were the top clairvoyants in our House. They could create a field or plane of shared sight, and bring Maya into it, where her dream would be like a broadcast to study.

The day worsened.

By noon I was engaged in an emergency meeting with the other Rulers. Every one of them had received dozens of reports about strange spheres found throughout the city—even in Old Forest, and out across the farmlands. Made of brittle black polymer, the spheres were the size of a pomegranate. Most were broken but a few had been brought to our scientists intact. Whatever the contents, they were long gone, dispersed through many tiny holes in the spheres. But there was surely residue.

"It's got to be some sort of attack. But we won't know what until the scientists report back. The Knights should be activated immediately. " Ruler Kenna was firm and we all nodded agreement.

The Knights of Atlantis were our first line of defense countrywide, and usually, all that was needed. Primarily peacekeepers, they were assigned two to a town, more for the larger cities.

High City had a force of fifty. Crimes were reported to the Knights and they took care of it, locating the offender and dealing appropriately with them. Normally, some sort of healing work was done, and then the offender would perform reparation for their crime. If a Knight didn't feel clear on handling a case, he or she could assemble an objective council, and ask for their judgement or recommendations.

Elite fighters that rose to the top of our military forces, Knights were men and women of extremely high personal frequency. Holding positions of absolute authority required exemplary compassion and integrity. They were re-tested every six moons and rotated out as they themselves, or others, saw the need. Though crime rates were low across Atlantis, Knighthood was one of the most taxing jobs.

"The military is already on alert. Inner Harbour's gates were immediately closed and extra units are guarding the outer harbor. Aeros are being vetted before entering our airspace, though it'll be difficult to maintain tight security with so many leaving after the Festival." Eirene, our Foreign Relations leader reported. "The Belial Ambassadors report nothing new, but I'd like to send them directly to Mardu and ask outright if he has anything to do with this. Or what his desires or aims are."

Again, we all silently nodded agreement.

"Maya had a dream I believe is related." I proceeded to tell them of Pawns examination of it, ending with "The dream indicated a biological attack. Other than finding a cure, our focus must be on the origin and purpose of the attack. I'll contact every spy in every country, and ask for aggressive intelligence."

All of our faces were tight. So much was just conjecture until we knew what was in those spheres.

"Has anyone gotten reports of spheres outside High City?"

Heads shook around the table. Murmurs in the negative.

We adjourned, hurrying away to press our various Houses, councils and staffs into full service. Not an easy task on a national holi day.

Ahna was waiting for me outside the meeting room, hair bright and straight as sunbeams around a fine-boned face full of questions. "Will you contact the Inner Harbor guard? They won't let the Alexandria ships leave because they're carrying so much sensitive cargo. Harbormaster said we're on high alert…?"

I nodded and filled her in as we walked down the hallway. "Where's your sister?"

Ahna held the door for me, as we entered the domed common room of the Oracles sanctum. "Ruler Kenna called her away from the Hall of Records a few hours ago. I had to finish overseeing the loading by myself."

"Come on." I made for my office. "Let's get those ships released, then maybe you can help me with the spy network. I need to get a day's worth of messages out in the next hour."

Maya—back to her unruffled self—was waiting for me in the office, along with the other two members of my small council, and my entire large council. Everyone already knew of the ruckus brewing. I was glad for the help and spent the afternoon and evening assigning tasks, gathering reports and summoning various Oracles who could assist the investigation.

It was nearing midnight when the message came to meet with the Rulers again.

The Ruler who oversaw Science and Technologies had invited Rizelle, Head of the Healing Temples to this meeting, along with a few more key leaders. "The spheres look to have been carrying a punch-bowl of viruses that will most likely cause illness outbreaks" the Ruler announced gravely. As with all the Rulers, she was the essence of calm. We only let our fears show in the private safety of each other. "Curiously, they're inactive at the moment and we've no idea what may activate them. The list of possibilities is apparently endless. Scientists are combing the records, but so far we've found nothing like it. They're working with plants, marine life and rodents to determine what it might affect and how. They have too little of the substance to test to the extent they need to."

"I'll issue an update to the Healing Temples so they can prepare. At least ready their staff." Rizelle said. I'd never seen her worried before. She left, after inquiring if there would be anything else discussed that concerned her.

"I'll get the news out across the country." Our suave, copper-haired

Communications Director spoke. "Wish we had more to tell them. There'll be fear—which won't help matters." Even understanding what reactions were probable, we rarely withheld information. In exchange, our people gave us absolute trust and loyalty. We all nodded gratitude to him.

Ruler Kenna offered a couple suggestions on urging the people to resist jumping to conclusions, before he excused himself.

"It's time to talk about the fact that only one other nation could come against us in this way." Ruler Eirene, as usual, brought us back to the center of pragmatism. "The spheres had to be dropped from an aero—anything else would have been reported as an anomaly. Even without proof, we all know there is no one else besides Belial with this ability."

"Could they have found out about the Mutazio army strike? Perhaps this is retaliation." Ruler Kenna's comment hung in the silence for awhile.

"It's possible the spheres came from within... some refugee or immigrant. Even an Atlantean with a grudge or mental illness." I reminded, though I highly doubted it.

"I'll have aero tracking reports compiled before we meet in the morning. Maybe we'll get lucky." Ruler Eirene replied.

Exhaustion adjourned the meeting, and we all had tasks to complete before we would rest.

"So this is how it begins." I muttered to myself two hours later, falling into bed for a few hours of respite. "Ready or not, here we go..."

6

THE CURE

9,970 BCE HIGH CITY, ATLANTIS

"I will not tell you our love story, because-like all real love stories-it will die with us, as it should."

— JOHN GREEN, THE FAULT IN OUR STARS

SILENA

"Still can't fathom why I kept you!" OldMother Silena muttered, blinking up at the dusty silhouette—and then sighed at her self-deception.

Because the artistry is perfection—beyond anything else in this over-wrought hulk of a temple. Why do I still try to con my own self? You have to care about something to lie. Aren't I too old to care?

She'd kept it because of *him*. For the love they once shared—perhaps a reminder of the bottomless dangers love carries.

From the beginning he'd been a rebel of the worst sort; the kind who flaunted it, laughed at admonishment, charmed, seduced or lied his way out of consequences. Unfortunately, by the time she'd realized all this, she'd already fallen—drowned in her own sticky-sweet needs, the frantic, insatiable mess that people called love.

"Obsession." Silena whispered to the gloom. "You were my mad obsession."

She'd overlooked the dark music he played in all minors, to seductive, off-kilter beats. Quietly, she removed or dismantled his ever darker sculptures and paintings; attempts to make ghastly modes of death beautiful, or ascribe great meaning to common mania. It was easy to cover up his works, since he was a scientist only dabbling in the arts, not a real student in the Temple of Beauty.

But his illegal science experimentation was what she couldn't tolerate. Time travel was where she drew the fatal line.

He'd come to her one night, ecstatic and secretive—more than usual—wilder than ever with his great lust for her. Bringing a trolley full of flowers, he'd torn off their heads, built a pyre from the petals and consumed her, body and soul, upon their fragrant silk. While she was admiring him, limp and satiated, he whispered that he'd been successful after a lifetime of trying. He'd travelled to another time... and returned, intact.

Time travel was forbidden in Atlantis—the study or pursuit of it even. So they fought then, as flamboyantly as they'd loved. "We're not meant to meddle in destiny!" She'd shouted, with fear and fury at his crossing of a line she could no longer ignore.

"Stop trying to control me! You've never supported who I really am." He snarled back, yanking on clothing. "Can't let anyone else rise higher than the *great* High Priestess Silena can you? You always have to be in control!" He'd flung the words at her and didn't even shut the door after he left.

The next morning she betrayed him. Reported his string of careless secrets to a Knight, believing it was the only way to save him. "It won't be so bad." She told herself. "Sure, they'll require him to rehabilitate in the Aades of Sacrifice, but clearly, he needs help."

He'd disappeared—somewhere in the realms of time maybe—instead of going to the Aades. He'd even managed to strike back at her in the language they once used to express undying passion, adoration and devotion; the language of Art.

She stared at it. This half-man, half-beast statue had appeared suddenly inside her sanctuary, her Temple of Beauty. *A vile idol. He's mocking me, or threatening.* She'd decided. That was the same day she'd met Drey's twin girls. Sweet Drey, who was dead now.

Habitually slipping a hand into the pocket of her favorite cloak, Silena removed the ball she'd already forgotten was there. Spying the strange sphere one morning, cradled on top of a rose bush outside the temple, she'd soon learned identical spheres had been found all over High City. The scientists were puzzling over them still, trying to figure out this plague that had everyone feverish and coughing. Some were dying.

Silena slipped the lightweight ball from one weathered palm to the other. Black and riddled with pin holes, it bore a strange symbol, stamped in grey; a solid sphere encased inside a thin circle that was broken, or incomplete maybe, from the bottom middle to the right middle. Overlaid on this was the equilateral cross of time and space, tilted to form an X. The bottom right cross arm shooting out through the gap in the circle.

Considering it, while the statue loomed over her, it suddenly seemed terribly odd that she'd come here for solace. Here, in the musty storage space where broken or never-finished sculptures waited perpetually to die. Here, at the back where she'd ordered his beautiful, monstrous sculpture kept—for what purpose she couldn't articulate to anyone.

But then she didn't have to. She'd been High Priestess of the Temple of Beauty. Now she was just OldMother, too old and worn out to keep up with those unending duties. She'd retired to the simpler title, the easier life, the boring anticipation of passing on. She felt utterly useless.

"Ah. We understand each other finally." Silena spoke aloud to the giant, dust-caked shapes around her. "We're both only waiting to die, clawing desperately towards our own end." Extending her hand out in a dramatized grasp, a girlish laugh escaped. Her hand dropped to stroke the top of the sphere again. "Well here's to me. I win." She cackled loudly this time, raising the sphere on one palm as if it were a wine goblet. "See, the whole city out there is sick. The very young and very old already dying in droves. That's me—the very old. I won't survive it. *You've* all got another century or three ahead. It's been lovely sharing this one with you th—"

The sphere rolled off of her up-stretched hand and bounced on the floor, coming to rest against that gorgeously wrought miniature city.

Hobbling after it, she bent over meaning to pick it up, squatting instead, settling her creaky old bones on the floor to study for the first time, how accurately depicted the little city was. Oh, much had changed by now, certainly, but at the time he must of molded and carved it, this was how High City had looked. She'd forgotten about some of the long-ago buildings, replaced with newer ones, or parks, or done over with expansions.

"You were so talented my love... " Tears gathered unexpectedly and one rolled, following deep lines down her cheek. " ...so talented." She looked up at the angel of darkness. "It's how I think of you, you know. Such an angel, so much darkness. He even looks like you. Did you think I wouldn't recognize it as a self-portrait? Did you mean to haunt me?"

The sculpture of half-man, half-ox stood upon the little glittering High City like a thousand foot giant, it's shockingly beautiful wings spread wide, muscular arms poised to smash a perfect pyramid of sparkling black crystal down on the city. The face... *his face...* leered a manic joy.

"How did you capture the exact degree of your insanity so well?" She wondered aloud. "You must have studied your reflection for days... weeks—what's this?" She struggled up off the floor, trying to move closer, wishing for more light. What was that, there on the underside of the lofted pyramid?

She stepped onto the city, uncaring if she broke it. He was perpetually threatening to, why couldn't she?

Squinting up, she willed her cloudy old eyes to focus. She was shorter now, precarious spine drooping a little more every day, and she'd never been taller than most twelve-year-olds anyway, even at the height of her youth. The angel of darkness rose at least ten feet with the pyramid raised above his head. A good lot of space separated her and the odd marking she'd never noticed before.

She looked around for a ladder. Nothing. Only ruined or aborted statues on wheeled bases for easy moving. Aha! "There was a staircase here once... now, where did you go?"

She tottered off the city, and teetered around in the gloom, peering between and behind the forest of shapes. "It was a ridiculous piece, I remember that much. Never wondered why your creator gave up on *you*... must've had more air than brains inside his melon. There you are!" She veered to the left and began shoving aside pieces that were two and three times her size. They rolled easily, bumping into each other until something crashed a little ways off.

"Oh dear!" She stopped to peer around a minute, before deciding it didn't matter. "Don't the rest of you get your hopes up though." She muttered between pants, as she pushed and shoved the huge staircase piece towards her angel of darkness. "That was an accidental mercy killing. I intend to beat the rest of you to the exit."

Finally, the partial staircase was as close as she could get it. Only about two feet wide, its ragged steps had differing heights and depths. On the second to the top stair perched a single human foot. That's where the artist had stopped; above the ankle of a common, bare foot fixing to descend a crooked stairway. "Boring!" OldMother snorted, taking the first step up. "Absolutely dull." The sculpture moved a little, and she stepped back down, stooping to lock the wheels. "Don't know why I bother!"

Only halfway up did she notice the lack of a railing. Here she was, well over a hundred years old, climbing a narrow, precarious staircase made of plaster, with no handholds and nothing to pad her fall. Shrugging, she took another step. "Good a way to die as any. I'm not coughing or feverish yet." The realization had depressed her when she woke this morning.

She'd been counting on dying soon for quite some time, but the years kept ticking stubbornly by, adding only more aches and less reason to live—as everyone she loved passed on.

Swaying slightly near the top, she reached toward the pyramid with both hands, realizing, now that she was so close, it was probably quite heavy. Possibly even attached permanently to the hands that wielded it.

"I'm... going... to find ...a way ...to steal ...your ...weapon!" She promised, grunting one word at a time, hefting and pulling the huge stone towards herself.

She almost had it before it slid off his palms. Almost.

Instead, it glanced off two steps below leaving a cavity behind, and landed on the miniature city it had been threatening since its creation.

"Curses!" She'd been hoping it was her that fell. Oh well.

She set about picking her tedious way down the rail-less stairs, losing her balance half a dozen times but always caught by some invisible hand. Reaching the floor, she bent double over the pyramid laying on one side.

The mysterious symbol glowed obligingly up at her in the gloom. She frowned. "I do believe I'm finally losing my mind. It's about time!"

It was the same symbol as the one on the mysterious sphere.

"Older than dirt. Feeble. Bones frail as rotted paper... " she muttered as she hobbled, peering around. " ...where might that ball have rolled? Not a bit useful to anybody on the planet, and yet I survive the plague *and* the stairs of death. Like a cockroach." She croaked a rickety laugh. "The great High Priestess Silena turns out to be of the roach family... Ha!" Picking up the wayward sphere she carried it back to compare.

She stared at the two identical symbols. "Not losing my mind after all. I wonder... " Even the grey color of the etchings looked the same.

Out of the top of the upended pyramid spilled grains of something white, a sort of yellowish white, "Or maybe my vision is finally going. It's about time... " She wet a finger and dabbed the powder, brought it to her nose to sniff, then to her lips to taste. It had no smell and was slightly bitter.

"With any luck, I just poisoned myself." Her mutter was hopeful, but her sharp mind knew better. She knew it was still sharp because everyone remarked on it often, and with an insulting degree of surprise.

Digging a handkerchief from the pocket of her cloak, she grunted, bashing at the pyramid's chipped point with a turquoise oval that had served as a miniature Hall of Records. More of the powder spilled out. Scooping as much as she could with gnarled fingers, into her handkerchief, she tied it into a pouch and headed towards the giant warehouse door.

"Perhaps I've been wrong all these years, my dark angel. Perhaps you came not to destroy, but to save…"

7

INVASION

9,970 BCE HIGH CITY, ATLANTIS

"Bran thought about it. 'Can a man still be brave if he's afraid?'
'That is the only time a man can be brave,' his father told him."

— GEORGE R.R. MARTIN, A GAME OF THRONES

AHNA

"OldMother Silena saved us." Rizelle, lead Healer at the Temple of Healing was taking Ahna's temperature, gently probing swollen glands and lymph nodes on the underside of her chin. "It's odd they call her OldMother… she was never a mother, no shred of 'motherly nature' either. Farthest thing from it!" They both chuckled knowingly. "Anyway. I don't know details, but she mysteriously produced a cure and the scientists—those well enough to stand—are reproducing it as quickly as they can."

Rizelle had summoned Aiela, asking her to take a supply of medicine to Poseidon's Palace and treat people there. With every healing temple in the city packed to overflowing, they'd long ago run out of healers. Aiela brought Ahna both for treatment, and to assist in Rizelle's request.

"Everyone in the City is sick to some degree." Rizelle continued. "Administer medicine to the worst—prioritize Knights and soldiers of course. We're getting an aero full of the cure anytime now. Other towns and cities are making it, though they're using it too. The whole country's infected. Every traveler here for the Festival carried disease home with them. I'm distributing as fast as I can to treatment centers but there's just not enough yet." She paused to pat Ahna's cheek after her examination and quick lymph drainage. "You'll be fine. Medicine will kick in by day's end. Hop up now. I need you both to work like the wind…"

Several thousand people had died already, mostly babies and elderly, but also some warriors, healers and just hours ago, Ruler Kenna.

Rizelle had explained. "Those in stressful positions succumb first because chronic stress depletes the immune system." It was a battle and there weren't enough weapons, nor people to wield them. The mourning would come, but presently the entire country was in survival mode.

"How do I—" Aiela began, but Rizelle was already leaving her tiny office with the cheerful poppy-colored cushions, and a tea collection that would've earned Auntie Sage's sincere approval.

"Trust your intuition dear." Rizelle answered the unasked question. She looked haggard and weary. "I'm sorry. I've no more time for you." And she was gone.

Aiela took a determined breath, provoking a coughing fit. She'd started on the medicine yesterday. The only remaining symptom was congestion. "Well I guess we'll get started then." Her voice was hoarse and her eyes red and puffy from little sleep, too much exertion and the slow shock of losing people to death.

Ahna groaned, rolling up to sit, and then stand. Her head felt over-stuffed, bouncing dull pangs back and forth between her temples when she moved. She had to breathe through her mouth.

People lined the walls inside the Temple, waiting for treatment.

Those who couldn't sit, lay side by side on blankets or towels spread across marble floors slick with tracked in rainwater.

She followed Aiela listlessly, stepping over and around miserable bodies to make their way out.

Outside, a light drizzle aggravated the fever chills, making her skin ache. The weather people hoped to wash the air and ground of the infectious diseases. It'd been raining for three days straight.

Trolleys were lined up waiting to drop off patients too sick to walk. Aiela hailed one after it dropped off an elderly lady whose mate had to be carried into the Temple. "Will you pull around back and help us load medicine?" She asked the pale trolley driver.

He nodded, coughing. "Surely Miss. And where to?"

"Poseidon's Palace."

Ahna desperately wanted to be curled in her bunk under the cozy green and purple quilt Mama made. Instead, she helped carry boxes, pots and canisters full of the white powder. Packing the little trolley full, she and Aiela stuffed more on top of themselves before setting off. Damp to the skin, she shivered, and felt grateful when the unorthodox burial by cargo began reflecting back her own body heat.

"The canals are so full." Aiela remarked, as they crossed a bridge arching over water running smooth and swift, lapping at the top of canal walls. They could hardly see the usual sparks of red orichalcum lining.

"Lived here all my life," the trolley driver replied, "and I've not seen them like this."

The great stone slabs of the streets, normally brimming with activity, were empty and quiet save for occasional passing trolleys. The constant, heavy dripping of water from trees and houses, and the small rivers streaming along street gutters sounded loud in the void of usual noises. The whole world was muffled in gloom, and a desperation to stave off death.

"When will they stop the rain?" Ahna muttered, her sore throat balking at use.

Aiela leaned out to look at the sky, causing boxes and bags of medicine to shift. "Soon as they've sufficiently cleared the air I guess. Sunshine would assist the healing. Hopefully they know that."

A lone Knight of Atlantis huddled beside the east Palace entrance. Loud metal shrieks protested as he opened the tall, intricate gates for them to pass.

"Never seen these gates closed either." The trolley driver said. "Nor guarded."

Aiela called to the Knight. "Have you been treated yet?"

He stepped closer, eyes searching for the source of the voice speaking from the loaded trolley. "No." He croaked, finally seeing her. Violent coughing ended with him spitting a glob of mucus on the ground.

"What are you doing out here in the rain? You should be in bed! Or at least staying warm and dry." Aiela was struggling to get out from under the precious cargo.

We shouldn't stop to treat him now. Ahna wanted to say. *It'll take more time than if we get set up first and send someone out to him.* But she knew her sister wouldn't leave someone ill when she had medicine at hand. Anyway, her throat hurt too much to try talking Aiela out of it. She studied the Knight instead.

He towered over the trolley. Ahna had only been this close to a Knight when the one that covered Chiffon came round to visit classes once a year or so. Their Knight had seemed big, but this one would've dwarfed Chiffon's, even hunched like he was now against his hacking cough, and the miserable sodden breezes that stirred it up. Tall as she was, Aiela barely came to his chest as she stood close, mixing powder into his water jug and sternly ordering he drink all of it. He looked mythical somehow. Like the gods that begat Atlantis.

All the Knights wore armor of course, but it looked merely ornamental until it was unfolded. A cuff covered with glyphs wrapped the left bicep. The right arm carried a piece that covered it from fingertips to shoulder. This was a Knight's primary weapon, integrated into their nervous system so that it gave them the strength of ten men, and responded to very individualized commands and movements. Contained within it was the capacity to stun, bind, maim or kill with light and sound. Should this weapon fail, Knights carried an array of others. These were a matter of personal preference, but might include electric darts the size of needles, a speaker that amplified the human voice into an unbearable pain, or a long, thin sword that sliced metal like frosting. These would be worn on a wide belt which pointed up like a mountain at mid back. Boots came to the knee. A band round the temple was double pointed with it's downward point almost covering the nose and the upward one rising well above the top of the skull. When activated, each piece unfolded into flexible lightweight armor that covered the entire body. The material was transparent in its native form, but painted dark matte purple for the Knights.

Ahna remembered how the children would gasp and giggle at the Chiffon Knight's demonstrations. How fast the armor transformed and locked into place. Sometimes, the Knight would let them poke at him with a dagger to show how impenetrable it was, assuring the boy who swung at his thigh hard enough to leave behind a faint scratch, that it was easily fixed. "We practice every morning," he'd explained, "hacking and chopping at each other. Paint job's the only thing that can be hurt when we're wearing armor."

Aiela's current, loud indignation at the towering Knight made Ahna smile, " ...ridiculous! You'd recover rapidly if you'd just rest! If you stay out here you'll only make yourself worse. When you're *well* you can actually protect us!" Aiela's voice always escalated when she argued.

"Two thirds of us cannot even stand guard right now." The guard muttered back between gulps, coughs, and sour grimaces at the taste. "I can. It is not a choice."

"There's been no Knight at these gates since anyone can remember! Another half a day won't mat—"

Fogginess flooded in and buzzing filled her ears, as a vision flashed and was gone before Aiela finished her sentence.

They looked like dogs but walked upright, shiny black and swarming up from the canals and harbor. Bombs exploded taking entire buildings down. Light guns flashed at everyone they saw. It was still raining...

"Aiela!" She croaked, trying to be loud enough. "EL!"

"What?!" Aiela swung back to see why Ahna was interrupting just as the guard was faltering under her onslaught.

"Leave him be. I saw... an attack, dogs, still raining. I saw it..."

59

They both stepped close to listen as she described the tiny sliver of images. Fear turned her rigid. Panic bloomed.

"*It was still raining.* Don't you see? This could happen tonight!"

"Go!" The Knight commanded, "Get back to the Palace. Have them summon every soldier to High City immediately. I'll get word to the Knights."

Frightened by what he'd overheard, wanting to get home to his family, the trolley driver helped Aiela unload while Ahna hurried through the halls of Poseidon's Palace searching for Ziel. He wasn't in his apartment or his office.

A few Oracle and Ruler apprentices were dragging half-heartedly through the hallways, trying to maintain their daily routine. Most were in their beds or gone to a healing temple for medicine.

"Maya!" Ahna felt relief, finding beautiful, capable Maya behind her desk. She would know what to do. "Where's Ziel? I've had a vision just now about an attack with big walking dogs—I know it sounds crazy. And it was still raining and—"

"He's with the other Rulers. In Kenna's quarters." Maya cut her off, already standing and grabbing her Comm. "Come with me."

"The Knight said to summon all soldiers to High City... "

Maya spoke into her Comm as they walked. "Well get them *out* of bed! They can direct weapons even sitting. We need as many in place as possible. Right now!"

"They came from the canals." Ahna whispered loudly.

Maya nodded at her. "Post troops and Knights along the canals outside the gates." She stopped and listened for a moment, one hand on her stomach, face tight with pain. Those whose respiratory systems weren't affected had stomach sickness, and those who didn't have stomach sickness had skin rashes and a yellow-tinted pallor.

"Yes I'm speaking for the Rulers." Maya dropped the Comm and doubled over, retching into her hands.

Ahna cast about for a receptacle but Maya was already retrieving her Comm.

"Don't worry, there's nothing left to come up. I haven't kept anything down in two days."

"Aiela and I brought a load of medicine. You should go to the Oracle offices and get treated."

Maya nodded as they entered Ruler Kenna's suite of rooms, and a hush of mournful chatting between the remaining six Rulers stopped abruptly. All of their eyes were wet and rimmed in red. Several coughed still, but were clearly on the mend. Ruler Kenna, like many others, had passed too quickly for the medicine to save her.

When Ziel saw Ahna he came to embrace her. "What is it? Aiela—?"

"—is fine. I had a vision..."

After being in the deserted world outside with its padded, rain-blurred edges, the room felt stuffy and loud, with a din of sniffles, sneezes, coughs and discomfited shifting. They listened without a word until Ahna finished.

"I've no idea what to do about it..." She admitted bluntly. "...so I'm going to go now. Aiela needs help." Unburdened of future terrors or trying to protect against them, she was desperate to get out from under their weight. Seeing everyone's worst nightmares coming was bad enough. Deciding what to do about it, absolutely unmanageable.

"I FEEL A BIT BETTER." She smiled wanly at Aiela, who, in the midst of supervising a dozen apprentices, maintenance people, and cooks handing out medicine, stopped to scrutinize her.

Satisfied with what she saw, Aiela moved on rapidly from one medicine distributor to another, as they had questions or needed to consult an actual healer. The orderly lines of those who lived or worked near the Palace, come to get treated, felt calming in the midst of it all.

Following, trying to stay out of the way, Ahna continued, "I'm just glad I'm not responsible for what comes after I see something catastrophic."

"Which is why we have Rulers." Aiela paused to survey the room. "We need a bigger space... the dining hall. Can you go tell them we're coming—if there's even someone to tell. I'll get everyone moved."

"And then you have to eat something." Ahna held her sister's tired gaze until she nodded.

"If anybody's cooking, we might as well serve the patients coming through too."

It was another hour before Ahna made Aiela sit to eat a bowl of soup. The large vats had simmered all day in the kitchens since these plagues began. A growing scarcity of cooks left the kitchens eerily quiet, and the few who remained, simply tossed in more ingredients as needed.

"Can you find someone to take food out to the Knights at our gates?"

Ahna considered the effort of assigning it, versus doing it herself. "I'll take it." Something was gnawing at her exhausted twin. She could feel it. Something beyond hundreds of patients filing through, or the fact that they would run out of medicine by nightfall. Something deeper than even the pandemonium and carnage of an entire diseased country. "What's worrying you?"

"Turner's ships are back. A man told me they've been docked at the inner harbor since this morning, and they'll likely sit for days until there's workers well enough to unload them. But where might Turner be?"

"Maybe he stopped to help somewhere. Or heard about the illness and took his men away so they won't be infected... "

Aiela was shaking her head. "He'd never do that without telling me first. Illness or not."

"What if the harbor master gave orders to turn everybody out who's not infected? Sent them away in aeros or boats?" She was grasping at threads, but in this chaos all of it was possible.

Aiela drank the remaining broth from her bowl and stood. Someone was waving and calling to her. "When we run out of the cure, I'll take a trolley to see if there's more at Healing Temple yet. I'll look for him then."

"But it'll be dark and—"

Aiela was already halfway across the room.

Carrying jugs of hot chunky stew, Ahna delivered them one by one to the Knights at four Palace gates. By the time she reached the east one, night had closed in. "You're still here?"

It was the same oversized Knight, patiently opening and closing the still shrieking gates for sick people who'd heard they could get medicine at the Palace.

"No one to relieve me. What we've got is massed along the canals outside the city gates, or at the outer harbor. Those numbers are too few." He gulped the soup, not even pausing to chew.

"Have more soldiers arrived like you asked?"

He was just a shape and barely that, a mountainous presence sucking at the upturned jug, and she realized he probably hadn't eaten all day. "Sorry. Don't answer, you're hungry... "

It hit her then. Without sunshine the last three days, solar paint, which virtually covered the city and lit it at night, had no charge. There were a few outside lights across the city that ran off storage cells, and some illumination spilling from inside of grid-powered buildings. Everyone was so used to the city buildings and streets— even tree trunks—being completely lit from the solar paints, trolleys didn't need guidelights on them anymore.

She looked up. Rain still misted the air, and cloud cover further muted the night. "We won't even see them coming, especially if they come from above." She muttered.

The Knight lowered the jug, looking skyward with her. "Yes we will. Pray to the gods any enemy comes by aero. Our radar weapons can clear a whole sky full of craft faster than I drank this excellent stew." He stepped close to return the jug. "Maybe the weather wizards didn't consider how dark the city'd be after three days of rain. Not to worry though, plenty of soldiers are here and they've lit up the canals outside the wall. Every light we've got is being placed out there, alongside the weapons. Should these, ah, dog-people somehow make it past our troops, you're familiar with the size of our wall?"

She knew he was trained in reassurance. A Knight's job was to calm and control. This one was good at it.

"Thank you for bringing hot food. I've been surviving on water and bars."

"You're welcome. We should've thought of you sooner. How long will you be out here?" She already suspected the answer.

"All night, all day tomorrow… " He shrugged. "However long there's a threat." He opened the gate to let her back through.

Ahna bowed. "Thank you for keeping us safe." He probably felt as rotten as she did. Pity mingled with respect that he refused to abandon his duty.

The low hum of an approaching trolley took his attention, and Ahna trudged back uphill to the shadowy Palace. Damp, achy and chilled, she wondered if they were all stuck inside some dream world; one shrouding a coiled intensity, just under the numb anguish of everyday death.

Aiela

"I'll just check. Maybe he's still on the ship. Maybe they won't let him leave."

"Sleep first." Ahna begged. "*Please.* I know you're worried, but if he's there, he'll still be there in the morning. It could even be a mistake —the report of his ships being here." She sat on Aiela's bed, sipping warm lemon water, swallowing with difficulty still.

"I have to get more medicine anyway." Aiela dug through a pile of clothes, looking for her heavy leggings.

"You don't even know if they have any to spare tonight! Wait till morning. You'll be able to help more people if you're rested."

Aiela looked up exasperated. "I can't just go to bed when there's so many who need medicine! I certainly can't fall asleep when I don't know where Turner is. What if he's out there, sick and dying somewhere?"

"He's not—"

"You don't know that!"

"*Please!* Don't go." Only Ahna's pathetic hitched voice kept the angry retort from coming out. Mercifully, Aiela found the leggings and began pulling them on. They smelled sour but she would need their warmth.

Ahna rose, wincing as she coughed. "Where's your other cloak?"

"No." Aiela faced her sister. "You're definitely not coming. No way. Get in bed. I'll be back in an hour and then I'll rest. I promise."

"You can't stop me... anymore than I can stop you. If you insist on going, so do I."

"Don't be stupid. There's no reason for you to come too. You're just trying to win now."

"I'm not the one being stupid! Or trying to save everybody!"

Aiela rolled her eyes. They never fought anymore, yet here they were facing off like they were five. "Fine." She snapped. "You win. I'll sleep first." Maybe between the shock of her ugly tone and the misery of illness, Ahna wouldn't notice she was lying. "Get back in bed. I've got to go pee."

Ahna rolled her eyes this time. "Like I'm going to fall for that."

"I promise I will come straight back after I pee." She recited it with as much sarcasm as possible.

Ahna crawled back under the quilt. "I'm just scared for you..."

"I know." Aiela was already half out the door. She *would* come straight back. She'd wait till Ahna was asleep and then leave again.

THANKFULLY, a few trolleys sat abandoned outside the Palace. Aiela rolled up to the east gate and checked on the Knight. "I brought you warm broth. Keep drinking. It'll help flush your system. Remember to take another dose the next three mornings." Already she felt chilled, and she thought about how he must feel, having been out here since this morning.

He took the jug. "Be careful. City's real dark."

She'd told him the Healing Temple was expecting her to pick up more medicine. Yes—even at this late hour, because people weren't going to stop dying just because it was nighttime. He'd been coughing in fits, clearly miserable, and she'd spoken with great authority.

It was hard to see well enough to drive. Interior lights flicked out inside homes and apartments as people went to bed. Offices, laboratories and markets had been dark inside since the city fell ill. She slowed to a crawl to keep from running into things. Even as her eyes adjusted, navigating was hopeless. Accustomed to her sub-conscious mapping the city, she felt lost in these foreign shadows. So she concentrated on going downhill. Half a dozen wrong turns later, doubt joined exhaustion. The headache that had poked and pinched at her all day, became a vigorous off-beat chopping. Shoving down the urge to cry in frustration, she continued on.

High City's inner harbor was along the east canal just inside the city walls. With only six bays that each fit two large vessels, it was meant for quick loading and unloading of cargo ships. She'd been there a few times, but the city had turned unfamiliar with only ten feet of it visible in the starless night. It began to feel like a maze.

Water covering the streets had turned into mud and thickened as she got lower, closer to the wall. Slowing to a stop to look for anything familiar, the trolley slid on the unmistakable stench of sewer. The system was probably flooded, or broken somewhere, from too much rain.

Above her, the night grew brighter from lights reflecting off of clouds, boomeranged from the other side of the wall. Occasional shouts and calls invaded the sleeping city interior, and three aeros suddenly lit the rain-soaked night as they landed atop the thirty story wall.

It was that brief light that saved her.

Movement snagged her peripherals; the sneaking, stalking kind. A two-second glimpse showed black forms moving towards her like a wave. Tall dogs walked on human legs. Then the light was gone, and unspeakable dread froze her. How'd they get inside the walls?

Ahna! They're here.

An explosion fragmented the quiet night, followed by another and another. She realized they must be advancing from every side of the city.

Just down the street, a man carrying a light sphere, stepped out of his house to see what the commotion was. Flashes hit him. What was left of his body crumpled to the ground.

This, finally, rocked her into motion.

Turning the trolley she drove uphill as fast as it would go. *If I can't see them they can't see me.* Shouted commands and the lights of aeros filled the night behind her as she sped, uncaring if she crashed into something.

Ahna wake up! They're here! Ahna! Letting instinct take over, she turned the full force of her mind to rousing a connection with her sleeping sister. Realized she was panicking, not thinking straight.

Explosions continued, almost in regular timed beats. She needed to concentrate on getting back alive.

Behind her, more and more flashes of light were accompanied by loud, wicked hisses like water droplets hitting hot oil. Cries, screams and garbled wails began too, but she didn't slow, or look back.

Atlantean troops realized their error quickly, pouring in through the impregnable city gates that hadn't been closed for protection in centuries.

But they were easy targets, grouped and unprotected. Those who got through, motored up the canals with spotlights, and hovered low in aeros to shine and shoot upon the moving black forms with the tall pointed ears.

But the Anubis were too well armed. The canals became circles of fire, and aeros came spinning down, crashing in deafening explosions.

With this shocking light, Aiela knew where she was, and the Knight at the east gate was fully armored as he let her inside without a word.

Lights already glowed all over the Palace as she flew through the halls to her room. Ahna was waiting, face white and frozen. "C'mon" Aiela gasped, "let's go! Bring my extra cloak it's at the bottom of the chest."

"J-just like m-my dreams." Ahna's teeth chattered as they wove through hallways full of sick and terrified people. "It's happening and I didn't know where you were."

"I'm sorry." She grabbed Ahna's ice cold hand tight, realizing that her own was trembling.

Ziel stood at his window watching plumes of fire jump high and then disappear. Aeros crowded the sky, frequently exploding in balls of blinding white. He was talking to a hologram of air controllers that shone from his Comm base across the room. "We can't take that chance. Warn the pilots to stay low. Go ahead and fire on anything else that gets close to High City. Let the rest go. I'm coming over there."

He snapped off the Comm and turned to them, putting a steady hand on each of their shoulders. Darkened cerulean eyes bored into them forging an iron calm. "Good. You're already here. This is what you're trained for. Packs on. Do not leave my rooms. If the Palace is compromised, go to the Crystals. I will stay in touch."

"Wh-where are you going?" Aiela hated that she sounded like a scared child.

"Air Control has no commander. Missiles are headed this way and they're afraid to counter them with all our aeros in the air." He said it like he was going to advise an apprentice on meditation. "Being severely short staffed is throwing everybody off." He smiled sadly and touched both their cheeks. "You know what to do."

8

OLD FOREST

9,970 BCE OLD FOREST, ATLANTIS

"I learned that courage was not the absence of fear, but the triumph over it. The brave man is not he who is not afraid, but he who conquers that fear."

— NELSON MANDELA

CHARIS

*L*ong after the watered-down sun had abandoned them to their fate, Charis stood disbelieving on her balcony. A string of tremendous explosions ricocheted grating sounds, throwing dust into clouds that reflected back flashes of fire. First a plague of illness, now something more terrible. Invasion.

Every bed in her spacious tree home, every cushion and even the rugs were pressed into service. People had come pouring out of High City before dawn, desperate to escape the only home most had ever knew. "Strange dog-like people wearing black armor, blowing entire buildings apart, killing everyone in sight with their light guns!" came the reports from shell-shocked lips.

A full scale battle had been waged between the dog people, and

Atlantean soldiers and Knights. Bodies littered every street and clogged the canals. Overflowing gutters and spillways, now ran the rusty color of blood. Many, still too sick to get out of their beds, had died in the first waves of bombing. Then the Belials arrived. In underwater capsules they'd come, wave after wave of them infiltrating, and systematically taking over High City. Atlantean soldiers and Knights fought valiantly, but their numbers were too few.

Those High City citizens who were well enough, had packed what they could carry and fled. "Only about half of us made it out alive." A sobbing husband reported. His mate was part of the half who didn't.

"It's said Mardu took the Palace." This from an Oracle apprentice who'd been at the Temple of Healing when the Belials came. "I heard he killed every one of the Rulers." She wiped at wet, exhausted eyes. "I don't think it's true though. I still sense them."

A severely wounded soldier who'd been carried out by a man and his teenage sons, was half-crazed with pain. Still, he felt responsible. Responsible for losing the city. Responsible to protect his country unto death. "They'll be spreading outward soon. We're not safe here for long."

Terror-stricken people are a study of animalistic reactions. Charis had observed them clinically while she fed, bandaged, and pressed them to rest. Studying the fear of others held off her own. Some froze, with no ability to think, speak or act. Others couldn't stop talking, babbling imagined conclusions hysterically between bouts of tears, anger or even denial. Every one of them who'd run, knew somebody who had stayed to fight, refusing to give over their piece of the city easily.

It was all so confusing. Should they all flee? Make a plan to fight back?

"What should I do?" She whispered now, from her balcony into the night of dust and fog. But neither the abrupt black, nor the dripping shelter of ancient trees offered an answer.

Sounds of plaintive crying reached her after the boom of explosions collapsed. A light glowed between branches where a young family had recently moved in. Charis had gone to them yesterday, concerned for their two tiny children who'd taken ill like everyone else. Bringing teas and potions that had relieved her own symptoms, she'd nursed the family; made a pot of soup, cleaned their beds, bathed them. The father was the worst.

She would go to them again. But first, she checked her Comm. A short national broadcast awaited, and she wilted with relief when she recognized Aiela's strong voice speaking from the Comm.

"To all Atlanteans," she began, "High City was invaded 24 hours ago by an army of hybrid human-dog soldiers known as the Anubis. Poseidon's Palace has now been taken by Mardu and the Belials. Our Temples are being blown apart one by one, and they threaten to raze High City in its entirety unless we—the people—submit.

Our soldiers are still fighting. I believe they will continue to until they no longer can. I do not know the state of the Rulers, but they are most certainly prisoners if they have not escaped the Palace.

We will continue updates as long as we can. My advice to you who cannot fight is; evacuate. It's believed attacks are happening across Atlantis and we will advise as to where, in the next broadcast. For now, the mountains and countryside are safest. Better still—leave Atlantis altogether if you can. Peace and hope to us all."

Charis breathed deeply, feeling balance return with even this small bit of news. Hope sprouted too, despite the bleak report. If she knew what she was dealing with—even a little—she could choose how to respond.

Astonished that any sort of joy could still reach her, she actually smiled with pride. Her beloved cousin's twin girls were not only safe, they were active. Ahna and Aiela were the closest family she had left. They'd come to see her at least once a moon since starting their apprentice in High City, and she treasured these times, remembering Taya, watching them both become ever more like her.

How they came to be in control of the grid was a mystery, but it meant she could communicate with them. If they could resist from the midst of this battle, she could certainly do something too. A plan began to form.

But first, the crying children next door.

Dressing warmly, adding Bren's long leather cloak, she gathered tinctures and tea. Hurrying across the uncertain night, she pushed open her new neighbor's door and stopped to bar it behind her before climbing up into their treehome.

Half asleep, the mother huddled beside two fussy children, little more than babies, singing to them in a voice strained and hoarse. Seeing Charis, she looked ready to weep with relief.

"I'll make tea." Charis suggested. "Then we'll get everyone clothed in case we're not safe here. It's best to remain ready to leave at any moment."

"Where would we go?" The mother seemed doubtful, hands holding tight to her small ones.

"There's a large underground facility not far away. We forest folk use it to store nuts, dried herbs, mushrooms and such through winter. A local sap gatherer stores her barrels down there. It's best if we're ready... in case."

Sharp coughs sounded from the bedroom and Charis took elderberry syrup to replenish the bit she'd left here yesterday.

The father was still feverish and she lifted his shoulders, helping him sit. Tall and stringy, he shivered despite the sweat sheen on his hairless chest. Pressing a mug of soup into his hands, she whispered the little she'd seen from her balcony, the broadcast update and her own instructions. "Don't worry about your family, I'll help. Once you're dressed, go back to resting. I will keep watch."

There was a deck built high in the old tree and she obsessively ran up half a dozen times to see if anything had changed. By the time they all wore layers, with bellies full and warm, the mother drowsed beside her sleeping children.

Charis made piles of folded blankets and baskets of food, between bouts of watching. Finally settling in with a pot of tea, she wrapped herself in Bren's cloak on the high deck.

So far the trouble seemed contained within the city walls. How long before it spread to Old Forest?

We'll prepare. Charis determined. *I'll send everyone on to any other destination they might have. The rest of us will serve. We'll shelter underground, stock food and clothing, coordinate with the twins and any others in High City who are serving. We'll be a way-station for those fleeing. The key is to get organized. We'll be ready.*

9

ATLANTIS IS MINE

"Power is the ultimate aphrodisiac."

— HENRY KISSINGER

MARDU

Stabbing a finger at five richly garbed men, Mardu ordered, "As my envoys, you'll follow my Generals. Specifically, you'll send back aeros full of medicine and healers. Offer whatever it is they want—threaten them—I don't care what you have to do. Just get everybody working round the clock. I need medicine for the Atlantean workers if I'm going to get anything done around here."

High City facilities that would have produced the cure to his Chimera were in rubble, along with the Healing Temples. Too stupid to think about preserving this city as their new King's Capitol, the Anubis had demolished too much of it.

His worthless, short-sighted advisors had neglected to account for this scenario, nor given clear directives on what to leave untouched. Too many of the remaining population were still violently ill. People he needed were fleeing. And Belials certainly weren't going to improve the country—for that he needed Atlanteans.

He pointed to Jaydee. "Choose Atlanteans to go with these envoys. Well-spoken, influential ones. Then gather the Elites. I'm ready for them next." His spies had been compiling lists for years on who would be sympathetic to the Belial cause. Who would join them. Which of the old aristocracies that claimed ancient Atlantis heritage, would swallow his bait of forming the new ruling class of people.

"Yes my lo—." She swallowed the endearment when he threw her a disgusted look. How many times had he told her not to be a fool. Just because he could openly use her anytime he wanted to now, didn't make him hers. He might find a suitable mate when there was time, and it sure as hell wouldn't be her. Her usefulness would eventually wear out.

"Are we finished here?" He asked the room at large, glancing around the elaborate, lapis lazuli hall. It pleased him to use the same space Ziel had, for weekly Oracle reports.

Conversations paused, people shrugged and looked at each, no one answered. "Be on your guard. Some Atlanteans will continue to fight. Report back to Jaydee twice a day. I'll be making decisions based on your reports. You're dismissed." These envoys would leave shortly from atop the Palace. He'd already had the Observatory equipment cleared so more aeros could come and go. Outbursts of resistance in the ruins of High City threatened anyone trying to get to the aero lots atop the walls.

Four days ago he'd taken Poseidon's Palace, capturing four Rulers of the High Seven. The minor Sound Eye made them wholly biddable. The Rulers themselves had ordered any remaining Knights and soldiers across the country to stand down, assuring the population in a national holographic broadcast that this was merely a change of regime.

"It's not a disaster. Belial desires simply to reunite with Atlantis. Mardu is committed to finding common ground. Do not forget, he *is* one of us." Consistently this message was repeated during instructive broadcasts transmitted to the population thrice each day.

Montauk, the Dark Tower mad scientist, hadn't been able to replicate the minor Sound Eye, but the one taken from Ziel's young Irish assassin had gained Mardu much useful information. He only needed the right people to put under its spell, and fortunately he held a majority of the Rulers. They had given sole rulership of the country to him. Under the Atlantean's own laws, this made him legally their King.

Only Ziel and Eirene, the Foreign Relations Ruler, had eluded him. Kenna was dead. No matter. He'd find Ziel eventually, and use him like the others. Once he'd ripped and plundered everything Ziel knew, he'd enjoy some long overdue revenge. Ziel would atone extravagantly for his sins, and die bearing the humiliation of utter failure.

Early this morning, the combined forces of Anubis and General Pompeii's troops had overpowered the main military compound north of High City. He'd simply had to steadily fire missiles at it from his own military bases, and wait until the compound ran out of power for their deflection laser. It helped that High City was low on solar power after days and days of rain, trying to wash away his plagues.

His scientists had been working to disrupt the crystal grid. Surprised when the military base power faltered after only four nights and days, he'd been elated to awaken to General Pompeii's communication. The deflection laser itself had been hit, then the main garrison of soldiers—probably regrouping to launch a counterattack. It was believed to be led by the missing Ruler Eirene.

"We've taken the compound and imprisoned all remaining troops. I've heavy losses." General Pompeii reported. "Half my men are dead or wounded, and three-quarter of theirs. The Anubis are all but wiped out."

"No matter. We don't need them any longer." Mardu inhaled deeply, leaning his head back. "Well done Pompeii. Ensure we've the right people in place to protect against attacks from remaining bases. I want you to take command, direct my Generals where to go next— probably Pyramid City, it's Atlantis' next largest. I'll leave strategy to you. I'm overcome with duties here."

Overcome was an understatement. He had not one, but two nations in an uproar. He'd armed any Belials who were interested, and let them loose on Atlantis to take what they pleased. Utter chaos would continue for a time. When it eventually settled, he'd press them all into the molds he chose. He had so much to accomplish and it all needed doing at once.

Already, the team who'd developed the technology for a protective dome over High City, was working to install its generators. The dome shield would require a huge amount of power—more than they'd had to spare in Temple City. But soon as he had control of the crystal grid there'd be power aplenty.

Besides quelling the remaining Atlantean troops and subjugating the people, he would take control of the Second Moon, use it to threaten Greece into joining their military to his.

He ordered High City's three best remaining architects be brought to him. Immediately they had begun drawing up plans to renovate his top Palace level into private quarters and a throne room. That would be the moment his victory was complete, ascending his well-earned throne...

Picturing a cavernous, gilded room, packed with his newly formed elite class—those who were worthy of his new Atlantis—brought a thrill. Over and over he replayed the scene that had driven him for almost three decades; He'd ascend stairs that reached almost to the ceiling. Perhaps he'd have them raise the roof so that his throne could be even higher—

"Your Elites are assembling my love." Jaydee interrupting his daydream.

He spun and backhanded her. Hard enough to knock her to the gleaming blue floor. A diadem she'd been wearing skittered away and she gasped, looking up at him with stupidly confused eyes.

"No one else is present... I-I-I thought—"

"You never listen. Love has nothing to do with how you serve me. Never speak that word to me again." He turned away.

The throne itself had been waiting for several centuries; an ultimate reward for his long-suffering—his dogged persistence toward this self-made destiny. Onus Belial possessed a massive chunk of meteorite. It was believed to be part of the comet that had impacted Earth, and ended the second epoch of humanity. Onus had it molded into an elaborate throne. Carved above the head piece was, *Nire boron-date munduko arauak.* My will rules the world.

Mardu had gladly stolen his predecessor's dream. He'd accomplished what the great Onus Belial never had. Now he would ascend the throne Onus never did.

"Get up!" He pointed at Jaydee, still sulking on the floor. "Go see when the feast will be ready. I want the ultimate luxury for my Elite. The finest of everything. Check the girls, make sure they're exquisite. I want plenty on hand so my guests can have their choice. Make sure they're well-versed on what's expected. And bring some smokes and wafers here. We'll get started with those before the feast... *what?*"

Still on her knees, Jaydee had put her diadem back on, but was shaking her head. "Dominus Mardu, I want only for you to be the most successful King of Atlantis. You know that. Pardon my input but this is not the way. It's too abrupt, too foreign, too *Belial.*"

She was bowing before him now, speaking carefully, head down. "There is much you'll require, much of your plans that you need *Atlanteans* for. It'll all go much easier if they *want* to serve you. They'll only accept your way if it comes gradually. These men who will be your elite, they're Atlantean to the core. They'll see the use of women as despicable. They'll think mind-altering substances destructive. They'll resist you, if you begin this way."

"What are you suggesting?"

She raised her head to meet his eyes. "Everyone craves comfort—security for their loved ones, especially when their world is falling around them. Everyone has some amount of greed inside—more so when they've lost everything. Start with those. Give them many reasons to like you, time to imagine the world they could build with you. Let them think they'll be kings too. Let them believe they hold power."

Sauntering to the wall of glass doors, Mardu stared out over High City; this place he'd lusted to own and rule for so very long. Dampened sunshine turned all the destruction depressing. Maybe half the buildings remained intact, but those blown apart littered once immaculate gardens with ruin. The vibrant colors that had always adorned High City were gone. Remnants of buildings which had stood for thousands of years, clogged canals that were supposed to blaze with the sparkling fire of orichalcum linings. Instead they overflowed with trash, creating lakes of sewage and rivers of decay, swamping the city. Splintered wood and twisted metal poked out of structures missing top halves. Entire sides of buildings had been sheared off, jagged holes ripped open.

He inhaled deeply, hating the anticlimactic reality of it all. Wet garbage smell still underlaid the singed incense smoke he'd ordered at eight points around the Palace.

What Jaydee said made sense. The more internal allies he had, the sooner Atlantis would be rebuilt, and the stronger he would be for it. This was his Capitol now. Time to start acting like its King.

Carver

Under a beaming spring sun Carver stood, watching workers raise collapsed building rubble from the canals. Often as not, a body—or several—floated up, mangled in the ruins. Grotesque with injuries, the damaged bodies were magnified by bloating.

The smell of rot lay on High City like a blanket, shaming invader and defeated alike. Piles of carcasses grew into morbid mountains, as workers cleared roads and waterways. Some mourned as they worked, for dead friends, neighbors, and coworkers who would be transported outside the city and burned.

"Incredible!" Carver muttered under the scarf covering his nose and mouth. A man right beside him was using only his highly trained mind to raise mangled metal frames. These oversized skeletons of once-majestic architecture rose in the air, streaming water, carrying debris that had been beds, artwork, animals and people. No wonder Mardu coveted the abilities these Atlanteans had. In Belial they'd be using conrectus, or slaves and camels for this sort of work, but here they had myriad ways of defying gravity. Handheld devices beamed energy into cracked blocks three times his size, changing the quarried stone composition so that even a child could lift it. Musical groups played the same twenty-four tones over and over, levitating broken columns of marble, quartzite, jade and lapis lazuli.

Even Atlantis' carnage was beautiful.

Every day, more citizens recovered enough—or maybe just got

curious enough—to venture out of their homes. Most wept as they first walked through their ruined city, especially upon seeing the demolished temples.

Upon seeing, more workers joined the effort to clear away the attack. Already, some were rebuilding.

"I want you to report to me the pulse of the City." Mardu had commanded. "Find a way to organize the clearing and rebuilding and do it fast! I don't want *ruins* for my Capitol."

"High City citizens are already working hard." Carver replied. "I'd like to reward their efforts, encourage desirable behaviors. Show them your benevolence."

Preoccupied, Mardu waved him away. "Do what you think. Yes, fine... "

Mostly, Carver was looking for Ahna and Aiela. It'd been a week now. Questioning workers in the Palace gained him the knowledge of where their rooms had been. Their clothing and personal things remained, but everyone claimed the twins hadn't been seen since the invasion. He'd located Ziel's little quarters, and he slept there now. Ruler apprentices, Oracles and palace kitchen staff alike, had answered his questions with short words and terrified eyes.

The Palace gates were heavily manned. Some of the staff, caught trying to escape instead of staying to serve their new King, were hanged. It had taken exactly six examples to subdue the rest. But plenty had made it out during the Anubis invasion. The twins must've been among them.

And what would he say if he found them? I'm sorry that I couldn't figure out a way to warn you? I'm sorry my father has wrecked your life and killed your people? I'm sorry to be one of the invaders...

Every day that passed brought a blacker despair. Much as he'd tried, he'd changed nothing. The whole point of abandoning the one person he loved was to save her. Yet he'd failed in that too.

Who was left to give inside information to? Besides the twins, he knew nobody here. Trying to help the imprisoned Rulers was too much of a risk. Likely as not, they'd mention it while under the Sound Eye's spell.

The best he could do now was make sure the twins had escaped.

Perhaps they were with Ziel, and already far far away. Part of him hoped so. The other part wondered how long he'd watch for them, search for information about them, before leaving here himself. Maybe he should go to Chiffon. Perhaps Ahna and Aiela had returned home.

"You're doing excellent work." Carver clapped the telekinetic man's shoulder, smiling in a friendly way. "I'm in awe of your abilities! I wish I could've seen this fine city before it was damaged. I hear it was the prettiest city ever built."

The man stepped away, shrugging off Carver's touch. "This country belongs to those who built it, passed down to those who maintain it. Only thieves break in and pillage, then *claim what was never theirs.*"

Carver nodded. "Yes. You're right. I'd like to help y—" His attention snagged on a passing trolley. Healer Lira! She was riding inside the little box on wheels as it wove slowly between heaps of shattered stone, ashy mud and bodies. He ran after her, catching up easily, waving the driver to a halt. "Healer Lira!"

She raked swollen, red eyes up and down him, shuffling cases and bags nervously. "Yes... who are you?"

He pulled the black scarf down, realizing it marked him as a Belial. The Atlanteans refused to protect themselves from breathing the dust of their despoiled heritage, or the stench of their lifeless beloved. "It's Carver... from the Ireland trip... do you remember me?"

She wiped at her nose. "Carver. Yes I remember you."

Belatedly it occurred that she was grieving, that it was the fault of his people. Carver glanced at the driver and another passenger, both glaring at him. Three more trolleys were piling up behind this one, growing restless at detainment. An armed Belial soldier patrolling this section of the littered street started his way. He leaned close to Lira, speaking low. "Is there a place I can talk to you? Private?"

She seemed slow to comprehend what he wanted. Finally nodding. "Come to what's left of the Healing Temple. I'll be there."

He stepped back. "Go ahead. Thank you." Then thought better of it. What was he waiting for? There was no more reason to hide. Mardu was too busy trying to jumpstart his empire out of utter chaos.

Every Belial was taking advantage of it. "Wait! He called to the trolley and ran to catch it. Stepping onto a running board, gripping the frame he smiled. "I'll just go with you now."

No one seemed happy about it but they continued on. They passed workers of every age, and no doubt every occupation, many still coughing, moving slowly as they labored under bright sunlight to clear out debris. Others brought jugs of water, or baskets of food to the workers.

Fresh food had been scarce following the invasion, with the established supply lines interrupted. But Ramon was working on that. Already he had aeros arriving from farms and orchards. He'd opened storehouses that protected the country from famine, and had fishermen bringing in three hauls a day instead of their usual one. Atlantean farms seemed to have endless supplies of reindeer, fowl of all sorts, sheep, goats and even elephants that could be slaughtered. Two small markets had re-opened. What the Atlanteans referred to as "scarcity" was still more abundant than what Temple City lived on daily.

Belial soldiers were thick patrolling High City—an ever present threat parading around, brandishing weapons. Across the rest of the country, Belial soldiers and citizens pillaged homes, and overran towns, taking what they wanted. But those in High City had been ordered to leave Atlanteans alone. Mardu decreed these were his people, and would be left unmolested—primarily because he needed a willing workforce. Still, they passed occasional soldiers rifling packs and bags, or patting somebody down, furtively cramming their own pockets full. No doubt this looting was hidden from the commanders. No doubt some of the commanders overlooked, joined, or even encouraged these abuses.

Then Carver saw a soldier pressing a girl against the wall, a hand on her breast. She struggled while another soldier watched and laughed. Her hair was light as flax and she was small.

"Stop!" He ordered the trolley driver.

Striding towards the scene, he stooped to pick up a broken corner of brick. Rage knotted cold in his belly as he swung it hard at the preoccupied soldier's ear. The soldier, younger than Carver, went flying sideways.

He came up bleeding and roaring. The other one who'd been leering, recognized Carver and put a restraining hand on his companion's chest.

"Go home." Carver said softly to the trembling girl, deflating with relief that it wasn't Ahna. She couldn't have been older than thirteen. "Report to the Palace if this happens again."

Carver stared the injured soldier down. "Mardu will hear of this. Who is your commanding officer?"

Blood ran from the soldier's ear. "I *earned* 'at—an a whole lot more! We was promised spoils of war! Whatever we can take is 'spose to be ours. It's why I joined. Otherwise, coulda got more stayin' in the gangs." He spat and it hit the tip of Carver's boot. Three more soldiers had gathered round, drawn to the uproar.

"Give me your gun." Carver held out his hand.

"No! I don' take no orders from you, I got a commander an—"

Carver used the broken brick one more time. Putting his weight behind it, he jabbed short and hard at the soldier's throat.

Clutching his throat and gurgling towards breath, the soldier slid down the wall he'd had the girl trapped against.

Carver bent to yank the requested light gun from his belt. Straightening, he glanced at the clustered soldiers watching with widening eyes. "Mardu's orders are to leave High City Atlanteans alone—especially the girls. Anyone who disobeys will be shot." He shot the young soldier. Walked away.

Killing always haunted him—but word would spread quickly among Belial troops. Hopefully his unhesitating savagery would save more than a few Atlantean girls from similar, and much worse, attacks. Girls like Ahna and Aiela.

Healer Lira's trolley hadn't waited for him.

THEIR CENTRAL HEALING Temple must've been magnificent. A swell of something between guilt and sorrow engulfed Carver, as he entered the cracked arch over a doorway void of doors. Gigantic shards of blue pectolite, and the clear quartz dome that was once the roof, blocked much of the central space. Smaller fragments crunched under his boots. Jagged peripheries of the bowl still held graceful pods that looked more like art than machines. No doubt, soon as the canals were cleared enough to stop damaging the broken city further, clearing and rebuilding crews would begin here.

Two of the arm-like buildings remained intact, packed wall to wall with people suffering horrific injuries. Several appeared to have died while waiting. "Healer Lira? Do you know where she is?" He asked anybody who would listen. Most ignored him. Others shook their heads, eyes pain-dulled or hollow with loss.

A young male healer administering medicine to a child with a bandaged head, pointed back the way Carver had come. "She's in the other wing, treating your lot. None of us want to."

In spite of the despising tone, Carver bowed. "Thank you. In case you haven't heard, envoys were dispatched across the country to bring healers and medicine to help you. I will see if I can get some clearing crews in here today. Make more space... "

"There's not enough healers or medicine in the world to fix the damage you've done." The healer bit out more words but Carver back-tracked, as much to get away from the shame welling inside, as to find Lira.

If the stench outside was bad, what filled the air inside was ranker still; personal and vicious, like a quarrel between bitter rivals. Stepping carefully between moaning, weeping, broken people, he noticed that even clean drinking water was scarce. Sending warm food, water and extra helping hands, would do much to ease this strain. He'd bring it all from the Palace himself if he had to.

Healer Lira was working midway down the other building arm. He was pointed into a room where she held a heavy looking machine over the crushed leg of a struggling Belial soldier. "Lie still! You have to stay still or I can't help you." Her pale blue robe was grimy with stains, hair pulled back from a sweaty forehead. She flicked exhausted eyes his way when he entered the tiny, makeshift surgery room.

"Give me a few moments to finish."

He nodded. "Of course! Can I help you with... this?"

"You could hold him still. He's in a lot of pain—which I can't do anything about. I have no hypnotist, no drugs, no nerve pods—my best healing crystals are broken. What I can do is mend the bone, but the leg needs to stay perfectly still, else it'll do more damage."

"Do you know who I am?" Carver asked the whimpering, writhing Belial soldier.

He wore an officer's uniform and stared out of pain glazed eyes, yiping when Lira adjusted his injured leg. "Don' think so." He slurred.

"I'm Carver. Son of Mardu."

The soldier looked confused, wincing, and sweating in his effort to focus on Carver's words.

Healer Lira glanced up sharply but said nothing.

Carver laid a hand on the soldier's chest. "So you'll do as I say. I'm going to strap your leg down with my belt. It'll hurt, but not as much as losing your leg—which looks to be the alternative. Scream as much as you need to."

Luck was with them. When Carver eased the belt tight around the man's upper thigh, he passed out. Together, he and Lira held the machine as still as possible over the man's leg.

It glowed and hummed loudly. Lira noticed him staring. "Usually, this is mounted and the patient is in a special bed that holds the body motionless." A three dimensional hologram on the top showed pieces of bone fusing slowly together. "We weren't prepared for... catastrophe." It wasn't an accusation, but guilt still wrapped around him.

He spoke in a low voice meant only for her. "I'm so sorry Lira. For all of this. I tried to help, to stop it, but I-I... failed... " Tears burned inside, and he felt one rolling slowly from the corner of an eye. She didn't look at him. Didn't respond.

"Mardu is my father—but I *hate* what he does! I despise him, his cruelty, his plans... " At this, her eyes came up to meet his. She blinked, went back to concentrating on the machine.

"Have you seen Ahna? Do you know where they are—if they're safe?"

Again, her eyes flicked up but she shook her head. "No. I pray they got out before... this."

She was lying. Her body had tensed, shoulders curling in slightly, eyes blinking too much while she said it. He didn't blame her. What reason had she to trust him? Still, it gave him hope. If they were dead, she'd have no reason to lie. They must be alive, possibly even close.

He pushed gently on the soldier's good leg, making sure the man was still unconscious. "If you see them, or hear from them, will you pass along a message?"

Lira didn't respond so he continued. "Tell them Turner is being held prisoner and I'll need their help to get him out. Tell them I'm on their side. That I want to help, any way that I can."

Minutes passed. A green light glowed on the machine. Lira set it carefully down, and faced him. "Why should they trust you? How can you expect anyone to?" She didn't say it with malice. Just stating a fact.

Carver thought for a moment. "Tell them it was me who sent Drey's journal." Lira pressed all ten fingers into her low back, staring blankly at him. "It's how our Mutazio army was defeated in Greece. The twin's father, Drey, made a node that controlled our—Belial's—mutas. Also could kill them. I sent—"

A tall, slightly plump woman opened the door. "Lira! I need you." She frowned at Carver. Her eyes took in the soldier, unconscious on the table. "Right now."

Lira nodded. "Yes Rizelle." And walked out the door without another glance.

THE MAZE

"Into the darkness they go, the wise and the lovely. "

— EDNA ST. VINCENT MILLAY

AHNA

*W*as Carver dead, killed by her own countrymen only days ago? Or perhaps weeks ago in the Greece invasion. Was he here in Atlantis somewhere? Out there in High City—close, yet impossible to find? Shivering, Ahna tugged her mantle's hood up, but not before Aiela's soft sob pierced her. Not the sound—not in this cacophony of Comm chatter—just the feeling of it. Aiela cried most nights from missing Turner, trying to believe he lived still.

Ahna fought to keep her eyes open, dragging her focus back to the row of Comms arranged beside the platinum Crystal. She must hold her vigil. The Belials didn't yet know their Comms were always listening, their viewers always watching. The Crystals saw and heard everything that happened in proximity to a Comm.

Day and night were all the same down here in the maze, so they tracked that through the Comms too. Daybreak was announced by Atlanteans rising early to meditate, often contacting each other by Comm to check in, give updates, assure those they loved they'd be together again. By mid morning, Belials stumbled bickering from their beds and began searching for food. Afternoons, the Belials spent exploring more of the city, watching Atlanteans restore it, taking what they wanted and moving into spaces they liked, whether or not they were vacant. Evening brought an absolute frenzy of Belial activity, usually involving all the wine they could lay their hands on, fading out around midnight as those above ground fell back into their beds each night.

She and Aiela monitored snippets of conversations, watched people fight, cry, eat, work, mate, comfort each other, and die. They passed intelligence to remnants of Atlantis' military, warned those they could on movement of Belial troops, and issued instructions to those trying to escape High City.

A few hours sleep, and then up to do it all over again.

They'd changed the maze again tonight. Eventually, Mardu would get something out of someone about the Crystals that powered the grid. Surely he must be searching for the Second Moon controls.

Ahna startled awake when her head dropped. Giving up, she began to shut off the Comm's screens, turning down the sound one by one. That's when she heard the music.

It should have been buried in the tangle of voices from a dozen scrolling Comms, but music wasn't played anymore, and it sounded as misplaced as birdsong at midnight. Listening intently, she singled out the Comm emitting the soothing melody. Touching a button to hold it to this frequency, she brought it to her ear.

The strumming was light, hushed, and familiar. A dulcimer.

Cross-legged on the floor, she took a deep breath and pushed another button for image. When the holograph sprang up before her, she gasped, staring at a distant corner of the outer Oracles offices; the room she used to greet and schedule those who came for a reading or dream interpretation, or astrology chart. Even dimly lit she recognized it, and just at the edge of that image was a hand strumming across a dulcimer. This instrument wasn't black or battered, but the colors of a tiger—gleaming and exquisite. Abruptly the music stopped and the player leaned forward, resting elbows clad in black onto knees, both hands in full view.

"Carver", she breathed.

She'd know those hands anywhere.

He was *here*! Ahna's heart thudded. *So close after all this time.*

Yes, and he left. No contact at all. Just turns up with the enemy. Why would I trust him? Threads of doubt invaded her excitement. His very presence here was a betrayal... wasn't it? He'd come against her nation, probably killed her people. And there he sat strumming a pilfered dulcimer in the Palace he'd stolen from her. He'd known exactly where she was the entire time they'd been apart. He knew she'd be in danger. Yet here he was, playing that song he'd sang to her so long ago on the beach in Ireland.

"It took two to light the fire.
Then her green eyes made it grow.
Burning higher and hotter,
while the crab pot simmered slow.

Well I've never met a girl before
who could light up the whole night.
Until I came to Ireland,
where she got me in a fight... "

How did she still remember the words after all this time?

Maybe there's a good explanation. He's playing my song. He must be thinking of me.

Despite sore muscles and the ache that never left her heart, she wouldn't fall asleep—not now. She had to know.

Aiela slept their usual sleep of despondent exhaustion, while Ahna buckled on her belt again, the one with five slim throwing knives, three vials of poison, and a laser gun. Waving off the lights, she slipped onto a hover trolley and sped off through the tunnels in the direction of the Palace.

She stopped a dozen times to disable traps and move walls so she could pass. Finally, she stood, breathing hard, at the secret door to Ziel's rooms.

Who might be on the other side? Who might she have to kill before finding Carver? And what might happen when she found him? She had no evidence at all that he still cared about her—and plenty of evidence that he didn't.

Waves of doubt grew. This was stupid. Worse than going all the way to Belial to find him. Had she learned nothing? She couldn't leave Aiela all alone to face what was happening. She wouldn't.

Turning, she made her way carefully down the long stairs, to the trolley, and back through the maze, berating her own foolishness every time she stopped to reset traps and reposition walls.

Rolling into the pallet next to her sister in the oppressive black of a soaring cavern, she fell asleep mid-thought; *We'll meet again Carver of Belial. And then we'll see what you have to say for yourself.*

"UNBELIEVABLE! What is *wrong* with these people? They're just giving up!" Aiela stalked back and forth across Crystal Cathedral, midnight braids chaotic behind her as her arms flew wildly this way and that. Soft boots made of fleece-lined camel leather, insulated her feet against the constant underground chill. "And we're not much better! We've lived down here for two weeks now. Two weeks! And for what? We can't raise an army like this! Who's going to call our allies if we don't? More and more the people are turning, caving, losing hope. We've got to do *more...* "Her footsteps were soundless despite stomping across the gleaming white marble tile.

Ahna sat on the same chilled floor, back resting against the Universe Crystal, green eyes following her sister's movement. For all Aiela's ranting, her constant movement was soothing.

Beside her, Sila's pale head, nearly big as a horse, swiveled back and forth too, following Aiela's fury. The snake looked more lavender every day, as though the grey gloom of the maze compelled her to show her true colors. Whether from the endless spaces of the maze, or a steady diet of rats, moles, bats, groundhogs, and no doubt larger creatures that wandered in from time to time, she'd grown rapidly. She'd claimed the spot dead center between the towering Crystals, coiling there whenever she wasn't hunting or patrolling the tunnels. Her massive coils pressed against all three Crystals, as if they were a glittering bed just for her. Ahna rested a hand on Sila's hard, cold scales and could feel the vibration thrumming through them, same as she felt inside herself living in close proximity to the 'Heart of Atlantis.'

Aiela was still ranting. "He must be brainwashing them. One day they're ready to sacrifice everything to resist and the next they're validating Mardu's madness!"

"Shht! I can't hear." Ahna pressed the Comm speaker closer to her ear.

" ...mandated Atlanteans of High City to attend. It is of much importance to our honorable King, Dominus Mardu, that everyone offer input into our newly united nation." Speaking, was the Ruler who'd headed the House of Education.

One by one, the captured Rulers had issued national broadcasts, imploring the people of Atlantis to "accept the change of regime as good and right". Giving instructions for peaceful "transitions". Assuring they, the former Rulers, "were now part of Dominus Mardu's overlord council who would advise his Greatness on building a stronger, brighter Atlantis than had ever been known. One that will again, rule the world."

As the broadcast ended, individual contacts pinged between Comms by the thousands. People were using their Comms to communicate like never before. Probably due to the separation caused by the destruction. Families and friends had been split apart in the exodus between the Anubis invasion, and when the Belials overtook Poseidon's Palace. Belial soldiers had quelled the exodus by shutting the city gates. But supplies still had to be brought in. Rubble and bodies had to be taken out. There were still ways to escape.

" ...will go. Sounds like a fair deal to me."

"Not much choice unless we go along."

"If the Rulers trust him... "

" ...not well enough yet. Something seems very very wrong with...
"

Voices drowned each other out until Ahna couldn't distinguish what anyone was saying. Aiela's restless pacing had been interrupted by her personal Comm, and she was talking rapidly to someone.

Ahna's lit up.

"Ahna? It's Felicia," said a quavering voice, "I've heard Aiela's broadcasts... been trying to reach you."

"Felicia! Yes, we've—"

A harsh sob exploded, cutting Ahna off. "Th-they're killing them!"

"What? Who's killing who?"

"Our elderly. A-All of them!" Felicia wept too hard to speak. Ahna waited, face tight, stomach even tighter, until the hysterics lessoned.

"They required everyone over the age of sixty to attend a special meeting at our Temple of the Sun. They *bombed* the temple Ahna! Killed everyone inside. Now they're going house to house searching for those who were too ill to attend. They're j-just... dragging them outside to the riverbanks—killing them—dumping them in the w-water." Felicia's voice ended in another sob. "Right now!" She whispered. "It's happening right now!"

Ahna's eyes filled as she tried to imagine what she could possibly say or do to help this sweet girl, reaching out from the midst of heinous assault, hundreds of miles away.

She'd missed Felicia after the Ireland trip, had spoken with her twice, seeking comfort from the grief of returning to Papa and Mama's death. Felicia lived in the City of Pyramids, a large metropolis that centered the northern half of Atlantis' continent. Ahna had only seen pictures. It was built entirely of large, medium and small pyramids, interconnected, with walkways in between the higher parts. One of Atlantis' more strikingly beautiful cities, set at the foot of the Central Mountains, its shapes imitated and glorified nature's noble, rugged peaks carved by eons of wind and water.

"Our rivers already ran red with the blood of High City's defeat. Now they're clogged with bodies... our wise ones. Our grandmothers and grandfathers. I wish I had died in Ireland. I *can't bear* this." Felicia's weeping was heartbreaking.

"Belial soldiers are doing this?" Ahna wanted to be clear. Sila nudged her face, long body stretched behind her as she made figure eights going back and forth between her and Aiela. Ahna pushed the snake away.

"Yes. They came in aeros. We resisted as long as we could. Our Knights fought to the death—every one of them—some of our people too, but we're not trained to fight. We've no real weapons. The Belials just kept coming—too numerous… "

Aiela was beside her now, listening wide-eyed to Felicia's horrifying report. They looked at each other, communicating silently. "Felicia, Aiela's here too. We want to comfort you but it's more important that you hear a bigger truth. Your life was spared so you can help. You lived—against all odds—for such a time as this. Do you hear me?"

The sobs quieted.

"What is *wrong* with you? Settle down!" Aiela hissed at Sila who was restlessly making circles around them, huge head bobbing, tongue flicking the air rapidly.

Ahna's mind was spinning. "We will get the word out so all Atlanteans know what is happening. Your elderly are being killed because they have energetic powers and the knowledge to resist Mardu. Pyramid City is next largest to High City. With a little planning, it could've mounted a massive resistance. Likely they'll try to wipe out Atlantis' entire elder population. We'll advise people. You've given us information that will save thousands of lives. *You* did that." She waited, hoping her words would have the intended effect.

Felicia sniffed noisily. "Wh-what do I do?" Timid, yet entirely sweet on the Ireland trip, she'd become close to both sisters, and then had very nearly drowned in the crossing between Ireland and Scotland.

"Do you know how to do a citywide broadcast? Or someone who can?"

"It would have to be from the Governor's pyramid… I think he's dead."

"Get there. Go as fast as you can. Warn the city to hide their elderly right now. Go!"

"Al-alright. I will." The voice was stronger now. "I'll go."

"Contact us again when it's done."

Ahna and Aiela looked at each other with a new horror.

"Get on the Comm." Ahna said quietly. "If it's happening there, it's happening other places—or will be soon."

"What shall I say?" Aiela had the same helpless eyes she'd had when she thought Felicia was dead in Ireland. She'd done her best for days now, to keep the nation informed, to keep hope alive. Despair, and the strain of trying to support Atlanteans was wearing them both thin.

At first, reports had trickled in of farms being ransacked by Belials, of Atlantean families being turned out of their homes so Belials could live there. Of town after town being subdued by the Belial military. By now, the trickle had become a torrent. Every few minutes a new atrocity. This though... this introduced a new focus of terror.

Atlantis' elderly were their foundation.

"Just report what's happening in Pyramid City. Tell them everyone over the age of sixty must evacuate the continent now. Or go into hiding at the very least."

"Sila, stop it!" Aiela dodged the snakes tail, whapping relentlessly against her thigh, movements frantic as she darted between the Crystals and back to nudge or nuzzle the girls, so big and insistent she almost knocked them over.

Ahna's Comm lit again.

"Ahna it's Charis, they're dynamiting our tr—"

A far off rumbling barreled in from all sides, undulating in a hollow roar through miles and miles of maze tunnels, drowning out Charis' distressed voice. The earth under Ahna began to shake. She looked up, watching the Crystals, fearing they'd topple if the shaking grew too violent. But the eighty foot crystal columns stood their ground, rooted deep enough in earth to move with it.

Sila had buried her head in a mountain of coils.

The earthquake seemed to go on and on, but probably lasted only seconds.

"What? ...can't... you!" Charis shrieked from the Comm.

"Hang on Charis. I can't hear you either. This'll be over soon."

They moved to the little area set up with bedrolls, food and water. It was a strange sensation, settling on the earth as it shivered and shrugged. Sila moved so her head rested on the floor right next to them.

"*That's* what Sila was trying to tell us." Ahna said. "Remember how Mama always knew when an earthquake or volcano was coming? Because Sila would warn her." She leaned over and kissed the giant snake's head whispering, "thank you."

Aiela found a jug of water, drinking deeply. "Wonder what has Charis so upset?"

"I don't know." Ahna closed her eyes, more weary than she could say. "I don't know if I can take anymore of this."

Charis had stayed in close contact as she hosted escapees at an underground waystation in Old Forest. People found ways to sneak out of High City, but often had to go without even basic provisions. Charis and her entire community in Old Forest did what they could, feeding and housing refugees, providing what was needed for the journey to somewhere safe. She was the last person Ahna expected to ever panic. Yet her voice had definitely sounded panicked.

The earth stilled, but there would be aftershocks. Atlantis was no stranger to earthquakes. They were as common as monsoons in the south or blizzards on Mount Atlas.

"Ahna?" Charis' voice came through loud and clear now.

"We're here Charis. Go ahead."

"They're dynamiting the trees!" Her voice shook with the effort to calm herself. "Belial soldiers are out here right now. They're shouting about traitors helping other traitors escape High City. They're *exploding* the trees. Our homes are being blown to bi—"

The earth trembled again. Once, twice, three times. Like belches from a pot running out of steam.

"I know you can't do anything about it but I wanted you to know. You can at least get the word out. It's not safe to come here."

"What will you do?"

"Stay underground. Wait till they're done… " Charis paused. When she spoke again her fear had hardened into anger. "And then we'll keep doing whatever we can. I'll let you know when it's over. How are you two holding up? Anything happening there?"

"Too much, yes. Aiela's fixing to do another broadcast. They've started killing the elderly in Pyramid City. Underground is the best place for you to stay Charis. Warn your people."

"Oh dear." Charis sounded somewhere between a whimper and a groan. "Why would...?" She let the question hang.

"Because you're our best chance at resisting whatever their plans are. Without our older generations—wisdom, experience, stronger psychic powers, leadership—we stand much less of a chance."

Aiela leaned over to take the Comm. "Charis?" She began, "You'll need to lead the Old Forest people in healing from this. Take some time to connect to each other from the heart, then to Earth. Mourn the loss of your homes, of the trees, but give the people reason to continue. Find hope, and focus on that. Don't let fear rule you or them. We'll be waiting to hear from you when it's over."

"Alright. Yes, I can do that. My love to both of you. You girls are doing a big job. I'm so proud... " She trailed away, sounding teary now.

"You are too Auntie Charis. We're all doing what we can."

"Have you heard from Sage?" Charis always asked this. The answer worried them a little more each time.

"Not yet... "

Loud commotion sounded from Charis' side of the contact. "I have to go. Talk soon." And she was gone.

Aiela made the necessary connections between her Comm and the crystals, then gave a brief, informational broadcast of what they'd learned. "Find hope." She urged nearly half a million people who would listen to this as they could. "Focus on what you have, who you have, what there still is. Let go of what's gone. Peace be with you."

Ziel arrived on a hover trolley just then. Ahna pressed her lips together trying to hide the smile but a snicker sneaked out. Aiela didn't even try. She burst out laughing.

He was dressed as a woman, silver hair curled and pulled into a fancy configuration on top of his head. Intricate black designs surrounded his eyes, and color bloomed from all the right places on cheeks, lips and eyelids. A delicate gown and matching jewelry completed a fiction that was as funny now as it was when he left hours ago. He slid off the hovercraft and stood, smoothing a trimmed and shaped eyebrow, watching them shake with much needed laughter. Aiela rolled howling to her side on the white marble tiles. He shook his head and began unloading his bulging pack.

"Alright." Ahna was breathless with the intense release. "We should get hold of ourselves." Laughter could just as easily turn to tears in the midst of this madness. So many emotions had assaulted them in the last two weeks, they felt raw and wrung out most of the time. Laughter was strengthening, soothing, so much better than the usual terror and grief. "Let's see what he managed to get. I'm hungry." She helped her sister up, though Aiela was still swiping at her eyes between giggles. "Pew! We both smell. Next order of business, bathing somehow."

Ziel eyed them defensively when they settled onto bedrolls beside him. "Sorry we laughed... again." Aiela said, not sounding very sorry. "What did you bring?"

His face softened when he saw how eager they were for fresh food and news of what he'd found in High City. "Lots of fruit. Some fresh roasted goat—what's happened?" He studied Ahna.

It had struck her that even his disguise wouldn't save him when they started exterminating the elders in and around High City. Making him into a woman was one thing. Making him young... something else entirely.

Going back and forth, she and Aiela relayed the news since he'd left. By the time they finished with the telling, his eyes were wet and his head bowed. "Eat something." He forced deep breaths. "I'm glad you got a broadcast out already. Gave them as much warning as possible. I'd hoped Mardu would continue his farce of civility longer than this. He seemed intent to win Atlanteans to his regime. Killing our elderly, mutilating Old Forest will guarantee a stronger resistance... unless..."

"Unless what?" Ahna didn't like the look in his eyes, could feel the defeat of what he was thinking.

"Rumor is, he plans to use psychotronics on the people. Then, there'll be no resistance at all."

HEALING BROKEN THINGS

"If you desire healing, let yourself fall ill, let yourself fall ill."

— JALĀL AD-DĪN MUHAMMAD BALKHĪ (AKA RUMI)

LIRA

*T*rue to his word, Carver set to work. Just hours after he helped her in surgery on that first surreal day of his appearance, he returned with two dozen Palace workers, Oracles and Ruler apprentices mixed in. Bearing gallon upon gallon of purified drinking water, vats of soup, even mattresses and blankets, they pitched in making patients comfortable, doing whatever the too-few healers bid. Clearing crews followed, and builders constructed a temporary roof over the central dome, rendering it usable at least. Aeros soon arrived, landing right on the littered lawns to disgorge medicine and healers, captured from other cities.

Lira's suspicion that Carver was just trying to gain her trust to get to Ahna, deepened. But also a tiny hope took seed; his motives with

Ahna might possibly be good. He certainly sweated and labored alongside the help he brought, day after day and night after night.

She hadn't contacted Ahna and Aiela, despite Carver's daily pleas. Partially because she hadn't a spare waking moment to spend on it. And would Ahna foolishly come to him? Lira couldn't take the chance yet. Hadn't decided if he was good for her. Was it true that he only wanted to help their cause? That he could pass inside information to whoever could use it to support the Atlantean people? That he would make sure the twins escaped? Or were these just paper promises fluttering off skilled lips?

Would it change anything if he knew the girls were at the center of Atlantis' communications, practically leading resistors? Would it anger him to know they were responsible for creating the increasing chaos and disconnect in Belial transmissions?

Too many questions. Hardly any answers.

Lira felt as fragile and temporary as wish paper these days. It was good to be so busy. Too busy to think beyond the emergencies lined up in front of her.

Her mate was gone. Dead in the swift and shocking slaughter at the military base just north of High City. She had a sister in Pyramid City. Her brothers were back home on the northeastern coast where her parents, grandparents and many cousins, aunts and uncles still lived—or she hoped they did. It'd been too long since she'd contacted them to see if Belials had invaded there yet. She was increasingly afraid to know. Was there a point where a person couldn't bear anymore loss? And what happened when you reached that point?

She finished splinting the arm of a six year-old boy, wrapping long strips of woven hemp round his chest. Affixing the arm sling to his little body would hopefully keep the pain bearable. His collarbone, three ribs and the humerus had been broken during the invasion. He'd waited so long for treatment, she had to re-break both humerus and collar bone to fuse them properly. His mother had died beside him in the explosion. He didn't know where his father was. "Papa's a sodjure a'till he comes back." The child would reply when asked of his parents. Nobody had the heart to tell him that his Papa would likely never come back.

"Count him out." Lira nodded at the hypnotist. Methods of pain control were scarce after the invasion wrecked most of the machines, and much of the medicinal plants and crystals. The hypnotists had died or fled. What they had left was reserved for surgery. Thankfully, two hypnotists were among the healers delivered in aeros, practically prisoners, given no choice in coming. Still. She was grateful for their help and they weren't at all grudging in their assistance.

Poking her head into the hall, she beckoned two young women. "It's done, you can go in. The hypnotist is bringing... " she searched for the boy's name. Gave up. " ...him up. He'll hurt for a few days. Keep him quiet as possible and have him chew peppermint and hemp. It's the only pain relievers we have in abundance. Make a tea of lavender and any mint, alternate that with lemon and turmeric. When the pain goes away, remove the splint and have him use the arm as much as he can." The women had three other children waiting with them.

In some gruesome mix and match game, the injuries and deaths of the invasion had produced altered families. Orphans were claimed by those who'd lost their own children. Men who'd lost mates found plenty of others in need of protection and help. Women and girls of every age stepped silently into sorrowful holes left by mothers and grandmothers, comforting, nursing, providing shelter and food.

After answering their questions, Lira walked to an exterior door, craving sunshine. She'd barely set foot outside the Healing Temple since the day Carver spotted her. The day she'd learned she had nothing left of the life she'd built.

Thankfully, every spare bit of floor space was no longer crammed with the endless tide of patients. Today, she might even be able to sit and eat between treatments. Patients still flowed in and out, but in a triage sense, these were the low priority ones. No longer did she have the guilt of dozens of deaths everyday because she couldn't get to them fast enough. Clinics had been set up in three other places, relieving much of the pressure.

Settling on a sun-warmed stone veranda, back resting against the building, she turned her face up to soak in blazing bright rays. It felt like a psalm of comfort, as if the sun had been joined by all the taken souls, to beam back a simple message of reassurance. Distant music floated between small breezes that smelled less of garbage and corpses today. Wafts of the old scents were returning: foods, flowers, trimmed grass. Surviving musicians had been encouraged to perform. They played while the sick got well. They played for mass funerals, and while people labored night and day to clear out the rubble. They played to bring familiarity and well-being back to their people. Lira sighed, embracing this temporary contentment. Perhaps the world as they knew it wasn't ending after all. Sleepiness tugged.

"Sorry to interrupt... "

Startling violently at Carver's voice, she huffed in annoyance. Other than sleeping for a few hours on Rizelle's poppy-colored office cushions, she had few moments to herself anymore. "What?!"

"Sorry... " He muttered again, squatting on booted heels beside her. The breeze lifted his shining black hair away from a disconcerting jawline. Bronzed skin glowed warm until she came to his eyes. Today they looked blue in the sunshine, but in most lights they looked grey. Either way they reminded her of ice or steel. Having come to know him better, she realized it was merely a cultivated absence of emotion. He was carefully blank, except for anger, which he used as intentionally as any weapon, and it made him seem cold.

"I brought you these." It was only tulips. Just a simple bouquet of bright spring colors he'd picked from a park whose flowers hadn't all been crushed. Or perhaps a garden that escaped the trample of war. He couldn't have known that her beloved had always picked tulips for her. That their home had been awash in them before...

Tears surged, as sudden and unwelcome as a rising flood. "NO." She forcefully pushed them away. *I cannot weep. Cannot. If I start I won't stop.* But still the emotions broke and though she cast around looking for something to dam them back up, there was nothing. Nothing but the understanding warmth of a carefree sun, and the furious cradle of foreign sounds. All day long, thousands of people moved things, cut things, pounded and built things, hollering and bustling about, all of it confined inside gleaming, inescapable walls. She tried to focus on these changed sounds of the city, grasping towards it like a lifeline, but it was no good. The tulips hovered in front of Carver's chest.

Long keening sounds shuddered from her depths as she let go.

There simply wasn't strength to hold it in. She'd lost so much, her mate, and their child that had been inside her. The tiny, half-formed baby they'd planned so carefully, and conceived so joyfully. The home they'd designed together was in rubble—possibly even cleared away by now, reduced to nothing. Only a memory to go back to. She'd even lost both cats, faithful companions of many years.

The pain of it bent her in half. Why she'd somehow lived through the explosions that took everything else was a mystery. Some sort of sick miracle that she didn't want.

Forehead nearly touching the stone veranda in front of her crossed legs, the long-delayed hurricane finally hit. Torrents of loss. Gusts of forceful tears. Why wasn't her chest caving in under such weight?

She surrendered to it, let it out and out and out. And still there was more.

Something feather light wrapped around her. She sobbed and choked and rocked and wailed odd, hollow little sounds, gulping breath before the next onslaught. It felt like entire ages passed while the grief found its vent. Like the sorrow of several lifetimes converged and collapsed around her.

Still the wrapping remained, and eventually, a realization that it was Carver holding her. That he knelt, long, bronze arms circling her shoulders, helping her rock when she needed to. He smelled like tulips. No, that was just because his gift had gotten crushed between them.

They stayed like that, resting between explosive bursts of sobs that should have dissolved her away to nothing—just like the bombs dissolved her home, her lover, her baby.

She felt him wave off someone who approached. The sun was no longer on her face but directly overhead now, the shadow of the building, a thin line that promised to grow. Still she wept and still he stayed, silent as a backdrop.

Eventually, miraculously, the grief storm waned. Had it been hours? Minutes? Days?

Calm—some sort of new emptiness—lured her outside herself to notice the Temple's cool shadow covered them. She straightened, and

Carver released her in careful degrees. His arms shone wet with tears and mucous.

Glancing up, expecting probing, unspoken questions from his icy blue eyes, she was relieved that he was staring off across the lawns. Watching distant workers as if it were completely natural to have someone you barely know come apart in your arms.

Wishing for a tissue, settling for the already grimy sleeve of her robe, she mopped her face. It felt swollen and gritty but oddly good to feel again. "Thank you." She sought out Carver's gaze but he turned further away, swiping at his smooth jaw. What she could see of his cheek was wet. Empathy. He wept for her loss, without even knowing it's breadth. "Carver."

Finally he looked at her. Red eyes—not icy—held such misery she touched his hand. "I will get your message to Ahna. We'll see what she says." Tiny, detailed muscles rearranged his face, but she couldn't tell if it was relief, or regret, or repressed anger he was feeling. He seemed to catch his breath. Nodded.

"The—" he cleared his throat and started again. "The dome gets launched tomorrow. It'll drain much of the available power until Mardu gets control of the grid. He's hoping the shutdown of needed utilities will force those controlling the Crystals to hand them over. The Rulers tell him there are three mega Crystals that generate and direct the power at the center of the grid. That only one of the Crystals is being used, because it's always been more than enough. They don't know who's in control of them. No one knows how to get to them."

"A what? Dome? What will it do?"

"It's a shield. Nothing gets in or out. Picture a thin membrane that acts like a laser beam—disintegrates anything it touches."

Lira's eyebrows rose. "Over Poseidon's Palace?"

Carver shook his head. "Over the entire city. The generators sit at the foot of the wall, so the shield forms a dome from the wall to about three thousand feet at its highest point."

"Won't that disrupt air flow? Birds? Weather?"

He shrugged. "Probably. The scientists aren't sure what all it will disrupt. Mardu tells them to learn and adjust as needed. It's experimental but he doesn't care. It provides him absolute protection from anyone who would come against him."

Lira's mind was trying to engage. If this dome sucked up most or all of the available grid power, the few machines they had left for healing wouldn't function. Lights, cooking, heat and such were all solar powered but anything more wouldn't function. Most of the newer aeros, trolleys, factories, even farm machines wouldn't work if the grid was drained. The country would be largely dependent on human labor again.

"That's not all." Carver was watching her reactions as he spoke—probably afraid she'd break down into another hours-long crying spell.

"Do you know what psychotronic weapons are?"

She shook her head.

"I didn't either." He admitted. "My understanding is limited so I probably won't be able to answer your questions, but Mardu says the psychotronic plan will go into effect once the dome is up. From what I understand, psychotronic weapons generate frequencies that have a certain effect on people. Specific emotions can be caused. Thoughts can be implanted. Mardu aims to create apathy in the people—so they stop caring what happens in their country—and of course acceptance of his rule, of the Belials."

"But that's... that's against the laws of humanity!" Lira sputtered, trying to form words. "It overrides free will! It's nothing less than pure evil!"

"Yes." Carver paused, letting it sink in further. "That's why I'm willing to do anything it takes to stop him." He shook his head, shoulders slumping. "So far I haven't come up with a way... "

"Where... " She tried to think what she should be asking. What would Ahna and Aiela need to know so they could get the information out? "Will these psychotronic weapons be only in High City or in other places too?"

"Here—just here—at first. But there's other things... apparently a way to encode visuals and sounds inside holograms or broadcasts. Messages our brains and subconscious can receive without us knowing. It's been used in Belial since Onus Belial's time. You've noticed they're encouraging music and performances—making sure they get broadcasted constantly? Whenever anyone is watching entertainment, they'll be influenced, brainwashed in a way, by these undetectable messages that are hidden in the sound and image. That'll go into effect across Atlantis. They've already introduced chemicals into food and water supplies—and just releasing into the air. These chemicals affect the mental behaviors. Wear down the will by making people unstable."

Chills broke out on Lira's skin. She felt the fear take hold. "What... " She pushed away the urge to sob again. This time in complete defeat. "What does he want?"

Carver considered before answering. Gallant angles of his face turned stony. "He wants the world to serve him."

"But... he's breaking it." She whispered.

Carver rubbed his temples hard, and started to rise. "That's not how he sees it. He thinks he's fixing it."

"That's insanity!" Lira gathered herself to stand.

"Yes." Carver said simply, reaching down a hand to pull her up. "It is."

"Tell her... " Carver said, just before Lira opened the door leading back to endless tasks, " ...tell Ahna she doesn't have to see me... I'll understand. But we need to get Turner out. Mardu will remember, will soon have time to—we have to get Turner away from here and I can't do it. Too many know me. I can arrange an aero, weapons, whatever is needed, but I need help. I don't have anyone I trust. Surely they'll know who can get him out if I tell them how." His tone edged into desperation.

Lira's eyebrows were high again. "Is Turner hurt? What's his condition?"

"He's weak, but he can walk. I'm doing all I can for him without raising suspicion."

"Alright." She had more questions but he was already headed off across the lawn.

She'd do it now, try to contact the girls right away. Her Comm was in Rizelle's office, the only home she had left.

GOODBYES

"*I will love the light for it shows me the way,
yet I will endure the darkness for it shows me the stars.*"

— OG MANDINO

ZIEL

I'd made ignorant moves. The problem was I had little actual experience in the caustic madcap called war. No one else in Atlantis had seen it and though I'd been alive during Onus Belial's uprising, I'd been young, watching from the sidelines, so to speak. It'd simply been too many centuries since an enemy came against us.

In earlier epochs Atlantis warred far and wide, conquering much of the known world, tucking it, somewhat willingly and very neatly under Atlantean rule. It was a wholly good rule, based on justice, equality and abundance. Our current "golden age" was the peaceful fruit of those times, cultivated and refined down through hundreds of generations.

As the Law of One gained in followers and our understanding

increased, we returned rulership to the local peoples. Because our Law of One teaches free will—even if that free will fosters chaos and darkness—no longer do we force righteousness on all the peoples of Earth.

Atlantis provides a place for souls to learn harmony and live in light. The rest of the world offers suffering at various levels.

But now, I'd made mistakes that weren't just stupid, they were fatal.

First was not requiring the Rulers to have a gatekeeper program. Something that protected them from *giving over the country* when they fell into enemy hands.

Second was letting the minor Sound Eye leave my possession. I'd wanted the twins to have a powerful weapon as backup when they undertook their mission to annihilate the Mutazio army. I'd been so desperate to protect them I hadn't paused to consider every possible consequence.

Third, and most calamitous of all, I failed to foresee that Mardu would plan around our weapons stationed along the borders, outside the City gates, and even the Second Moon, focused like a hawk on the airspace above us. That he was more cunning and determined than predictable. That he'd use a ruse as old as violence itself; cloaking the enemy in friendly vessels. I've often complained of the naivety of Atlanteans, never suspecting the truth; I am the most naive of all.

Because of this, because of my distracted, ignorant moves, my home houses an evil I hadn't imagined, my beautiful jewel of a country lies in ruins, and my people answer to a vengeful slave master. Every night hides a thousand bitter tears that I save up so the girls won't witness my utter defeat. Laying here in the unforgiving bedroll surrounded by a dark so foreignly black it keeps me awake, I let my mistakes replay as though flogging the ego that led me astray.

They're so resilient, the twins. So clever. That, at least, I did right. Breathing through my mouth because weeping always clogs my sinuses, I turned, grasping toward this thought like a field of sunflowers following the sun. Despite daily setbacks, reports of things so atrocious they can only listen and shed hopeless tears, the girls work till they drop. Every morning they awaken more resolute, talking strategy, how to better direct the people of our beloved country, how to block Mardu and his Belial savages in their reign of terror.

"Ziel."

I startled, not expecting the whisper, the small sphere of light appearing from under Ahna's heavy, leaf-green cloak. In a black as total as the maze offered, even a little light set us to squinting, blinking like owls with our hugely dilated pupils. I sat up, wiping furtively at wet cheeks. "What is it? Why aren't you sleeping?"

A shadow moved from behind Ahna and they settled together by my bedroll, cross-legged, tugging their hooded cloaks around them. Always it is the same chill down here. We've taken to wearing several layers. The one constant we can control for.

"I can't sleep when I know you're in despair." Ahna put icy fingertips on my arm, trying to soften her words. "Don't bother denying. I can feel it."

I'd always pictured myself being noble when trouble came, wisdom pouring forth, surprising myself with unknown depths of hidden strength. Instead I felt addled, overwhelmed, capable of very little. Even my psychic abilities seemed dimmed and useless.

Aiela yawned loudly, speaking in garbles before the yawn ended. " ...get you out of this... pit. It's not doing any of us any good. If you'll stop trying to hide it, we can help you. I'm a healer you know."

Embarrassment kept me from meeting their eyes. I should be bolstering them, not the other way around. Common sense made me nod. "Alright. Do what you will. And I'm sorry—"

"Oh stop!" Ahna muttered. "No apologies either. You're doing the best you can, just like we are. Lower your expectations of yourself for one minute and you'll see your pride's getting in the way. This isn't who you really are—but it is a reasonable human response to what you've been through. It'll pass if you'll let it. And one more thing; You don't get to claim total responsibility for Atlantis' defeat, so stop trying to. There are thousands of other people involved you know."

I blinked at this startling speech. It wasn't like Ahna to lecture or be so blunt—especially to someone who'd been training her not so long ago. It pierced me and I felt the ache in my heart soften a tiny bit.

"Bring your bedroll." Aiela said softly. "Lay out and get comfortable by the Terra crystal. I'll get my things to work on you now."

Meekly I complied, not daring to say anything lest it bring another tangent of words so true and telling. Failure, as usual, offered more lessons.

"Be careful." Ahna called, monitoring the Comm chatter. Behind her, Taya's snake, grown to astonishing proportions, was dancing slowly back and forth as if waving.

"Bye!" We both lifted a hand, cheery with anticipation of escaping our vast dungeon. This time Aiela and I were going. We'd been going out for food, water, baths, sunshine, changing out fuel cells and other necessities almost every day in combination of twos. Our stockpiles, so far, remained full and we were determined to keep them that way as long as possible. It wouldn't take much to cut us off. The problem now, was how far we had to travel to get out.

The girls had collapsed the main entrance to the maze as per protocol, soon as they'd come down here on that awful awful night. That was the only entrance the Rulers or anyone else was aware of. It'd been rigged since the day it was built.

Several other entrances existed. There was of course, the secret Palace entrance, which we couldn't chance, and a ponderously long tunnel that led to Old Forest, which we'd been using exclusively. I'd only imagined Old Forest to be an escape route should the others be compromised, but with High City sealed so thoroughly now, it was our main outlet. The tunnel was deep, cutting under two canals and the wall. It was also old. Part of the networks crisscrossing beneath High City since ancient times, it ran over eighteen miles long. Though a small distance for our hovercraft, eighteen miles would quickly become a major obstacle without them.

Mardu had already deployed his energy dome over High City. Glowing red, humming day and night like a million rankled hornets, it kept the grid nearly drained.

Our hovercraft were powered by the grid. We'd been supplementing the grid with additional power for short periods, while we used the craft, but didn't want to continue doing so. Mardu's people would soon realize there was more power available at certain times and probably use it for some new atrocity.

Controlling the power supply was a major coup for us. The girls and I had discussed cutting it off completely since our people had little of it to use anyway, forcing Mardu to live the same way everyone else was. But I wanted Mardu to believe his dome was really protecting him. Already he'd sent more of his troops out of High City —which didn't bode well for the smaller towns and villages, but made it easier for those Atlanteans trying to rebuild our ruined Capitol. We'd leave the dome intact until the time was right, until there was a concerted effort to come against Mardu. Then we'd pull the plug on its power.

If nothing else, communications throughout the continent remained strong and though it took little actual energy, it was only possible via the grid. Between the three of us, we'd figured out how to disrupt communications between Belial Comms. Theirs had different frequencies than Atlantean Comms, and we concocted a simple program that allowed us to listen in, or cut off the Belials. It was causing havoc. Especially now that many less aeros were usable.

"You brought an extra pack?" I asked Aiela, who was hanging on for dear life as we flew at high speed between earthen walls. They'd narrow further once we hit the old section.

"Two." She replied. "In hopes there's more fresh food." We were both weighted down. Her pack sagged with depleted cells for our heaters that we'd exchange for the charged ones we'd left in hidden spots of sunshine. Mine had empty water jugs.

Today we planned to bring a trolley back with us. Trolleys ran off of rechargeable cells and it was only a matter of gathering up what remained of those I'd had specially made to fit the maze tunnels. Most had been at the main entrance and were buried now, but all we needed was one or two. Long as we could recharge their cells regularly, we could use trolleys exclusively, though the going would be slower and rougher, especially in this tunnel leading to OldForest.

I worried too about the integrity of the maze. Tremors and earthquakes had almost doubled since Belial moved into High City. What-ever their projects, they were unsettling our already fragile area. We'd long had the major and minor fault lines mapped and knew how to work with, and around them. I doubted Mardu had given so much as a thought to them.

"Ahna really knows nothing of Sage?" I asked, unable to refrain any longer. I'd been waiting to speak to Aiela alone. Ahna had a lifetime of practice at holding secrets but Aiela's was only recent. I feared Ahna wouldn't tell me if she'd visioned something bad about Sage. Espe-cially if it meant I'd do something that might compromise myself. The twins' biggest fear was losing me, though I can't imagine why. I'm not contributing much.

But Aiela might tell me. She's as terrified at Turner's disappearance as I am at Sage's. We've heard nothing since before the invasion. Of course it's been just as hard on both the girls, imagining all the reasons why Sage hasn't gotten in touch. At this point, I'm making up stories and grasping at straws.

"She's had no visions and heard nothing. I promise. We're as worried as you, but it doesn't really help to talk about it, does it?" Aiela's tone was clipped. She knew full well my manipulations.

"I wouldn't do anything without talking through what's best with both of you." I said, just as shortly. "I hope you know that. No matter what we found about Sage."

"We're counting on that." I felt her rest her head against my pack.

Her night had been short. I'd fallen asleep while she was doing healing work on me, and I'd no idea how long she'd stayed at it. I did feel markedly better this morning. For the time being at least, the depression had cleared. I'd not realized how weighted I was until I woke without it.

Some time later, inhaling the muted smells of earth, I slowed as we approached the exit.

Stepping outside into fresh air, was itself an elixir. We stood breathing pine perfume and moss musk, letting sunlight warm our faces, soaking in rays like plants kept too long in the dark. The tunnel came out on Old Forest's south side, not far from Squirrel's Nest.

Devastation from Belial's attack on Old Forest broke my heart anew every visit, though we'd been going and coming amongst it for days now. Majestic trees that had housed thousands of generations of Atlanteans were torn asunder, thoughtlessly mutilated as punishment for the suspected harboring of those escaping High City. Much of Old Forest was impassable now except on foot, with toppled, fractured trees whose branch reach easily covered multiple acres. It was its own sort of maze, and we'd spent half a day crawling and climbing, making our way to Squirrel's Nest the first time we came out after.

Miraculously, Squirrel's Nest still stood. A quarter of Old Forest's trees remained, but they were the ones that didn't appear to be homes. Even these lucky remnants had been damaged from the neighboring trees crashing against them, crushing parts of any that were actual abodes. Squirrel's Nest was small to begin with, taking up only the barest of space within the central branches. For this reason, it remained intact.

Charis had supplies delivered there regularly and we arranged our fuel cells on high branches where sunlight formed pools of renewal and comfort, invisible from the ground.

Aiela and I sighed with relief to have sky above us and oxygen-rich vegetation around us, as we started climbing in silence. We rarely talked outside the maze for fear the wrong person might overhear. I was, as usual, disguised as a woman. Most everyone knew my face. If I was recognized it would be reported, whether by well-meaning folk or not. Mardu had offered a choice of rewards for me.

Because Atlanteans weren't particularly motivated anymore by threats of death, the Belials had taken to bribing them. "Your family may remain in your home if you report on your neighbors." Or, "We guarantee safety and plenty of food for your children if you turn over the elderly."

The genocide of the elderly continued, only now, they were brought to High City first. We'd had reports that Mardu himself sometimes oversaw the selection process, keeping those who seemed useful, condemning the rest to death. Other reports said he'd taken to mining them for information. The thought of it threatened to unhinge me at times.

As we walked, I trailed fingertips along fallen trunks, the ridges of tree bark separating rugged valleys so deep small critters could hide in them. Entire colonies of bugs formed miniature metropolises in fist-size craters. Leaves bigger than two hands, had only been touched by birds, butterflies and insects before now, and I wanted to exclaim at their luminescent green. Thriving and lustrous, they didn't seem to know yet their life source had been cut off.

All three of us craved the feel of anything besides dirt and stone, anything of the outside world. The replenishing warmth of sunshine, the freshness of breezes that knew no boundaries, had become a treat greater even, than special food or material things. "Incredible", I remarked, with not a small amount of grief, "how much I took for granted."

Heaving my aged body awkwardly over smoother branches with three foot diameters, I ducked under an evergreen that showered us with musky-sweet smells of sap, not minding the prick and scratch of their dust colored needles. Birds flitted here and there, their calls uncertain and mournful. My gown disguise was horridly impractical but I scarcely noticed anymore. Aiela was trailing behind me, no doubt lost in her own sensory wonderland. And that is what saved her.

I felt her grab at me just as snapping branches and shouts filled the air. Two Belial soldiers charged in like angry, puffing rhinos, pointing light guns at my chest.

"It's only a old woman!" One shouted, as two others crashed through surrounding downed trees to get to us. The four of them looked around and I exhaled when they decided I was alone.

I could have shot them. Slipping a hand to the light gun resting at the bottom of the gown's deep pockets would go unnoticed. I could take out at least two before they retaliated. It would cost me my life for certain. But even then, after all the killing and atrocities, I could not bring myself to violence, and I wondered; Given the chance to overcome Mardu by killing him, would I then?

Aiela must have hidden well. I didn't dare look. Apparently she wasn't willing to trade my life for any number of theirs either, as no spitting hisses of her light gun came to disintegrate my captors.

"Who you with? What you doing?" They demanded.

I shrugged, trying to look decrepit and lost, pointing to my pack.

One of them jerked it off me, examining the empty water containers. "She jus' gettin' water."

"She sure ugly!"

"Mus' be why she out here all alone." This started a campaign of crude jokes at my expense, but I maintained a slightly batty, uncomprehending expression as they searched my pockets, finding and exclaiming over the gun. One of them struck me on the back of the head with it before they led me out of OldForest into waiting trolleys.

Only a few skilled craftspeople knew of Squirrel's Nest. I worried immediately someone had given it up, but after no indications of recognition, I realized these soldiers were merely lucky. They'd been tasked with patrolling Old Forest and happened on us at random.

I analyzed my options all the way to the Aades of Sacrifice. The soldiers thought me mentally flawed, just another elderly person to be rounded up. I could've run. Like as not, they'd shoot me. Would that be better than someone discovering who I am?

Or I could simply tell them and get on with the showdown that surely must come. No. Better to let this play out. Who knows what opportunities lay ahead. If it came down to my execution, disguise intact, I'd reveal myself—not to avoid death—I'd always known I wouldn't live to see Atlantis saved. But first, I had things to say to Mardu.

The Aades' underground was crammed with old people. The closest thing to a prison Atlantis had, each underground room was full enough that we could barely lay down at night.

Mostly, I was angry to be stuck back inside Terra's bowels. The maze had ruined me forever to living within dirt and darkness.

Belial soldiers filled the top floors of the crystal-sheeted pyramid above us. It's beautiful rainbow reflections were cracked and marred by the invasion, but it was built tougher than the rest. It had endured as explosion after explosion rocked the rest of the city to ruins.

That first night we were allowed water but little food. Those in my room seemed an odd mixture of nostalgic, indignant and afraid. Elderly people rarely fear death, but we care deeply what happens to those we leave behind. This was the cause of fear and indignance both.

I couldn't afford to reveal myself yet, so I didn't talk. But I did listen.

The soldiers divided each group brought in, distributing them between rooms. This intentional separation was particularly harsh for couples, and many already mourned the loss of their mate. Some of them worked out a system of passing messages back and forth, spoken from room to room. Things you'd expect like, "Please tell Bella to stay strong. We'll see each other soon—one way or another. Tell her she's always in my heart."

It was first thing the next morning, shuffling along the fringes of a bedraggled handful of elderly, that I saw her. Cream-colored hair half fallen down. That face I'd loved all my life, looking worn with worry. My stomach churned and hope died a little more. They'd found her.

Here was my Sage.

Bold and insistent, I demanded to see an Atlantean guard. Plenty of our own people had joined the Belials, had given up fighting them and chose to improve their own situation any way that they could. It was frustrating, but I understood. People will do anything to keep those they love safe, to clutch tightly any bits and scraps of comfort.

Eventually, that evening, a young man was brought. He was impudent and looked down at me as though I were less human than he, though it was all pretense, learned from those he answered to now. I didn't care.

"There is a woman named Sage," I described her, claiming she was my sister. "If you let me have some time with her and then release her, set her free in Old Forest perhaps—or anywhere outside the wall, I will lead you to Ruler Ziel."

The guard studied me doubtfully. "Who are you? How would you know where Ruler Ziel is?"

I held his gaze, using every bit of mind control power that I had. "None of that matters. What matters is the reward you will get when you bring Ruler Ziel to Mardu."

He looked dazed for a moment, then nodded. "Yes. That is all that matters."

Ten minutes later I held her in my arms. Crying and clinging together, I still managed a small laugh, as she disapproved hugely of my disguise. All that evening I held her. All night we whispered of the twins, of Sage's mishaps and misfortunes in trying to reach us. We planned and argued and wept together.

Then we said good-bye.

REUNIONS

"Sometimes we find others in that darkness, and sometimes we lose them there again."

— STEPHEN KING

AHNA

"*H*e could be anywhere in the Palace! It could take days to find him."

"We'll just pretend to be apprentices." Aiela agreed.

In this they were united; retrieving Ziel before Mardu extracted information from him.

"Who knows what drugs or weapons or tools they have. The other Rulers are under *some* sort of influence—probably the minor Sound Eye. What if it works on Ziel too?" Ahna was afraid he'd give the Crystals over. With the Crystals came control of the Second Moon, and with such weapons, girded by an unlimited power supply, there'd be no stopping Mardu.

Aiela was afraid Ziel might accidentally inform Mardu about

them, even if he was programmed—as they were—to reveal nothing about the maze or Crystals.

What neither could bear though, was the thought of losing him.

"At least Auntie Sage is safe with Charis for the time being." Aiela's voice held enormous relief. "Soon as we figure out how to rescue Ziel, we'll go to her. Maybe hide her down here."

"It seems" Ahna pondered, "that we've traded one colossal worry for a bigger one."

After Aiela had returned from Old Forest, agonized and unraveling over Ziel's capture, they'd waited, searching communications, contacting everyone they could think of who might know something about where he was taken. Then Charis comm'd to say Sage was discovered at Squirrel's Nest, waiting fretfully to be found. "She's been trying to get here, get to you girls and Ziel for weeks, but then she was seized for being elderly. Here, she wants to talk to you." Charis spoke fast, over the usual ruckus in the background.

Auntie Sage was hoarse, as though her excessive supplies of tea had suddenly run dry. "Ziel bargained for my life. He gave himself up so that they'd release me." The words came forlorn and frayed. "I can't think why, and he refused to even talk about it. So now Mardu has him." It barely sounded like Auntie Sage's voice and the girls looked at each other, eyes brimming with worry. She sounded so broken.

"We will come to you as soon as we can." Ahna assured her. "Just rest Auntie Sage. Get strong. We're going to need you."

A resigned sigh was the only reply.

"Are you hurt? Do you need me to come right now?" Aiela asked.

"No." Sage exhaled, sniffing, attempting to compose herself. "No. As long as I know you girls are alright, I'll be fine. Of course I want to see you for myself... when you can. Ziel said to keep on with what you're doing." A modicum of strength crept into her tone. "Under no circumstances are you to try to find him or help him. He can take care of himself and he won't have you risking yourselves for him. He said you're much too important and you are to put the welfare of Atlantis before him."

"WHAT SHOULD WE WEAR...?" Aiela asked. Their choices were few and increasingly shabby. "How do we conceal our weapons?" They settled on tunics and leggings under brightly colored meditation cloaks, to hide weapons, and how dirty their clothing was. Without laundry facilities or even sunshine, washing clothes was unreasonable.

"What time should we go?"

"Better chance at night to avoid people, but harder to blend in..." Discussion of every elusive detail continued as they prepared. Mostly, Ahna knew, it gave outlet to their crippling nervousness. They were going into enemy territory, with no idea where Ziel might actually be.

Sila was curled in her usual spot, ignoring them. Bigger than ever, she seemed unaware their world was falling apart, piece by devastating piece.

"Keep an eye out Sila." Aiela joked half-heartedly, patting the cold lavender coil closest to her, before climbing on the hovercraft.

The snake lifted her head, watching them leave. As if to say, "I always do."

It felt like moons instead of weeks since they'd travelled the familiar route to the Palace. They'd gone back and forth between Ziel's rooms and the Crystal Cathedral exactly three times between the Anubis invasion, and when Belial marched into the Palace and declared it theirs. Pandemonium had set them dizzyingly adrift during those deathly days and nights. It was Ziel who docked them firmly underground, declaring them Atlantis' last hope as keepers of the grid, the Second Moon, and the center of communications. As astonishing as the speed and breadth of their lives turning upside down was, even more startling was how quickly they'd adapted to it.

"We're here." Aiela's whisper bounced off the walls in the deep underground silence. They slid off the hovercraft to finish on foot, climbing climbing climbing. Ahna breathed heavily. The weapons she'd strapped to her body, and a slim canteen, weighed like stone. "You're the better fighter." She'd told her muscular, fierce sister. "I'll carry backup weapons and water. You should stay light and limber."

And then the nearly invisible door was before them. They stood still until their breathing evened and deepened. Both drew a light gun.

They stared at each other, sharing the jitters of adrenaline, reaching for and pulling in calm. "Ready?" Ahna whispered.

Aiela waved off the light. "I'm always ready."

The little bedroom was dark and they stood listening until they knew it was empty. Dawn should be well on its way by now. Entering under darkness would aid them—as would the masking bustle of daylight. They'd chosen to use both.

Aiela cracked the door into Ziel's main room, peeping out before pulling it open. Her empty fingers curled in beckon. No one out there either.

They crept across soft carpets, cat-eyed and careful in the first glow of day. Someone had been here. Clothing heaps bristled with weapons by the single tall window. Three dirty food plates were stacked on the tea counter, and fruit, cakes and boiled eggs waited in a basket on the pretty rosewood table. They studied it for a moment, remembering hours and hours spent here.

"Should we check his room?" Ahna whispered so close her lips brushed Aiela's ear.

Aiela nodded towards the weapon in her hand. "Be ready."

Ahna was pressing the door handle when she registered movement on the other side. The latch disappeared under her hand, abruptly yanked open. She almost pressed the trigger, so great was her shock. Almost.

"Carver!" Her voice sounded tinny and disfigured, barely audible. He froze, backlit by sphere light, staring mutely at their shapes.

"Carver?" Aiela said louder from behind her. "Is that really you?"

He sucked in a sharp breath, then his face lit. A smile suffused those icy eyes, melted the stone carved lips, relaxed coiled tension of surprise, and he put a finger against his mouth. "Shhh." Stepping around her, he strode toward the door of Ziel's suite and Ahna thought to wonder why he was *here*—and should they stop him? Was he going right now, while they trustfully watched, to sound an alarm?

For no reason at all the smell of Ziel's rooms registered. As if the part of her that identified scents illogically clicked on after a long outage. Lingering still in this color-comforted room was the quintessential musk of Ziel, fresh yeasty bread undercut with honeysuckle.

Carver was checking the locks—already secured. Returning in three swift strides, he lifted her off her feet in an embrace. "I can't believe you're here. Is this real? Is this happening? Did Lira tell you? I missed you so much it hurt. Where've you been? What—"

Ahna felt disoriented, afloat in the formless, otherworldly logic of dreams. "Carver," She fought to stay stiff inside his arms, "put me down."

He did. No doubt registering her board-like quality, the fact that she wasn't returning the embrace.

It was too much. The shock of finding him in Ziel's rooms. The sincerity she felt from him as he greeted her. Moons of yearning for him rushed back like a sneering wrinkle in time, but so did bitterness at his refusal to stay in contact with her. All that she'd done to try to find him, all that it cost her. And now, what could possibly be the meaning of him... *here*?

Carver; part of the invasion. Carver; participating in the brutal reign of Mardu.

Aiela

Dark gods! This could be sticky. Aiela had literally forgotten about the possibility—or probability—that Carver might be here in the Palace. She'd forgotten what Turner revealed during all the chaos of going to Temple City in Belial to retrieve Ahna, followed by the terror of wiping out the Mutazio army in Greece. Carver was Mardu's son. *Mardu's son!*

The realization sent hope spiraling through her. Turner had also insisted that Carver was good, wanted to help them, still longed ("pitiful much" Turner had chuckled) for Ahna. If this was true, if Carver's allegiance was what Turner claimed, it'd be more succor than they could've imagined. They were about to find out.

Ahna backed away from Carver, fingers clenching and unclenching the light gun, emotions massing like thunderclouds on her face. She was winding up and Carver had no idea the storm he was in for. Aiela almost grinned. This should be interesting. But then Ahna's gun hand began to twitch and jump in jerky movements.

"Ahna." Aiela said evenly. "Best hear him out before—"

"What are you doing here?" It was a hiss. Each word bitten off.

Carver's face sagged when he realized there was no long-awaited welcome. He began to look terribly uncertain. "I can explain... will explain... do you want to sit? There's quite a lot. To say. It'll take awhile. So much has—"

Ahna was nodding, tight little shakes up and down, blazing green eyes trying to skewer him. "There certainly is! I can't even think—are you part of this? All this... *butcher* and *desecration*? You *invaded* my city! I will kill you—" The gun hand lifted.

"NO!" His hands came up. "No, I didn't want—I tried to stop it. I swear it! I couldn't do that... this, I love y—"

"DO NOT SPEAK TO ME OF LOVE!" She lunged forward a step as if to hit him, gesturing with the gun instead. Waving and stabbing the air like punctuation. "You don't *ever* get to say that word to me again! You... you... you *liar! Warmonger! Murderer!*"

Aiela cringed. Who might be nearby to hear the too-loud accusations?

Still. This needed to happen. There was simply too much between them.

"Fine. I won't, alright? I won't." Carver's tone was quiet, though husky and desperate. "Please can we sit? I will answer every question you ask. There's so much to tell you. Can you just—"

"I don't believe you." Ahna's eyes narrowed and if looks could kill, Aiela thought, Carver would be withering right this minute. "How am I supposed to believe a thing you say? Look at you! Here in *our Palace,* in Ziel's room no less, acting like it's yours! You've something to do with all this or you wouldn't be here. You think I'm stupid? You think you can just act like you're glad to see me and I'll, what? Just fall into your arms and believe whatever camel dung you shovel? Is that what you think?"

Carver shook his head, shoulders slumping. Opened his mouth to reply, then closed it again. Crossing warily to the rosewood table, he sank into a high-backed cushion chair, the one Ahna usually sat in. Aiela followed him, taking her own usual seat. This could clearly go on awhile.

Ahna paced in short, stiff steps. Her small frame seemed three times bigger, as chaotic waves of emotion rolled off her like the bulging swells of displaced sea after winter storms. They were dark red, almost grey.

Aiela selected a peach from the basket. Might as well eat while she could. Ahna's rage wouldn't last long. It burned hotter than anybody else she knew, but it ended quicker too. And when it did run out, they all had a lot to talk about. The peach wasn't ripe enough yet, but she didn't mind the tart, or crunch. She grabbed a cake to offset it, thinking about making tea.

"Fine." Ahna finally said, stabbing the gun at him like an accusing finger. "Talk then. If I think you're lying I might... hurt you."

You already have. Aiela could've pointed out. She'd known the truth of Carver's allegiance soon as he'd stood, stock still in the doorway, upon realizing who they were. His energy had lit up like the Palace at Winter Solstice. That vibration, those colors, could only be love. He did love Ahna. He would do anything for her. But Ahna needed to figure that out for herself. She'd feel it soon enough, soon as her volcanic anger cleared out. And Carver probably deserved some of this fallout.

"I'm Mardu's son."

Aiela stilled halfway into a bite. *Nothing like starting with the worst part.* She watched Ahna's gun hand twitch again, tap-tap-tapping against her thigh, eyes narrowing to slits.

"There's five of us. I'm the youngest. I hate my father." He recited it in a rush like unimportant trivia. "I sent you your father's journal, didn't Lira tell you? The one that explained how to defeat the Mutazio."

"You mean the one that explained how *your father* stole mine away, forced him to do things against his will, abused and tried to kill him? That's your proof? You could've got that information from the Rulers —the ones you've been *brainwashing.*" Ahna ended with a careless touch of sarcasm. "And how does Lira figure in?"

Carver looked puzzled. "You're not here because of her? I've been helping her at the Healing Temple. Asking her to contact you. She wouldn't even say if you were still alive or still here. I figured she would've told me if you weren't, so I kept asking."

"No. Lira hasn't said anything. We're here because of Ziel."

"Oh." Carver said quietly, defeat drifting like a cloud across his features. "Yes, Mardu has him. I'll tell you what I can, but first, there's something else you should know." His eyes switched to Aiela. "I've been trying to protect Turner, but he needs your help."

Aiela's heart stopped beating. Or felt like it at least. "What do you mean help? Where is he? Is he alright? What happened? He hasn't been in touch at all and that's not like him. I've been so worried, I knew something was wrong..." She stopped, realizing Carver could only talk if she let him.

"He's being held on his own ship in the harbor. He's not in great shape. Mardu knows Turner killed the Mutazio and he wants... revenge. He's just been too busy since we... got here."

Aiela started another question but Carver kept talking over her.

"I've been checking on him, making sure he has water and food at least. I couldn't get him out without help, or outwardly betraying Mardu, but I'm ready to now. I've only been staying here—doing whatever I can—to find you two. Together we can get Turner and go. I never wanted to be a part of this! I have aeros, supplies, we can go wherever you want. Anywhere far away from here."

"How did Mardu get him? How did he know?" Aiela's belly felt like she'd swallowed rocks instead of peach.

Carver sighed. "That's a long story." Faced with both their mutinous glares, he decided to abbreviate. "There were descriptions of a curly-haired Irishman from the border people. Mardu imprisoned the entire crew from the fleet when they came for the crystals, hoping to get information on who it might be. He figured out pretty quickly that Turner fit the description. Turner confessed and Mardu hurt him pretty bad. Killed a bunch of the crew... "

Aiela felt her heart cracking. "I have to get to him! We have to go right now! What if he's dying? Take me to him!" She was on her feet, concerned only that Carver agree to her demand. She'd make him—however she had to.

"Yes. Alright." Carver was eyeing both girls nervously. "But we'll have to plan it carefully. He's under guard…"

"What about Ziel?" Ahna reminded. "Can we get him first? Then get Turner?" They both looked to Carver.

He was shaking his head. "Mardu has Ziel with him. We'd have to go through all of Mardu's guards. It's… impossible—right now anyway. Maybe if Mardu gets done interrogating, puts him somewhere else. Might be possible then."

"But we can't *let* Mardu interrogate Ziel. That's the whole point! We need to get him out before he talks." Aiela was careful not to mention the Crystals, or what else Ziel could reveal.

"I'm sorry." Carver scrubbed his hands over his face. "Unless you have some army in waiting, some plan that involves more men and weapons than Mardu has, there's no way to stop it."

"But—" Aiela began to protest.

"You have one choice right now." His voice hardened with impatience. "Get Turner out—or not. Ziel is lost to you."

Carver

This was all going so wrong. His fears were happening right before his eyes. The sisters were still in the city and Ahna despised him. How had he thought she might still love him after all this time—after he'd abandoned her—taken so much from her people? It savaged him to see that sensitive face full of shocked betrayal. Her tight, accusing frown confirming he really was a horrible person.

No time for self-pity. He stood. Too many other things to deal with. He glanced at the pile of clothes and weapons. "I'll dress while you decide." Stopping squarely in front of Ahna's angry green eyes, he looked down on her and raised an eyebrow. "Either shoot or stop pointing that at me." He'd forgotten how small she was. How her hair glowed like the finest strands of sunlight.

She defiantly shoved the light gun against his chest, the force of her fury venomous and chilled. "There's still the matter of trust. You didn't tell the truth in Ireland—not even in the midst of professing your *great love*. What truths aren't you telling me now? I won't be a fool for you twice."

His own anger rose, mercurial, broiling. "You want the truth? You want to know why I didn't tell you who I was in Ireland?" He leaned into the gun, his face inches from hers. "You would've judged me soon as you knew. Wouldn't have bothered trying to understand—"

"You don't know that! You don't know the first thing about me!"

"Oh really? I know you would've seen me only through that lens, been as suspicious then as you are right now!"

"You've taken everything from me Carver! How can I not be suspicious?!"

She blinked back furious tears and all his ire died, right there on the spot. "Alright." He took a deep breath, pushing away a lifetime of hyper-vigilant defenses. "I will tell you the whole truth. You won't like it, you'll have plenty of reason to get rid of me and I wouldn't blame you. But when I'm done, you're going to have to decide. Either use this", he wrapped a hand around hers and the gun, pulling it tighter against his heart, "or trust me—because it won't work otherwise, I can't help you like this."

He glanced to Aiela. "I made a deal with Turner's father, while we were in Ireland. Mardu sent me to contract for their ships. At the time, he said it was to transport crystals from our mines. Now I suspect he'd been planning the invasion even then. I swear to you I didn't know about his plans—Mardu is too paranoid to tell anyone anything until it's about to happen."

Aiela started to speak but Carver kept going, switching back to Ahna. He needed to get it all out. "The rest of that trip was more true and real than any part of my life before or since. Mardu punishes, controls and abuses, by threatening anything a person cares about, so I couldn't risk him finding out that I cared for you two, or Turner." He didn't even blink. "If I'd told you who I was you could've found me. I'd either have to hurt you by rejecting you or he'd know—and always be a threat to your lives."

"Maybe you could've told me all that and—" Ahna began.

"Maybe." Carver cut her off. " Probably. I've failed in a hundred ways—I'm sorry. It's the best I could do at the time. You three are the only true friends I've had and I'm unskilled with friendships or trust… " he said it roughly, without pity, meeting Ahna's eyes, recklessly refusing to shrink from any of it, " …or love. But that's not nearly the worst… " he flinched saying the next words. "Mardu had your parents killed."

They physically startled as from an invisible impact, but he forged on, words barreling fast. "He informed me when I returned from Ireland. I didn't know of any connection before. He'd sent Jaydee to spy on you—which I did know when Jaydee revealed herself to me towards the end—but I didn't know *why* yet. Turned out Mardu was gauging whether you were aware of your father's work with the Mutazio nodes, whether to have you assassinated too. It wouldn't have taken much for him to do it out of sheer paranoia. I convinced him you were both brainless and harmless. I knew nothing of any of this until after. If I had, I would have done more to protect you. And yes, I should've at least warned you about Jaydee. Another failure." He stopped then, feeling wrung out, an empty relief.

Ahna's gun hung limp at her side and Aiela had curled into herself at the table. Both of them stared at him in wordless shock.

"I'm sorry." Regret started an acid burn inside when he saw their shattered expressions. "The only thing I could think to do was get your father's journal to you. I knew you'd have Ziel to help, be able to do something about it. That was my first attempt to stop Mardu from coming against Atlantis."

Ahna shoved the gun into its band on her belt, wiping away tears with both hands, seeming to release the breath she'd been holding since he'd opened Ziel's door and prayed the image of her standing on the other side wasn't just another dream.

"All that and you're not going to kill me?" He realized then that he'd been pushing her. That he'd been trying to prove how much he deserved her wrath, her disgust at his weakness, her ultimate rejection.

She shook her head. "You're telling the truth." It was matter of fact, but the icy edge was gone. "Is that all?"

He emitted something close to a laugh, almost buoyant with her acceptance of his confession. A strange new sensation. "Yes. That's all. That's every vile secret I was most ashamed to speak."

Ahna glanced at Aiela in the way they communicated without words, before replying. "Most of it wasn't your fault. We don't hold you responsible for Mardu's evil. Thank you for your help. If you hadn't sent Papa's journal, it might be far worse. At least Greece is still our ally... " Her eyes traveled over him, awareness rising suddenly between them and he remembered he was wearing only loose pants. Something else flickered across her face but she turned away before it could ripen.

Gods he'd missed that encompassing gaze, that pointy little chin that lifted like a queen proclaiming judgement. Crossing to his clothing, he wondered what might come next. At least he'd greeted her like he'd wanted to, hadn't waited for permission to hold her. Should've gone ahead and kissed her too—might never get the chance again.

Pulling on his black pants, armor, shirt, and boots, he listened to the murmuring behind him. They sat close together, a whispered discussion going back and forth. Strapping on his own guns, his blades, poisons, money and Comm, he thought about how to get out of the Palace without seeing anyone who mattered. The girls would help, hopefully knew it better than he did. He still got lost at least once most days.

"We're going to trust you—not that there's much choice." Aiela spoke quietly when he settled again at the table. "We do believe you and there's much to tell each other but—"

"You need to get to Turner." Carver nodded. "I agree."

The three of them strategized, sharing food from the basket, careful and awkward with the fragility of uncertain alliance.

He'd arrange one of the aeros that still worked, and supplies. The twins would get Kane, cousin of Turner, and apparently, fight instructor to Aiela. The plot was as simple as possible. He felt his spirits lift. So close. By this time tomorrow they'd be well on their way to... somewhere else. Eventually Ahna might fully forgive him, realize he'd risked his life a hundred times for her. He'd have the rest of their lives to prove that he loved her.

"Between the four of us, some luck, sleepy guards and darkness, we should be able to pull it off." Carver said. "Then we'll be gone for good. Does Kane have family? Anybody he'll need to get out?"

Both girls stared at him queerly. Finally Ahna said. "We—we're not leaving. After we get Turner out, we'll send him away in the aero with Auntie Sage. You should go too if you're set on it, but we can't."

It felt like a brick dropped in his stomach. "What do you mean you 'can't'? Of course you can—you have to! It's the whole reason I'm doing all this; getting you two and Turner to safety!"

Ahna was shaking her golden head, but compassion softened those frosty green eyes. "We will not leave Ziel behind." Each word enunciated very clearly.

"What if we can't get him out? What if there's never a chance?" He hated that it sounded like a whine.

"We'll find a way." Aiela replied firmly. He knew then, that he wouldn't be able to change their minds. And that they still did not understand fully what they were up against in his father.

TURNER

Turner coughed, and it felt like something tore loose inside. His chest rattled with every inhale and exhale, but to cough enough to clear it was excruciating. Carver said his collarbone was almost surely broken, and probably several ribs.

His face throbbed—though nothing like the raw stabs of pain for days after the beating—and his right arm was still swollen and useless. The only part of him that didn't hurt was his left leg. The knee on his right had been kicked brutally and he'd only lately been able to put slight weight on it again, for which he was thankful. He'd graduated from being unable to get up at all, to crawling, to now shuffling slowly, balanced against the wall.

The worst part was being so close to Aiela, yet unable to get to her. Carver knew nothing of the twins either. Every day he despaired a little more, hope seeping away.

Waving the sphere on for light, he struggled to sit and then stand from his prison bed; a pallet on the floor of a stuffy room, deep in the hold of his father's ship. He needed to relieve himself. He needed to drink water and eat something. Staying alive felt like an endless torment and there'd been plenty of times he'd decided to give up. If it hadn't been for Carver's regular visits, bringing soft foods, insisting he had to hang on because help was coming, he'd have let his body expire. Sure, and it'd been trying mightily to for weeks now.

Dizzy and chilled, Turner urinated in the corner bucket, sipped lukewarm water that tasted brackish, and took the last peach back to his bed. He felt ill. The last several days he'd been weakening again. How much longer before his broken body was incapable of going on?

SHOUTS WOKE HIM. Banging, footsteps running, more shouts. He waved the light on wondering if this was a fever dream, and lay there listening, but all had gone quiet again. Head spinning, he waved off the light just as he heard the voice.

"Turner?" It was female. Sounded too far off, no way would his answer be heard. Still, he tried. "Here! I'm—" it was a croak that ended in a fit of coughing. He moaned, holding his ribs, trying to still the spasms.

"Turner!" Closer this time. He looked wildly around, grabbed the light sphere, the only hard object he had, and banged it against the wooden planks.

"Turner? Is that you? Keep banging. I'm coming."

He banged harder, ignoring the slicing pain, bashing the stone light sphere against floorboards with every ounce of strength left.

It was Aiela. He'd know that voice anywhere.

And even if this was a dream, he was going to see her, damn it. He was going to look into that exotic face again. He banged until he heard footsteps outside the door, banged while the lock rattled and frustrated curses were hurled.

"Are you away from the door? I'm going to have to shoot it."

"I am." He called faintly, coughing again.

She must have heard. A blinding flash of light accompanied the loud, electric hiss and then she was in, rushing to his side, "Turner! What have they done to you?" She put too much weight on him, trying to embrace him, pulled back immediately. "I'm sorry love. Gods you're in so much pain." She stopped then, waved the light brighter, looking into his eyes, her own already filling. She caressed his face lightly, examining it, ran her hands down over his chest, splaying around the ribs. "How are your legs?"

"Left is… fine." He coughed again, shrinking from the pain of it.

"Don't talk. Just nod yes or no. We need to get you out of here quick before anybody comes. Can you walk?"

He nodded yes, struggling to sit. Wishing he could ask all the questions running through his mind. Was she here alone? Had she killed the guards? Where was she taking him?

Aiela helped him to his feet. He groaned and coughed, but lifted a hand to her cheek. "Loove ya."

"Shhh. I know." She said, tears falling freely within her focused calm. "Plenty of time for all that later. You're alive and about to escape. Save your strength for that." She moved to his right side, laced his arm across her shoulders and held him up. "Put as much weight as you need to on me."

They set off, him hobbling, leaning heavily while Aiela talked low, answering his unasked questions. "Ahna's keeping watch above. There were only two guards, probably because it's middle of the night. They saw us coming and we missed a couple shots—had to fight our way in—thank the great goddess for Kane's training." She was breathing hard with the effort of his weight, but did not falter. "We finally found Kane, to help get you out, but he's hurt too. Fought both the Anubis and Belial during the invasion. Got shot, quite a lot of damage to his shoulder. He's too weak still—already in the aero. All we have to do is get you to it. Auntie Sage will take it from there."

He didn't like the sound of that. "Yer comin'?" He grunted, trying to lever himself up the narrow stairs. The coughing fit doubled him over, nearly sent him toppling backwards. She wedged herself between him and the stair wall to steady him, panting as she strained to help him climb. The slight silhouette of Ahna waited at the top, and he stopped after stepping up on deck, trying to inhale, coughing with the effort. City lights turned the night pretty, all of it capped with a ruby red glow in the shape of an overhead dome. He wished he could enjoy this fresh air for the first time in too long.

Ahna put a hand on his arm in greeting.

"He's in a lot of pain and very feverish." Aiela updated her sister. "I'm not sure how we're going to get him to the aero. He needs to be carried."

Ahna thought a minute. "How about a boat? I'll go see if Carver can find one. You two just work on getting off this one." She ran off, disappearing down the gangway.

Aiela talked while they took laborious steps, speaking barely above a whisper. "There's so much to say but we don't have much time. Ahna and I are living in the maze, controlling the Crystals, the grid and communication. There's a comm you can use to contact me when you're better. Auntie Sage is taking you to Chiffon, she'll be able to heal you there. We'll stay in touch but you can't stay here and I can't leave—there's too much we have to do. Mardu has Ziel. Belial has taken over the entire country, but we have a fighting chance if we can coordinate the Atlanteans and weapons we have left. We have allies— Greece and Egypt, maybe India and China—who will come to our aid if we can get word to them. I'm hoping once you're better, you can help people escape. Maybe get word to your father, have him send ships and warriors?"

They'd made it past the fallen guards and were off the ship, looking about for any sign of Ahna. The inner harbor was deserted, but they stayed in the shadows anyway. "Don't talk." Aiela knew how desperate he was to ask questions. "It'll make you cough and we can't risk drawing attention. There'll be plenty of time later, once you're away." She caressed his neck, leaned in to kiss him so very gently on the lips.

He put a hand on her face. It was too cruel, having her for this little bit and then losing her again. "Ya come with..." He tried to tell her, beg her to come with him. But he only coughed and hurt until the long tunnel of darkness started closing in. At least he knew she was alive and well. At least he had the chance of healing. He'd come back to her —whatever it took.

"You're terribly hot!" Aiela worried over him, helping him down to sit on the ground, while they waited. "Infection somewhere... " He reached for her, wanting only to hold her, feel her, but she was digging in a pouch at her waist, pulling out bottles. "Here, drink this. It'll help with the pain." She tipped the tiny bottle against his lips, just a sip, and he gagged a little but forced himself to swallow.

"And this. It's for infection." That one was even worse. He fought the coughing. Aiela tucked both bottles into his shirt pocket. Laying her hands across each side of his ribcage, she stilled then. "I'm directing energy to your organs. They're sluggish and we need them to keep doing their jobs."

The buzz of a small engine sounded below and a light sphere waved on and off from the canal. "It's Ahna. Let's go."

Everything started blurring together then. He tried to tell Aiela about it as she and Ahna maneuvered him into the wee boat, but she shushed him. "I know. You're feeling the drugs I gave you. It'll be alright, just rest."

The world tilted and spun slowly, combining with the movement of the boat to make him nauseous. He registered the twins speaking low and rapid, what seemed like a never-ending time of motoring along waterways.

Then Carver was there, leaning over him, and both the girls were stretching out on the hard boat bottom beside him, their warmth a balm against his aching chills. "Try not to make any noise mate. I'm going to cover you with a tarp while we get through the gate."

The tarp smelled like bad fish. He retched, coughed, but Aiela steadied him, holding his head against her chest, stroking his hair. "Shhh." She breathed. "You're alright. I've got you. Just relax, it's a little ways to the aero. Relax all of your body... there, that's it. Open to me, let me help you. I love you my Turner. I've missed you more than you know."

He felt her strength flowing into him somehow. Felt the constriction in his chest easing just a little. He drifted away on her whispered words.

The next thing he knew they were lifting him out of the boat. Carver under one arm, Aiela under the other, they carried him, his feet dragging. It was the pain that brought him back to consciousness.

"Stop." He gasped, coughing with the effort to get his feet under him. The pain eased a bit once his full weight wasn't dangling.

"Sorry." They both muttered. "Is that better?" Carver asked, as they all repositioned.

He nodded, registering the dark shape of an aero ahead. Everything was still in the night, and a bright swath of stars shone overhead as they walked slowly towards it.

14

ZIEL

"So many of you believe that everything happens as it should happen, as it is 'meant' to be. Dear Ones that is not always the case. Things happen as they happen, as a set of many potentials. You are creators of your event horizons.

— METATRON, VIA JAMES TYBERON

ZIEL

*I*n the beginning Mardu used the minor Sound Eye, holding it six inches from my nose, clearly accustomed to its workings, and I knew; this was how he had the other Rulers doing his bidding. I'd suspected as much.

Surprised to speechless rage at my silence, my impenetrable obstinance even under the spell of his new toy, he set his boy on me, perhaps thinking I was withholding on principle alone.

Balek and his band of sneering guards, or friends, or whoever they were to him, kept at me day and night. I don't think there was as much as a square inch that escaped their fists, boots and eventually, their clubs.

The realms of meditation served me well as an escape. Outer events faded to background like one of our yearly hurricanes raging far off in the distance, held at bay by our weather machines. Physical pain had not been a part of this lifetime—until now. It occurred to me that Atlantean's ability to withstand pain of any sort, is severely limited by our total inexperience with it. We've arranged life to exclude pain completely.

DELIRIUM'S an odd state of mind. I studied it's essence, the textures and edges of it, from my semi-lucid state. Time didn't exist anymore. Everything had coalesced in one endless presence of bottomless pain. Quick as I registered the word, sensations followed and my mind galloped off again, running running running. Don't go near it again!

I—this me who'd been fairly cohesive—had shattered to pieces, each piece having its own experience, like a broken mirror that reflects varied distortions of reality.

Reality; now there's a misunderstood concept.

"...this can stop Ziel, anytime you choose to cooperate. Where are the Crystals?" Mardu's voice was dull, his frustration had frayed him to a state not that different from my own. Determined to win, he still battered me because he didn't understand. He thought no one could bear so much pain without breaking—but I *had* broken. I'd broken long ago. Splintered. Crushed. Fragmented. I literally could not do what he asked. It was impossible.

I'd been programmed with a gatekeeper personality years before I'd programmed the twins. Once triggered, the personality shut everything down. He might as well be speaking in a foreign tongue. I didn't know what he asked, my mind went as blank and confused as a small child. It was in between his persistent tortures that other pieces of me came and went.

It must've been the use of my name that summoned me momentarily out of my sweet delirium.

I wasn't in my body. From a high corner of the room, I saw the fragile naked form cowering on the floor. He'd sheared me with his

135

knife and large patches of scalp still hung off my bloody head. He'd known that hair acts like antennae to the psyche. Was that moons ago? Or just hours? The knife had flashed again and again. Half of my fingers were missing pieces or split lengthwise.

Now we know gatekeeper works very very well. This floating part of me gloated. I clung to any victory, any triumph.

Thin tendrils of foul smelling smoke rose from Mardu's current handiwork on the body. I dived back into delirium, terrified, as that pale form started to squirm and scream.

◎◎

LIFE WAS EBBING AWAY. I felt my body struggling to breathe, to pump blood, unable to keep up with the wounds or stave off infection. This realization bloomed in my inner darkness and I pondered it. Death's door was opening up before me and I was grateful—but along with it came a sense of now-or-never, which lent a crushing urgency to my muddled mind.

Working to clear it, I decided the best I could do was mislead, lie well and extravagantly. Fortunately, I've had a lifetime of practice and since I'd endured to the end, Mardu would likely believe me. He was so desperate to defeat me he'd probably jump on anything I confessed, especially if my death followed.

Soft, rhythmic slapping came from nearby. Female whimpers turning from fear to discomfort. "Please... stop." I knew that voice, forced my eyes open. It was Frond.

I was a heap on the icy marble floor, chained to the foot of Mardu's bed. The noxious ruination of my body began to register and I returned inward, forcing my mind to focus, to concentrate on thoughts. *Shut everything else out. Make a plan and do it quick.*

"Mardu!" I yelled, but it came out like a squeak. The slapping stopped. "Mardu, I'm ready to talk." I gasped at the sensations flooding in.

"Good for you. I'm busy." He sounded breathless and the bed shook.

"I won't talk unless you let her go. You won't get a single word."

A pause, then Frond came flying off the bedside. Naked, she landed painfully on the floor, saw me and started to crawl towards me. Her beautiful chestnut hair was knotted and tangled. "Ziel, you're awake..." Her lip was bloody.

Mardu stepped off after her, half-dressed—missing only his shirt, pulling his pants together in the front. He kicked her in the chest with his boot. "Get out."

Her yipe, like a small puppy, broke my heart. "Go!" I commanded with every ounce of strength that remained. "Go now!"

She did, eyes wild and unfocused, scrabbling away on hands and knees before rising to run off in the darkness.

He turned to me. "That's all it took? Fucking one of your little bitches, making her squeal?" He laughed. "All that time and effort and... mess, half your body cut away, but play rough with a *woman* and you crack like ripe melons! Where's your sense of self-preservation? You know I'll have her back in here soon as we're done..." He squatted down to look at me in disgust. "You're such a little squid of a man. No, not a squid... a shrimp! That's what I meant."

I could smell the alcohol on his breath. It was making him wordy. Hopefully gullible too.

"And to think, I once looked up to you. How have you ever commanded such respect? If they could all see you now—and they will! We'll have a public execution I think, leaving no doubt in their minds, no misguided hopes they've anyone left to look to but me. So..." He rose and walked to a chair, dragging it right in front of me, it's ornate metal legs shrieked irascibly across the marble. "...talk."

I breathed as deep as I could—but that ushered me too fully into my body. My pitiful, mutilated body... "The Crystals are in an underground cavern exactly one hundred, twenty seven miles due west. We accessed them through tunnels that began under the Palace—which I've collapsed. There was a maze—gone now—but there's another way." I stopped to catch my breath. An agony of pain was crowding in and I didn't have long before it became too much, before I'd need to find respite again. "You'll have to start from the central mountains in Crystal City—the ruins. You'll easily find the opening... parts of the tunnels on that side need repaired but you surely have people to send. Once it's repaired, stay northeast. True northeast. It'll get you there."

"Are you the only—"

"I'm the only keeper of the Crystals left. Everyone else is gone." I lied quickly. If he activated the gatekeeper personality, I'd no longer be in control. "Taya was the only other and you had her killed already." I watched his face, just needing to confirm it.

"How did you know?"

"Doesn't matter now." I gasped as a new level of pain marched forth from the tattle-tale nerve center of my brain. "I've permanently shut down the Crystal's remote control. Was coming from that last task, headed to the Crystal City ruins when your men found me. There's nothing left now but to get to the Crystals and manually program them. There are three—though I've only allowed one to power the grid since the invasion. Each around eighty feet in height. Instructions will be in a hidden drawer in the wall, 27 degrees left of the cavern entrance." Precise details rounded out my lies.

"Why are you telling me this now? Why not before?" He seemed truly curious.

I thought fast, my body sensations excruciating now. Letting the pain register fully on my face, I allowed its sounds an anguished escape. "My… " I closed my eyes, summoning appropriate emotions to accompany the lies. "my lover is gone. Dead. The only woman I've ever cared for, the one person I had left after your… wreckage of my country. It happened just hours ago. She has plagued me—constant dreams and visions—since." I let my outrage show and it pleased him. Then I let tears come. It wasn't hard, my body had little control left to it. "Your *horror show* against the elderly has taken her. So what, I ask you, is there left to live for?" I slumped, willing my body to dissolve in the sobs that shook it. "You've taken it all. I want to join her. If I give you the Crystals, you don't need me. Consider this my surrender."

Mardu shook his massive, black head, tongue clucking lightly. "Still, you *have* wasted so much of my time… " He stared in silence for a beat. "I'll keep you around until I find them. You can stay alive that long—I've a bet going with the guards."

How is it possible, I wondered, fading back into oblivion, *to discon-*

nect this completely from your own humanity? How can one be so thoroughly dark and cruel?

THE NEXT TIME I opened my eyes, the night was darkest. But morning always followed.

Mardu slept deeply from the sounds of it.

High City glowed, outside banks of floor to ceiling windows in this stolen room where hundreds of generations of Atlantean Kings and Rulers had slept. If only I could crawl, look upon my beloved city one last time. Both knees were crushed though. The rest of my body couldn't move anyway, all strength leached into the cold of this glossy white floor.

It was time. Vital organs were injured beyond repair, too much blood lost. I'd lied well and convincingly here at the end, deterred Mardu as long as I could. May it be long enough. May the twins find their way. *"Bourne of lightning and fire,"* I whispered, giving them eulogy here at my end. Mardu's snores came heavy from above. *"One shows the way. Mark the hour of early birth with crimson flower."*

I'll visit Sage in her dreams and give my farewells. Then the girls. Probably, I can guide them even better in spirit form without this needy, confining body.

"Darkness flayed in breast of men, given now the way to mend." I whispered it like a prayer, mind working to detach, concentrating on the silver cord which had bonded me to this precious body for so very long.

"Heed the two, follow One and light prevails before end."

The sensation of death was like being an air bubble trapped on the lake floor, rising swiftly to the surface, going back to where I belonged.

Suddenly, I was free.

15

THE METEORITE THRONE

"You need power, only when you want to do something harmful.
Otherwise, love is enough to get everything done."

— CHARLIE CHAPLIN

AIELA

*H*er tears dripped onto Turner's limp body. He'd lost the last shred of consciousness halfway to the aero. It had taken all three of them to get him here, to lift and lay him out on the worn carpet scantily padding the metal aero floor.

Relief that he was alive butted against worry of what could happen next, and impotent anger. She absolutely hated sending him away. But High City was too dangerous, and he needed a healing temple, not the chilled gloom of the maze, or the frenzied comings and goings of Charis' underground haven.

She might've been able to bear it better, think more clearly if she weren't so exhausted.

Clinging to him despite the stench of sickness layered with sweat and urine, she rubbed his icy arms. Normally solid as the great pyramid foundations, his body was wasted from being beaten and held captive. She pictured him as he was when they met in Ireland, robust and cheerful. That's who her Turner was. Who he'd be again.

"Wear this—all the time." Carver demanded softly beside her, slipping his monstrous Belial ring into Auntie Sage's hand. Crafted from rich yellow gold was the head of a man. Diamond fangs spiked from his screaming mouth, red ruby eyes stretched wide, and black horns jutted out both sides of the gleaming head.

Auntie Sage recoiled, but Carver was insistent. "It's the only way you'll escape the elder cleansing." He nodded at the black aero, sitting with wings folded in. "The only way you'll escape period if Belials try to take this from you. It's too big, too loud and too old, but it'll run on naught but saltwater. Hide it and everything in it when you get where you're going. You can live out of it if you have to. This ring; any Belial will know it, will do your bidding if you invoke it."

There hadn't been time for lengthy introductions between Auntie Sage and Carver. "He's the one I told you about, from the Ireland trip." Ahna had explained. "He's Belial and helping us."

"It's too heavy." Auntie Sage's mouth turned down in distaste when she slid the deranged ring onto her middle finger. The thick gold overspread the knuckle and splayed out her fingers. "I wish you girls would come home too. It's what Ziel would advise."

"I know—and there's nothing we'd like more." Ahna consoled. She wrapped both skinny arms around Auntie Sage and it hit Aiela like a physical force, the roles were all reversed now. Ziel and Sage were the vulnerable and it was up to her and Ahna to protect them.

"Heal fast." Aiela whispered in farewell, touching Turner's matted curls. Rising to face Kane who mutely watched it all, she offered a sad smile. "You'll look after them?"

"Ya know I will!" Kane winced every time he moved, but didn't seem to care. "Next time ya see the spoilt wee bugger, he'll be good as new." He lowered his voice, nodding toward Carver. "Didna think there was such a thing as a trustworthy Belial. Ye're sure aboot this one? I kin still knock him aboot e'en wi' oney one arm..."

"I'm sure." Aiela reached to embrace Kane's thick neck, feeling for the long braid that always hung down his back. "Thank you for going with him…" She bit back more fear words, hating the thought of both these men being so far away. "…and teaching me how to fight."

Kane snorted. "It's me's gettin' saved here while ye're headed inna the fray again. Yer fists are as fierce as yer heart Cailin. Wi' that, ya cannit fail."

"I'm… *desperate* to believe that." She pulled back, feeling his iron faith flow in magnetic waves. "Farewell Kane."

He swiped an oversized paw at her head, grunting with the pain it cost, and Aiela blocked it easily with a forearm. Kane grinned, and bowed to her the traditional Atlantean way, "Farewell yer wan."

Turning to Auntie Sage, Aiela felt tears threaten again. "Don't let him come back for me. At least not until I need him to. If he should be captured again…"

Auntie Sage raised doubtful eyebrows. "I'll do what I can." They stared wordlessly at each other before collapsing in a fierce hug.

Please stay safe, Aiela might have said.

Come back to me, both of you. Sage might have replied.

But neither would ask for something so frivolous as a promise.

"Time to go." Carver was nervous someone might happen upon Turner's escape, might raise alarms in the night. "Best we're back in the Palace before those dead guards are found."

Aiela looked back from the little boat, watching the aero lift off, its clanking racket drowned out by a bellowing engine. Even after it disappeared from sight, they could still hear it.

"It's sturdy and swift." Carver assured her.

They would land in Chiffon, where Auntie Sage could heal both Turner and Kane. Unexpectedly, some huge relief settled inside, almost resembling hope. She turned her attention to the awkward silence hanging between Ahna and Carver.

Ahna

The hurt part hadn't fully forgiven him. *But forgiven what?* Ahna argued in her head, *his lack of trust? He did what he had to.*

As Carver steered the little boat along the canal toward the bright red dome crowning High City, Ahna studied his silhouette. He seemed more confident. And why not? He was a prince of Atlantis' new King. There hadn't been princes of Atlantis in thousands and thousands of years. Atlantis was practically prostrate at his feet—of course he'd be sure of himself, no longer the wary, dark hero who'd rescued her, protected her, made her breathless with sweet lust, and tearful with tenderness.

Power changes people faster than any other force on earth and that's what worried Ahna. Carver's newfound confidence triggered some thread of anger—because it came at devastating cost to her—and yet, it was irresistibly attractive too. What a bother.

"So that's done. What now?" She asked Aiela. They'd been debating since this morning how much to tell Carver. Was is safe that he know about the maze and Crystals?

Aiela yawned, shaking her head. "I've got to sleep or I'm going to lose my mind. That's about all I know. If he can get us back in, let's rest in Ziel's rooms."

Ahna agreed, weariness overwhelming her too. It'd been well over twenty-four hours since they'd slept.

The lines differentiating Belial and Atlantean were blurring to nonexistence. Belials loved the exotic, plumaged High City styles, the endless richness of form, material and color. Some Atlanteans had started dying their lips and tongues, defying the former demureness they now claimed had been forced upon them. By appearance alone, they'd become indistinguishable. Ahna wondered if any of the healing temples had agreed to Belial's extravagant genital enlargements yet.

"Use poor grammar." Carver reminded as they motored up to the gate. "Be indifferent and rude. Only way to tell the difference anymore."

City gate guards barely glanced at them after seeing Carver. In the sleeping night, the sound of the boat's quiet motor bounced around inside the smooth, arched tunnel that ran through High City's fifty feet of pure, white wall.

Inside the walls, the dome turned a crescent moon ruby-red, and the Second Moon into an accusatory blooded eye. The buzz of the laser generators filled the air with sounds of angry wasp hives.

Hailing a trolley by Comm, Carver escorted them to the slumbering Palace in silence. Even the Palace guards seemed lackadaisical and half-asleep. "With the dome up," Carver explained, "nobody thinks we're in danger."

"That's good." Ahna whispered back, trudging through deserted hallways. "Easier to mount an attack if nobody's expecting it." She studied Carver's energy as she said it, hoping to divine his true feelings, expecting resistance—no matter how slight. After all, she was speaking of his family being ousted and killed, not just his nation.

Carver veered close so she could hear him whisper, locking metallic eyes into hers. "I like the sound of that. I have some ideas how to get troops in. If you gather forces to take High City back, I'll support them from within." Hope filled his words and seeped from his pores. He smelled of damp earth.

She wanted to dance like a wild woman—managed to smile instead.

Unwilling to forego a hot bath, she and Aiela hurried through it, encountering no one.

"I fell asleep in the water." Aiela yawned, toweling dry.

Ahna fought to keep her eyes open. "We should be terribly worried about Ziel but I'm too tired for even that."

Back in Ziel's rooms, Carver had hot tea waiting. "You two can have the bigger bed, I'll move to the small one."

"No!" They chorused, startling Carver with their vehemence. "We prefer the small room." Aiela said, sipping tea. "It's... special to us." Ahna added.

Carver eyed them strangely. "Well, good night then." He turned towards Ziel's room.

"Wait. Carver." Ahna went to him and wrapped her arms around his ribs, pulling his guarded body to hers. "Thank you." He held her as though she was made of glass, returning the embrace.

When she stepped back, the old Carver stood there. The one who'd looked both uncertain and insatiable every time she touched him.

His chin dropped. "I haven't done enough yet... but I will. Once I know what to do."

She touched his cheek. "Help us get Ziel back. He'll know what to do—now that we have you."

Carver

Dread infused every cell of his being. "Are you sure?"

The serving girl in the kitchen looked perplexed. "Course I'm sure! Didn't you hear about it yesterday? Everybody was talking of it! Interrupted the preparations for today even."

"And…" Carver was half afraid to ask, "…what's today?"

The young girl smiled as if he was playing with her, or testing her. "Today's the day Dominus Mardu ascends the meteorite throne!" She sobered, absentmindedly patting over-coiffed hair looped into an absurd flower bouquet at the back of her head. "See, since Ruler Ziel has so tragically died, Dominus Mardu will make a memorial to him, instate his statue on the Palace alongside all the greats of Atlantean history. It's to be part of the Throne Ceremony. A symbol that we can turn from the old to the new. Since Ruler Ziel was found, and joined Dominus Mardu, we've been awaiting an alliance, believing peace would be restored. And now the Dominus promises it has happened! Though Ruler Ziel was too ill to broadcast, there are dozens of witnesses—including the surviving Rulers—who swear he bowed to Dominus Mardu and placed his own diadema of wisdom upon our King's head. Apparently, he asked only to be the new King's Oracle advisor." The girl's bottom lip quivered and tears welled. "No chance of that now… it would've been so perfect. Ruler Ziel assisting Dominus, er, King Mardu. Two nations coming together. *Such* a historic moment."

Dazed, Carver left with the basket of food. How was he going to tell the twins about Ziel? He'd failed them. Again.

Thanks to the immensity of the Palace, he'd managed to avoid Mardu—seeing him only when summoned. Most of the time, he'd stayed immersed in the rebuilding; a perfect guise for searching for the girls. Thrill raced through him even now—even under this new dread. He'd found Ahna! There was hope. She'd softened to him so much in just one day—an endless day for sure—but at this rate, he'd have her back, really back, in no time.

With Ziel dead, what else would they need to stay here for? The thought brought hope and guilt in equal measure. They'd be devastated. Might even decide they wanted nothing further to do with him.

Then again, maybe he could finally take them back to Chiffon where Turner and Kane were. They could all go somewhere else, build a new life. Ireland maybe?

But first I have to tell them.

෴

AHNA AND AIELA were nowhere to be found. The door to their little room stood wide and the unmade bed was empty. Were they bathing again?

Sharp raps on the outer door brought a servant with summons. Mardu wanted his sons assembled to break their fast. They were to be dressed by professional tailors, made ready for the Throne Ceremony.

Carver debated leaving a note for the twins, dithering about dangers it might present, finally deciding not to risk it. He left the food basket on the tea counter.

Hurrying to the top floor of the Palace, he wondered where Ziel's body was. Perhaps he could find out what was to be done with it, have something to tell the girls when they asked.

Mardu's opulent living space was overwhelming. Rooms had been remodeled to cavernous proportions, with few walls and elaborate pillars supporting the roof. The new "King's Quarters" sprawled on and on, dwarfing gaudily gilded furniture, statuary and art—much of it gifts from Atlanteans hoping to curry favor. Belial guards, outfitted like Knights of Atlantis, but with armor of red and gold, stood in the shadows, while servants hurried around a table being laid with food so pristine and colorful it might've been a painting, but for the enticing scents rising on whorls of steam.

"Apparently," Mardu announced, pacing back and forth along his lineup of offspring, "Atlanteans *like* the notion of having princes again. I'm told it brings to life ancient times when Poseidon's sons romanced the whole land." He stopped to sneer. "Imbeciles! Heads softer than rotten melons! But if that's all it takes for quick acceptance as their King, you'll play the part well enough." Royal blue silk, intricate with embroidery, lent him a certain nobility. He seemed different, Carver thought, less crude. As if he were stepping into the refined expectations of High City.

Balek snickered into his hands, then bent double, laughing in shrill fits.

Mardu stopped, scowling stiffly, in front of Balek until the eldest son righted himself. "What's funny?"

"These dummies..." Balek flung a boneless arm towards his line of brothers, "bein' prinshes..." He dissolved into another fit of hysterical giggles. "It's *prefect.*" Balek singsonged as he swayed drunkenly, "Pretty pussy prinshes, peckers in a row—"

Mardu backhanded him. The force lifted Balek off his feet, sent him flying to skid into a heap on the white marble floor. "You will stop your drugging and drinking."

Balek's laughter had turned to whimpers. His mouth and nose streamed red. He stared with bulged eyes at the slick warmth he caught in his hands, slipping on bright smears across the floor when he scrabbled to push himself up.

Mardu watched him fail to rise, booted him in the ribs, and bent to yank his head back by a fistful of unwashed hair. "I've had enough of your stupidity. Next time I see you drunk when you're meant to be serving me, I will replace you."

Balek's mouth opened, closed, and opened again as tears ran down to join the blood. Probably, Carver decided, from the pain of half his body being held up by his hair.

"Y-y-you can't jush g-get another *son!* I'm the *eldesht!*" He blubbered, sounding very much like a young child.

"I can. I can do anything I want." Mardu released him with curdled disgust and straightened. "You stink! Get out of here! Bathe and sober up."

"The rest of you," Mardu turned to point, "sit. My master of ceremonies will lay out the plan while we eat. Then the tailors will be brought and you'll get ready." Despite Balek's drunken display, true excitement lit Mardu's eyes. Eyes that were steely blue-grey at the moment. Eyes that Carver had hidden from since he was born. "If it's princes they want, it's prince's they'll get, and all the better! You'll charm them, rule them, fuck them and make more princes. You'll distract them while I turn their world inside out and build a dynasty." He smiled then, and Carver realized he could probably count on his fingers the times he'd seen his father sincerely smile. Joy and ease hadn't ever been a part of this household. They wore it awkwardly.

Mardu watched as a servant filled his plate, pointing to this dish and that. "It's all much easier than I imagined! Thanks in part to the psychotronic weapons. The Atlanteans are more subdued than I remember, eager to have me, panting to be ruled—like a woman pretending to fight what she really wants most."

"It's rather poetic." Sarim remarked, as they took chairs on both sides of the massive table. "Poseidon had five sets of twin sons and you have five sons…"

Mardu ignored him, waving the servants to serve them.

"Look who knows their *Atlantean* history all of a sudden." Ramon taunted. In Balek's absence, he was the eldest, already stepping seamlessly into Balek's vicious role.

"Someday we'll rule as the five kings." Norse said. He was carefully neutral, always sidestepping the conflicts his brothers created. "Poseidon's sons were the ten kings—we'll be half as many and twice better."

Mardu glanced sharply at his fourth son, cutting a bite of rare reindeer veal, blood pooling off the meat. "Or maybe I choose just one of you to succeed me. Maybe none of you." At a snap of his fingers, a middle-aged man with styled, wavy, copper hair and a precisely trimmed beard stepped up. "This is my master of ceremonies. He's devised the order of events for today. You'll do as he says."

The man was tall—though the fiery, rust color of his hair attracted attention far more than his height—a bit gaunt, and dressed better than any of them, save Mardu. Some Atlanteans could never be mistaken for Belial. Jeweled rings decorated long, pale fingers and a silver diadem glittered round his temples as he unrolled a scroll, clearing his throat. "Palace gates open after midday meal. We shall fill the Throne Room with Dominus Mardu's elites, the lower levels and outer courtyards for the... common folk." His crisp dictation commanded attention. "Music will entertain the people before the former Rulers inform them how Atlantis is to be ruled hence. More music—newly composed for this sacred occasion—then each of you shall be introduced as a Prince of Atlantis, starting with the youngest." He paused to glance around the table. "And who might that be?"

Carver swallowed before speaking, sat up straighter. "That'd be me. I'm Carver."

The man made careful note of their names as they sounded off in birth order. "I will speak with each of you to determine how best to introduce you. Next I shall introduce Dominus Mardu as Atlantis' new King. The lengthy ceremony shall commence, and end with the joyous ascension of the throne... "

Carver ate, only half-listening as worry about Ahna grew. Where were they? What if they heard Ziel was dead before he could tell them? This whole ceremony nonsense would delay his return. He needed to explain, wanted to comfort her sadness—if she'd let him.

Thoughts of being close to her again took over. The unexpected embrace last night had opened a door to moons of carefully suppressed desires. Emotions he'd thought long gone had come raging back as he tried to fall asleep. Waking early, his world held elation again, returned like springtime after the frigid death of winter. He'd bathed and dressed carefully, gone to the kitchens for a food basket, planning to pick a bouquet of flowers to greet her with. But news of Ziel—"

Thunk. Warm, bloody meat bounced off his cheek. "Pay attention." Mardu growled.

All his brothers, and the very orderly master of ceremonies, stared at him expectantly.

"Sorry, what did you say?"

"Your escort. Is there a girl you prefer to use?"

Carver shook his head. *Escort? Why?*

"One shall be assigned then." The tall, red man said in clipped, indifferent tones.

. . .

149

Aiela

"We can't just keep disappearing and not tell him why." Aiela bundled foul-smelling clothes from their dank sleeping area in the maze center, while she argued. She'd send them to the Palace laundry. *Ahhh to have fresh clothing again! The things we take for granted...*

"What else can we do? Move into Ziel's rooms and... what? Abandon our duties down here? No! I don't care what he thinks about our absences—we'll tell him when we're good and ready."

"Liar." Aiela cocked her head. Ahna was trying so hard to pretend she wasn't being torn apart by Carver's reappearance. Desperate to trust him, but afraid. "You do too care what he thinks." Her voice gentled and she stopped working, faced Ahna. "You don't have to pretend with me. I know what it is to love."

Confusion sprouted in Ahna's green eyes. "But do I love him? Mostly I feel... stupid. Like wanting him still—now that I know who he is—means I'm gullible. Like he's broken my trust somehow. But he hasn't... not really. I understand everything he has done, more than I want to."

"Maybe it's easier to stay angry than to forgive. Easier not to risk loving again."

"Maybe." Ahna looked miserable, clenching and unclenching her Comm, turning towards the Crystals. "We better see what's happening out there."

"I'll try Auntie Sage." Aiela dropped the Carver subject for now.

"I'll check in with Felicia, then see if I can get Healer Lira."

To confirm Carver's story. Aiela left it unsaid.

"We're here safe and sound." Auntie Sage sounded tired, but relieved. "Chiffon's full of Belials, like everywhere else, but they haven't bothered the cottage. Probably too far out of town. Too humble."

"How's Turner?" Aiela wished she could care about other things right now, felt guilty for placing her worry over Turner at the top such a mountain of dire concerns, yet could do nothing else.

"Sleeping again. I'm waking him every few hours for fluids and medicine, but sleep will heal what those don't. He has nightmares...

I'll work on those later. I was doing energy healing on him while he sleeps."

"And Kane?"

"Strong as an ox that one! Charming... *terribly* disobedient. Tries to help more than he should. Getting him to stay still long enough to heal will be the problem!"

Aiela laughed. "Knowing he's there with you helps me worry less."

"Worrying is useless, you've better things to do with your energy. Can you check in every day?"

"I plan to." Aiela sighed. "I love you Auntie. And I don't have to tell you how much I love that crazy Irishman you're putting back together."

Neither of them mentioned Ziel, some unspoken pact weighing heavy in the vast distance between them.

Ahna was already listening to Comm chatter, switching back and forth between Atlantean and Belial frequencies.

Sila had unfurled from her usual mountain of coils between the three Crystals, and was standing tall and solemn beside Ahna as if listening intently too. She was still growing rapidly, thriving on the poor creatures who'd made the maze their kingdom. "Getting fatter every time I see you." Aiela murmured, stroking the lilac scales. "At this rate you'll be big around as these Crystals soon." Sila bobbed her arrow-shaped head, tongue flicking to graze Aiela's cheek. "Oh, feeling affectionate today are we? I guess you missed us. Good thing! You're very nearly large enough to swallow me whole."

"It's all anyone can talk about," Ahna frowned, when Aiela settled beside her. "The Throne Ceremony. Mardu becomes King today."

Aiela raised her eyebrows. "What are they saying?"

"Everyone's clamoring to go. Apparently, there's been a line outside the Palace gates since early morning. I can't *believe* how many Atlanteans are just... accepting it. Much less, wanting to attend!"

"Should we go?"

Ahna frowned. "For what? And if someone recognizes us? Anyway it's to be broadcast, the whole country can watch."

"Probably safer not to. We can watch from Ziel's rooms."

Ahna listened awhile longer while Aiela sent out a broadcast, like she'd been doing at least twice most days.

Her tone was curt, her words cursory. "A false king will take his throne in High City today. And each of us has a choice to make. Will you accept this king, or will you resist the evil he spreads? Will you go along with greed and self-gratification and unlove, or will you remain true to the Law of One no matter what it costs you? I know you are suffering. We've all lost loved ones. It would be easy to stay discouraged, but that too is a choice. No matter what happens inside our nation, can you—each one of you—live in love, and be a pillar of harmony and light? I pray that you can. I pray that you will. You've been given many tools. Now is the time to draw on your knowledge. Remember who you are.

Tonight I will explain the psychotronic weapons being used all across our continent, by Mardu. I've inside information. Every Atlantean needs to know how to protect themselves against this technology, because it is designed to break us down. These weapons implant thoughts, whisper words only your mind can hear, and present images only your subconscious can see. Tune in later for more specifics and what to do about it."

"How do you always know exactly what to say?" Ahna absently tickled Sila's chin as Aiela shut off her broadcast Comm. "You sound so much older when you're... leading."

"I *feel* older." Aiela had been wondering herself. "It's almost like the Crystals—or somebody—is talking through me. Is that possible?"

"I'd say when it comes to the Crystals, it's *probable*."

Ahna

From the time they re-entered Ziel's rooms, the crowds clamoring at Poseidon's Palace were deafening and offensive.

Outside Ziel's single window alcove, all they could see was bodies. Masses of people dressed in glittering colors, cheering, shouting, scuffling, singing drunkenly, dancing and even fighting. Throngs surrounded the Palace as far out as they could see, filling all of its courtyards. Verandas and lower hallways too by the sound of it.

"Where did they all come from?" Aiela asked.

"Must be Belials... " Ahna replied, feeling the overwhelm of a crowd, " ...but how did they all *get* here?"

"Look at them! They just *hit* each other. Or elbow or shove... "

"Or kiss, or grope... "

The mass pitched and yawed this way and that, disharmonic and bellicose. Like an ant pile that has been disturbed, bodies moved at odds with no discernible pattern.

Ahna shuddered. "Their energy feels so aggressive. Foreign."

"You should see their auras!" Aiela's eyes scanned rapidly, trying to take it all in.

"It's like watching some other world."

"Displaced." Aiela named it for both of them before inhaling appreciatively. "Look. Carver left us food."

With a shudder, Ahna turned away from the window to fix a pot of tea, while Aiela unpacked the basket. The marble, stone and metal of the Palace interior amplified the sounds into an unbroken din, echoes that didn't stop or fade.

They sat at the rosewood table, sipping tea, eating buttered millet cakes, first-harvest peaches, and cold mussels spiced with peppers, feeling the bizarreness of doing something they had done so many times, in a world completely changed. Ahna turned on Ziel's Comm base, tuning until she found the Belial broadcast.

Constant chatter accompanied fast-moving images and Ahna turned it up. "This, my happy fellow Belials, is the throne room, where today—on this long-awaited, majestic day—King Mardu will ascend his Meteorite Throne... "

Aiela squinted at the panning images and gasped. "That's Ruler Kenna's old quarters! There's Ruler Eirene's and the meeting rooms the Rulers all used... he's made the *entire north side* into his throne room!"

The image passed over the heads of loud hordes, pausing on newly gilded pillars supporting the raised roof, and steps the width of the cavernous hall's front wall, led up, up and up. Rich swaths of satin and velvet looped and swagged from above.

"... sacred and holy of holi days will henceforth be celebrated on this day! This day our very own Dominus Mardu sets us *truly free* as a continent. No more separation or condemning those of us who want to live as we see fit. No more keeping the best of everything for those considered righteous... "

"Empty propaganda!" Aiela spat. "Trying to convince everyone how much better off they'll be now that the Law of One is usurped." She turned down the sound. "I can't listen to it."

"They're incredibly bold, telling people what to think. First they do it subconsciously via psychotronics, then they do it consciously, and people agree because they've already been having these type of 'thoughts'." Ahna observed darkly. "Maybe now is a good time to look for Ziel. Mardu will be busy once the ceremony starts. Everyone else will be attending, or focused on it too."

"We'd just be lost in the crowds." Aiela agreed.

"We'll wait until it starts, then go?" Ahna ate faster.

"We've at least two hours—if it starts at sundown as promised."

"EL, WAKE UP! EL!" Ahna shook her sister awake. They'd both nodded off waiting for the ceremony to begin. There had been an endless parade of people being introduced, new councils—*dozens* of them— and what they'd be doing. Elites, that were Atlanteans and Belials somehow deemed important or of "purer" bloodlines, were brought up. They were to be "lords", overseeing dozens of new Atlantis regions. Governors had been chosen for cities and towns, most of them Belial. There were so many people in charge of things, Ahna wondered who was left to do the actual work. "Look, it's Carver." She turned the sound back up.

" ...first Princes of Atlantis in centuries! And aren't they handsome! They'll be introduced in due time but for now, let's watch for the entrance of our highly anticipated, savior King, the Great Dominus Mardu. He must be—"

Ahna stared. "There's a girl with him!"

She was almost as tall as Carver, wearing the latest fashion. Layer upon layer of orange and yellow poofs, matching the girl's hair, done into something resembling a setting sun with rays spiking out.

Aiela rubbed her eyes. "Well he couldn't exactly take you. He better be careful, her hair could poke out an eye. Looks like all the 'princes' have a girl on their arm. Those must be his brothers."

But Ahna's eyes stayed on Carver, reading his body language, reaching for his energy, finally determining he barely knew this girl. The escort clung to him and smiled vacantly, face swiveling between him and the crowd. "Why not? The Belials don't know who we are. If we joined the Palace family, we could do more."

"That's jealousy talking. Too many people here know us."

Abruptly, the image shifted to the exterior of the Palace, panning across crowds that waved and screamed drunkenly, then zooming in on a lit statue. Ahna and Aiela leaned closer to the holographic image as if that would make it clearer. "Is that...?"

"Turn it up!"

" ...former Ruler Ziel will be commemorated after Dominus Mardu is Kinged. His statue was placed without delay, at the behest of Dominus Mardu, to be honored in the sacred traditions of Atlantis."

The image switched just as abruptly back to the throne room where a tall, red-haired man was giving instructions to the crowd of richly dressed Belials and Atlanteans.

"They're lying! Ziel can't be dead." Aiela stared at her sister, eyes pooling with dread.

"Carver would have told us. Surely there would've been talk of it on the Comms... " Ahna sounded less sure, even to herself. Something was niggling at the back of her mind. Something she desperately ignored.

Back inside the throne room, the tall red-haired man was introducing the "former Ruler, now titled simply, Head of the House of Education."

Though outfitted in elegant finery, she looked drugged, eyes half-lidded, shoulders drooping as if sleep-walking. Without even glancing at the audience, she began reading from a single page. "We, the former Rulers of Atlantis are pleased to approve this reunification of two great nations, and overjoyed to present to you our decision to unite the Atlantean continent under a King. Many of us have long known that a change was needed, that our formerly glorious country has sunk further and further into segregation, fundamentalism, stringent regulations, and…" her voice was rote and heartless, droning such words as 'overjoyed' and 'glorious'.

"He's making them read this scripted garbage!"

The three remaining Rulers stood beside the robotic Head of Education, waiting their turn.

"Ziel isn't there." Aiela noted flatly.

They studied the panning images. Every time a former Ruler mentioned the King, the image hovered on the meteorite throne; A twenty-ton chunk of meteorite, shaped like a fan with cold, silvered-black hues, polished to a refined gloss. Indented seat and armrests were molded so gracefully, it looked like yards of silk draping something sharper or uglier underneath. Carved in flowing script gilded with orichalcum were the words, *Nire borondate munduko arauak*. "My will rules the world".

No one else was on the high dais where the throne waited, hunched between deep red velvet curtains drawn to each side with golden cords. At least one entire story high, the dais was reached by steps the width of the room. Halfway down the steps spread a lower dais where Mardu's sons sat, and the red-haired Master of Ceremony and the former Rulers spoke from.

Belial guards, outfitted in red and gold, stood shoulder to shoulder across the base of the steps.

"It's hideous." Aiela snapped.

Ahna only nodded, studying all the mismatched color that clashed like discordant notes.

16

CHIFFON

"The pieces of a puzzle look utterly strange, but they still fit together in the end."

— HOODWINKED

TURNER

Sage had worked miracles. Turner remembered only bits and pieces of arriving in Chiffon; the bracing, salted air, bitter things being trickled into his mouth, Kane and Sage struggling to move him into the little cottage perched between forest and sea.

It was idyllic and charming here. Picturing Aiela as a child, barreling happily around saving broken animals, was a balm to his spirit, sure as Sage's endless teas and oils were a balm to his body.

If only his thoughts weren't on Aiela day and night, wondering if she was still safe. If she missed him as desperately as he missed her. If the time might come when she'd agree to go home to Ireland with him. Maybe Carver and Ahna would come too. His father would be only too happy to shelter Atlanteans. Especially those who knew how to heal like this!

Sage had taken him to Chiffon's Healing Temple three times. Each visit left his jaw sagging at the ways they'd mastered the human body. He'd thought the widespread rumors of Atlantis' miraculous abilities to be overinflated. Now, he'd experienced it first hand. Sage had done much to heal him, but the machines that mended broken bones and lacerations to his organs were beyond anything he'd known was possible. Only because of Sage's influence did he get a small bit of time with the machines, with power supplies running too short to serve all who needed it. Healing Temples functioned at night now, since the grid was drained during daytime.

Turner ate eggs that Kane had scrambled with tiny hot peppers, wild mushrooms and chives he'd found around the cottage. Sage came in from shearing the llamas.

"Sure an' I'm good as new, thanks ta yer healin' magic. Time ta get back ta the girls don't ya think?"

Kane hovered to hear her answer. Turner'd been yammering on about it for days.

Sage shook her head. "I want to go back as badly as you. Perhaps more." She picked off tufts of llama wool clinging to her hemp tunic. "But it'd land you right back where you were before—or in an early grave. You know you can't take the chance. What good will it be for you in High City, not even able to show your face? There's plenty to do here if you want to play hero."

Most of the villagers of Chiffon were being used as servants to the steady influx of Belials taking over homes, businesses and even some outlying farms. Atlanteans who fought back were eventually over-powered, always outgunned. These peaceful country people had no weapons, save those fashioned from tools and household items.

It was only a matter of time until some Belial came out here. Sage had Turner and Kane harvesting spring crops, though the produce was small and young yet. They hauled in fish to clean and dry, moved chickens and blankets to Cherry Island, preparing for the day they'd have to abandon the little cottage in the woods.

But that wasn't all. Every few days, the three of them flew the old black aero up and down the coast, bringing back any boats still sound enough to float. Often they stole Belial vessels, concealing them as best they could. "There's a reason I've ended up with two brawny sailors!" Sage proclaimed. Much like Charis in Old Forest, they were helping Atlanteans escape the tyranny that had become everyday life.

Every second or third day, some person or family would appear out of the forest, weary of hiding and surviving in the countryside. Most of them were on the run from brutal Belials who'd taken everything, and now demanded the Atlanteans serve them for the right to eat what they'd cultivated, or sleep under the roof built and furnished by their own hand. Rumor had it, some were being kept in chains so they couldn't run.

Sage would make a pot of tea for the ragged Atlanteans who stumbled in, directing Turner and Kane with calm instruction. "Fix these ones a hearty meal while I pack food and clothing." The fugitives would be bathed, given anything Sage could spare, and sent on their way in a boat—if there was one to hand. If not, they'd walk south along the coast where other Atlanteans had formed small holdouts, or had sea cruisers to ferry people across the sea to Merika.

Not a week ago, Turner had a spate of luck and hailed a ship headed north. He'd been fishing when he glimpsed its familiar outline on the horizon. Thinking to get word home, so his family knew of Atlantis' plight, he strained the little motor to catch up to the old timber vessel.

The Captain was from the far northern continent where glaciers covered much of the land, but the southernmost parts were lush and fertile. He agreed to a stopover in Ireland. "We'll need to put in anyhow for freshwater and foodstuff. Your port'll do."

Thanking him profusely, Turner scribbled a note and prayed Da would respond with haste.

"Da, Send every ship you can to Cherry Island. (approximate coordinates.) Ours and any else you can hire. Atlanteans in dire need of vessels to evacuate. Belial rules now, stealing Atlantean homes, enslaving many. I'm well. Will return home once Aiela is with me. All my love, Turner."

. . .

FUMING NOW, at Sage's predictable answer, he took another bite of eggs. She was right, but he didn't have to like it. "Have ya any idea when Aiela might contact us again?" He longed to hear her voice, to be assured she was well and free.

Sage shook her head. "Today, I hope." Worry furrowed between her brows and Turner felt sorry he'd inquired. She had enough concerns without being reminded of Ahna and Aiela's peril.

He stood from the table made from lightning-twirled cherrywood. "Si' doon and eat. Yeh've no' taken a rest all day. We'll be needin' ya hale an' hearty, ta boss us around. I'll see ta the baggin'." He grabbed the cotton sacks she'd pulled out of cupboards and headed outside before she could refuse. Aiela would certainly not forgive him if he didn't take care of Sage. She laughed lightly, patting his cheek as he passed.

"You're a good man Turner. My girl chose well."

SLEEK AND DARK—LOOKING at first a shadow sliding across the restless ocean—a ship was coming in. Turner folded the rich auburn and black fleeces before stuffing them into sacks, one eye tracking the vessel. It was a shape he'd only heard tell of from sailors who spoke in fearful tones. Long and narrow, its prow curled high into the likeness of a dragon head, the other end a spiked tail. It was blue, deep as the twilit sky or the ocean depths.

"Banpiro." He muttered darkly to the freshly shorn llamas placidly chewing their cud. "So the tales are true."

Finished bagging the wool, he went to warn Kane as the ominous ship dropped anchor at the mouth of their crescent-shaped inlet.

Sage and Kane came outside to watch. A small rowboat hit the water with a splash and what looked from this distance to be a female, climbed down into it. Each of them wondered, as they stood shoulder to shoulder, ready with weapons from Carver's aero, if this was help or harm sailing to their door.

She was beauty personified. Tawny as a panther, she moved with inhuman grace and speed. It was all he could do to keep his light gun hidden in a pocket instead of wielding it like a shield. Every cell registered danger. Beside him, Kane was tense and poised, but Sage murmured, calm as ever, "If this is who I think it is, we'll want her on our side. Don't threaten her."

Stopping in front of them, the woman studied each one with light gold eyes. "I am Nadya, come from England. I search for an Atlantean friend who is named Drey. He was supposed to live here." Her accent was fierce, deliberate. "Where can I find him?" She prowled back and forth and Turner half expected to see a tail.

Sage stepped forward and bowed. "Nadya, I know who you are. Drey lived here with his family until... he is gone, dear."

Nadya frowned. "Where did he go? I come to help him and his family. We hear what is happening in Atlantis. I owe him a debt—"

Sage was shaking her head, voice thick. "He is dead."

Nadya stopped. Her stillness seemed as dangerous as her movement. Absorbing the news without expression, she finally nodded. "I am sorry. Are you his family?"

"Yes." Sage smiled sadly. "Come inside for tea, if you please. There's much to tell you. Drey spoke so fondly of you, you know, even though you both suffered. He held great love for you always."

Turner and Kane bowed awkwardly as she passed to follow Sage towards the sand-washed cottage. Feral eyes took in each man in turn, a gaze lacking human emotion or expression. Turner felt a shivering in his abdomen.

The short story of Drey and Taya's death flowed out of Sage as she took pinches of dried things from canisters, crushing them together inside sachets while the water heated. She told of Mardu's takeover as she brewed tea in two tall pots. Turner set out mugs and Kane scrambled more eggs. Finally, when all four were seated, Sage ended her story with, "Ahna and Aiela are Keepers of the Crystals you see. They stay in High City to protect them, to find a way to overcome Mardu from within."

"Who are you?" Nadya's glowing eyes held Kane's wide ones.

"I'm—" Kane gulped and started again. "I'm his coosin." His head tipped in Turner's direction.

"You're Scots." She looked at Turner. "And you, 'his cousin'?"

"Sure an' I'm the mate—almost—o' Aiela. We plan ta wed, ya see, but Mardu took me... em, hostage. An' all hell broke loose after. She broke me oot o' my own ship, Aiela did, wi' Carver's help an' me half-deid. Carver's the love o' Ahna." He scratched his ear. "I wouldna call them mates joos' yet. Carver's a Belial so it's all a bit confused at the moment ya see."

"You're Irish." Golden eyes flicked between the men. "Drey would consider you his family?"

Sage answered for them. "He would. If he'd had the chance to meet these two, he would've been proud to call them family. For certain, they're family to Drey's daughters."

Kane pushed the platter of eggs towards Nadya. "If yer hungry...?"

He's entranced. Turner realized, grinning inwardly. Never had there been a time he'd seen his older cousin so uncertain, or cowed. *Prob'ly the first time he's met someone stronger, an' it's a woman ta boot!"*

"I am Banpiro." Nadya said. "I do not digest human food well."

"Aye, thought as much." Kane pulled the eggs close and started stuffing in spoonfuls as if to prove something. "Ye dinna eat human food. Wha' do ye eat?"

She had the grace to blink at least. "Blood. Mammal, winged creatures, sea cows—whatever is warm."

"Human?" Kane asked, eyeing her around a mouthful.

"Kane!" Sage snapped. "Mind your manners!"

"Only when I have not other choices." Nadya held Kane's eyes still. *Some sort of sparring match,* Turner decided.

Sage noticed too. She cleared her throat, pouring Nadya more tea. "The question now I think, is where do we need your help the most?"

"High City." Turner said promptly. "If I'm stuck here," he glanced apologetically at Sage, "the least we can do is send help ta the twins."

Sage nodded agreement. "How do you feel about going to High City?"

Nadya considered this. "I will do what it is best for you, Drey's family. I regret being too late to help him. Yes, I will go to your High City, but I do not know what to do there."

"I do." Kane said quietly. "I know exactly what ye can do thair."

"You still need time to heal." Sage protested.

"We'll be needin' yer help here mate." Turner knew well what Kane was angling at.

"Ach, I'm plenty well healed." Kane said. His large calloused hand covered Sage's in thanks. He spoke to Turner next. "Ye cannit go ta help our lasses, but I can. Nadya knows noothing o' High City. I do. Together we can do more'n either one aloone."

"I am not alone." Nadya said. All eyes turned to her. "I've brought my family."

NIGHT OF RAIN AND STARS

"It's the heart afraid of breaking, that never learns to dance.
It's the dream afraid of waking, that never takes the chance.
It's the one who won't be taking, who cannot seem to give.
And the soul afraid of dying, that never learns to live."

— AMANDA MCBROOM, THE ROSE

AIELA

*A*iela watched the Throne Ascension ceremony all the way through, disbelief devolving into fear that gripped and grew.

Mardu didn't even *walk* to his throne. He'd been carried into the throne room, seated on a sparkling orichalcum chair. The litter was carried by soldiers in the midst of a parade of at least a hundred military Generals and Officers. Drums were playing a deafening beat that throbbed inside the cells of her body.

At the base of the steps, a contingent of Atlanteans stepped forward and used some small technology to levitate the litter all the way up to the meteorite throne. Mardu stood, raised both arms, and the very palace shook with the stomping, applause and shouts of those who filled it. It went on and on. Finally it died, and there were more long, pompous speeches from everybody that mattered in this new mad order.

Every one of them proclaimed officially that Mardu was henceforth King of Atlantis.

And what did she have to fight the Belials with? Control of the country's power supply? The ability to communicate with a people overwrought, desperately fighting for homes, families, survival?

Belials killed Atlantean soldiers or Knights on sight—or suspicion —with or without proof. Those still alive had fled before some former friend gave them up in exchange for the promise of a paltry protection. Atlanteans were fast turning on each other, unsure who to trust in this purloined peace, where the price of security was betrayal.

Fear turned to panic when they brought out Ziel's body.

"Looks fake." Ahna whispered, as six Belial guards lugged in a coffin, almost as an afterthought. Mardu had pontificated at length about how great Atlantis would become under his reign. He'd introduced his Generals who'd "won him a united nation", and acknowledged his councils and "elites"—basically all the overdressed people filling the throne room.

Ziel's body was robed in faded blue, an orichalcum diadem resting 'round his temples. They set him at the foot of the steps leading up to the throne. The simple box was fresh-cut wood, unvarnished, unadorned, monastic in the midst of that glittering, pretentious place.

Mardu didn't bother to descend from the throne. Didn't even stand. The holographic image had to switch between him and the dead man. "It is with great sadness, I memorialize my old friend Ziel. I know the great love this country holds for him. I'd hoped to give him a place of honor... "

Aiela wouldn't believe it. "It's a ploy. Mardu's trying to steal our hope. Their scientists could have made somebody to look like Ziel. I've never seen that robe, or diadem before." It was flimsy proof. Not nearly as flimsy as her waning faith.

"They're *parading* him, showing off! Being vulgar and disrespectful on purpose!" Ahna voice rang with the unfamiliar. Hatred. Atlanteans did not look upon the face of the deceased. Memorials were about honoring the life of the individual, not the decaying shell of a body no longer inhabited.

Together they watched, fighting bouts of rage and tears, as Mardu made grandiose claims, mostly about himself and all he'd done for Ziel throughout their supposedly long "friendship". He ended with a brief mention of the statue already erected on the Palace exterior to honor Ziel.

"Do you think it's true?" Aiela's voice was thick and flat, already resisting the answer.

Ahna stared in mute despair, gave the tiniest of shrugs. "My mind doesn't want to accept it... but I feel it. It's him."

And then the tears fell like rain.

Carver found them there, sobbing and trying to figure out what to do next.

He knelt on the floor between the floor cushions they curled in, touching both their hands in the gentlest of gestures. "I tried to find you this morning, as soon as I heard. You weren't here." Aiela could see deep sorrow cloud his aura. "I've failed you yet again and I don't know how to make it right."

"There is no right anymore." Ahna said bitterly, pulling her hand away.

"Then we must create it." Carver insisted quietly.

"I'll have to tell Auntie Sage." Aiela rose, all the weariness of the ages settling on her shoulders. Drying her eyes with the hem of her tunic, she steadied herself with the mundane task of heating water. Plenty more tears would flow later when she spoke with Auntie, and Turner. For now, she welcomed the familiar numb. She caught Ahna's eye while the tea brewed. *It's time to tell him of the maze.*

Ahna shook her head. *Not now.*

Fine. Then you make up the story of where I'm going. Aiela busied her hands with teapot and cups.

Carver got to his feet. "I'll go to the kitchens for food, but first I need to change out of this nonsense." He looked very well, Aiela thought, wondering if Ahna even noticed. The satin of his long, formal tunic shone like dew gathered on plums, shimmering silvery light on top, a deep color massing underneath. His eyes looked more silver than usual with his hair styled back, highlighting the raw structure of his face. Tall boots made of serpent skin were sheened with the same dewy finish.

If Ahna wouldn't patch things up between them, Aiela would have to take matters into her own hands. With Turner, Sage and Kane so far away—without Ziel—they needed Carver more than ever.

Once Carver had shut the door behind him, she crouched next to her sister, telling her as much, in a voice gone razor shrill with the shock of this new loss. "Forget about loving him—can you at least make friends?"

"I know we have to tell him... trust him." Ahna rested her face in her hands. "It's just all too much; trying to balance the horror, the chaos, the planning, more horror, and the... the chemistry of attraction in the midst. Romance doesn't fit with all this. I've no *capacity* for it!" She wiped the wetness from her cheeks with the backs of her hands. "You go ahead. Give Auntie Sage my love, Turner too. You need to hear his voice right now, it'll give you strength. I'll deal with Carver."

Relieved, Aiela drank her tea, rummaging for snacks to fuel her body. "I'll try not to wake you when I get back."

Carver

When Carver returned with the meal basket, Ahna sat alone, glass-blown and still, a tiny stone mug nestled between her palms. Red-rimmed eyes studied him but she offered a fragile smile. Carver glanced toward the room the sisters shared, door standing open into darkness. "Did Aiela go to bed?"

"No." Ahna uncurled. "Sit... please. Do you want tea? There's things I need to tell you."

"Yes, alright. And you should eat." She looked hollow. How was it he still found her the most desirable woman in the world?

He laid out supper brought up from the King's feast, a bowl of fire-roasted quail in a rich merlot gravy, plates of spicy peppers stuffed with creamy melted cheeses, tender spring vegetables lightly steamed

167

and buttered, pastries filled with fruit and cream. The Palace throbbed with music and voices, as parties grew more boisterous by the hour.He shuddered to think how it must clash against Ahna's newest grief. Relieved to have escaped without notice, from the throngs that filled every common space to bursting, Carver filled a teacup and sat, waiting for her begin.

She lifted her chin. "El and I are Keepers of the Crystals. We wanted the small room because there's a secret door where we come and go through a maze beneath the Palace because we coordinate communications—"

"Wait," he interrupted, holding up a hand to stop the barrage. "*The* Crystals?! Do you mean the center-of-the-grid *power* Crystals?"

"Yes and there's a maze—"

"Who else knows this?" Fear, old and foul, clenched his gut. Mardu was putting every bit of intelligence he could muster into finding the central Crystals, and whoever controlled them. The grid and the Second Moon remained holdouts, the last things not under his power.

"Nobody." Ahna reached for a pastry.

How could she eat right now? Did she not realize the danger she was in? When Mardu found out—and he would—

"Why are you so afraid?" She seemed truly puzzled. "Literally nobody else knows—besides Auntie Sage of course. And Turner."

"Not one other single person? There is not *one* person who could tie you to the Crystals?"

"Not one." She said firmly, a little blob of raspberry cream stuck on her upper lip. "Do you want to know about it, or not?"

"It's just that if… *when* Mardu finds out about you, there's no limit to the pain he'll inflict. He's a psychopath, a masochist, more evil than you'd think a man could be!" He was desperate to make her under-stand. "You don't know him. The thought of—"

"Enough!" Ahna leaned close to him, still unnaturally calm, touching his hand. "Fear isn't helpful right now. I need your strength."

It stopped him cold. *I need your strength.*

He took a deep breath, coming back to himself. "S-sorry." Real-izing his deepest childhood traumas lay beneath this overwhelming fear, he turned deliberately away from it. He watched her eat, fighting back the panic. "Tell me about the Crystals. I won't interrupt again." His voice felt strained.

She eyed him doubtfully, finishing the pastry before coming to some unspoken decision. "There's three. Huge. We're only allowing one to power the maze. With the dome sucking up so much, we figure it limits the amount of power Mardu can put into other things. Worse things—whatever that might be. I'll show them to you, but not tonight. Aiela needs some time talking with Turner. He sets her right." She paused, taking a bite of pepper. "The maze is hundreds of miles long, er round, more like. We've lived in it since the Anubis invaded. Ziel did too."

"Where's the entrances? Is there any chance Mardu could find them? Who all knows where they are?"

"We collapsed the main entrance during the invasion." Ahna's eyes were far away. "There's an entrance from Old Forest, and the one here." She shrugged a wraithlike shoulder. "I don't *think* anyone knows of the Old Forest one. Theoretically, it could be found—though it's pretty well hidden... "

She told of learning to navigate the maze, their training as Keepers of the Crystals, the communication system they'd co-opted, and the pockets of Atlanteans who were actively resisting as Belials took their country away, home by home, village by village.

The precise cadence of her voice calmed him in increments.

More than once, watching her lips shape words, pause to sip tea, or smile at a memory, his mind flashed back through months of fantasies. How much he'd yearned to see her again, kiss her, feel her body wrapped around him.

The elegant, inner steel he'd glimpsed in Ireland when she decided to fight the islanders, had returned as she talked. He grinned when she spoke of scrambling Belial communications.

"It's been driving the Generals crazy, you know. Often as not, the troops don't move when they're supposed to because they can't get through to each other. Supplies are not being delivered. Soldiers are deserting en mass because they can provide for themselves better on their own than staying with the troop. You two are playing havoc with the entire Belial military!"

He reached to wipe the blob of cream off her lip, not expecting the tingle of desire at such tiny contact. Not expecting her eyes to suddenly smolder back at him. This was the look she'd worn in Ireland so many times, leading up to their single night of lovemaking.

I need your strength.

He licked the cream from his fingertip and—unwilling to consider the wisdom of it—leaned to kiss her.

She met his lips with equal pressure, responding to the pull of desire, then drew back a fraction. Green eyes held his and he shivered with the sense of being exposed to the soul.

"I'm giving you everything—you might have noticed." She said it so matter-of-factly, pressing a hand along the side of his face. "I'm now totally vulnerable and I want you to understand that it's a choice. I won't doubt you anymore—or make you prove anything. I've *decided* to love you. Aiela said earlier, 'if I couldn't love you, could I at least make friends with you'. I realized then which I wanted. Lust is easy, infatuation is just instinct. But love can be hard. That's what I'm offering. A partnership. Not because of the situation we're in. Not because of either of our sexual or romantic needs, but love for the sake of love. The deepest sort of exchange that exists between two people. Total trust. The commitment to care for each other no matter what—even though this is the worst possible timing for something like this."

He blinked back the tears blurring his eyes. Pangs of relief mixed with fear of not deserving, and the utter joy of being seen and accepted. "I… love you." He couldn't hold back the stupid grin, even as he tried to push away the barrage of emotions. "It began the day I met you, and it hasn't stopped."

"Which day, exactly?"

He shrugged. "Pick one. The day I watched you hug your parents goodby on the dock in Amaranth. The day on the Seacruiser when you stared at my hands like you were addled—and then acted all stuck up. The day I carried you, and you bled on me. The night I first played music just for you, the night we made love… or any of them in between. Each day we were together I fell in love with you all over again."

Reaching round her waist, he pulled her off the cushion chair, bringing her onto his lap. Forehead to forehead, they settled, re-learning the feel of each other. He breathed in this dream held so long, embodied now, unexpectedly. She kissed his eyes and the planes beneath them, before settling on his mouth. His hands caressed her, meaning to offer comfort even as his body responded to the shapes of her. He tasted fruity sweetness as she rested her lips on his mouth, her hands threading into his hair.

"Well I'm all yours now. Again." She whispered.

He pulled back, needing her to see his eyes, hoping to express the depths of this feeling he had carried for so long. Mostly he needed to see if she really meant it, like a child returning again and again for reassurance. "Thank you." It came out a pitiful mumble—but it made her smile. And that smile was suddenly worth the world. Worth every day and night of yearning and worry and the raw grief of thinking he'd never see her again.

'I need your strength', she'd said. But he needed hers even more.

"Don't thank me yet." She kissed him soundly. "I'm going to be more trouble than I'm worth." This time her smile was mischievous and that's when he saw it.

The light had to be just right, and he hadn't thought to look for it before. A long, pale line, finer than a strand of hair, ran from her temple to her chin, barely missing her mouth. He traced it with a fingertip. "You kept it. Why?"

"It'll sound stupid. I… it was like some sort of connection to you. I couldn't just erase it." She looked away. "It faded more and more, and so did you. So did my memories of you, and I could barely stand it. When I went to Belial to find you—"

"You *what?!*"

Blowing out breath, she shook her head, green eyes tired and sad. "It's… a long story and I'm not sure I have the strength right now… yes, I kept my scar. Sometimes it's been the only proof you ever… "

"…loved you." Carver finished for her, tears springing up again though he swallowed again and again to force them back. He kissed the beginning of that fine line, and worked his way down it.

She sat very still, eyes closed until he reached her chin. Then she opened his shirt, hands roaming inside, resting her head on his shoulder. "I need you so much." She sighed then, lips on his neck, and they set to kissing in earnest, caresses turning to gropes, restraint falling away.

I need your strength.

Awkward in their haste, exchanging small pains, laughing at their own desperation, their sexes finally came together, melding hot and wet, hard and soft until he came in waves that rose up over him. Breathing hard, he uncovered her breasts, licking and caressing, moving against her until she orgasmed with those little mewls and sighs he'd thought of for so long.

Joined together, her head on his shoulder, he kissed her hair, stroked her neck, her half-clothed back. He muttered hoarsely, "Will you sleep with me tonight?" and felt her nod against him.

Standing, he carried her to his bed, their half-shed clothing tripping him, still-full platters of food forgotten on the rosewood table.

She waved off the sconces as they went, arms and legs wrapping him like a delicate glow in the darkness.

He wished for stars overhead, and a singing Scottish ocean, but was plenty content with bursts of soft conversation, a hundred questions asked and answered.

Twice, bouts of sudden and violent tears shook her, and she burrowed into his arms, mourning losses he couldn't imagine. Then would come the passion, as if to celebrate the fact that they, at least, were still alive.

I need your strength.

"You have it." He vowed as she sighed in sleep. "As long as I've any strength left, it's all yours.

18

TWICE BETRAYED

9,970 BCE HIGH CITY, ATLANTIS

"Extinction is the rule. Survival is the exception."

— CARL SAGAN

JAYDEE

*J*aydee fingered garments with growing disdain, in a spacious tent of the once-luxurious clothing market; the first shop to reopen after the invasion. This one, she had always counted on for any special occasion. But that was before.

"Do you have *nothing* new?! These are all the same!" She yanked at the robes, gowns, tunics and cloaks on display, as proof to the nervous merchant fretting in her wake. "Worn-out styles! Used up colors! The King won't like it when I report your lack in pleasing me... "

It wasn't at all the truth. Mardu could care less about her, though she eagerly served at his beck and call. These days, Jaydee preferred her own carefully-filtered reality. Mardu's slights and insults and abuses didn't hurt so much if she told herself—and everyone else—a different story. Pretending things were exactly as she wanted them, had been a way of life since she'd met him.

"There simply isn't anything new *coming* to us." The pale, painfully thin man whined softly, attempting to soothe. "Imports are slow with Mar—er, since the King has closed High City. Chiffon, Pai, Venuska, Georgia, none of our best suppliers are manufacturing. Too disrupted with—"

"I don't *care* about all that!" Jaydee tossed her long silky hair. Next she would visit the Palace beauty people. "Bring me your best dozen of these *rags* then!" She flounced towards the mirrored rooms, already unbelting her form-fitting robe. Mardu was bored with her—and no wonder—the Belial women were somehow finding fabulous things to wear—stealing all the best things before they got to market no doubt, pilfering the Atlantean wardrobes they'd overtaken. *Of course he's going to look at them, want them at his side and in his bed. I must do better.*

IT WAS on the trolley ride back to the Palace that she recognized them. She'd spied for Mardu half her life. Paying attention to details was a deeply ingrained habit.

Generous hoods covered their heads but something about the way they walked caught her eye—closer than most pairs—confidant, purposeful strides in the midst of a cowering populace. "Aiela." She whispered. "And the other one, the small one... " but she couldn't recall the name.

"Stop here." She poked the driver, a young man who was quite stupid and dull. She'd ordered him to smile a little instead of looking on the verge of tears all the time. "Make sure these get delivered to my rooms in the Palace." Her wave encompassed the back seat stuffed full of gaily wrapped packages. "If they aren't, I'll hold you responsible and you don't want that. I'm soon to be your queen."

"Yes. I will do as you ask." He let her out, almost running over her delicately slippered toe when he pulled off. *Ignorant, sad-sack, ugly...* but her attention returned to the two figures disappearing up the street. Leaving her fury, she followed.

Wishing she'd dressed in something a little plainer and a lot more comfortable, Jaydee ducked behind half-repaired buildings, wove among workers, stepped in some sort of nasty spillage.

After the twins entered the Palace gates, Jaydee summoned a guard lazing about. "I need someone to follow those two! Quickly! I mustn't be caught and they may be a threat to the King." The guard looked at her doubtfully until she thrust the Belial ring in his face. She didn't wear it openly, it was hideous, but it did come in handy to get the slothful Belials hopping. Mardu wouldn't give her one no matter how many times she asked, so she'd stolen Balek's, seduced him during one of his frequent binges, and taken it. Let him worry about replacing it.

"Do it now or I'll have you punished!" She barked.

He shouted to three other men inside the gatehouse and a young guard stepped out.

"Follow those two." She hissed, pointing. "Tell me everything they do, where they go, who they speak to. Do not let them see you watching. It is of utmost importance. The King will reward you for a job well done. Hurry up!"

"HE DON'T WANTA SEE you now! I got orders to follow." Mardu's personal guard puffed up and towered over Jaydee, to show he wasn't going to let her pass.

She nodded, smiling prettily up at him. "Of course you do and you're doing a mighty impressive job. Just give him a message for me? Please? I'll wait out here for his reply."

The burly big guard stared with a hardened expression, and finally nodded.

"Tell him I know who's doing the Atlantean broadcasts. He'll be interested." At least she hoped he would. It seemed she barely knew him anymore. A few days ago he'd threatened to toss her out of the Palace altogether if she didn't leave him alone. Bothering him came with no small risk. But surely he'd want to know about this.

Back when they first started, the voice giving daily broadcasts to Atlanteans had seemed familiar but she hadn't realized why, until seeing those spoiled twins from the Ireland trip again. Not only did she know who it was now, she knew where to find this voice that had been spreading lies about Mardu, giving warnings of Belial movement and convincing Atlanteans to resist. They'd been operating from right here within High City. Maybe even the Palace itself!

Surely Mardu would see now, how valuable she could be.

"Two minutes." The returned guard growled, holding a door that must've been a foot thick with wood and steel. "No more."

She bowed at her King's feet, giving the respect he'd certainly earned. "It's the twins, remember the daughters of Drey that I followed to Ireland?"

"Get up." Mardu said irritably. He was at table, eating a late supper. The air smelt of fried onions and charred meat. Two stunning young girls sat on either side of him. Atlantean girls. Though food sat before them, they looked too scared to eat. "Go." He told them. "Wait outside my quarters." He pointed at the guards standing in shadows behind him, and one took the arms of both girls, escorting them out. No doubt to hold onto them until Mardu summoned them back.

"Of course I remember. What about them?" He cut a bite of meat. Chewing, he gestured at the fragrant plates of food with his knife. "Sit. Eat if you're hungry."

Jaydee talked while she moved to obey. "They're here in the Palace. I happened to see them while out—er working for you, and I followed to see what they're up to." She ate a bite, pleased at her reception. How long had it been since she'd eaten with her beloved? "So I thought, why in the world would they be *here? Now?*" She let the question hang only a moment. "They seem to be staying *with Carver*. And did you know he occupies Ziel's old suite? Of course you do! I misspoke. The twins returned there, yesterday afternoon, and haven't left since. Carver brings food to them… "

Mardu snorted. "So? He liked fucking one of 'em in Ireland as I recall. I even told him he could have her again—if she lived through High City's fall. Sounds like he's doubled his pleasure." He smirked indulgently.

Jaydee smiled sweetly back, rising to refill Mardu's goblet from a decanter of rich purple wine. "I don't know what Carver told you about Ireland. But I can assure you, he truly cares about the little one… what was her name… even if he pretends not to, pretends to have used her, I swear to you, he was not himself on that trip. He couldn't stay away from her. And the fact that Turner is missing—after murdering your Mutazio—he was the lover of Aiela, the dark twin. Did you know?"

Mardu went very still. "No. I did not know that."

"My fault." Jaydee bowed her head. "I neglected to tell you because I hadn't thought about those two in so long. Hadn't connected them anymore… "

In truth it was one of the little facts she hoarded until it became useful. Now it had.

"Put together, I think it is too much coincidence to ignore." She waited quietly for him to consider this, glad she'd taken extra care in dressing, had visited the beauty people before coming, even had her skin smoothed and tightened yesterday. The older Mardu got, the younger his bedmates seemed.

When he didn't respond, she plunged ahead. "I also believe Aiela is doing the Atlantean broadcasts that are keeping resistance alive, spreading information that only fosters rebellion." This would surely provoke him to giving her what she sought.

They ate together in silence. If she'd learned anything, it was to read his moods.

"I'll send three of my guards."

She startled when he finally spoke.

"Wait until after midnight. Put them somewhere fairly comfortable. I'll find out what they're about. If it's nothing, I don't want Carver fretting about some girls he wants. Gods know, he hasn't wanted many. I've an interest in keeping him happy."

"Take just the girls?" She was so close to having revenge. Carver had been terribly high-handed, so brutish and smug to her in Ireland. Ignoring her completely since the invasion, he'd acted as if she were invisible, except for the occasional look of disgust. It was time he learned some manners.

"Carver too. Separate cell. I'll question him myself tomorrow."

A warm tingle of thrill filled her. Anticipation of the look on Carver's snobby—

"And none of your sneaky antics." Mardu squinted a glare. "Probably I'll get nothing from him and then he'll go back to being a Prince of Atlantis. You'll not want him as an enemy. Still," Mardu spoke begrudgingly, draining his wine glass, "it's worth investigating. What makes you think it's this particular girl doing the broadcasts?"

Emboldened by his acceptance of her information, Jaydee moved behind him, massaging his shoulders. "I recognize her voice. It seemed a little familiar but I couldn't place it. Not until I saw Aiela again. She imagines herself quite a leader you know. On the Ireland trip, she literally just walked up and announced herself leader of the group."

"And they accepted her?" Mardu sounded more weary than interested. He'd stopped eating and closed his eyes, leaning into her kneading fingers.

"Readily." She breathed closer to his ear, sensing an opportunity. "You're so tired my king. Entirely too much is resting on these broad shoulders... "

He sighed, just a little, with pleasure, his tone less begrudging. "Push harder."

Jaydee put her back into it until he flinched and groaned. He always had liked things rough.

Mardu

Certain jobs he couldn't delegate. It was wearing him out, the work of re-making a country, with so few to trust. In Belial he'd at least known his people, how to rule them, how to control them in the ways that mattered. There had been established norms. This chaos of mixing Belial and Atlantean was yielding unpredictable outcomes. At least the psychotronic techniques were finally beginning to pay off. Slower than he'd hoped, but Atlantis was melding into the form he wanted.

"He better be able to talk." Mardu snapped at Montauk, who stood beside Carver's prone form laid out on a bed. Montauk was proving infinitely useful—but Mardu still despised the man. Thought he was smarter than everybody. Amused himself by irritating people until they lost control.

"Well able." The scientist's white hair was longer than usual, sticking up every which way, but his sardonic smile was the same. "He just needs the right motivation."

"And he won't remember... ?"

"Not a thing." Montauk bowed as mockingly low as he always had. "Jaydee tells me this is high secret... " He nodded at the lockbox Mardu carried. "Trouble within the royal family." He clicked his tongue and Mardu wanted nothing more than to rip it out and feed it to the obnoxious, cocky ass. Instead, he turned away.

"I'll leave you to it then." Montauk deflated when he didn't get a reaction. "Summon me when you're done and I'll bring him out."

Mardu set the minor Sound Eye on a table, the only other furniture in this tiny room besides a bed. Montauk stepped out, closing the door behind him, as Mardu put on eye shields and unwrapped the stone.

Carver looked to be sleeping. "Open your eyes." Mardu commanded.

Carver's eyelids fluttered open. His breath was shallow and slow.

"Look here." Mardu tapped the stone, holding it right in front of Carver's face. Obediently, the half-lidded eyes fixed on the stone. "I'm going to ask you some questions and you're going to tell me the truth, all of it, leaving nothing out." He rewrapped the stone, locking it away. His was the only key, which he wore around his neck at all times. Looking around for a chair, he swore. "Move over." Forgetting Montauk's drugs acted as a paralytic.

Carver strained with the effort to shift his unresponsive body, eyes bulging, face growing red until he looked like he might pop veins.

"Stop. Be still." Mardu shoved at the dead weight of his youngest son and sat on the bed, trying to ignore how much Carver looked like himself at that age. Nostalgia didn't sit well. There was nothing in his past that he wanted to remember.

"Do you have Drey's daughters staying with you?"

Carver didn't hesitate. "Yes. They like staying in Ziel's old rooms."

"And what are they doing here? Why are they staying with you?"

"Ahna and I love each other. We had sex. We will have more. The twins are keepers of the Crystals. Ziel's extra room has access to the maze where the Crystals are."

Mardu was shocked to utter silence. Such small sentences. The answers to his most pressing concerns.

"The Crystals that power the grid?"

"Yes."

"How do you get to them?"

"I don't know. Through the maze surrounding them."

"Have you seen the Crystals, or the maze?"

"Not yet."

Frustration welled. Stupid bitch Jaydee. If she'd just waited a bit longer, had a little patience, they'd have all the information they needed. Still. He could easily question the girls next and get it all. *Ziel you rotten, conniving liar! Too bad I can't cause you more pain for this.*

Mardu had sent almost a hundred of his best people to Crystal City, looking for the tunnels Ziel claimed led to the Crystals.

"Tell me everything you know about the Crystals, the maze and the twins."

"Ziel trained them... " Carver began, and talked for a long time, telling anything the girls had told him. The whole story came out in his rote, evenly timed voice with no emotion, no inflections, nothing but the facts.

The whole story except what mattered most: Where exactly were the Crystals and how did one access them?

19

GATEKEEPER TESTS

"It's like light expands and dark contracts."

— DOLORES CANNON, THREE WAVES OF VOLUNTEERS

AIELA

*A*iela was furious. "That evil, camel-faced, worm-infested, wrinkled hag—"

"If only she was here to hear your insults… instead of me."

"Jaydee's an *Atlantean*! Does that mean nothing to her? It's one thing to side with Belials and save yourself, but to betray others? To put your country mates in harm's way—and for what? What could she possibly get for telling… whomever she told… whatever she told them about us?"

Betrayals like this were happening all over the country. They'd heard stories every day since the invasion. But the actual experience was like someone sneaking up and knocking you flat from behind.

"She has nothing to tell." Ahna replied, already weary of the circles they'd been talking in since Belial guards ordered them out of their bed in Ziel's rooms. "Jaydee knows nothing about us. Not really. The best they could have is suspicions."

"Carver knows." They stared at each other, faces glum, fear rising.

Carver was being dragged from his room as the girls were hurried out the door. He was fighting, trying to get to his weapons. Jaydee, slithering about with a gleaming smile, ordered the guards, "Shoot him! If you can't control him, shoot him!"

"Nooooo!" Ahna had screamed, already out of sight in the wide, gently curving hallway that used to be such a welcoming place, and now seemed harsh and threatening.

They hadn't felt they were in any particular danger, now that Mardu was firmly ensconced, now that High City was the province of beggars and thieves; those Belials directly serving the King, and Atlanteans who couldn't leave.

But danger had never left.

IT WAS TWO DAYS, by Aiela's estimate, before they saw any soul besides the silent guard who delivered their meals.

At least they got meals. He'd tossed in a bucket when they asked to relieve themselves.

They didn't bother asking about bathing.

Their prison had most likely been someone's office—empty now. It had plenty of space to pace in, plush carpets to sleep on, the smallest one put into service as a blanket, and even ornate murals of countryside and beach scenes adorning three windowless walls. The fourth was covered in an exquisite tapestry depicting the ruins of Crystal City. Nothing here could be used as a weapon, or to escape—though they'd tried.

Only one guard had brought the first meal, swinging the door open to set a basket inside, barely glancing at them before closing it again. Taking their food to the far corner of the room, they plotted in whispers while they ate.

"Look! Half a roast fowl! Save every bone. We'll break them, sharpen them if we can."

"Our guard isn't very big."

"Think there's only one?"

Aiela shrugged. "Probably. As far as they know we're harmless little Atlantean girls."

Ahna lifted an eyebrow. "I'll distract him, maybe even blind him, with our lovely smelling bucket."

Aiela grinned. "I'll take him out at the knees. Then use a little bone spear to punch a few holes in his neck."

The plan had worked better than they'd hoped. He hadn't even had time to shout for help before Ahna had thrown the bucket contents into his face, while Aiela knocked him to the floor and punctured his trachea.

They'd been wrong about there being only one guard. In fact, there'd been three, playing some game just outside the door. Guarding, as it turned out, several doors lining the narrow hallway. Upon seeing the girls, those guards had drawn weapons before even rising from their seats. Sound wands knocked Aiela unconscious. Her head still pounded from it.

"As prison cells go, it could be much worse." Aiela reminded herself now.

"I'm glad we have lights in here." This from Ahna, the exquisite tapestry rolled around her like a glorious shell that trailed dramatically behind her. She gazed at the four light spheres inset high above them in the ceiling. They'd been waving them on and off, judging morning by the sounds of the Palace coming to life outside the room, and settling down again at night.

"I'm glad we get to be together." Aiela said for the umpteenth time. They played this gratitude game to keep their spirits up, determined not to let fear and worry lend any useless opinions.

The door banged open and Mardu himself strode in. He stood staring at them while five guards streamed in behind him, filling the room, setting three cushioned chairs to face each other, a small bamboo table between them and a locked box on the table.

Aiela's heart sank. She hadn't seen that box since the day she returned from killing a hundred thousand Mutazio; the muta army that belonged to this huge, dark man whose savage presence seemed to suck all the air from the room. This was the monster who'd ordered Turner tortured, and was, most likely, looking for him still. Anger began to build its fire in her belly.

Wearing a tyrian red robe that was cut to fit his broad shoulders perfectly, a wide, ornate diadem encircling his bushy black hair in gold, he wrinkled a blunt nose in disgust. "The stink. Take care of it." Trailing from his shoulders, a brilliant gold cloak continued moving even when he was still.

A guard hurried to obey.

Aiela got to her feet, bristling up to her full height despite wrinkled nightclothes. At her side, Ahna still clutched the tapestry 'round her. Aiela lifted her chin. "Why are we prisoners?" It was her most imperious and mature tone.

"Sit in those chairs." Mardu pointed as if she hadn't spoken. "Do anything but what I tell you and I'll break something important—not just a finger. I haven't time to waste on you. The sooner you tell me what I require, the sooner you can go free."

Aiela understood finally, why this man had commanded a country for so long, had easily taken over the most powerful city in the world. He was absolutely sure of his own strength. As if there was nothing he had not done, or could not do. As if the entire world existed to serve him.

"You'll just let us go if we tell you... what?" Ahna moved towards the cushion chairs. Mardu's resemblance to Carver was unnerving.

He didn't reply to Ahna either. Just went to the locked box and opened it, putting on eyewear she hadn't seen before.

Panic disrupted her breath. "Turn around." She said to Ahna. "Don't look at it." She pressed her forehead against the bare stone wall where the tapestry had hung.

"It won't matter." Ahna's voice was even. "He can make us."

Before Aiela could reply, a hand grabbed her thick bundle of braids, dragging her to the other chair as Ahna shrieked, "Stop it! You don't have to hurt her!"

"There's only one painless way for this to go." Mardu sounded annoyed now. "And endless *painful* ways." He handed eyeshields to two guards. The rest left the room.

Ahna reached for her hand, sending waves of calm. *All is well. Whatever happens now is out of our control. All is well. Pretend.*

The stone was just as she remembered, Milky white, with blue veins spidering through it. Mardu screwed only the first section of its staff on, like a handle, then brought his chair to sit so close their knees almost touched. "Do you know what this is?"

That's when she realized she was feeling no effects. An energy field spread horizontally from the stone's beveled center, like a pool of rose-orange light that encompassed the room. A gust of elation came from Ahna through their linked hands. "It's the minor Sound Eye." Aiela answered.

Mardu's eyes narrowed, going back and forth between her and Ahna. "How do you know that?"

"Because Ziel told us about it." Ahna had gotten the message across; Answer as if they were compelled to.

"Ziel trained you. For what?" Mardu's voice was forceful.

How does he know that?! She swallowed. "Yes. Ziel trained us because I'm a Ruler apprentice and Ahna's an Oracle apprentice. Ziel was both."

"Liar!" Mardu snarled, shoving the stone closer. "Look straight at this... " The guard crushed her head, holding it from behind, as if she wasn't already looking at the stone, "... tell me the whole truth! You are keepers of the Crystals at the center of your big fucking maze, aren't you? You *will* hand it all over to me... "

A great rushing filled her head, washing her outside herself. The sensation wasn't like a sound, or a light, or anything else she could describe. There was simply the rushing. And then she knew no more.

"EL! El wake up! He's... they're all gone now, come back. El!"

Aiela woke to Ahna's urgent whispers and tried to force her eyelids up. Only one complied, and only a little. The room lights were dim, but still stabbed inside her skull like the piddly bone shards they'd almost killed a guard with.

Ahna sat beside her, blotting her lip with a corner of the tapestry.

The room spun in a slow waltz. "What... " Her voice rasped against a raw throat. "Drink? Water?"

Ahna shook her head. "There is none. I'm sorry. I'll go ask for some, now that you're awake. Do you know what happened? I blacked out... or... something. I don't remember anything since the stone and... Mardu's questions."

She seemed as disoriented as Aiela felt. Sitting up, the pounding in her head tripled and she couldn't seem to open her left eye, no matter how hard she tried. "What's wrong with my... "She put a hand to her face, yanking it back when the touch brought sharp pain.

"Don't do that. Your eye is swollen shut." Ahna told her, leaning in close to study it. "Turning colors already—there's blood on your ear." She reached to blot at it.

Aiela pulled away. "What happened? Why is your lip bleeding—and so swollen? Did Mardu do that? Gods, my body hurts all over!"

"Your ear!" Ahna's face took on a look of horror as she carefully held Aiela's hair away. "Your ear is missing some p-p-pieces!"

But Aiela's one eye focused on the underside of Ahna's thin white arm reaching up from inside the tapestry. "What happened to your arm?" She took Ahna's wrist, gently rotating it. They both stared at the burn marks lining its tender underside from wrist to armpit. Then the smell registered.

Gagging, Aiela sank back onto the floor. *What happened to us?!*

Not knowing how she got them, the wounds, pains and marks took on an insidious taunting, became a disembodied terror that haunted her as she tried to sleep.

Water was brought when Ahna asked, and food—though they had little appetite.

"How can something like this happen to my own body, and I don't have a single memory about it?" They asked this question of each other a hundred different ways. "Did we tell him anything? Do you think he has control of the Crystals now?"

But no matter how many questions they asked, no answers came.

20

BANPIRO LOVE

"The world was on fire and no one could save me but you.
It's strange what desire will make foolish people do.
No I don't want to fall in love, (this girl is only gonna break your heart)."

— CHRIS ISAAK, WICKED GAMES

KANE

*A*djusting the single, large sail, into a broad, black sheen that bulged full, Nadya waved to the oversized man at the helm, some sort of gesture inquiring if it was positioned correctly, Kane guessed. The man waved back from inside the sloped forecabin and she began tying off ropes.

Obsessively, Kane watched this queer creature. Her movements were at once fluid and precise. She looked like a woman—mostly—but didn't act much like any he'd known.

He'd known quite a few, being raised in a household of sisters, aunts and grandmothers. Scottish women were brawny and brazen, very much the center of their homes. Always in charge. Steady as the moss-patterned rocks which Scotland provided en masse to build with.

Nadya seemed both sultry and savage. Especially compared to the women of High City with their endless frills, nuanced moods, and fussy attention to perfecting every detail of their own beauty. Kane had not taken a mate in his new country. There'd been plenty of lovers, but no one he'd particularly connected to. It had been simple curiosity between two opposite people, that drew the abnormally gorgeous females of High City to their cheerful instructor who taught them the art of the fighting dance.

He couldn't quite say what it was about Nadya that made him feel like he was in some glittering trance, wholly focused on every move she made, every small expression and shade of character. She was exquisite—and entirely foreign.

He hadn't really believed Banpiro existed.

Sailors told tales of these creatures who looked like humans, but were not. Supposedly, they drank warm blood—animal and human alike. Supposedly they didn't die. But sailors told a thousand odd and unbelievable tales. Who could say which ones were true, and which had been hatched in imaginations over-grown from too many days and nights on the surreality of an endless ocean?

"You will need to prepare your own food." Nadya's distinct and proper enunciation drew him from his trance.

"Aye. Ye dinna have a proper kitchen aboard either I suspect." He smiled, watching the setting sun reflect in the gold of her overly wide eyes.

A corner of her mouth lifted. "No kitchen. Not even food you might consider proper."

"I've brought eggs, roots an' bread. Fishin' will do me well an' fine, but wha' sustenance fer you?" His tone was playful, as hers had been. His curiosity about her knew no bounds.

Without blinking, she considered him a long while. "I've everything I need aboard."

A chill ran up his backbone. Surely she didn't mean... him? That look had insinuated... something.

"Aye. Good... good." He shuffled from foot to foot on generously knotted, black walnut planks, searching for something else to say, some clever action or words to hold her attention. "Where do ye hail from?"

Glancing around her neat, dark ship—magnificent with its dragon-head prow arcing aggressively towards the horizon, and a slightly lower, undulating tail forming the stern—she pointed towards the small, aft-cabin. "Would you enjoy some wine? The answer to your question is lengthy and I will likely give you more than you bargained for."

Again, chills tingled. He fought to contain his blind eagerness. "I would. Yer no' needed out here?" She'd been working on deck since they set sail from Chiffon, near on three hours ago.

Vaguely waving a hand towards the bow, she ducked under rigging to head for the cabin. "No, I am done. Yulio will shout if he needs me."

For all its shadowed beauty, the ship was compact, not more than 60 feet in length, with depth enough for standing room in the hull. He'd been below decks just long enough to toss his bag of necessities into a darkened, boxy space with a bunk.

When he boarded, Yulio, the huge, silent helmsman, had clasped Kane's arm in greeting. Straw-blonde hair reached his shoulders and he looked stout as an oak. It wasn't often Kane felt outmanned, but Yulio rose over him like a great blonde bear. It didn't take long to figure out he was shy. Watching intently as Kane showed them his Atlantean weapons, Yulio couldn't bring himself to ask the questions hovering in his eyes. Kane had left the bag of weapons in the fore-cabin, so Yulio could examine them to his heart's content. Nadya mentioned two more members of her family, "sleeping so they can sail the night shift". They'd been a crew of four and he made five.

"I am from Avalon." Nadya began now, pointing her chin at a quartet of chairs carved with flowery faces and vines, well-cushioned, arranged around a matching table. Kane sat obediently while she rummaged in a cabinet, bringing forth ornate silver goblets. "Avalon is within Leonesse, the adopted country of my people—the place we coaxed and carved from the wilderness, whence we were exiled from Atlantis." Her tone hinted at pride and bitterness in turn. Prying open a crate of small clay jugs, she selected one, and set about peeling a wax seal, removing the cork with an effortless pop.

"I've no' heard o' this place." With glaciers melting, inside the last few generations, freeing more and more habitable land, there were plenty of colonies and countries he'd not heard of.

"You would not have." Nadya glanced at him before pouring. "We seek to keep it unknown."

He waited until she stoppered the jug and placed the drink before him. "Why?"

"It is best if you let it breathe a while." She swirled plum colored liquid inside her goblet and sat beside him. Close beside him.

"Because we have much riches. Our homes will stand for three thousand years and beyond. We have more animal herds than we will ever use. Our people are excellent craftsmen, with talents developed over lifespans that appear to be without end. They craft with jewels and precious metals, create artwork that takes away the breath. Those who know, call us 'little Atlantis'. Men the world over would covet what we have—possessions I mean... " Long golden eyelashes lowered halfway as she sipped, savoring. "... and the kiss of a Banpiro that stops time."

As if possessed inside a dream, Kane reflected her movements, sipping from his own cup. It was exceedingly potent wine, but well-balanced. "What is it ye mean by *that*?"

"I mean," Nadya fixed those molten, unblinking eyes on him again, "we can stop time for certain humans. They can become Banpiro. Most die from our blood-taking—but some live, and we do not understand why. I became a scientist to study this phenomena. It is something to do with the brain—some ability to rewire itself and let the body become other than what it was—or not."

Most die from our blood-taking.

So it was true then. Kane's heart pounded like a huge skin drum announcing battle. He'd last felt this odd mixture of excitement and danger, preparing for combat as a youth in Scotland's clan wars.

He only noticed his goblet was drained when Nadya moved to replenish it.

"You like our wine." She brushed against him in rare, cat-like approval. A black silk tunic, longer and finer than any wares of High City, clung to the musical curves and angles of her body. Thin black leggings painted a sheen over shapely calves. Pouring with steady hands, even as the ship moved beneath them, her scent was strong and heady as the wine. Cloves and spices first, orange and vanilla underneath. He hadn't noticed it in the sea-tossed breezes outside, but here, in this cramped room, it pillowed around him like desire distilled.

"Yulio is... ?" Kane let the question hang while he sipped once, twice, three times from the goblet. Metal tang joined the deep notes of red wine.

"Yulio is my brother." Nadya seemed amused at his unfinished question. "My family is rather sprawling. They are not blood. Not as the family you would think."

"Ye mean ye've no 'real' family then?" What he really wanted to ask was "No mate? Children?"

"I did. Mahlia was my sister. Born of the same mother. Together, we survived the atrocious experiments of Onus Belial while our parents died from them, while our two sisters died and our brother. Together we survived losing those we loved—and next being outcast from all that we knew. Mahlia was all I had... everything left to me." The golden eyes shone with tears now and Kane wanted to weep for her.

"Wha' happened?" He whispered it.

"Balek killed her." Flat tones, no expression whatsoever.

Kane's head tipped and swirled inside, sure as the carpet-clad deck did under his feet. "Balek... ?"

Nadya sighed, deflating at the remembrance. "The eldest son of Mardu. I was taken—we've had dealings with Belial over the centuries, so I trusted when they asked for my help. I hoped we might be returned at last to our homeland, our birthright. At the very least, I wanted our colonies to be recognized as the part of Atlantis that they are. My people have never lost hope that there might be a cure for us." Nadya's face hardened and Kane instinctively leaned back a little. *"They* did this to us. They should find a way to return us to the natural rhythms of life... " She splashed more wine into her goblet. "... and death."

"So I kept faith with Belial and then they did *this...* " She told the story of being taken to Balek's stronghold, being forced to develop brain nodes that would control their Mutazio, and meeting Drey. Her voice thickened, turning monotone as she spoke of the fatal night Mahlia was burnt to death and stolen from her. She even told of Balek's brutal misuse of her in his stone-lined bedchamber.

Kane was shocked to silence by the time she finished. He hadn't touched the rest of his wine.

Nadya reached to tip a tear just below his eyelash onto her finger. "You weep for me?" She said it wonderingly, truly curious.

"Aye." He chanced taking her hand. It felt both strong and silky, but cold. "It's a terrible, tragic tale. It's honored I am, ta hear it. Honored ta be sailin' wi' a... a heroine."

She smiled and he saw up close the elongated incisors that added breadth and form to her prominent mouth. The now-familiar shiver set him wondering if this liaison was wise, but then she leaned over and kissed him. Placed cool lips against his own and used them like one might a fingertip, caressing, exploring. She tasted like spiced wine.

"It is I who am honored... " she said matter-of-factly, withdrawing, "... to have you assist in my revenge."

He suddenly felt the need for more wine. "Revenge." He repeated it stupidly but she merely smiled again, pouring the last of the little clay jug into his half-full goblet.

'Yes. I gave my word I would not take revenge while Drey lived. Now he is dead and I shall have it." She spread a hand suggestively on his thigh, caressing upwards, her body coiling towards him. "I shall take it with *pleasure.* Belial has forgotten what it is they created, who it is their *sheitan* son has abused!" This time her kiss was both harsh and demanding. "But we never forget. I bring my brothers to avenge me. And I bring you to show us the way." She ran fingertips down the side of his face, laughing softly when the chills visibly shook him.

"Drink. It is good for you hot-blooded creatures." She straddled him, tipped the glass to his lips, then to her own before she set to kissing him again. When she moved to his neck, he held his breath.

She nipped lightly as she worked her way down to his chest, baring his skin as she went.

He thought of all the animal species where the female consumed the male after they mated. Danger made him harder than even her perfectly-shaped body. The skill of her touch made him dizzy. He had no will left.

Kane, the Scottish warrior who taught graceful fighting dance and gave women everything they wanted most, was powerless, as Nadya, the seductive Banpiro took all that she wanted from him.

21

DEFEATED BY THE MAZE

"Let them be hunted soundly. At this hour, lie at my mercy all mine enemies."

— WILLIAM SHAKESPEARE, THE TEMPEST

MARDU

"*A*ll *fifty* of them?!" Mardu stomped back and forth, one two three turn, one two three turn, breathing hard with rising fury. "You're sure they're not just lost?" This was taking up too much of his precious time! He needed to be planning the takeover of Greece, issuing an invitation to meet with the Ruler— to threaten him with the Second Moon if he didn't comply.

Not to mention, forming his new army of combined Belials and Atlanteans to begin drills. Once he had the Second Moon under his control, it still wouldn't solve every situation. He'd need an army too.

"I'm sure, my King." The Belial General hesitated to provoke further anger. "Their trackers stopped moving. We found all but one of them, dead by some device or trick. Drowned, crushed, buried… one of the rescue teams even perished, tripping a second trap while digging out bodies." He shook his head. "That's twice we've wasted groups of the best, smartest, most motivated Atlanteans we could find. All of them defeated by the maze."

"Get a hundred this time! Make maps. Go slower. Use throwaway people—prisoners, old people, children. Use monkeys if you have to! Do whatever it takes. Force every Oracle and apprentice you can find into service. There has to be someone who is gifted enough, who can sense their way to the Crystals. This is Atlantis!" Mardu stopped to think a moment. This could take moons. They'd already wasted an entire week and were no closer to finding the power center of the grid.

Those twin bitches who were supposed to be Keepers of the Crystals, had some sort of protection from the Sound Eye—same as Ziel had. A sorcery that even Montauk did not understand.

"Bring Balek to me." Mardu ordered a guard.

"Go!" He shouted at the General, livid at how slow and stupid his supposedly best and brightest were. "It is *impossible* that a simple maze can defeat you with all of our technology, and all of the knowledge of Atlantis at your fingertips… "

That's it! He realized. *There could be answers in the Restricted Archives.*

As the General scurried away to gather more maze breakers, Mardu sent for Montauk too.

"Break them!" Mardu snapped. "Any way you can think of. I've got too many priorities waiting, I can't waste anymore time on increasing our power supply. If we can't get to the Crystals, we'll have to install new ones. Create our own grid." *Which still won't solve the problem of controlling the Second Moon.*

Balek's weasel face split in a grin. "Thank you my King." He bowed. "Thank you for entrusting me with this honor. I will not fail you." He stopped on the way out of the room. "Er… why me? Why not ask Sarim? Or Ramon?"

"Carver likes fucking the blonde one." Mardu's attention was already turning to Montauk, being ushered in by a guard. "He'll hate the thought of you abusing them. Might inspire him into cooperating."

"Can I... kill him? If it comes to that?" Balek's eyes, arranged much too close together, held a spark of mania. Mardu understood. He was asking permission for the ultimate triumph over an adversary.

"Only if it delivers the power of the Crystals to me. Otherwise, he's more valuable to me than you are—even with this betrayal." Mardu pointed at his eldest in warning. "If I find you've harmed your brother with no good cause, you'll suffer in kind."

"Montauk." As Balek left the room, Mardu addressed his most brilliant scientist.

"King Mardu." The uneven white hair that stood perpetually on end, almost touched the floor as the man bowed double. Sarcastic, secretive eyes hardened as he smiled during his rise. "How may I serve you today?"

"Go to the Restricted Archives under whatever's left of the Hall of Records." Mardu hated how much Montauk's face lit up. How was it that he was making so happy the people he most despised? "The maze surrounding the Crystals is resisting Atlantis' best minds. I'm loathe to waste any more who can serve me in useful ways. Look for anything that might aid us."

Montauk's tone and expression lost their mockery for the first time since he'd come to Belial many years ago, begging asylum. Atlantean Knights had sought to imprison and reform him for his crimes. "For so long I've wanted to know what's been kept from us down there. Truly, Dominus Mardu, I can never repay this gift."

"Oh, but you can." Mardu waved away the stupidly sincere gratitude. "You can find a way to power my nation. Bring me the key to the maze."

"Your bath is ready." Orja, his favorite servant, pressed a goblet of juice into his hand. It was bright red and fragrant. She paused, meeting his eyes instead of hurrying away to prepare his clothing like usual. Though she'd run his entire household in Belial, he kept her close here in the Palace, because his enemies could be anywhere. Her only duties now, were seeing to his food and daily care. She'd aged, he suddenly noticed. Lines between her eyebrows and around her mouth mapped long decades of serving him. Silver glinted from her feathery raven hair, yet she still seemed beautiful to him. She was the first person he'd sent for from home, once he'd taken the Palace. Her presence was calming, reassuring. Until she spoke again.

"I dislike you setting the boys against one another."

It was the first time he could remember Orja expressing an opinion on his actions. He frowned. "I didn't."

She flushed, but stood her ground. "I heard you giving over Carver's friends to Balek. You have locked up your own child as if he is your enemy, and now you're giving the ones he loves over to his tormentor. By torturing those girls, you're alienating the best of your sons."

"Carver betrayed *me!*" Mardu felt rage rising. What right had she to question him, especially about his own offspring? "Those he 'loves' are my enemies! How dare you—"

"What you are doing will be your DOWNFALL!"

Her shouting stunned him so much that he actually took a step back. Orja was defying him? Now, after all these years?

She was looking down, and her lip trembled. "Your boys are the nearest thing I will ever have to sons. You must understand. I care very much for each one of them. I don't want to see them set at each other's throats. Carver will not stand for it—not anymore." A tear rolled down her cheek as she looked up at him, whispering the last part. "He will destroy you." She turned, and walked away.

Balek

Somehow, they'd become a sort of confidant to him. Balek gazed at the twins, thinking how he didn't really want to kill them—or even cause them pain. But he must. He must do what it took to fulfill his father's desires. Mardu's approval was an even greater craving than the comforting company of these two beautiful girls.

He'd spent almost two days with them, and he was allowing them to bathe now. It was their reward for being nice to him, for trying to help him.

Even though he'd hurt them at first, they smiled at him, begging him to stay, insisting they wanted to help him—if only they could. It was confusing. His only friends were the parasitic Belials who liked him only as long as the wine and drugs lasted. But here, there were no drugs, though he did order wine brought with their noonday meal.

Hours ago, he'd sent away the guards who had held the girls while he hit them. Just as Mardu had warned, both girls went eerily blank whenever he asked about the maze, or the Crystals. It was like they turned off, even though their eyes were open, tracking him without expression.

No. Too many marks on those pretty naked bodies. He didn't want to hurt them anymore.

All three dressed in fresh clothing, he escorted them back from the palace baths and Ahna inquired hopefully about food. "You'll order us something hot? And tea?" Her hand was on his right arm. They seemed to always be touching him. Not recoiling, flinching, disgusted like all the other Atlantean girls he'd known.

"Of course." He stepped out of the little cell to give orders to a guard. "Bring plenty and it better impress me." He barked, shaking his head to clear the muddle. "I'll be dining with the prisoners again."

He'd already had comfortable chair cushions brought. The girls had pushed theirs close on either side of him, asking many questions about who he was and what all he did for Mardu. They stroked him and giggled at him, telling him he must be so very intelligent and strong. "Eldest Prince of Atlantis." They called him. "The Next King."

"When you're our King," Aiela inquired, serving him first, once the food had arrived, "what is it you will do with Atlantis?"

"Oh, my father will have done it all already by the time I take the throne." Balek boasted. "My job will be to enjoy it. I'll have to maintain it of course, but it'll be a well-built machine by then."

"Machine?"

"Sure. With access to the Restricted Archives, Montauk will be able to replicate the Sound Eye. Improve on it. We'll use Atlanteans— they'll be willing slaves by then—to build as many aeros, ships and weapons as we need. Our armies will be beyond counting as we conquer every nation." Balek felt his chest swell as he thought of it. "The will of every human on the planet will serve me by the time I take the throne. Mardu has big plans for re-making it first. Creating better humans."

"How do you create better humans, exactly?" Ahna smiled, but her tone was sharp.

"Program out emotions, differences, preferences." Balek shrugged, chewing some sort of fish stuffed with creamy herbed vegetables. "Mardu hasn't explained it all—and I'm *much* too busy with important matters—but we've already begun the master plan."

LATE THE NEXT MORNING, Balek took a seat in Carver's stupid little suite. "Orja is gone, did you know?"

Carver shook his head, face wary. "What do you mean 'gone'?"

"Bloody gods, you're slow! I mean Mardu can't find her. She left a note, and no one has seen her, or knows where she went or how."

"What did the note say?"

Balek shrugged. "Mardu burned it. Even if I cared, I wouldn'ta asked. He was in a mood black as hell itself." Turning to a guard, he ordered food brought to break his fast.

"I've spent the last two days with the twins. Since I can't decide which one I want most, I'll just have them both." Balek goaded Carver, chewing overcooked reindeer veal just arrived.

Carver looked away, but his whole body was vibrating and tense. He'd been confined to these rooms, with guards posted inside and out, until Mardu decided what to do with him. But Balek had his own plans. His men were done digging the pit, putting the finishing touches on it right now. Carver needed to learn his place.

"They *like* me. That should make you feel better." He'd left the twins last evening feeling magnanimous and benevolent. They shouldn't be prisoners. He'd have to do something about that.

This morning, he realized he'd been under some spell. He'd deal with them soon enough.

"You should see them, can't keep their hands off me. I'd like to use them rough—they'd put up a worthy fight—but they could be much more to me than just throwaway bed toys. Maybe one of them could be my mate... if they cooperate—lead me to the Crystals." He laughed, thinking of it. "One could be my queen, the other my whore. Or maybe I'll have *two* mates. Atlantis would love me with an actual Atlantean ruling at my side."

Carver made to leave the table.

"What, you're not eating?" Balek stuffed another bite into his mouth. "Aiela's more queenly, don't you think? She inspires loyalty, makes you *want* to bow down and swear to serve. But Ahna's got that perfect little body... golden hair between her le—"

Pain exploded. An unbearable torrent of sensation blossomed outwards from his nose, as Carver slammed his face into the rosewood table. There wasn't even space to release the scream building inside. A hand grabbed his hair and flung him to the floor. Carver's knee ground into his back, an arm around his throat, pulling back too far.

Guards were shouting, fighting to get Carver off, motions that only made the throttle jerk tighter. So much weight was crushing him, boots and elbows striking him in a hurricane of blows.

Carver wasn't letting go. As a guard stepped back, lifting his sound wand, Balek tried to shout "NO!" but had no breath. *Fool! It'll hit me too!*

The room was going black. Then Carver let go of his throat, grabbed either side of his head in a violent, neck-snapping jerk—

A guard tackled Carver.

Violent pain—so bad Balek still couldn't draw breath in, even with the weight gone. Coughing, choking in air, desperate—he found he could still move. His neck wasn't broken.

Rolling to his back, he spit out blood, too much flowing from his nose, lips, and teeth.

Carver was fighting the guards.

One guard fell stiffly back, a butter knife planted deep in his eye socket.

NO! You can't let Carver win! He wanted to shout it. Couldn't. It was work just to breathe.

Only two guards left. Balek tried to call for more, still couldn't get any sound out.

Another guard fell, forehead bounced off the single alcove window. He lay still, stunned from impact as the glass cracked, spidering rapidly outward.

Carver was hitting the remaining guard, raining vicious blows to face and stomach, so fast the guard was driven back, arms up, trying to defend. Stumbling over a body, the last guard fell violently back towards the window—and through it—in a shower of glass shards.

Carver turned. Cold, raging eyes pinned on Balek.

Balek crawled toward the door. So hard to make his body work, not enough breath yet. Had the bastard permanently injured his windpipe?

Bending to the guard—still twitching with the knife buried in his skull —Carver reached for the light gun, fumbling with the holster. Behind Carver, the guard with a bleeding forehead raised his sound wand.

Balek was too close to Carver, but he welcomed the blast of pain in his ears. And then nothing.

THEY WERE CARRYING out a body when he woke; the guard, dead from a blunt knife. Another still bled from a hundred small glass cuts. The one who'd shot Carver was giving orders.

Carver was propped against the wall, bound hand and foot, still unconscious. At least he'd taken the brunt of the sound blast. Balek had been shielded. He sat up. A stretcher was brought, bearing him to the King's own healers, quartered on the third Palace level.

His intense pain was addressed first.

Two hours later, his voice was only a scratchy whisper, but it worked well enough to have Carver taken out and thrown into his prison pit. Sharpened steel spikes lined the bottom except for a space in the middle, barely big enough for a body to curl in.

The guards were being careful, trying to lower Carver's limp body into the space without spikes. But the pit was too deep.

"Drop him!" Balek sounded like his throat had been shredded. Felt like it too, but he didn't care just now. The drugs were doing their job well. "Just throw him in! Why're you being careful? Do you *see* what he did to me?!"

They obeyed, watching as Carver's unconscious body collapsed in the shallow water pooled at the bottom of the pit. One leg splayed out mid air and a spike caught it, piercing through the calf.

Balek felt the tiniest crumb of satisfaction. Hopefully, it had broken the fucking bone.

"Shut it." He rasped, stepping back so the guards could drag the heavy metal plate over the pit. There'd be no light in there. And no chance of escape.

Now to get the two bitches. He wanted them to watch when Carver woke.

VISIONS AND DECISIONS

They're lining up the prisoners and the guards are taking aim.
I struggled with some demons, they were middle class and tame.
I didn't know I had permission to murder and to maim.
You want it darker, we kill the flame.

— LEONARD COHEN, YOU WANT IT DARKER

AIELA

*B*alek stood across the room from them this time. When Aiela tried to get closer, the guards shoved her back against the wall. *Guess he suspects we're influencing him.*

"What happened?" Ahna asked, still speaking in the sotto cadence they'd been using to charm him.

"Nothing." Balek's voice rasped painfully and he flinched. His face was severely bruised, both lips split and terribly swollen, nose noticeably crooked. Somebody had beat him badly.

"I'm a healer you know." Aiela stepped towards him again, uneasy at the ominous color of his energy.

He wouldn't even look at her.

She tried again. "I can help you—"

"You're a fucking whore sorcerer is what you are!" He flinched even more this time, trying to scream it, clearly costing himself more pain. "Bring them!" He wheezed at the guards. There were four—one to bruise each of their upper arms, gloved fingers digging in, unnecessarily jerking this way and that, while they walked, as if they were resisting.

Aiela was behind Ahna as they followed Balek through the halls and outside. He led them down the mountain to one of the gardens just inside the Palace walls.

A huge, rough metal lid lay on the ground. Three of the guards strained to shove it aside, revealing a pit. Aiela swallowed. *Was Balek throwing them in here?*

Then the morning sun hit its depth.

"NO!" Ahna reacted so violently she escaped her guard's grasp, came at Balek swinging. "You get him out of there! I will never tell you about the Crystals if you hurt him! Do you hear me? *NEVER!*"

One guard grabbed her from behind and yanked backwards, pinning her arms behind her back. Another guard hit her twice with closed fists.

"Stop it!" Aiela thundered, struggling towards her sister. "I will tell you! Leave her alone!" She screamed it at Balek.

He lifted a hand, signaling the guards, a smirk of pure enjoyment flowing across his grotesquely colored face. He came to stand in front of her. "You will take me there? Right now?"

"Y-you have to let them both go first." She stalled, trying to think.

Ahna was shaking her head. "No El. Don't do it."

"You have to send my sister and Carver somewhere safe before—"

"No." Balek rasped. "I don't! If you give me what I want, I will *maybe* spare their lives after."

"No deal then." Aiela squared off, eyes narrowed as she leaned as close to Balek as she could get, putting every ounce of loathing she felt into her words, and throwing them at this vile little Belial. "I will not negotiate. It's my way, or *no* way." She knew, at that moment, she would die rather than give in to him—to any of them. Stubborn was a label she'd started earning at birth. She wouldn't give him what he wanted. Not for anything.

"We'll see about that." Balek turned and walked away.

The guards chained her and Ahna by the ankles, fastened to the large metal rings that served as a handle on the huge pit lid. "You *might* be able to wander around... a little." Jested one guard.

"It'll be slow going." Smirked another.

And then they were left alone.

"Are you alright?" Aiela examined Ahna's face. Fresh red marks showed over old bruises from Mardu's last visit—or Balek's mistreatment, before they were able to cast their spell over him.

"I'm fine." Ahna muttered, squatting down at the edge of the pit. "Carver?"

He didn't move. Metal spikes surrounded him thick as riverbank reeds. One was stuck in his calf, suspending his leg midair.

"Carver!" Ahna shouted it this time. "Wake up! Carver!"

No response.

They sat beside the pit, discussing what to do next. Even in these circumstances, it was nice to sit in bright sunlight after so many days in a windowless room.

It was an hour or more before Carver finally stirred, eyes blinking open. Lifting his head with a groan, he slowly took in the pit full of spikes, and his leg with the spike through it. "Wh-where... ?" His eyes lifted to their two faces peering down at him. Widened. "Is Balek dead?"

"No." Ahna was casting around, trying to find a way out for him. "He's plenty bruised though. Was that you?"

Cursing, Carver let his head drop back in the sloppy mud. "I tried to break his neck."

"What happened?"

He told the story three words at a time, clearly depressed that he'd failed at killing his brother. Being thrown in a pit and impaled on a spike didn't seem to bother him nearly as much as Balek still being alive.

Thirst lessened their conversation by mid-afternoon.

Carver had roused long before then, grunting and gasping as he maneuvered, trying to get his leg off the spike, nearly passing out with the effort of balancing and lifting, in so much pain. They were crotch-height, and anchored firmly in the ground. No amount of pulling or pushing moved them a bit. Blood poured out when he finally wrenched his leg up and off.

"Put pressure on it." Aiela instructed. "Both sides, hard as you can. Is there something you can wrap it with? No, don't let go—keep holding it until it clots."

Though thirst-inducing, the sun was hot enough to dry out Carver's pit. At least he didn't have to sit in the soupy mud he must've been in all night.

By the time night had fully fallen, Aiela and Ahna huddled together for warmth, trying to joke about whose stomach growled loudest.

They took turns asking Carver questions. Explaining how they'd used mind control and touch programming to make Balek treat them well, how Balek told them about Mardu's plans for Atlantis—for enslaving the world, for genetically modifying humans.

Carver told them about each of his brothers.

Several times, they strained and heaved, trying to drag the metal lid, to see if there was any chance of escape under cover of darkness—not that they'd get past the guarded gates—but they had to try. They were barely able to move it.

Then it started to rain.

Aiela and Ahna jumped up and down, swinging their arms and legs, moving rapidly as possible to keep the chill from settling in deep. Carver tried, but discovered movement set his leg to bleeding again. His voice shivered badly. "The w-w-water's p-pooling ag-g-gain." His dull tone echoed the hopelessness creeping around them like a fog. Filling them up with every breath.

Eventually exhausted, all three of them curled up tight, hoping to sleep.

Aiela lay with her back against Ahna's, fear overwhelming her. She tried to push away despair's hungry claws but they were too sharp and too many, reaching from all directions. Where was the way through? Was there one? *We need help... and there is none. Help...* Finally she let the tears come, appreciating their warmth as much as their release.

"MAMA!"

Strong arms wrapped Aiela, melting away desperation and discomfort.

Papa added himself to the bundle and Aiela wept uncontrollably. "I can't do this." She sobbed into Mama's shoulder. "I need you. We're stuck! There's nothing else—nowhere we can go from here. I've failed." She cried out the trauma, the misery and terror, resting in the presence of her dead parents. They cradled her, rocking, soothing.

When she'd calmed, Mama took her face between her hands. Mama's eyes had always been like the ocean depths.

"Aiela." It was both a blessing and a command. "You're not done yet. This is not the end. My precious girl, you've done so well and you don't even know it! You are meant to save this world from a fate it won't recover from. If Mardu succeeds, humanity is completely lost. But he won't. You and Ahna will stop him. It is already written, and you only fail if you don't get back up and keep fighting."

"But how? And... and what if I can't?" Mama was surrounded in moving flowing waves of color, like rainbows. "I don't think I have much strength left."

"Then just be." Papa spoke for the first time. Behind him, rapid scenes flashed, scrolling through people, some she recognized, most were utter strangers. Foreign places, hundreds of faces, loving, straining, scowling, shouting, weeping, laughing. He let her watch it for bit. "See? It's just a play. All life really is, is a stage."

"I don't understand." Aiela felt foggy, tried focusing on Papa's radiant appearance. They both looked younger than she remembered them. Fresh and beautiful.

"It's not as serious as it seems." Papa explained gently. "In some ways, this life is all pretend. What matters, is that you do your best. That you act with courage, be always in love, hold on to joy."

Aiela shook her head. "There is NO JOY in this! Don't you know what's happening here? Atlantis is lost... to evil! Thousands have fallen to darkness...

millions more will fall the world over. They have no power to fight it. I can't fight it either. I am not enough to stop this great fall... " Tears of shame spilled out. "Ziel was wrong about me. I'm not special."

Again, simply loving her, holding her, they let her cry until she felt cleansed.

"Let go of emotion." Papa suggested. "Look back on all this from the other side, without fear, without regret or anger even. See what is happening, like it's a game of moves and countermoves. Like you have no responsibility for any of it. Just see the game... "

Magically, the emotions melted away and Aiela was able to see it, just as Papa said. She studied it from new angles, perspectives shifting.

"Now," Mama said, "do you see something you could do next in this 'game'?"

An idea formed. "Yes." Incredibly, new strength sprouted inside. "Yes, I think there's something we could try. But it wouldn't save Atlantis... the opposite in fact."

"There's more than one way to save Atlantis. You're playing the 'long game' here." Papa smiled. "Sometimes, letting go of what we love, is the best way to save it."

ᏇᏇ

AIELA OPENED her eyes to a spectacular sunrise washing the entire sky in brilliant color. "Ahna." She whispered. "Ahna wake up." Though shadows cloaked the rain-soaked ground beneath them, glory sang and danced in sunrise colors calling to them from above.

Aiela told about the dream of Papa and Mama, and the plan—the countermove that had appeared.

"I dreamt too." Ahna whispered urgently. "About the *beginning* of all the destructions of Atlantis. It was the Crystals. They did it every time. They set it all in motion. The Crystals tore apart High City to save the world—*and we programmed them to do it!*"

Aiela stared at her. "The same solution came to us in two different ways."

"We have to." Ahna said. "I've seen what happens if we don't; Mardu kills us and digs his way to the Crystals. He starts using the

Second Moon against other countries, damaging more of Earth's grid each time. China and India start fighting back so he goes after them, only they're out of range so he uses the Crystals to ramp up the power of the Second Moon and extend its reach. But the power is too much. He starts a chain reaction that shatters the planet and collapses the *Universal grid*. The Universal grid El! This entire planet—and I can't even comprehend how many more. We have to stop him!"

"We will." Aiela felt the steel of this resolve. "It's why we're here. And now we know how."

Deep in thought, they sat under the canopy of majestic fire-washed clouds that morphed to shocking corals and blue-tinged purple.

"Bet you we won't live through it."

"Bet you we will."

They grinned at each other, whispering in rapid bursts. As the Palace grounds came awake, as the solar colors of High City faded, and warm sunlight beamed a new beginning, they formed a plan.

23

THE DEATH

9,970 BCE. EASTERN COAST OUTSIDE HIGH CITY, ATLANTIS.

You say I took the name in vain, I don't even know the name.
But if I did, well really, what's it to you?
There's a blaze of light in every word. It doesn't matter which you heard
The holy or the broken Hallelujah

— LEONARD COHEN, HALLELUJAH

KANE

"Where is it we go now, Kane?" Nadya, along with the blonde giant Yulio, and two Banpiro men, both dark and gaunt, surrounded Kane. Nadya's dragon-prowed ship, anchored in deep water, was far enough out to not be seen except on the clearest of days. They'd rowed ashore and hidden the rowboat, catching their breath as they sat on an outcropping of rock. All four Banpiro gazed at him expectantly.

"Froom here we walk." Kane looked west. "That way." Peaceful and lush, the remaining treetops of Old Forest were just visible on the horizon. "And pray god we dooen't encounter Belial soldiers."

He set off, trying desperately to walk without wincing. Nadya was at his side, the others trailing behind. It'd been years since he'd had a night that left him this tender.

"Who exactly do you pray to?" Nadya asked. She seemed to be walking just fine, which irked him a little. They'd fucked every which way—including ways he hadn't before. And he still had all his blood.

"I dinna mean a *actual* god. Jus'... any powers o' good that exist."

She was incredibly literal, and naive in some ways—definitely not in others though.

"We have not any fear of soldiers my lover Kane. Belial or other." Nadya smiled at him. Never had he seen a woman look both patronizing and hungry.

Crossing the south river canal was the only time they encountered Belials, but they weren't soldiers. Just common thugs out to rob or molest anyone they happened upon.

Two Belial throats were slit, bodies sinking to the bottom of the river so fast Kane had only time to gape. The other four were drained, alive until their hearts arrested, and Kane vomited his own breakfast remnants into the sluggish water.

Nadya looked a bit sheepish as she washed the blood from her hands, and lips. "I am sorry my lover Kane." Lithe shoulders lifted in a slight shrug and she met his eyes. "It is who I am."

They reached Charis' underground hideout by midmorning. Sage had provided precise instructions and Kane was so relieved to be among humans again, he hugged the aging lady much too tightly for much too long.

"It's nice to meet you too." Charis gasped, within his crushing arms. "Can I make you tea?"

Taking time to eat, and report news of Sage and Turner, Kane listened to Charis' worries. No one had heard from the twins since five days ago.

"I am not sure of the exact location of the maze entrance." Charis apologized. "I can only go on my instincts, my knowledge of Old Forest, and the little that Ziel or the girls hinted at when they were coming out regularly for food and such."

She spread a crudely drawn map out on the barrel turned into a table. "It's somewhere around here... it almost *has* to be... " She eyed the four Banpiro waiting patiently by the door. "Hopefully they're as useful as legend tells. The maze is terribly dangerous. You come back to me, Kane. We've lost too many... too many. You remind me of my Bren." She patted his stubble-rough cheek in farewell.

IT WAS miles of walking once they'd found the entrance. Distributed between their packs were charged light spheres and torches, water, white pebbles, weapons, and eggs for the huge snake who roamed the maze.

"Sila was Taya's pet." Sage had explained. "The twins tell me she's become queen of the maze. Her favorite treat was always eggs. It's worth a try to find and befriend her, maybe she'll guide you safely through."

Kane let another pebble fall from his hand, spacing them as far apart as possible, close enough to still catch the light. At any rate, all five of them knew accomplishing their mission this way was improbable at best, perhaps impossible. Sage was certain the maze's other opening went right into the Palace—in Ziel's suite of rooms. But if they could find their way through from OldForest, there'd be no High City gates to sneak through, or Palace grounds to infiltrate.

All day they walked—near as they could tell without the automatic cues of sunset. Time was thoroughly blurred by the monotone darkness underground. He was dragging too far behind when Nadya finally called a halt.

"You must eat and rest." She said sternly, as if it were his fault she'd force-marched him into exhaustion. He couldn't tell if the other Banpiro were tired too, or if they were just accommodating him. With a can fire, he boiled eggs, adding rations of dense grain cakes and dried fruit to the meal, flavoring the boiled water with tea, which soothed his mind and body with its comforting heat. Sleep claimed him fast.

He woke to angry hissing and the dim outline of four Banpiro blocking the tunnel in front of him, weapons poised. With their backs to him, he couldn't make out what it was they faced.

The hissing deepened by the time he struggled out of the blanket and peered over Nadya's shoulder. "Ach! It's bigger than Sage said! Sure an we mean ta make friendly wi' the great monster! Pu' doon yer weapons, yer makin' 'er nervous."

Slipping between Nadya and Yulio, Kane held out his hand, offering two eggs. "Tsk, tsk, wha's all this hissin' and spittin' now, loovely Sila? We come ta make yer aquaintance." He went down on one knee, keeping eye contact with the gigantic thickness that, pray god, was the supposed friendly pet snake. Otherwise they were in for a wretched fight. Even with four Banpiro and weapons at his back, this was the stuff of nightmare; the reptile was thicker around than his torso. Its length spread so far into the darkness beyond, he could not see the end of it.

"C'mere Sila snake." He crooned. "We're meant ta be great friends ye see? We need ye ta take us ta Aiela and Ahna. We'll rescue them t'gether, wha'd'ye say? Ach, these are fer you, tha's it Sila, c'mon now, et up."

Her hissing had stopped and she bobbed her head towards Kane, fractionally slow. Eventually, her forked tongue flicked out, testing the air.

"Eggs, Sila! Fer you! C'mon an' get em'. An' more where tha came from." His tone was friendly and even, like talking to the great, moody aurochs or sour and paranoid billy goats back home. Like caring for the placid worker elephants here in Atlantis.

"The trick is ta be confident." He spoke in the same voice to the Banpiro party hovering nervously behind him. "Shoulders back, head up, bu' no' threatenin'." They must've moved, because Sila drew back sharply, emitting another ear-splitting hiss.

"Ah Sila. Ta be sure, ye're a wicked one!" He didn't flinch back, though it took every ounce of concentration not to. "Wha'ever ye're doin', mabbe don't?" He suggested to the Banpiro. "Ye could roll up my blanket and pack our things. Once she takes the eggs, we'll need ta move out."

Only when they'd turned away from her and occupied themselves, did she come to him. Her head was twice bigger than his own. She looked a pale ghost in the dim. Nosing his ear, she lowered to gulp an egg, then the other. "That's it Sila. Can ye take us ta the twins? Ta the Palace entrance?"

"Do you think she understands?" Nadya's tone was low and even.

Kane shrugged. "We've no' much choice ha' we?"

Sila warily watched the Banpiro shuffle. Watched Kane shrug into his pack and guzzle water. She stood tall in the tunnel, head grazing the ceiling. When they all stood ready, she turned back and began to slither in graceful, and terrible undulations.

Kane followed, feeling a mite sick when they passed a long lump in the pale lavender body. "Do ye think it's a human body?" He whispered to Nadya.

She shrugged. "Most likely. I do not know what else that large would be roaming the maze. Unless there are things Sage and Charis do not know about down here."

Kane shivered, preferring not to imagine what else might be hiding or hunting in this endless blackness. Dropping pebbles religiously, he spoke little, conserving his energy for the unknown miles ahead.

Yulio was the tallest of them and had to duck as he walked, to avoid scraping the earth and rocks above them. Sila stopped now and then, nosing junctions where up to four tunnels converged until she was satisfied, and set off again in one direction or another. Kane took advantage of her uncertainty when he could, drinking water or pissing it, digging small snacks from his pack.

Twice, he offered Sila another egg, the last time, taking the liberty of stroking her.

She tensed when the Banpiro made any move towards her, but seemed to watch Yulio with more curiosity than hostility. "Ye like the big one aye?" Kane crooned. "Ach, so do I. It wouldna hurt ta make some friends here. We're all on yer side, ye kin?"

"Sila," Kane called hours later, jogging to keep up, "Ye're in a mighty rush—an' I pray god ye're takin' us somewhere—but I ha' need o' rest." He stopped still, and eventually she came back to nose at him. She'd increased their pace for the last little while, and he was so out of breath he felt faint. "I hae' ta rest!" He repeated. Panting, he leaned to put his hands on his knees.

"Sit down Kane." Nadya ordered. "I'll get the fire. You should eat a real meal and try to sleep."

Sila seemed restless, not settling even as her five companions did.

Kane had just curled in his blanket and closed his eyes, the tea again working it's magic, when Nadya went tense beside him.

"Did you hear that?" She looked at the other Banpiro. They nodded, heads cocked, all crouched with weapons already in hand.

"Wha' is't?" Kane hadn't heard anything.

"Voices." Nadya whispered as Yulio brightened the light sphere. She helped Kane up. All grogginess fled as they set off after Sila.

She sped, slithering rapidly off into the darkness, but stopping to wait for them every hundred yards or so.

Ahna

Balek's guards dragged Ahna through the familiar, no-longer-secret door in Ziel's rooms. The slab of marble wall, with its fine-tuned mechanism, had been completely removed.

Panic and dread had been building to a fragile, knife-sharp edge for what seemed like hours.

First they'd taken Carver, his pain echoing off the palace walls as they hauled him roughly up from the spiked pit and made him hobble ahead of them. When he fell, they kicked and struck him. He'd been caked with wet mud, shivering violently.

"I think his leg is broken." Aiela had whispered, wincing as she described the colors of the energy surrounding his wound.

"Tell Balek we'll take him to the Crystals!" Ahna had screamed after the guards. "We're ready to now! He doesn't need to torture us anymore. Tell h—"

"Shut up!" One of the guards stopped to backhand her—their first acknowledgment that the twins sat here shackled and parched. The

215

force of it stunned her into painful silence as the guards, bored with prodding Carver, began to drag him.

Next they'd taken Aiela.

"Tell Balek we will take him to the Crystals!" Ahna insisted, clutching at the guards, clinging to Aiela, both of them repeating it over and over like a desperate mantra—and then she was gone. Physically pried apart from her twin, with no idea what might happen next, Ahna wept, terror rising. What was he doing? Why wasn't he listening? They were perfectly willing to give him what he wanted.

"Mardu!" She began shouting as anger rose to replace the terror. "Mardu, I will take you to the Crystals!" She screamed and shouted until her voice wore out. It was better than the tears, better than her mind making up stories. But nobody came. No one even acknowledged her hoarse and broken pleas.

DOWN THE UNEVEN staircase inside holy mountain, Ahna willingly followed the guards now. "Where is my sister? What have you done with her? Where is Balek? I demand to be brought to them both right now!" Her overused voice grated and squeaked.

"Shut yer cursed mouth!" One of the guards huffed at her. "We are taking you to them!"

This brought a measure of comfort until they reached the bottom of the long staircase and rounded the corner. A room had been hollowed out where once the tunnels had begun. It was lit up bright, but all she saw was the stone slab, balanced across two large rocks. Like a crude alter, it dominated the space.

Aiela lay bound upon it.

Balek stood beside her, a look of manic joy on his face.

"What are you *doing*?!" Ahna tried to shout but it came out a tired screech. "I'll take you to the Crystals, you don't need to hurt us anymore, we're ready to comply, we'll take you there right now. Please! Stop whatever it is—"

"Shut her up!" Balek screeched.

A guard clamped his gloved hand over her mouth, too much of it covering her nose and she struggled to breathe.

"You *will* take me." Balek said, and she realized he was intoxicated. He was slurring and his eyes were stretched unnaturally wide. He raised his hand to show her the dagger and she began to struggle violently, causing the guard's hand to slip and a muffled part of her protest escaped. "NO!"

"Oh yes!" Balek shouted back, his voice almost as high and scratchy as her own. "Yes! Yes! Yes! First your beloved whore of a sister will die and then your *beloved!*" He did a little maniacal dance, and behind him, Ahna saw that Carver was slumped in the corner. Blood crusted most of his face and Ahna struggled again. *This can't be happening! I can't lose them both! HELP!* The plea went upwards and she stilled. *Think, think, think...* But the hand still covered her mouth and restricted her breath and there was nothing she could do or even say.

"You think you're so smart working your whore sorcery on me. Well *I've* outsmarted both of *you*! She wouldn't give me what I want without you and now she gets to *die* for her refusal. I was going to make her my queen, but now I'll kill her to prove to you I do what I say. Then I'll kill Carver if you don't take me through your little traps. If you do, you'll get to keep him... *maybe.*" Balek cackled uproariously, waving the dagger above Aiela who strained against her bonds on the table.

Everything seemed to slow down then and crystallize into a single continuous moment. Aiela relaxed and turned her head to look at Ahna. She was gagged, but her eyes and energy burned bright into Ahna's mind. Brighter and clearer then ever before.

Do it Ahna. Do what we planned no matter what happens. I love you—

"NOOOOO!" Ahna lunged hard towards her sister, breaking away from the guard. Steel-like hands clamped on her from behind, arresting her head-long plunge.

Movement blurred from the corner as Carver sprang up, throwing himself at Balek, as Balek slammed the dagger point down, both hands wrapped around the handle, burying it in Aiela's chest.

Time overlapped... one image blurring atop another.

Ahna stood on the balcony outside her palace room. The crystals had woken her. *Horror and dread filled her at the single image burned across her inner eyes. Her twin lying on an altar. It was crude, a rough slab of dull stone, with shadows surrounding her—people perhaps—or something else. But her attention focused on one searing image; a knife planted deep in Aiela's heart.*

LIKE THE CATERPILLAR, THE COCOON WILL GIVE HER WINGS. BE NOT AFRAID.

It echoed, tone upon tone upon tone around her, reverberating, ringing so loudly inside her mind she almost fainted.

And then she came back to shouts, bodies piling in from... somewhere, hissing weapons and blinding light flashes, and she then was jerked backwards by her guard, around the corner where other guards knotted together at the base of the lower stairs leading up to Ziel's rooms.

"Go get the King! NOW! Hurry!" One guard shouted to another. Ahna heard boots pound upwards above them.

"Ahna?" A voice she didn't recognize called out. A male voice with a Scottish accent. The deafening commotion had abruptly stilled. "This is Kane. I taught yer sister Aiela. Listen, we've go' her now. We've go' yer sister." His voice reminded her of Turner. "The prince too... Ahna are ye there?"

The guards were arguing around her, while one leaned out to shoot blindly around the corner.

The hand was removed from her mouth. A harsh whisper beside her ear. "Answer them! Ask what they want."

"I-I'm here! This is Ahna. Which prince do you have?"

"Ach! There's more'n one prince here? What do yer captors want fer ye?" He spoke directly to the guards now. "Whoever ya are, we'll trade this beast o' a prince fer the girl."

They whispered ferociously around her.

"We must wait for the king. He won't want to let the girl go, she's his only link to the crystals!"

"We can't trade her."

"What 'bout Balek?"

"We wait for the king!"

"Take Carver with you!" Ahna yelled. "Take him and Aiela and go!

Leave me—you mustn't stay here, they're going for Mardu. He'll be here soon and he'll kill you all!" She marveled that the guards hadn't shut her up again. They were busy trying to peek around the corner, shooting, and still arguing about what to do.

Suddenly, they thrust her ahead of them around the corner. Her guard used her like a shield, one hand holding her by the neck of her tunic, the other wielding a light gun beside her ribs.

Ahna saw the altar slab was toppled, resting on one edge, sheltering several people, and the tunnel behind it. Aiela was nowhere in sight, though she thought she saw light bobbing away down the dark tunnel. Carver was no longer there either.

Balek was thrust like a rag doll ahead of Kane. The Scotsman was trying to say something but Balek began screeching incoherently, drowning him out. "You come get me right now! Do not let these idiots defeat you! Keep the girl and shoot them! Shoot them!" His voice strangled as Kane fought to control him and then Balek dropped like a sack of rocks, leaving Kane exposed.

The guard took the shot and Kane crumpled while Balek scrabbled on hands and knees towards his guards. A hand shot out from behind the slab, wrapping his ankle, yanking him backwards in one powerful movement, as a high, animal scream sounded.

A female, with beautiful reddish-blonde hair streaked out to lift Balek by his neck, forcing him up in front her. He wailed, arms flailing as if still trying to crawl to safety.

"You kill my Kane?" She thundered in a thick, strange accent, blind rage powering her words. "I kill your prince! Slow and painful—and still it is too good for this *sheitan!*"

All went quiet when Balek's eyes bulged, as the tip of a blade sprouted out the front of his abdomen.

One hand still gripped his neck, holding him up. "For Mahlia!" She spat.

The blade disappeared.

"And for *me!*" This time, the blade must have entered the vicinity of his anus. A bloody metal tip pointed upwards, emerging from the soft part below his sternum.

Then Balek screamed and screamed.

Ahna felt the shrill sound overtake all else in her head, as the panicked guards retreated up the steps.

Shrieks of agony and evisceration echoed endlessly around her, reverberating inside her, until she knew she was going mad, as she bumped and banged over the shoulder of a guard who carried her on the long trek upwards.

24

CHERRY ISLAND

The battle of Armageddon is fought over and over again in every age of the world's history.

— W. SCOTT ELLIOT, THE STORY OF ATLANTIS

AIELA

*D*reams *within a dream. Here, and not here.* Aiela's consciousness was at peace with this riddle, but her broken body strained. Strangely, her essence wanted to leave this peace, to return.

But I've already died, another part of her argued, *and all is well. All shall be well. I don't need to go back...*

From the moment the knife had plunged into her body, the journey here had begun. She'd been looking at Ahna, watching her struggle and fail, sending her calm, desperately trying to ease the red haloes of trauma spiking from her aura.

Do it Ahna. Do what we planned no matter what happens! I love you—

She'd shouted it with her mind, since the gag kept her from forming words.

The dagger piercing her chest was unexpected. She hadn't believed Balek would do it—hadn't seen it coming, focused so intently on Ahna.

Initially, the intrusion seared white-hot, and then death spasms shook her body, all pain ebbing away as her consciousness flowed out from it.

Calm, as golden light, infused her. She sensed at once that all was well.

Death was no stranger.

She was three when a kitten was stillborn and Mama explained the absence of spirit. At four, she lost her first patient and Papa helped her cry and bury the sea hawk. There had been Monkey, and plenty of other patients after that. Just before her eighth birth day, a village elder died of old age, and Auntie Sage had taken her along to the bedside. Each time, she'd curiously watched their auras fade away, or sometimes blink out quick, like shutting off a light. Death was a part of life and yet she had began to fear it. She'd had so much to live for— lots of things she wanted to do. The women in her family always died young. What if it came when she wasn't ready?

But now that it had, it wasn't so bad...

She sent the golden calm to Ahna in greater power, concentrating, as her spirit rose above the wreckage of the body, now lying so still on the stone slab.

No pain now, only the safety of Love. *Pain lies only in the human experience.* She saw it so clearly now, just as she did the glowing beings that enfolded her in an embrace of white light. *Here to take me home.* Even as she watched, detached from the pandemonium erupting, she felt only peace. Arms of light lifted her towards that place of all-encompassing Love. *Home,* her spirit sang. *Ahna, it's all alright, do not fear.*

Suffused with the great Compassion of being held in the arms of Creator's total Love, she rested. No reason to return to that dense, pain-filled place... was there?

And yet her body called to her, carried by strangers who worked urgently to keep it alive. Turner called to her, not yet aware she'd left the physical plane. Her twin, grieving to the brink of madness, unceasingly called for this not to be so. To not have to go on alone.

Would she stay in Love or return to pain? The choice was hers.

Carver

Hours of darkness and pain blended together, until Carver lost any sense of time. His leg burned and throbbed, but knowing he'd left Ahna behind, knowing she was in Mardu's hands... that was worse.

Someone carried him at an uncomfortable run—a male with a strange scent. What kind of strength did it take for such prolonged speed? The people who labored under Aiela's body and his own, spoke in thick accents when they stopped, urging him to drink.

The female, a strikingly beautiful woman administered injections to Aiela every time they stopped, fussing with the dagger still lodged in her chest, counting her pulse and breaths.

Twice, she gave Carver a shot, telling him it was for the pain. He faded rapidly into dreamless sleep after each one, so it must have been a sedative too.

At times, he thought he saw an enormous, ghostly serpent leading them, and his old childhood fears lodged at the periphery of his awareness. But surely it must have been hallucinations. They followed a trail of small pebbles that glowed white in the steady light. He slipped in and out of aching wakefulness.

Once, they halted, dumping him unceremoniously on the chilled earth while they gathered around Aiela, working with hushed and urgent voices. He did not understand their dialect save for a word here and there. When at last they took him up again to continue on, he asked, "Is she alive?"

"Yes." The female answered him curtly. "Just."

His leg was throbbing again, every beat a sharp stab, and he forced his mind to work ahead, drawing attention away from the pain. "What is your plan? Where will you take us?"

"To the isle of cherry trees, near Chiffon." The female again. "On my ship. I do not know if she will live long enough."

"I know where there is an aero. You could get her there in a few hours." He'd make them leave him at the closest healing temple. He had to find a way back to Ahna.

They considered it. A blonde man who looked giant next to the others, carried Aiela, cradling her in his arms and speaking little— same with the thin dark man who carried him with ease. But the female and the other male seemed to be arguing about it.

Finally she asked, "You can fly this aero?"

"Yes." Carver replied, heart sinking. Of course these foreigners wouldn't be able to fly an aero.

But Ahna... A voice argued in his head. *There's nothing I can do for her until I can at least walk. She'd want me to see Aiela to safety, no matter what.*

"Who are you?" He asked the female. "How did you come to be here and why?"

"I am Nadya of Avalon, in Leonesse. Friend of Drey who is father of this one and of the one you love. I owe him a great debt and I came to pay it. It is said Mardu killed him." There was an edge to her voice. "Drey was a great man. A man of excellence."

"Mardu's evil has no boundaries." Carver affirmed. "He's killed countless good men... and women. I would very much like to stop him." He felt a twinge of strength as he said these words. *I can come right back for her. Mardu still needs her. Please gods, may she have the strength to keep her secrets a little longer. Maybe Turner would come back with me. Maybe he'd even be able to gather enough Atlanteans and weapons for an attack. The girls had mentioned Atlantis' allies, perhaps there's already a movement underway to counter the Belial takeover...* His mind went in circles until he blacked out again in the uncomfortable rhythms of being lugged for miles, slung over someone's bony shoulder.

ACTING the young Prince of Atlantis, Carver commandeered a trolley in Old Forest, then an aero.

Belial soldiers readily obeyed his orders, believing his story that he'd been injured in an accident. Only Mardu's Palace guards would know of his recent imprisonment. Aiela's prominent dagger had been covered and he offered no explanation for her pale, prone form, or his eerie companions.

Mardu might get word of it eventually, but he'd be busy dealing with Balek's gruesome death, and no doubt still obsessively focused on gaining control of the Crystals and the Second Moon. He dared not think of how Ahna might factor into that obsession just now.

Carver was taking them up in the aero, gaining altitude as rapidly as was safe so he could push the old machine to maximum speed, when Nadya announced, "She is not breathing."

"Should we land at the next city and take her to their healers?" He *must not* lose her.

"I am a healer. Just not for her species."

Again the males had gathered around. Nadya directed them with streams of instructions in their language, her hands steadying the blade, while they took turns cautiously pumping Aiela's heart and breathing into her. Nadya injected something into her arm again and eventually, Aiela began breathing on her own, stopping and starting half a dozen times.

Carver felt faint and they brought water to him. His leg was an agony, but he knew there was no help for that, so he ate the grain cakes one of the dark men handed him, gritted his teeth, concentrated on studying the maps, and told himself to stop being such a baby.

Finally, he spotted the tiny crescent shape of Cherry Island floating in the deep blue sea below. Lowering cautiously, he looked for a clearing large enough to set down in.

Turner

Turner was fishing not far from land, when he saw the noisy black aero descend to hover over the island, then sink rapidly into the center of it.

Pushing the little motor to its highest speed, Turner slid the small boat right up onto the beach, took up his weapons and ran like the devil was chasing him—praying he wouldn't be too late. Surely Sage would stay hidden, or come to him. That aero had to be Belials. Atlanteans had lost everything of value or use.

Abandoning the wide path, before reaching the clearing where two huts had become their home, Turner wove through young sapling trees. Never did he expect the scene that materialized before him. Nadya and a shaggy blonde giant carried a body on a board between them. Sage hovered beside it, talking rapidly, though he couldn't hear what she was saying from this distance. Behind them, Carver hobbled between two strangers.

Catching his breath, Turner dashed after them.

"Carver?!" He yelled.

Carver turned and collapsed into him as he neared. "Turner! I'm sorry, I'm so sorry. She's alive, they kept her alive even when she stopped breathing but—"

"Whoa mate, slow down. Sure an' there's time ta tell the whole tale, aye?" Then he saw Carver's tears furrowing tracks, pale as death, down mud caked cheeks.

The tall, dark Belial slid to the ground, buried his face in his hands and sobbed.

Without a thought, Turner sank to the ground too, arms steadying around him. "Sure an' I've got ya now, go on, let it oot."

He held Carver's heaving body and crooned like to a babe, " It's a'right mate, it's a'right now", wondering what in the world his friend had endured—at the hands of his brutal father no doubt. Turner knew too well that fearful pain. Mardu had beat him near unto death.

And what news had Carver of the twins?

In moments, Carver quieted, struggling to rise to his feet, and failing. Turner lent him strength, helping him lift to standing, noticing then his leg. "Yer hurt mate, here, lean on me, I've got ya now, it's a'right."

"No my friend, it's not alright." He whispered in a low and defeated voice, swiping his eyes with shaking hands. "It's Aiela." He gestured at the huts where the stretcher party had disappeared. Balek tried to kill her… still might succeed. And they have Ahna—Mardu does."

Horror shot through Turner. He froze, body rigid, mind reeling. "Tha' was *Aiela*?!"

"Go. She needs you."

"Ya canna walk though...?"

Without waiting for an answer, he dashed towards the hut. *No no no no, not Aiela, no!*

Sage and Nadya were working over her, giving curt orders to the Banpiro who filled the small space. They hurried to build a fire and boil water.

"Turner my healing box, the bigger one, in my hut." Sage snapped, not looking up.

"Is... is Aiela a'right? Will she li—"

"Get my box." Sage stared the briefest of moments into his eyes. The message was clear. She didn't know yet. He ran back outside to the other hut, panic making him clumsy, fear numbing all else.

When he returned and set the large, heavy chest down, they didn't make him leave again, long as he stayed well out of the way.

Aiela looked so pale, unmoving. Her hair fanned out around her and he ached to touch it, to cling to her and somehow drag her back into her body. "Ya *have* ta live." He whispered. "Ya vowed ta marry me. Remember?" Tears ran freely.

Her right ear was mangled at the edges and bruises colored both eyes. Her arms were a mass of colors. He felt sick at the thought of what Mardu might have done to her.

Working together, Nadya and Sage removed the dagger from her chest, swiftly sealing the wound.

"She's not breathing." Grief quivered low in Sage's voice.

"The lung is surely collapsed now. We must mend it quickly enough. Can you do this? It is better if we mend it now, and begin her to breathe again after. Do you agree?" Nadya seemed so strong and sure.

"What if it's too long?" Already Sage had tools in her hands, was probing into the puncture wound. "I need more light! We need a healing temple! This is too dangerous to do here. I don't have the right tools. I don't have enough experience in surgery... " Sage's voice was tight as she worked, her entire focus on the small, deadly wound.

"Then we have my blood." Nadya had hesitated in saying it. She was handing tools to Sage, helping her perform the delicate operation.

Nadya suddenly turned and spoke to Turner. "Where is the Belial?"

Turner felt a bit of guilt. "I left 'im ootside." What sort of mate was he, leaving his wounded friend? But he needed to be by Aiela's side. What if she died and he wasn't here?

"Go and bring him in. Yulio can help. We must attend to the leg next."

"Put him in the other hut." Sage added. "He needs drinking water and a bit of light food. Nothing heavy. Make him some tea. Chamomile, lavender and lemon. Stay with him."

"I canna jus' leave Aiela—"

"You can do nothing for her except to pray. Go." Sage gave him a tremulous look. "Please."

Sage

"What do you mean 'your blood'?" Sage pressed Nadya the second Turner was out the door.

"Banpiro blood is regenerative. We do not age. Our wounds heal fast enough to watch."

"Yes, but it kills humans." Sage had heard plenty of stories.

"Not all of them." Nadya swabbed away pooled blood and helped her suture the skin.

Compressing Aiela's heart, Sage wondered why Balek had stabbed her in the right side of the chest. Had he not known where the heart was?

Quickly, she ran her hands over Aiela's body, feeling for broken bones. With so many bruises, welts and even some scabbed over places that looked like burns, who knows what might be damaged inside?

Nadya breathed into Aiela's too-pale lips, and Sage remembered watching those same lips when they were impossibly tiny, fluttering with newborn breath while she slept, always beside her sister. *And where was Ahna now?*

Again and again the breaths. The heart compressions. Sage used her healing crystals, setting one over the wound, another for the heart, the rest arranged around Aiela's body. She sang the life song, calling Aiela back into her body, asking her spirit to return to this plane. She laid her hands on Aiela, channeling the energy up from earth, down from the cosmos, feeling the currents run through her own meridians into Aiela's.

Again and again they stopped working to feel for the natural heart throb, the smallest whiff of air returned. But nothing.

Finally, she injected the heart. It was a last resort, a drug made from a plant that could stop a beating heart—or start one.

Still nothing.

Sage wanted to roar in protest. She'd lost too many of her girls. Surely not again! The anguish of so many losses lodged a silent scream in her chest. *Take me! Why must I always live to watch my loved ones die? Not this time! I will not!*

"What are the chances she would live if you give her your blood?"

Nadya looked so solemn and brooding, yet those great golden eyes held compassion too, when she answered. "I do not know. We do not know why some live and others do not. Maybe one in ten…"

"We can't just keep doing this." In desperation, Sage felt tears finally flow out. What to do? Was it worth the risk? Would using Banpiro blood condemn Aiela to certain death? Could they get her to a healing temple in time, and if so, was there even enough grid power for the machines? Or any Atlantean healers left to help?

"She is already dead." Nadya's eyes flickered to Sage's large box of healing tools, and back to meet her squarely. "The chance of saving her is one in ten." Nadya waited quietly.

Sage finally nodded. "Do it."

Nadya nicked the fresh sutures, reopening Aiela's wound and Sage wanted to protest. She kept quiet as Nadya drew a scalpel across the vein in her wrist, squeezing her blood directly into Aiela's chest. "It'll heal much faster this way." She spoke with no emotion, only deter-mined action. "Start a line into her vein."

Sage did as directed.

It wasn't much, just one large vial of Nadya's blood. They pumped her heart for several never-ending moments before Nadya whispered, "Look, she is breathing."

It was feeble and feathered with pauses, but her chest rose and fell on its own.

"Now we wait." Nadya said.

"For how long?" Sage's heart felt like it was made of stone. She couldn't let hope in, not yet. And next she must deal with Ahna's situation.

Nadya put a cool, gentle hand on her shoulder. "It takes a little time. The body must decide to accept it, must integrate the new information into her cells. Come. You should wash, and rest a little. Perhaps you can drink some tea to revive? I will stay with her."

It went against every motherly instinct, but Sage knew it was right. She'd go see if the aero could take them to the healing temple. And she'd need her strength, no matter what happened next.

GIVING UP THE CRYSTALS

"Ring the bells that still can ring. Forget your perfect offering.
There is a crack in everything. That's how the light gets in."

— LEONARD COHEN

AHNA

*R*ocking faintly back and forth, Ahna realized her mind was utterly blank. Maybe it was gone. She hadn't spoken a word since they'd... since Aiela was stabbed. She hadn't been able to walk. It was like her body refused to function. Someone must have carried her back to this room where Ziel had slept for... how many years? It had never occurred to her to ask.

This thought, this slight little interest in something, brought with it a thin ray of hope. She clung to it. How long *had* Ziel slept in this bed? She'd never actually been in this room before the night with Carver, though Aiela and her had spent countless hours in the other two rooms. Carver... no, she couldn't think of him yet either.

Someone had bathed her—she was starting to recall it. Two

231

women had exclaimed about her vacant stare, then gossiped while they washed her limbs and hair, dried her, dressed her in a soft robe. A guard had laid her here.

A glass was held to her lips at times and she'd swallowed the water.

As awareness slowly returned, she noticed the figure sitting by the bed. Light had shone under the door last night and there'd been sounds of people coming and going, no doubt cleaning up the mess from the maze. Maybe pursuing the strangers who'd taken Carver and...

"Are'ntcha hungry?" The male voice was not unfriendly. "*I* am." His armor made soft sounds as he rose, stretching, yawning loudly. Daylight flooded in when he opened the door and asked for something to break the night's fast. Male voices conversed but she didn't yet care what they said. The outer door opened and closed.

"King Mardu'll likely come an' see you this morning." The guard sat back down. "They says he was livid that Balek killed your sister without asking. Guess Balek paid in kind for *that* mistake, eh?" He chuckled at his own crude joke.

Ahna closed her eyes against the weight and sharpness of grief pangs. Tears squeezed out to drip down her temples. She curled towards the wall, trying to blot it all out. Go back into oblivion.

"Don't be tellin' anybody, but I'm *glad* he's dead. Never liked that fool."

Thankfully, the guard didn't speak again until food arrived. He scooped her up and carried her out to the rosewood table. "Don't weigh much do yah?"

Two other guards joined them, all of them eating quickly as if the food might disappear without notice. "She didn't sleep much." Her guard informed the others. "Probably ain't eaten since two days ago. Heard Balek wouldn't feed 'em while they was at the pit."

"Here." He held a bite of peach to her lips. The scent of it brought a sudden longing for tea. She accepted the peach and then stood in a jerky motion, surprised that she even could. It felt like her body had ceased to be hers. Almost like she didn't exist and this was all some dream mirage.

"Comin' back eh?" The guard raised his eyebrows. "That's good.

You're s'pose to let us know what'cha need. Orders are to treat'cha well."

It took conscious effort to make her limbs work again, and they were slow, like moving through mud. She heated water, rummaged through Ziel's cabinet until she found tea tins with something still in them. By the time she sat at the table again, the food smells had turned her ravenous.

She ate with her hands. Grain cakes sticky with honey, hard-boiled eggs rolled in black truffle salt, charred chunks of goat meat, two whole peaches. A full stomach felt wonderful. Slowly her other senses came back. Then her mind began to process.

Aiela. Balek killed Aiela.

Abruptly she burst into tears.

Somehow she ended up on the floor, rocking hard, crying harder. The same guard lifted her, carried her back to the bed without a word.

Wishing she could make her mind go blank again, she focused on the whispery sobs, such strange sounds coming from her own throat. And then it hit her. How did she still feel this whole if she'd lost everything?

This thought arrested her. The golden cord. She reached for it.

Found it.

Sitting straight up in the bed she let this sink in. *If the cord is still here...*

Would we still be connected if El is on the other side? Or does the cord mean El is still alive?

Then her mind raced. *If there was even the slightest chance Aiela was still alive, she must move carefully. But how could she be alive? She'd seen the knife go in, saw her die!...*

Nevermind that, her intuition said. Focus. Think. She fought to obey this smarter part of her.

Aiela would be expecting her to lead Mardu to the Crystals, would trust her to follow the last message her mind had blared over and over. *Do what we planned. Do it!*

Too many questions crowded in. Should she wait until she heard from Aiela? Or would that be too late? Should she go ahead at the earliest chance and follow their plan? But then she'd be condemning everyone to certain death, those she loved, all those who still followed the Law of One...

Still, their sacrifice would save the rest of the world—and many more worlds besides. She and El had already agreed on that.

Atlantis' great knowledge, the technology they'd so carelessly expanded, was too dangerous, too tempting to people like Mardu. Some of it never should have existed. Much of the restricted archives should have been erased, and all such technology eradicated. She knew this now. Ziel had been right. His words echoed in her brain. "Every time someone stumbles across such things, humanity needs to make the same decision—or face these kinds of consequences. The greater the power, the more vulnerable it is to dark uses. And there really is no noble reason for a technology that controls another's will." Her heart contracted again in grief.

There would always be people like Mardu in the world, desperate to dominate, savagely spreading their own self-hatred.

All morning her mind went in circles. Several times she tried to find Aiela, to communicate with her. But there was not even the slightest brush of contact. It was like Aiela was there, but without any awareness.

The guards left her alone except to bring meals and ask if she wanted anything—another bath perhaps? She shook her head, restlessly moving about the rooms, then collapsing in sudden exhaustion. Most important was to rehydrate, and she drank until she was about to burst. No matter what lay ahead, she would need her strength, and a very clear mind.

She was meditating when she heard Mardu's voice in the outer room.

Not waiting to be summoned, she went out to face him.

He studied her for a moment, in silence. His bronze face was creased with fatigue, and some grief-haunted shadow hung about him. Gilded robes hung like bitterness from broad shoulders, now slumped.

"I'd heard you were non-responsive. It appears you're recovering. Do you know where Carver is?"

She shook her head.

"Do you know who it was that killed Balek and took Carver?"

Again she shook her head.

"You understand they've stolen two of *my sons*—two Princes of Atlantis." Mardu bristled, the bully returning, expanding as his fury lit and began to burn. "They *butchered* my eldest—my heir! Killed him right here under *my Palace!*"

You were letting the one torture the other! She wanted to spit at him. *What kind of a monster does that, and then pretends he cares about losing them?*

But some part of her wouldn't let her mouth form words yet.

He flexed both hands and she wondered if he was going to hit her. Maybe hurt her like he'd done in the past, when he didn't believe what she'd said.

That's when it struck like a bolt of lightning; She held no fear of him anymore.

Taking the smallest step towards him, she began to really see him, to test, and feel his energy instead of blocking it. Carver had his father's eyes. For the first time, she wondered what it felt like to be this man's son. Her own father had been all that was love in the world. It was nothing short of a miracle that Carver had any good in him with such a brutal beginning.

Squaring her shoulders, she studied this hulking man who had become the very definition of terror. This man who'd rained horror and pain upon her and all those most dear to her. Letting this fact play through her mind, refusing to flinch from it, Ahna faced him fully. Not as a victim—not anymore—but as all that stood between evil, and letting it spread like the disease it is.

"You saw your sister die." His tone was mean as he met her eyes, a proverbial knife twisting.

Ahna nodded, knowing grief showed on her face. Letting it.

Liar.

Her body visibly twinged at the invading voice, though it came soft as a whisper. And just like that Aiela was back. What had always been a mere brush of mind touching mind became a full-blown voice inside her head.

I'm not dead and you know it!

A faint smile played across her face at the oh-so-familiar tone.

Mardu scowled. "You realize that you've lost? That I am going to get what I want, one way or another?"

Ahna felt herself smile a little more, one shoulder lifting in the slightest of shrugs. It was all so clear now. Darkness depended on a complete absence of light in order to win.

But she was light.

Mardu didn't stand a chance as long as she lived. Or El, or any of the thousands of people across Atlantis who would stand in the Law of One, and offer their light any way that they could.

She knew what her next step was. She knew Aiela wasn't gone. It was more than enough to renew her strength.

Mardu seemed confused and unsettled by her careless calm. "Even now my people are working down there. We're going to get to them and when we do, I won't need you anymore." Some part of him registered her lack of fear and she felt him grow nervous.

He stepped back, broke eye contact to address the guards. "Her mind's clearly broken. We need to take advantage of it. Go get Montauk." He turned and swept from the room.

When Montauk arrived, Ahna was ready. The tricky part would be to keep him from asking the wrong questions. If he triggered the gate-keeper program, her plan would fail. If his new and thought-to-be-improved Sound Eye really did work on her, the plan would fail. If she aroused any of his suspicions, didn't play her part well enough, the entire plan might fail.

It felt like setting off in an unknowable maze where a single misstep would spring the traps that she must weave between.

I'm going to need your help. She sent to Aiela. *Huge odds of failure, little of success.*

"I've got a special treat for you my dear." Montauk was in a buoyant mood.

The heavens and earth are full of those waiting to help. Aiela sent back.

"Don't worry, it won't hurt at all—assuming you don't resist."

Montauk smiled in a friendly way, holding out a vial. "First you drink this little potion... "

She accepted it, hesitant. Though bolstered by the surreal surge of support and hope from Aiela, she must act appropriate to her physical situation.

"... it might be bitter but if you hold your nose, you won't taste much." His flat hand reached out to support the vial towards her mouth. His touch brought a montage of his energy. Powerful intellect that he hid, so others couldn't usurp it. Condescension for other humans because they weren't as smart. Bitterness that no one recognized all that he was. The desire to be seen and known...

"There. Not so bad was it?" He smiled, turning to open the case.

Ahna moved closer. The stone had the same milky white color with blue veins. This Sound Eye was hastily shaped, its sloppy diamond shape slightly off kilter. She wondered if it would, in fact, work on anyone. While he was still lifting it from its velvety bed she began to speak. Letting her eyes fall to a lazy half mast, her gaze soften, each facial muscle relax, she followed the stone as if locked on to it. "I know what you want. When we go into the maze, I will lead you to the Crystals." Her voice was monotone and quiet. "When we arrive at the Crystal Cathedral I will show you how to program them."

"You'll show me—*and* do whatever you're instructed to?"

"Yes. I will do as you instruct."

"And we won't need the stone again will we?"

"I will respond to your energy signature without the stone. I see your energy signature—all of it. Your intellect is beyond what anyone knows. You resent how others treat you. You hide behind sarcasm and humor because you're afraid that—"

"Yes, well, enough about that!" The barrage of observations unbalanced him. "Is there anything else we need to know about our task together?"

"You need small trolleys to transport everyone. It is many miles. It is cold in the underground, and very dark." *There is an enormous snake that guards the crystals but she'll let you pass if you're with me. The Crystals have a will of their own so who knows what might happen down there...* Ahna might have continued.

LATE THE NEXT morning they set off. Mardu was in a foul mood, grumbling about how long it took to gather enough small hover-transports that could run off of solar cells, and technology that could map their path through the maze. They waited for his crystal technicians to appear. "If I didn't need them so much, I'd have every one of them whipped." He growled to Montauk.

"Plenty of time for that, once we're in control of the grid." Montauk replied cheerily.

Ahna could feel how much it pleased him to goad Mardu, to respond in ways that would most infuriate his king. Even the guards got nervous when Montauk was around. Like as not, one of them might end up bearing Mardu's rage. *Dangerous game you're playing.* She might have warned the mad-haired scientist. But excepting short monologues, while supposedly under the Sound Eye's spell, she didn't speak. It had just become easier not to. More and more, everyone ignored her.

She set a fast pace down the steps from Ziel's rooms, trying to manage the incoherent terror echoing, from the last time she'd been here.

In the room at the bottom, hastily chipped out of earth and rock, everyone piled onto hover tubes. Twelve people in all. She shivered, closing her eyes while the four guards struggled to move that stone slab out of the way. Riding with Montauk, they led the others.

She pointed left or right before they came to the turns, sometimes up, and then down down down. Montauk went slow. She could feel trepidation bunching him up like a stiff spring squeezed tighter and tighter. Remembering the first time Ziel brought her and Aiela down here, Ahna relaxed. It had felt like the earth swallowed them, digested them into some vast and terrible unknown. She was the only one not feeling that right now.

Last night, she'd fallen asleep wondering if Carver was healing, hoping he wasn't suffering still, contemplating the odds that she'd see him again. Likely not. Mardu would have her killed as soon as he had what he wanted. Her knowledge was too dangerous.

It'd be worth it if she could pull this off. She didn't mind dying in order to win. The price of freedom for the rest of them, she hoped.

Ultimately, she had it easier, knowing Carver and Aiela had been taken to safety. Theirs was the difficult part, wondering what she was enduring, trying to guess when her plan might be complete. *I'm following our plan.* She had sent to Aiela over and over. *I hope you're getting people out.*

Something else had happened with Aiela during the night. Still strongly connected, her voice was no longer as clear. Wishing fervently they could still communicate like they had yesterday, Ahna thrust a closed fist out to Montauk and he came to a stop. The other trolleys piled in behind them, as she slid off the tube and went to illuminate the Cathedral.

The collective gasp made her smile.

Ahna exhaled her own relief that Sila wasn't curled in her usual spot between the crystals. She'd worried that Mardu would order Sila killed if he saw her. So far, no one had seen her and lived to tell about it.

The crystal technicians gathered round, admiring the towering natural obelisks.

"They're bigger than I ever thought possible…"

"Incredible! Look at all the carvings!"

"Such power! Do you feel it? I'm all buzzy."

"I've never seen such brilliant colors in a large crystal!"

Seeing them anew through the eyes of these, their new masters, pride and pain twined together. They were impressive. She connected to the blue one. The one that had first opened its consciousness to hers. *Are you ready?*

Now is the time for our program of completion. Its reply came back. She knew they didn't experience emotion, knew their intelligence was something her human self could not understand. Still, it ached to think of their ruin.

It is not ruin, it is completion. Every creation has purpose and every purpose must complete. Then a new creation.

For once, their emotionless reasoning was a comfort.

Mardu and Montauk were examining the console that controlled the Second Moon.

"This is overly simple." Montauk sounded delighted. "Outdated even. I'd imagined much more sophistication for their deadliest weapon."

"Their no-kill policy crippled them long ago. We're lucky they never brought the thing down. Point it toward Greece. Target one of their large, important trade towns and obliterate it. Pick two more cities and burn only half. That should bring them falling to their knees before me. How long until it's in position?"

Montauk studied the screens, enlarging maps until he had selected a town. It was on the island of Crete. Their jewel. "Fifteen minutes, I should think."

Outrage swelled inside Ahna, protests screamed in her mind as she looked for options—any way to stop them. She had no weapons. The guards constantly shielded Mardu.

She focused on the back of his head. *Not yet. Wait. It's better if you wait. Not yet, not now...* But no matter how much she implanted thoughts, he didn't change the order. She'd attempted to influence him before and it just didn't work. His mind might be dark, but it wasn't weak. She couldn't find the chink. There would need to be doubts about his decisions, or some urge to do good that she could exploit. She couldn't stop him.

Acceptance melted into sadness at the loss of innocent lives. She was here to do something else. She was here for perfidy.

Focusing on the technicians, she showed them how to power the grid using all three Crystals. Her words were soft with defeat, her directions succinct.

Enhanced excitement made the four men and one woman standing at the control panels jabbery. Again and again they exclaimed over the brilliantly lit columns, ignoring her except for the occasional pertinent question.

Ahna wandered from Crystal to Crystal as she gave the instructions, running her fingers over them, loving their overwhelming beauty, silently saying goodbye. Grieving them already. The program she'd given the technicians was not what they thought.

These Crystal megaliths would power up to a degree they never had before—and it wouldn't stop. It would build and build. Such a simple program really. They'd charge, working off of each other to excite every atom, every molecule down to the subatomic particles that were pure light. Entire universes of information pulling in more, filling, filling, filling with power until finally, it could no longer be contained.

She watched Mardu approach the Crystals, reaching a hand to examine the platinum one. Saw his eyes bulge wide as he made contact.

Mardu

Barely had his palm touched the glassy chill of the towering Crystal when it felt as if his head was imploding, pain sucked into a tight point between his eyes and then exploded outward, lighting up every molecule of his brain. Was that hideous scream coming from him?

Fire was creeping all around. He could feel the scorching heat, as the hem of his robes caught and he looked up for a way to escape but the sky was falling. Earth and water rose above in a wave that blotted out the stars, and then it began to rush towards him.

He landed hard, splayed on the white marble tile, some anguished sound still sawing and grating in his ears. As everyone rushed to surround him, he stopped screaming, gasping for breath.

Two guards struggled to untangle from him and he realized they must have pulled him away.

"Wha... I saw... I saw... " He panted and gasped, barely able to form words.

"Get out of the way. Go back to your business! Give the King some space." Montauk's authority resounded in the cathedral and every astonished face turned obediently away, each person drifting off, trying to find something else to focus on.

Montauk helped Mardu to his feet. "Wh-what's happened to me?"

Ahna was watching him from beside the emerald Crystal, a knowing look on her fine-boned face. He stabbed a finger at her. "You didn't tell me they… " He didn't even have words to describe the experience. "… did that." He finished lamely midst knife points of fresh pain, though he'd meant it as a threatening accusation.

Hating Montauk and the guards, even as they supported him to the nearest hover tube to sit, he ordered Ahna and the technicians to come to him.

"The grid is fully powered?" Bloody gods he felt weak. And addled. His body still burned, but it was his head that was blinding him with furious pain.

"Yes. With what they're putting out, we could power a dozen grids, and bigger domes! You're going to have more power than you know what to do wi—"

"You've no idea what I know." Mardu snapped. "The little bitch gave you everything you need? All the… programs that we need for using them?" It was hard to think. Those terrible images were still burning behind his eyes. His entire body was rebelling against him, reacting to danger.

"Indeed. They have relatively simple systems, we can do a lot more with them, use them for many more functions if—"

"STOP talking!" His head felt like it was visibly moving to the beat of the hammering inside it. "Take me back." He ordered his guards. "I need a healer. You," he eyed Montauk, "finish up down here." His head was splitting open. "Make sure the technicians have what they need and set up a schedule—"

"Yes, yes." Montauk interrupted him trying to soothe. "I know what to do. Trust me. I'll report to you first thing when I return. I've everything I need." His smile was condescending, his deep bow triumphant.

Mardu hated him for it. But there wasn't much choice.

The guards were loaded on hover tubes around him when Montauk held up a finger. "Oh yes, and the girl? What shall we do with her?"

"Kill her." Mardu almost wanted to die himself just so this pain would stop. "Leave her in her precious maze for the rats and the worms."

CHERRY ISLAND II

"Nothing is so painful to the human mind as a great and sudden change."

— MARY WOLLSTONECRAFT SHELLEY, FRANKENSTEIN

SAGE

*S*age found Turner side by side with Carver in the next hut. She certainly hadn't thought she'd see him again so soon.

The dark and silent Banpiro men were feeding a small fire against the chill of a coming storm, while Carver talked intently to Turner. They all stopped, and turned their attention to her when they saw her.

"How is she? Is she... alive?"

Her heartbreak deepened at the anguish on Turner's round face, mop of curls drooping into his eyes. "She's breathing at least. We're waiting to see if the... treatment... works. Nadya will let us know, soon as anything changes." She pushed the hair back from his eyes before wrapping her arms around him. Already he felt like a son to her.

The giant blonde Banpiro, who was called Yulio, headed silently out the door, no doubt going to Nadya's side.

Carver slid down the bench, making room for her, leaving a steaming mug at her spot. "Here, sit. Drink." He grimaced as he re-adjusted his leg without comment.

He made her vaguely uneasy. Some long ago instinct from her own Belial origins perhaps. Turner seemed to trust him, which said much. If she weren't so tired and worried about Aiela, she'd be barraging him with questions about his people and their atrocities and what was he doing about it all?

"Carver's been fillin' us in on Ahna and what's happen't in High City." Turner's eyes were red rimmed and watery. "We lost Kane. They kilt 'im. An' then Nadya kilt Balek…"

Sage tightened the hug before releasing him. "I'm sorry." Too much was happening too quickly. Grief for the strong-hearted Scottish man would hit her later. She sank wearily onto the bench, and wrapped her hands around the mug in front of her, staring blankly at it.

Turner knuckled away a tear before it could fall. "Wer makin' plans ta go back an' get Ahna oot. I think ya should hear it, if yer feelin' strong en—" He cut off suddenly at her look.

What do these boys know of strength? She focused tiredly on Carver. "Thank you for getting Aiela here so fast." She eyed his leg propped up at an awkward angle, ripped pants spread open. "That's a nasty looking wound. A lot of pain?"

"I'll keep until there's time to fix it."

Listening as the boys continued their planning, Sage drank the tea, then brewed a new pot from roasted cacao husks and cinnamon. It would revitalize her, extend her a new energy. Just by looking at it, she could see the Belial's leg was severely infected. She'd need to get him to the healing temple before he went septic.

Though she tasted nothing and her stomach tried to rebel, she managed to eat some eggs and porridge, insisting the boys eat too. Her night was just beginning. She'd need steady hands and a clear mind yet.

Thankfully, Turner's fear for Aiela and grief for Kane was being redirected into action for Ahna, plotting with Carver, heads close together, how they might get to her.

Sage noticed the two darker Banpiro had silently disappeared. "I'll check on Aiela and gather some things." She looked to Carver. "Can you pilot us to Chiffon's healing temple? You'll heal fast with their machines. Without them, it'll be several days and I want Aiela to—"

Voices erupted, escalating curses and crashes coming from the other hut. Sage and Turner dove outside, nearly colliding with Nadya as she came, yelling for Sage.

"Your girl awoke already." Nadya's cultured voice was tight. "She is not herself."

Outlined by firelight behind them, Yulio's huge form fought to constrain a struggling Aiela. The other two Banpiro had hold of an arm or a leg, trying to contain her, their bodies thrown around by her rage. She was shouting obscenities, kicking and cursing them, clawing at his face. Yulio captured her free hand, as she dislodged the Banpiro from her other arm.

When Sage waved up the lights, she caught her breath, fear rippling through her belly.

Aiela's face shone stark white. The bones strained against skin turned translucent, veins running like tiny blue rivers beneath it. The whites of her eyes were bloodshot so heavily they looked a dull orangey red. *What have I done?!*

Turner was roaring at the Banpiro to be heard above Aiela's shrieks. "What're ya *doin'* ta her! Let her go!"

Yulio shook his massive golden head as Aiela's hand shot out and she lunged with terrible strength, half-freed, towards Turner.

Turner met her with open arms, but her hand clutched his throat. He gaped in disbelief at her wild eyes, before prying at her clawed grip as she screamed curses at him.

Nadya stalked into the melee to plunge a needle into Aiela's neck. It seemed like minutes, but could've only been seconds, before Aiela's body slumped, loosening her death-grip on Turner's throat.

"We need to bind her." Nadya looked to Sage. "I did not give her much of the sedative. Her body may not handle it well with all her systems already depressed. She may be unconscious only moments."

Sage rummaged in her chest for the straps she used as tourniquets. "Turner." She was shocked her voice didn't quaver. "Go get Carver. Help him to the aero. We need to get them both to the Healing Temple. Quickly."

◎◎

CHIFFON LOOKED DARKER FROM ABOVE, as they flew over, en route to the Healing Temple.

"You've my ring still... just in case?" Carver asked in a strained voice. He was fading fast, but Sage had little attention to spare him with Aiela thrashing and screeching lunatic things from the back. Yulio had trussed her with the straps, then bundled her in bedsheets until she looked like a mummy. A mummy that still managed to bang around something awful as they flew. Turner and Sage huddled together beside Carver in the second pilot's seat. The sight of them seemed to enrage her more, so they reluctantly kept their distance.

"Right here." Sage replied to Carver, digging the heavy monstrosity out of her pocket. "You should have it back."

He shook his head. "You're in charge... not sure I'll last much longer. Wanted you prepared for what we might face next... er who."

"Set down over there." She pointed to the east of the Temple as it came into view.

"I can't see where... "

The Temple itself glowed a soft dusty pink, lit with solar paint that matched its rose quartz exterior. Its lawns and gardens were dark, except for pathways cutting this way and that, like orderly swaths of starlight.

"You're going to have to trust me. That big space on the east side is a lawn. There's trees on the periphery, so aim for the middle."

He was breathing much too fast and sweating, but he did it.

They poured out of the aero, Yulio and Nadya carrying Aiela, avoiding her biting, snapping mouth. The other two Banpiro brought Carver, who'd promptly passed out soon as they'd touched the ground.

"I need a surgery room. Right now." Sage demanded to the first two healers they encountered. "And a pod for this one." She motioned to Carver's unconscious form.

"I'm sorry, we're fu—" The elder healer began, but Sage cut her off.

"I *know* you're full Vivla! I'm not asking. We'll use what we need with or without your consent."

Vivla glared at her, obviously knowing who she was, yet irritated at the intrusion. She glanced at the impatient Banpiros and their patients, then pointed stiffly towards the podroom. "Show them which one to use."

The younger healer led them away.

"He needs stabilized, and the infection treated before it spreads to his blood. I'll tend to the leg later." Sage called after them, already headed with Vivla in the opposite direction, motioning for Yulio and Nadya to follow her with the still struggling Aiela.

Vivla was extremely displeased, telling Sage so in tight, gloomy words as they rushed through hushed hallways. "This is the last thing we need! Can't you at least quiet her? You're disrupting very very sick people. People who've been waiting a long time to get treated."

Sage didn't respond.

Tall and droopy as a willow tree, Vivla ran the Temple now—without adequate grid power, despite shortages of medicine, healers, and everything else they required. It was an impossible job and Sage hated adding another hardship.

But Carver and Aiela represented salvation for thousands of Atlanteans. The country needed them whole. Not that Vivla would ever understand—maybe wouldn't even agree. So Sage let her gripe and grumble on about this intrusion, amidst the din of raging that echoed off the high, ornate walls of this beautiful , once peace giving building.

Sage interrupted Vivla as they neared the main—and best equipped—surgery room. "You'll need to help me with this. I don't know the surgery crystals like you do. She's been injected with Banpiro blood and I suspect it's mutating her cells. We need to stop the mutation."

Vivla stopped walking in an open-mouthed stare.

"You'll have to wait." Sage informed two healers, headed towards the room with an unconscious patient. "We'll be awhile."

They looked to Vivla, who managed to shut her mouth, and nod in confirmation.

"The blood got her systems going again." Sage continued briskly. "She was technically dead. Lay her on that floating table. The one that looks like stone." She pointed, and Yulio and Nadya obeyed immediately.

"The mutations saved her life, but we need to stop it before it..." She'd been going to say 'overrides her humanity completely', but Yulio and Nadya were still some percentage of human... weren't they?

"Alright." Vivla rallied. "Hold her still while I sedate her. I'll do my best."

It took a cocktail of three powerful sedatives, to keep Aiela still long enough for the array of crystal machines to do their work.

"Look at this! The Banpiro cells constantly mutate to overcome any effects we introduce!" Vivla breathed, peering at the screen, frenetic with the activity of the rapidly mutating cells. Her naturally dreary voice held excitement. Like any true healer, she was riveted by this unexpected discovery. "I'll want to keep some of their blood here to study...hers too."

Twice, the machines hiccuped, faltered, and powered down, as the grid power surged and faltered, even though it was the middle of the night. It took four full hours of trial and error before Sage, Vivla, and three more summoned healers, outsmarted the invading cells.

They couldn't be sure what percentage of Aiela's own cells were mutated. And though they had stopped the changes, there was no way to reverse them.

"Theoretically," Vivla intoned, weary, and back to her droopy self, "the master cells will pattern all replications to their original design. So it may just be a matter of waiting out her normal mitosis process. But replications *could* pattern from the mutated cells instead."

Ready to drop with fatigue, Sage knew she wasn't done yet. "Can you finish up here? I need to see to Carver. Soon as they're both stable, we'll get out of your way."

"Go and help her." Vivla instructed two of the healers. "She doesn't know our systems."

Already, Yulio and Nadya had proffered several vials of their blood. Vivla had accepted it as adequate payment for this disruption.

With Carver sedated, and stabilized by the pod, the healers worked fast to clean his leg. The bone was fractured but not broken, and already fusing back together. They used lasers to cut away dying tissue and infrared to kill infection which had spread to his bloodstream. With the healing crystals on it, the leg would be whole in less than an hour. The final procedure was seven points of transfusion, replacing poisoned blood with fresh.

Administering an internal tincture, Sage left Carver to his greatest healer; sleep, and went in search of tea. She found it, with Turner and the Banpiro quartet, in a healer's lounge.

As the sun rose, Nadya roused them all from too little sleep.

"The Belials will arrive once the sun is high, demanding all sorts of enhancements and beautifying treatments, all the day long." Vivla had warned them. "The only time we have to treat our own people is at night."

"We will go before then." Nadya had assured Vivla.

They woke Carver. Astonished, he shifted his weight from leg to leg."There's no pain! I don't feel it anymore!"

And then they got Aiela.

The vigilant Banpiro hovered over her, but she was bleary and quiet. All that remained of her fighting, biting rage was sullen irritation.

"I told you, I'm not hungry!" Aiela snapped, when Sage offered pears and a grain cake. But she was thirsty like never before. "Where is Ahna? I want to talk to her." She took in the spacious healing room with its pretty, polished quartz walls, glaring, seeming not to care she was back in her once-favorite place.

"You can't." Sage forced a calm voice." "Ahna is still in High City."

"How come I'm here then? And why's she not?"

Turner hovered at a distance, no doubt fearing another outburst, his eyes darting to Aiela and away again, like a wounded animal. Aiela ignored him.

Sage sent them all out of the room, the Banpiro men, Carver and Turner.

"We could only rescue you. There were many guards with your sister." Nadya balanced her, while Sage helped her wash off the blood and re-dress.

"Who're you?" Aiela's eyes were deeply confused.

Sage introduced Nadya as her father's long-ago friend, attempting to explain who the Banpiro were and why they'd come. Halfway through, Aiela interrupted, fretting over Ahna again. "But where *is* she?"

"We don't know. Carver only saw the guards carrying her away aft—"

"Tell me again how it happened? It's all jumbled in my head. Everything since Balek dragged me away from the spiked pit."

"Well *we* don't know much... " Sage began with a sigh, recounting the little Carver had described of her death, and the events around it.

By the time the others rejoined them, Aiela was beginning to make sense. She even gave Turner a half smile when she saw him pacing, fidgeting forlornly across the room. It seemed a bit forced to Sage, but it was all Turner needed. He came to her, folded her carefully in his arms, and muttered tearful, unintelligible Irish words while he held her.

Aiela pushed him abruptly back, swinging to face Carver. "Why would you just leave her there?! How could you?"

Nadya stepped in front of him. "It was not his choice. It was mine."

"Mardu needs Ahna *alive*." Face set like stone, Carver did his best to reassure Aiela. "If Ahna keeps her secret awhile longer, we can get back to her in time."

"But she's not going to! We made a plan." Aiela told of her dream visit from Drey and Taya while at the pit. Of Ahna's simultaneous dream from the Crystals.

"Ahna will take Mardu through the maze, use his own people to activate the Crystal's destruction programs. The Crystals showed her."

Her voice hardened, " It all has to be obliterated—everything—to save the planet, and keep the Universal grid intact."

They stared at her, not comprehending what she was saying.

Sage felt like her brain had simply stopped processing any new information.

Aiela spoke slower, sounding more like her old self. *"Listen to me. We have to leave here and get Ahna now."* Her words came measured, and full of conviction. "People must be warned and there's very little time. She'll have to make it look real— like she's finally handing over control—and who knows how long that will take. Once she does, Mardu will gather the right technicians, people to put in charge of the Crystals and Second Moon. At the earliest, they'll go into the maze tomorrow. We might only have two days."

She looked at each one of them until they met her eyes. "Two days before the Crystals dismantle Atlantis."

IN A HURRY, they'd piled back into the aero, to make a stop at Cherry Island for supplies, and be on their way to High City.

Everyone else was resting when Sage spoke privately with Aiela.

Aiela revealed bits and pieces of what Mardu had done to them— what they surmised anyway, from the bruises and burns left behind on their bodies—how he'd learned the words that triggered Gate-keeper and tried to work around it, Balek's boasting of his catastrophic plans. Finally, Aiela asked for the details of what had happened on Cherry Island. "How did you and Nadya bring me back? I remember being dead." She had little emotion over it. "I was on the other side for a long time it seemed."

Her eyes shone in the pale light of a new morning, and Sage star-tled when she saw the gold glowing in them.

ANOTHER KIND OF DEATH

"It is a power—to be damaged, yet still believe in love."

— RUNE LAZULI

AHNA

*M*ontauk used a silk belt from one of the technicians to bind her hands together behind her back. "This way I won't need a guard with me. Oh, don't look so innocent, I'm sure you were very well trained."

At least it was soft and cool against her skin when she started pulling and stretching, working at the knot.

"Hop on. Let's get it over with. I have duties to attend to." Despite his patronizing tones, Montauk hunched, as though carrying a thousand, unwilling pounds on his shoulders, as he herded Ahna towards the hover tube. "Any particular direction we should go? A special place you'd like to be buried? I won't leave you lying about for the rats. Don't worry… "

He was lying. Ahna tuned out his ramblings as they left the lighted

Cathedral, for the darkness of the maze. *It's done,* She sent to Aiela. *Get everybody out.*

Where are you?

In the maze.

Safe?

She didn't reply. What was she supposed to say? *Headed to my execution right now in fact. My future's never looked grimmer.*

Actually, that wasn't true. Losing Aiela had been much harder than her own impending death.

She hadn't wriggled a hand free yet, and her window of opportunity was shrinking. Ahna leaned back, steadied on her hands and drew her legs up, kicking with all her strength to launch Montauk off the craft. One heel struck his head, the other one his kidney. She went flying off the back from the force, as he crashed in a shower of dirt and rock, bouncing back and forth off the tunnel walls.

On her feet, she ran like the wind. Ran for her life.

But he got the craft under control and came after her before she had reached another tunnel opening to hide or lose him in. She felt the futility as he chased her, knowing he'd simply plow into her at speed, uncaring the damage he did.

She dropped flat so the craft passed right over her, but he'd been expecting as much. He was on her before she regained her feet, one hand gripping her hair, the other a fist that he buried in her belly.

She dropped again to escape his battering, this time with the breath knocked out of her.

He bent to grab her.

She came back up fast, using her forehead to batter his face. One foot kicked his knee viciously, and as he faltered, she brought a knee up hard into his crotch.

Even as he doubled over in pain, the light gun hissed, missing her by so little, the laser singed her arm.

"Wait!" She screamed, backing off. "Stop!"

Against all odds, he obeyed, groaning as he straightened, light gun aimed at her chest.

The hovercraft was a short distance off, light from its sphere almost swallowed by the hungry press of darkness.

He actually had the gall to smile feebly at her. "You certainly put up a better fight than I expected." One hand still covered his crotch protectively. "It's not often I underestimate someone." He inclined his head at her and stumbled as he backed up a few steps. His nervousness jangled around her.

"We'll just do it here. I'd be a fool to risk anymore antics in your tricky little maze."

"Why're *you* so distressed? Is it the dark down here?" She asked conversationally. "Or that you have to kill me?"

His face looked haggard in the strained light. "No need to be impertinent."

She wondered what her odds were of simply running off, of escaping his shots in the total black that pushed at the edges of this fragile circle of light. "You might just let me go." She pushed into his mind as she spoke. "What harm could I possibly do? Unarmed, no food or water, bruises and burns and internal damage from Balek and Mardu's beatings." She coughed pathetically, offering proof. "I'd likely not make it out alive anyway…"

A shape formed behind him, and she felt her eyes widen, as the enormous length appeared silently from the black. *Must keep his attention.*

"… but at least I'd die on my own terms, and you wouldn't have *this* on your conscience—"

"Suddenly so prolific!" Montauk lifted his hand to aim the light gun at her head. It shook, ever so slightly. "Any final words?"

"Yes… my ghost will probably haunt you." She shrugged, making her voice nonchalant. "Certainly, this will add a negative karma debt —" She dropped once more like a stone, flattened against abrasive dirt clods, as the gun spat.

Or was it Sila? *Something* made him glance back just in time to see the pale monster strike with lightning speed, knocking the gun from his hand.

Scrabbling backwards, and then rolling to get her bound hands in front of her, Ahna watched as Sila struck at him again and again, drawing blood like spontaneous blossoms on his face, his belly, his neck.

Shivery hissing shrieked along the tunnel, so high-pitched, it sliced at the ears. Serpent vengeance was noisy, and terrible.

Montauk screamed, flailing, with nowhere to run, as Sila's coils caught him, wrapping him with a speed that seemed impossible for her size.

The silence seemed abrupt, as that graceful, simple body wrung the breath from him. Bones cracked and popped—loud within the muffling, lavender coils.

Ahna looked away when Sila's head, big as a horse, descended, mouth stretched impossibly wide to swallow Montauk slow, starting with that wild, white shock of still-quivering hair.

"Ugh." Ahna felt nauseous. "Sila, you're a wonder to behold—and also disgusting."

She walked slowly, careful with her aching body as she straddled the hover tube. Trying not to look at Sila's silent eating ritual, she worked at the knot until her hands were free. Even in her peripheral, it was a picture she'd never unsee.

"I'll be back with Aiela." She muttered, talking to self-soothe. "We need to shut down the dome so people can leave."

She didn't look back as she sped off, whispering into the darkness behind her, "Thank you Sila."

Aiela

"Ahna Aigeron is dead, following the death of her twin, Aiela, two days previous. These foolish and misguided sisters were the last leaders of those false Atlanteans attempting to resist King Mardu. Now, at last, we can embrace the patriotism of unity. Together, we will commit ourselves to the illustrious plan King Mardu has for his new Atlantis. An Atlantis which will again become the glorious ruler of the entire world—"

"Lies!" Aiela spat, infuriated. "Turn it off. And *hurry up!* We need to go find her."

Charis didn't turn down the broadcast. "We need to monitor what's happening."

Aiela studied the faces busy around her. Except for Nadya and

Yulio, they were all wary of her now. Turner most of all. His silent expressions of betrayal and loss should create emotions in her, she knew that. But she couldn't feel it. She vacillated between numbness—wherein she tried to act as they expected—and frustration that devolved easily into black rage. Only thoughts of Ahna brought a sense of something that felt good. That invisible golden cord seemed the only link to who she'd been.

"Do we have enough weapons?" Aiela gulped water, as Nadya and Yulio loaded packs. They'd parted from the dark Banpiro males upon arrival in Chiffon, sent them to secure Nadya's ship and stock it with water and food. It was to be their rendezvous point once they had Ahna.

"No. Except for blades, we have only the two light guns." Nadya spoke with precision. It comforted Aiela somehow.

"We'll have to get what we hid in the maze then. The Crystal Cathedral will be crawling with Belials. After we kill them, I'll shut off power to the grid, bringing down the dome so people have a chance to get out. Carver and I will find Ahna, while you two and Turner help Lira and Rizelle evacuate the Healing Temple."

Sage and Charis, already on their comms for hours, worked tirelessly through a network of Atlanteans still loyal to the Law of One. Aiela went to listen in, as strangers multiplied around her. Those left in OldForest were arriving, rallying here at the underground headquarters to help spread the word before power to the grid was shut off. Then they must find a way to get thousands of people off the continent.

"Ruler Eirene is alive." Charis took a break to update Aiela. "She lost the use of her legs when the military base was struck. Still she has managed to gather what's left of her troops—not many. She'll launch every remaining naval vessel—says she's got enough soldiers to take back the outer harbor and seize the Belial vessels in it. They'll wait there for evacuees."

Aiela forced a grin. It's what she would've done before. "This is very good news."

"That's not all. There's a fleet of old aeros waiting. Once the dome is down, they'll land at the Temples in High City and across the midlands, to transport people to the waiting ships."

This time, Aiela felt something real. Tentative and narrow, hope began to shine, piercing through the slashes and cracks of her battered and changed spirit.

She wandered over to Carver as he and Turner loaded their packs from Charis' provisions. "Your leg still holding up?" He seemed to be walking fine, but she didn't want him slowing her down.

"Doesn't matter." Carver's eyes flashed steel. "I'm going to help find Ahna, with or without your permission."

Aiela shouldered her own pack, filled with water, thinking through what lay ahead. First they'd visit the emergency stashes she and Ahna hid in the maze so long ago. Retrieve poisons, blades and light guns. Get a trolley to travel faster.

"I'll wait for you outside", she announced to no one in particular. The smothering roomful of people and expectations prickled. Stalking as fast as she could out of the underground cellar, expanded into a vast warren of rooms and tunnels over the last many weeks, she ran smack into someone in the dim between light spheres.

"Umph." The smaller body sprawled backwards in front of her.

"Ahna!" Aiela reached to pull her up.

"Ouch!" Ahna grabbed her in a fierce hug. "You're here!! Already? And... whole?! How is it possible? Where's Carver? Did you bring Turner and Sage too?" It spilled out in one breath surrounded by haloes of color; fear, relief, desperation, sadness. And then Ahna stepped back, frowning. "What's wrong with you? You're... different."

Aiela heaved a sigh, not realizing until this moment how brimful of doubts she was, and some unnameable despair. The awkward disconnect inside of her seemed suddenly unbearable.

"I don't *know* what's wrong. I-I'm shut down, or shut off, or... something. It's like another kind of death." Normally, she'd be *sobbing* with unspeakable relief to see Ahna again—to be alive and together. Especially since Ahna was practically blubbering with happy disbelief.

"I can't believe you're alive. I knew you were, but how?! I've so many questions, so much to tell you—Montauk's dead, Sila *ate* him while he was trying to kill me and Balek's dead too. You should've seen the woman who killed him! It was savage and atrocious and I don't know who—"

"Her name's Nadya." Aiela interrupted. She's here. C'mon, let's go outside. I don't want to be with everybody down there just yet… "

Under an ancient Old Forest tree, they wept. Well, Ahna did, which made Aiela tear up too, though her emotion still felt small, and distant. Then they talked. Leaning against bark that thrummed with spirits older than Atlantis itself, they poured out all that had transpired in the short time they'd been apart. Consoling each other, restitching their frayed and tattered psyches, they reminded each other that they'd survived, that it must be for some grand and elaborate reason. This life-long ritual of sharing everything, began to reconnect Aiela to her humanity, as nothing else had.

"I don't think I could have done it without you." Ahna's eyes still shone wet as she scanned the trees, finding a pair of goldfinch singing a delicate concerto.

The summer sun shone down with all its might. More light reaching the forest floor than ever before, with all the downed trees. Neon green grasshoppers bigger than her thumb, clacked this way and that. Hummingbirds with radiant throats whizzed madly by, imperiously trilling their presence, while three iridescent dragonflies played around rainwater puddled in a leaf. Aiela wished she could rest for awhile, just leave her disfigured human reality and enjoy this warmth, the fragrance of trees, the oblivious hum of life going on around her, that she watched in every heightened sensory detail.

"We need to get going." Ahna was reluctant to leave this temporary respite too. "There's not much time left—and too much to do. If we don't get people out, we'll be responsible for as much death as Mardu himself. One way or another, by this time tomorrow, it'll all be over."

"I need your help first." Aiela reached for Ahna's hand. "Can you feel this? What's going on inside me?"

Ahna concentrated, frowning. "Do you have any idea how to heal it?"

"I think so." Aiela had one idea anyway. She ignored the possibility that it mightn't work. "I need you to connect to the Crystals. Can you do that? Channel the green one to me?"

Gripping both of her sister's hands, Ahna closed her eyes, inhaling deeply, and exhaling long.

The connection went through Aiela like an electric shock. A space opened behind her closed eyelids, vast and edgeless as the universe itself, full of energy waves in colors so brilliant and powerful, she instinctively squinted. Reaching for the purple waves, she directed them inside of her, down through the crown chakra, streaming into the darkened pituitary chakra, the energy center that had gone dull and lifeless, unable to keep up with the changing cells that Banpiro blood had introduced. Stifling the throat chakra, and then the heart, every one of her chakras were malfunctioning in different degrees. She felt Ahna tremble, registering the changes, as she held connection to the powerful Crystal energy.

"C'mon body," Aiela whispered, "I need you to adjust." Breathing deeply, she pulled in the crystalline energy, one brilliant color at a time, attaching it to her chakras like bloodlines infusing new blood. She became aware of the words of determined love, Turner had muttered while he held her tight, even though she'd pushed away from that love. She saw again the knowing gaze Auntie Sage had pinned her with, gripping her chin so she couldn't look away, saying "Aiela, this is nothing but your shadow come to life. You can fear it, or you can embrace it. You've spent your whole life with your face to the light. This darkness that's overtaken you, it is still *you*. You're just facing the other way, meeting your full shadow for the first time. Study it, use it. And turn around any time you're ready."

These touchpoints served her now, creating a container for the crystalline energies. Sluggish at first, her chakras began their spin, picking up speed as the colors fed them. Feeling her spirits lift, she squeezed Ahna's hands, and opened her eyes. "This will do for now."

"That was... incredible! All that color coming through me!" Ahna looked renewed too. Energized. "I feel so much better!"

Voices sounded before Nadya, Yulio, Turner and Carver appeared from the underground entrance. Turner stopped dead when he saw Ahna, Carver bumping into him.

"Sure an' ya've made quick work o' findin' yer—"

"Ahna!" Carver flew to her, embraced her, lifting her off the ground.

Ahna wrapped around him, laughing or crying maybe, or a little of both.

Aiela took Turner's hand, grinning into his eyes before leaning in for a tentative kiss—the first, since she'd kissed his unconscious lips and sent him off, half-dead in the aero. When *was* the last time they'd really kissed? She felt a rush of familiar emotions as she tried to remember.

She had returned from death a different person. Her world was literally falling apart. Yet this stubborn Irishman still had the power to move her. He touched her cheek and it felt as though he was reaching into her soul, pulling her up from the cold, sucking mire, steadying her as she readjusted to the light.

"How long will this take?" Yulio's little-used voice startled them out of the tender reunions. It was the first time Aiela heard him speak.

"He's right." She said. "We're together again—against a lot of odds. Every one of us should've died by now. Since we didn't, we've got our people to save. We can catch up on the way."

BRINGING DOWN THE DOME

"We are all ordinary. We are all boring. We are all spectacular. We are all shy. We are all bold. We are all heroes. We are all helpless. It just depends on the day."

— BRAD MELTZER

TURNER

"Dark as the divil doon here."

"I do not like it either. It is like being in the intestines of the earth. I feel as if I might be digested—just another organism that becomes a nutrient." Nadya did most of the talking, since Carver and Turner were breathless, just trying to keep up with the tireless Banpiro. "Returning is even more unpleasant than the first time."

Yulio mumbled something that Turner couldn't make out.

"I know that." Nadya replied. "My debt to the good man Drey is satisfied. And yet I cannot abandon his people in their time of need."

"I could." Yulio replied, clear enough for everyone to hear.

The twins had gone ahead on the hover tube, promising to return with another transport.

Sure enough, before long, faint lights appeared and rapidly closed.

They gave Turner and Yulio poison dart bows, dividing up among them an odd assortment of weapons. Heavily armed, with four light guns between them, and a dozen blades of various size, they squeezed three on the tube and three in the narrow little ground trolley, and set off again.

Every little while, the twins halted, moving walls Turner had thought simply tunnel sides or ceiling. It took all six of them to reset traps; there were pits to fall in, boulders to crush, water to drown in, dirt to suffocate, even fire to scorch invaders. Vast lower sections of the tunnels, they simply flooded.

"There must be no possible way back to the Crystals after we leave." Ahna explained. "Mardu will send troops to take them back as soon as we disconnect from the grid. There must be no routes left."

"How d'ya keep track of where ya were, and where ta go next?" Turner could not fathom it. Everything looked the same down here: an endless repeat of dirt, rocks and blackness.

"Was all part of our training, love." Aiela huffed, pushing a wall into place, squeezing his arm in passing, with a grit crusted hand. "C'mon. More to do still."

◎◎

NIGHT MUST SURELY HAVE FALLEN, far above the narrowing circles they traveled in, before Aiela and Ahna declared the maze ready. "The Cathedral is just ahead." Aiela's voice dropped to a loud whisper. "And so is Sila." She pointed to a mountainous pile as they came upon it.

The snake—"big as a sea serpent", Nadya had warned Turner—was resting, unconcerned about what might be happening in the world of humans.

"We'd welcome your help Sila, if you're inclined." Aiela trailed a hand along the fat coils. "She gets lethargic after she feeds." This, whispered in his ear, as they crept around her.

Scales big as his palm glistened, and every hair on Turner's body stood up. How had Aiela lived in this maddening darkness? What was it that enabled her to care for a creature he couldn't even bring himself to touch?

He turned his mind to the great and glorious relief of seeing Aiela return more and more to herself. Bit by bit, the woman he knew was resurfacing. He'd feared that all she'd endured had changed her forever. Mostly, he feared she might never come to love him again.

They stopped, when a glow broke the utter dark of the passageway ahead. Tip-toeing up to the Cathedral entrance, Turner stayed beside Aiela as they entered the cavernous space. Crouching low behind trolleys and boxes of equipment, the others fanned out along the shadowed edges of the room.

He counted only six people—no guards even—just technicians. At a console with maps illuminated on screens above it, two Belials discussed which country to threaten next with the Second Moon. Turner recognized maps of Greece on a side screen. A red splotch blinked. Ahna had described how Mardu had wasted no time in attacking Greece. Grief and anger tangled with helplessness, as he studied those pulsing lights that might as well be bloodstains.

Aiela waited until everyone was in position. Then they struck. Five Belials lay dead in seconds. The sixth had managed to hide behind the Crystals.

Sila came gliding by as Turner and Carver checked pulses. The twins fell in behind her massive length. She was a pale shade of lavender, he realized, seeing her for the first time in full light. What a queer color for a snake.

"Wait! No! No! Gods help me! Noooooo... "

He couldn't tell if the panicked shouts were male or female, but he knew what they were about. "Like as no', I'll be havin' nightmares aboot this." He focused on Aiela, refusing to watch Sila eat a human, even if it the enemy. "Ach, probably fer the rest o' me life!"

Aiela's face was stony. "We shouldn't be killing innocent people like this. It's not right. But I don't know what else to do."

Nadya and Yulio dragged the dead body away from Sila, piling it with the others.

Drawn to the towering columns of carved Crystal, Turner

marveled at their colors, at the intricate designs decorating their surface. "Yer Mum did all this, did she?"

"Ziel says she did." Aiela and Ahna were touching images on the Crystals, in some relevant sequence. Finished with the blue one, they discussed the emerald one before beginning its sequence.

Something nudged against Turner's leg and he watched Sila squeeze into the space between the three brilliant columns, curling into her usual pyramidal pile of coils.

"What are we going to do about her?" Ahna asked. "We should've got her out before closing off the maze."

"I don't think she'd go." Aiela leaned against Sila and reached up on tiptoe, stroking the huge head that slid down to greet her. "This is your home and these are your friends. You'd no sooner leave the Crystals than I'd leave Ahna, would you?"

Nobody mentioned that Aiela *had* in fact left Ahna, albeit, unwillingly.

Only just finished with the platinum Crystal, Aiela's comm lit, and she listened with only curt reply. "Good news." She relayed to the others. "Charis and Sage's network have gotten the word out. Already, those in the coastal cities and towns are leaving. They're taking back the boats and ships stolen by Belial. She says if we can get to the Blessings Service tonight, we could reach anyone who hasn't yet heard."

"What is this service you speak of?" Nadya asked.

"Poseidon's Jubilee is tomorrow—I'd completely forgotten—High City typically celebrates with games and races and all sorts of festivities. Auntie Sage says Mardu has co-opted it, changed it to his liking. There's always been a Blessings Service on the eve before. Those who still observe the Law of One are likely gathering, even though it's not part of Mardu's sanction. They need the support of each other now more than ever." Her face relaxed a bit. "And apparently, there's a funeral for Balek tonight too."

"Which means the important Belials of the city will be occupied!" Carver took a deep breath. "Finally! Something going in our favor."

It meant they wouldn't have to kill so many to get out of the Palace. It meant they had a prayer of getting out alive. Heartened, Turner breathed easier too.

"Goodbye then Sila." Ahna murmured. "Tell Mama we did our best."

Turner backed away, while the girls said their farewells, first to the snake, then the Crystals—which did seem eerily alive in some way. His whole encounter with them seemed almighty and surreal. And finally, he understood the bits and pieces of what Aiela had revealed, of the role Ruler Ziel had recruited her into. The role meant to be a great and dangerous secret.

"Everybody got your light spheres on?" Aiela called. "It's about to go black in here."

HALTING OFTEN to block off the maze, taking even more care between the Cathedral and the Palace entrance, the twins led them back to the space where Balek had killed Aiela—or tried to anyway—before dying a grim and grisly death himself. The spot where Kane had died.

Nadya had spoken of her vengeance on Balek with quiet pride.

Carver had described it to Turner in disturbing detail, surprised when his eyes filled with tears during the telling. He'd wept softly, hands covering his face, unable to explain this odd and unexpected grief. "He was my brother. Cruel... and the worst bully... but a part of my life since it began. I don't miss him. I don't know what this is that I feel."

Turner knew. " Sure an' who wouldna weep o'wer a broother lost wi' demons inside, an' then ta meet his end exactly how he deserved? The whole thing is tragic!"

An eerie feeling shivered through Turner when they passed the slab of stone propped out of the way. Were those dark streaks Aiela's blood, or just part of the rock?

The six of them crept, feeling their way up uneven steps.

Expecting to find guards at the entrance, they piled into the little palace room with weapons drawn, finding it empty. Voices sounded from the main room and they readied.

Two guards gaped mid-bite, from the pretty rosewood table, while Yulio and Turner put a poison dart in them. "Rest easy mate. It's no' personal." Turner caught the guard he'd killed and lowered him gently to the plush carpet.

Yulio didn't bother.

Ahna

"You know how to get to the rendezvous?" Ahna whispered to Carver.

Twice she'd begged him to stay with her. Not to do this thing. But he insisted that if he didn't, Mardu would find a way to escape. "He'll be the first to figure out what is happening. He always is. And then he'll simply take an aero and fly away. I won't let that happen." Carver's steel-grey eyes went hard, and she remembered how little she actually knew of this man. "He will pay for his crimes. It'll be a smaller price than he deserves."

Now, she could feel his tension. Fear of failing, determination not to, and the great weight of a ticking clock, was building a low-grade panic inside each of them.

"Yes." Carver smiled into her eyes. "I'll be there. Just make sure *you're* there to meet me." His palm slid across her cheek and then he was gone.

Yulio opened the broken pane of Ziel's narrow window, admitting a strong breeze to swirl in, fresh and cool, ruffling the room.

Ahna watched Aiela take a last look around this place where they'd spent so much of the last few moons. A mountain of loss waited patiently for both of them, out beyond this night of great and terrible deeds. She pushed it back. No time for that now.

In the uncertain light of dusk, it was easy to creep along the palace balconies, dropping finally to the grounds. They covered their heads with generous hoods, leaving through the east gates, weapons ready. But no guard was watching. Instead, they were pointing up at the night sky, arguing why the dome had disappeared and what they should be doing about it.

High City came aglow with the usual rainbow of solar paints, colors swathing every building and walkway as they moved through it. Nadya especially marveled at it. "All of this glory, and it is to be wasted by the ignorance of evil!" Bitterness echoed in her tone. "It is the loss of my birthright."

The Blessing Service was underway on the lawns of the Temple of Beauty.

"*How* is she still alive?!" Aiela exclaimed as they joined the crowd. On the small knoll, serving as a stage, OldMother Silena stood with palms raised, speaking blessings over the gathering of several hundred. "Older than days!"

Aiela and Ahna didn't hesitate, pushing their way towards the shriveled former Head of the Temple of Beauty. "Apparently, she's managed to survive the plagues, the invasion and even the elder cleansing. I'd love to hear *that* story." Ahna replied.

Silena stopped speaking when the twins stepped up, flanking her. "Who's this now?" She squinted at them, cackling with delight upon recognition. "You two are supposed to be dead!"

"So are you." Aiela replied, with a grin. They embraced the fragile-looking lady and turned to the crowd, rippling with murmurs, and rustling with movement as speculations spread.

"I am Aiela Aigeron." She began. "This is Ahna and we bring dire news."

"The King claims you both dead!" Someone called out.

"The King claims many things that aren't true—including his very kingship!" Aiela retorted. "I'm sure you've many questions, but there isn't time. Come morning, all of Atlantis will be gone. Destroyed. You must leave now. We have only hours left."

Dead silence met this announcement. They all just gaped, unsure whether to believe her.

Ahna stepped forward. "Ruler Ziel was murdered because he would not give over control of our power grid. The Crystals, which powered the grid, and the Second Moon were what Mardu wanted most. With them he plans to rule the world. He's already attacked Greece—surely you saw the beams coming from the Second Moon?"

Murmurs broke out in the crowd.

Ahna raised her voice above them. "He plans to force every

country to come under his rule. Many of you know that he has taken over the very will of Atlanteans via psychotronic weapons, even introducing chemicals into your food and water supplies, into the very air that you breathe. It's how he's ruled Belial for so long. He is using Atlantis for our unlimited technology, weapons, and slaves, to help him recreate the world as he sees fit. But eventually, he'll split apart the planet. Aiela and I have set the Crystals to detonate—"

A roar of protests broke out, drowning Ahna's voice.

"What gives *you* the right to make this decision?"

"This is our Country as much as yours! You can't just despoil it!"

"If you can set the Crystals, then you can *unset* them!"

"Where are we to go??"

"How many will die because you deem it better than Mardu's plans?"

"We can't leave! Every gate is guarded and no aeros left to us... "

An elongated, ear splitting whistle interrupted the din. OldMother Silena had two fingers in her mouth. "STOP ARGUING!" She shouted, as if to unruly children. "Are you all stupid? Has the evil Belial succeeded in turning you into *fools*? This is not a discussion! It's the Only Warning you're going to get. Heed it or don't—*I'm* not going to wait around to see what you decide. Let the girls finish, and then do what you will."

"Ruler Eirene is alive." As if to punctuate Aiela's statement, far off booms echoed back and forth between the walls. "That's probably her, with Atlantis' remaining troops, taking back the outer harbor." She raised her voice even louder, putting all the force she had into them, "Naval vessels are waiting there for you. Take all the food and water you can carry. Leave your treasures—you can't eat them. Get to the outer harbor—"

"HOW?" Someone shouted again. "How can we get out of the City?"

"The dome is down." Ahna pointed out. "We've shut its power off—"

"Yes but the guards—"

"The north gate." A familiar voice shouted just behind her. "Come through the north gate."

"Jai!" Ahna wanted to weep at the sight of her tall, beautiful friend. She hadn't seen him since the invasion, hadn't known if he still lived. Surrounding him were at least five more men.

"We can take the northern gate." Jai assured her fiercely. "Easy as pie! I've befriended a certain few guards. How do you think so many Atlanteans have escaped an impregnable city? Trust me." He winked at her with his usual gaiety, but she saw the gaunt edges to him, the new lines on his face.

Turner embraced Jai, conversing rapidly, then handed Jai every weapon that he carried. "Yer goin' ta need 'em more'n I mate."

Ahna and Aiela followed suit, arming Jai's friends as best they could.

OldMother Silena was already giving commands to the crowd. "You will make haste gathering water and food, spreading the word as you go. Use the north gate—and remember, we can't all fit through at once so don't leave it till the last minute. The ships won't wait long either." Her voice rang out like a beacon of hope. "May courage and peace guide us each and every one. May Atlantis live on in our hearts. Take her with you to your new homes. Be blessed!"

Contrary to direction, many of the people came forward to thank the girls.

"Thank you for making a choice that not many could."

"You're surely a gift of Light, returned to us from the Divine!"

"Blessings on you both. May your rewards be everlasting."

"I pray for the soul of Ruler Ziel. He sacrificed so much to protect us."

"Thank you for caring, for warning us. You could have simply left."

"Atlantis will remember you girls—all that you have endured."

Nadya and Yulio interrupted the flood of praise. "We go now. Your friend Jai may need us to take, and hold the northern gate. You should come too. Once soldiers see Atlanteans preparing to leave, they will try to stop it. It is wise to get out while you can."

"We have to go to the Healing Temple first." Aiela was firm. They couldn't leave before warning Healer Lira and Rizelle. They were probably working among the sick and wounded even now. "We won't be long. Meet you at the gate."

Nadya nodded curtly before striding off in Jai's wake.

Ahna, Aiela and Turner set off at a dead run towards the Temple of Healing.

OLDMOTHER'S REVENGE

"They always say time changes things. But you actually have to change them yourself."

— ANDY WARHOL, THE PHILOSOPHY OF ANDY
WARHOL

OLDMOTHER SILENA

*T*he streets were filling. It reminded her of how rapidly ash filled the air back in the old days, when Atlantis' frequent volcanoes spit and sputtered. Before they learned how to suppress them.

Conversations were harried as Atlanteans headed north, arms full of bags, packs on their backs, wide-eyed children stringing along behind.

Here and there, Belials staggered out from gluttonous dinners to see what was happening.

A large wave of revelers swept down from the Palace, where they'd supposedly been mourning the death of the firstborn, so-called, Prince of Atlantis.

"Already inebriated, the fools." OldMother Silena snorted, watching it all with beady old eyes. "First born prince pah! First one of you in the grave! And the rest of you soon to follow."

Her arms ached, holding their heavy load while she stood waiting for Yorn, her favorite trolley driver. "Where *is* that boy?"

Pleasure hovered inside, thinking about the interrupted Blessing Service—all those startling revelations.

As usual, everyone else had been full of questions and worries, all why's and where's and but-what-about's? But Silena knew exactly what to do. She'd had a plan before those brash twins had uttered their last word of warning.

Finally, she knew why she was still alive.

She'd wept for days, (weeks, or moons even—who keeps track of time at her age?) after the terrible plagues and the ensuing invasion spared her ridiculously prolonged life.

She hadn't any skills outside of art and music—no way to contribute. Uselessness had ravaged her more since the Belial takeover, then time ever had.

Encouraged by the elder cleansing, she had gleefully made plans for a flamboyant death. Spending extra time walking the City streets, loitering round the markets, she hunched and hobbled—more than was strictly necessary. While much younger Atlanteans were rounded up and exterminated across the continent, no one even looked her way. It was as if she was invisible. She'd come to think of herself as a cockroach. How many calamities could she possibly survive?

But now, death loomed, so comforting in its certainty. The entirety of Atlantis would perish, and she'd make certain she went with it. Silena twirled a pretty dance step, smiling to herself. This mission she'd undertaken for herself, was enlivening every ancient cell of her being.

"Finally!" She climbed into the trolley before Yorn rolled to a stop. Lifting a fist she shouted, "To the Palace!"

"But M'dam! We are to be leaving! I'm here to take you out the north gate and to the outer harbor where we can—"

"You will do all of that without me!" She interrupted. "I'm not leaving."

"B-b-but you *must!* Atlantis is going to be destr—"

"Yes, yes, I *know* Yorn. I'm not deaf. I've something very important to do and we must hurry."

"It's a *secret.*" She added smugly before he could ask. "Drop me at the Palace gates and be on your way. It isn't open to discussion." She glared at him fiercely until he sighed, giving in, meek as a kitten, like everyone who'd ever known her. Well—everyone except the unforgettable mother of those twins. Now what was her name...?

Taya! Yes, that was it! Clapping her hands together, Silena shifted the bomb she carried.

So many people were coming and going through the Palace gates, Silena had Yorn drive her right up to the doors. Soldiers and guards were streaming in. Mourners—most of them quite intoxicated with those horrible acids the Belials ingested—were streaming out. Silena clucked with delight at such a convenient uproar.

"Goodbye Yorn." She hefted her little bomb and hurried from the trolley. "Thank you for always letting me bully you into my schemes. Now get out of here. I'll see you in the next life perhaps." She rushed off before waiting for his answer.

Gossiping people parted and flowed around her like a rock in a creek, never even glancing her way. Everyone was worried. Machines that needed power didn't have any. The dome was inexplicably down. Atlanteans were leaving High City in a steady stream. King Mardu feared an imminent attack.

She made it all the way to the throne room, where she positioned herself amongst the curtains at the base of Mardu's hideously garish, double dais.

As much as she hated how he'd decimated her city, she hated him even more for his monstrous decor. This entire room was a sin against the hallowed sacredness of Beauty.

Was that supposed to be *art?!* She gawked at the sorry excuse for paintings and sculptures positioned nearby. Her classes of five-year-olds could do better than this!

Clearly, no one had given even a thought to the acoustics in here.

Probably couldn't hear anything but garbles in the back, when their supposed king spoke. And the throne! Like something a monkey might mold from his own feces!

The room was filling with Belial soldiers—plenty of Atlantean-turned-Belial-soldiers too, she noticed. Fickle, black-hearted bastards. *And who are you to condemn?* An inner voice asked impertinently. *As though you've never erred in any of your imperious and prolific judgements. Never sinned for the sake of self-preservation. Never turned your back on what you claim to love.*

Mardu entered—she assumed it was him, not actually able to make out features with her used-up eyes. He sat on his ugly throne, so far above them she worried her little bomb wouldn't reach that far. Still, it was terribly heavy. Hopefully that meant it was terribly destructive.

"Someone has failed me!" Mardu thundered. The room was full of soldiers shifting and jockeying for position as they fell silent. "The dome that protects us has no power!"

I was right. She thought smugly. *Acoustics couldn't be worse.*

"Rebellious Atlanteans are trying to leave High City. You will stop them! You will shackle them and keep them in the Aades until power is restored. Use the Temple of Beauty as a prison once the Aades is full. Those trying to escape will become the first slaves. We shall make an example of them."

Silena caught her breath. Vile, vile man, profaning her own holy Temple, enslaving the faithful who revered those sacred spaces! Now she was *glad* he would die by her hand. Delighted even.

She set the timer, peering at the dial, unable to make out its tiny numbers. Shrugging, she turned it only a little. What she certainly didn't need anymore of was time.

Mardu was babbling louder, hoarse shouts that echoed uselessly around this idiotic room.

"Those of you in command... every soldier... on duty until this threat has passed."

Inhaling deeply, Silena closed her eyes, a smile settling onto her lips. The only thing better than finally getting her flamboyant death, was taking Atlantis' evil conqueror with her. And plenty of his rotten warriors too.

"Commandeer aeros... usable without the grid... boats, trolleys, whatever you need... stand guard. Our large weapons are being... without power... useless. We may be... an invasion—"

She let the meaningless words wash over her and waited for the end.

A quiet tick sounded and anticipation surged through her weary body. Just as she was wondering if she'd feel it, a blast crashed into her eardrums.

Then OldMother Silena wondered no more.

30

A RECKONING

"But men often mistake killing and revenge for justice.
They seldom have the stomach for justice."

— ROBERT JORDAN

CARVER

*B*alek's funeral. Such an odd thought.

Carver shot a guard in the neck with the light gun as he rounded the hallway corner outside Mardu's quarters. Even as he dragged the body behind a lifesize statue of three leaping dolphins, his mind stayed busy, trying to sort through too many rapid changes. *Ahna and Aiela survived—survived both Mardu and Balek in fact.*

Stealthily gliding from shadow to shadow in the spacious rooms, Carver killed two more guards, the first with his blade, taking him from behind. The second was dozing, head lolling back against the wall. Carver shot him in his unprotected face at close range, the flat sizzle exploding out in blood and bone.

Satisfied that he was finally alone, he piled the bodies in a corner of Mardu's bed chamber, not readily visible unless one was looking for them. The trail of blood released by his knife, and the seeping organic matter released by the light gun, was harder to hide.

Positioning behind the doors, Carver studied a collection of finely cut glass decanters filled with fruited brandies. Deep purple, bright red, warm amber, and pale green, the colors were beautifully illuminated by specially placed light spheres. No doubt a gift from some groveling orchard keeper, desperate for the favor of the King. Four equally exquisite goblets stood on the hutch, just inside the suite entrance. Carver noted the varying levels in the decanters. Mardu would drink from these.

Opening the small pouch he carried on his belt, he removed dark vials no bigger than his smallest finger. *Which one would he drink tonight? Might as well do them all. No need to save these for a future use. One way or another, it ends shortly.*

"Just a little back-up plan." Carver whispered, as he tipped a few drops at a time into each of the decanters. "In case you kill me—or maybe just beat me and toss me out on my ass." It had happened more times than he could count as a child. He continued portioning the poisons until they were gone.

Pouring a glass, he left it ready, welcoming even. "Probably should have found a way to do this long ago... " How many lives would he have saved if he'd been braver, surer, stronger? He shook the thought away with the steady determination of purpose, "I'm here now. better late than never."

A knock startled him.

"Guards?" Jaydee's shrill call accompanied the opening door.

Carver shrank deep into a niche, wedging behind a diamond carving of a naked woman, taller than him by half.

"Where is everyone?" She pushed the door wide and crept in, gaze going 'round the opulent quarters. "Guards?" Loud this time, she teetered on high golden heels, clicking across to the door of Mardu's bed chamber. Outfitted in bright pink and yellow, her gown flashed with gemstones outlining strategically placed gaps that showcased heavy breasts, the curves of hips and legs.

Styled into a bouquet of flowers, her hair was colored to match the gown, the flowery perfume she wore assaulted Carver's senses. Finally satisfied there was no one about, she click click clicked back to the hutch, and picked up the waiting goblet. Her enlarged lips were dyed bright pink in the Belial style, no doubt matching her tongue and genitals.

Should I stop her? Carver stepped out from hiding, but she was already drinking in large noisy gulps. Glass drained, she poured another, drinking half before wandering back towards the bed chamber.

Carver followed. Just inside the chamber doors, he spoke in a low voice. "Jaydee."

She whirled around, dropping the goblet. "Who...?" Splashed wine and glass shards skittered across the marble tile. She slid and swayed, started to fall.

Carver caught her.

Her eyes were wild, staring at him. "B-but you're dead... " Confusion blurred her words. "... no, you're you're you're *gone*." Scrabbling to stand upright, her hands went to her temples. "Get away from me!—I, I'm... dizzy!"

"You drank a lot. Why are you here?"

"S-scared. Atlanteans are running, fighting to leave. Riots outside and... and... " Wilting as her body went slack, she stared at him with hugely dilated irises, fear outlining the bloodshot whites. "Wha's happening to me?"

Half carrying, half dragging her to Mardu's enormous bed, Carver laid her out on gilded satin spreads, pondering whether to tell her she was dying by pure chance. That her life was suddenly over because she drank poison meant for Mardu. It seemed cruel to just announce it.

"Rest here awhile. Mardu will be back soon."

Her eyes were droopy now, but she still seemed to take in the situation. Eyeing the pile of guard's bodies her breathing quickened. "You... *traitor*. Mardu'll kill you... you won't win." She sighed deeply as though this thought satisfied her.

More than likely she'd had a variety of substances at the funeral. How that would react with the poison was anyone's guess.

"Are you gonna k-kill me?"

"I hadn't planned on it." Carver said drily. "But you drank the wine... "

Her eyes widened for an instant. "Poison?" She struggled to rise. Failed.

He nodded. "Like I said. It wasn't meant for you."

"It's... it's a c-coward's weapon!" Trying to spit this last insult, she stiffened, whimpering as her hands clutched her belly. She fell slack then, sinking into either sleep or a coma, as death hovered near.

Bitchy to the last breath.

Unsure what to do, Carver settled on the foot of the bed, watched her breathing grow shallow. It might have been a long time that he stayed there, or it could have been only moments.

He wondered what Ahna was doing. Felt hope bolster him that he might get to be with her. Although neither of them had any idea what the future held or where they could end up, there was a very real possibility of being together. Even the possibility felt like a gift.

An explosion rocked the building. Deafening sound reverberated through Mardu's suite, and Carver catapulted to his feet, heart pounding. Waving up the lights, he glanced at Jaydee. Her eyes were half open. No movement of her chest rising or falling.

Loud creaks and groans from the buildings under him became sharp pops, and then a grinding sound, as Carver watched a split in the floor spider towards him, felt the marble shift under his boots. Feeling quickly for Jaydee's pulse, confirming she was indeed dead, he left the room.

Should he continue to wait for Mardu? Was there an invasion underway?

Running out to a veranda, Carver looked across the glowing city. But there were no invading aeros hovering over the Palace, no troops firing from below. From this distance, he could make out few details of the City. The streets looked full, movement everywhere, like an ant mound abuzz.

Hearing the suite doors bang open, he watched through the glass doors as Mardu stumbled in, breathing hard. Covered in dust and debris, blood trickling from several small nicks and cuts on his face, he looked around wildly, calling out, "Guards!? Guards?"

Bending over to catch his breath, he commenced the same inspection that Jaydee had earlier, except he stopped at the sight of her on his bed.

Carver slipped inside to bar the door. Where ever the guards were, they'd be here soon, looking for the King.

"Jaydee get up! Somebody *bombed my Palace!* My throne room is decimated and half my soldiers—or more! Where are all the guards? GET UP!" He was beside her, shaking her.

Standing behind him, Carver watched it dawn on Mardu that she was dead. Watched Mardu's overlarge body stiffen when he noticed the gruesome pile of dead guards. Watched his father belatedly fumble for his light gun.

Carver leapt forward, knocking it away. It bounced loudly across the marble, and Carver waited calmly to see what Mardu would do next.

Staring at each other, Mardu's eyes flickered fear for the briefest instant. It was the first time Carver ever saw it cross his father's face. He hadn't believed it possible, and it brought a rush of strength.

The next instant Mardu covered it with a snarl. "So the bastard whelp returns."

"Not a bastard." Carver replied evenly. "Bastards don't know who their father is. Unfortunately, I d—"

Mardu lunged at him, the blade in his fist slicing close to Carver's neck.

Sidestepping, Carver shoved to further Mardu's momentum, foot sweeping his legs out from under him.

Mardu landed hard, but sprang back up, swinging hard at Carver again. This time his blade tip sliced across Carver's cheek, one fist connecting viciously with ribs. Carver felt them crack as he brought an elbow down on Mardu's knife arm.

The blade dropped, but Mardu followed with a series of swift punches, chops and a knee to the groin. Carver blocked some, but not enough.

His father had lived a lifetime by the skill of his fists. And an ability to ignore pain.

And a bull-headed madness that didn't allow for retreat.

But Mardu hadn't had to fight four older brothers his entire life. He hadn't endured as much, or as long, as Carver had.

They battled furiously until Carver was half-blinded with blood and felt as if he couldn't draw breath into his lungs. Fury pushed him past all reason and he pummeled his father, driving him back and back, uncaring that he was sacrificing his body for the ability to punish, to avenge, to unleash his rage on this man who'd bullied and belittled and tortured his own child.

Mardu tripped backwards on the pile of bodies.

Carver hit him twice more as he fell, one fist sweeping up under the chin, the other landing solidly on his temple. Mardu sprawled on the dead guards, and finally, didn't move.

Working fast, ignoring the sharp pains inside every time he moved, Carver tied his father's hands behind his back, trussing his ankles together, slack enough to still walk. Gagging and blindfolding him, he wrapped extra straps around Mardu's chest and arms, the last went snug around his father's neck, for insurance.

Washing blood from his eyes, he used Mardu's pristine linens to staunch the flow from the knife cut, a mangled lip, smashed nose, splits and cuts around both eyes.

Limping, pain piercing with every breath, he woke Mardu with a decanter of the poisoned wine, dribbling it slowly onto his blunted, dark face.

Mardu stirred, then came roaring back to life, twisting and bawling and thrashing.

Well out of the way, Carver simply waited until Mardu calmed.

His father managed to wriggle away from the piled bodies and sat panting on the marble floor.

Carver grasped his bicep. "Stand up. We're going to take a long walk." His father outweighed him by more than he'd guessed, judging by the bulk Carver supported as Mardu struggled to his feet.

With a light gun in one hand, pulling his father blindly along with the other, Carver led him up to the old observatory on top of the Palace. Now an aero lot where Mardu and his Generals could come and go as they pleased, it was deserted and dark, except for the far off glow of High City.

Mardu cocked his head as the night air hit them, no doubt hoping to hear the shout of guards. There was plenty of shouting and cries, but they all came from below.

Carver couldn't see the damage, but he smelled dust in the air and the acrid tang of burnt things.

Halfway up the dirt path, Mardu managed to spit out the gag. "Take the blindfold off." He demanded. "Or are you *that* scared of me?"

"Walk." Carver replied, jerking Mardu forward by the strap encircling his neck.

It was slow going. His father limped badly, scuffling and wincing, stumbling on the uneven path he could not see. Not that he would ever admit it, or ask for mercy.

"Where are we going? Someplace you can kill me with no one around, like the scared, whimpering mutt you've always been."

"We're going to a place where you can watch what's coming." Carver hadn't known what he would do once his father was beaten. Some instinct guided him step by step. He continued conversationally, as if instructing on how to cook an egg.

"You'll get to enjoy all of it. The fruits of your violence. You'll get exactly what's coming to you, set in motion by your own cruel hand. There are wages of love and wages of evil—"

"And what is it you *think* is going to happen?"

How could a voice be laced with so much hatred? Carver wondered. Why were some people kind and loving and good, while this man was filled with greed, bitter rage and bottomless darkness?

He answered. "Atlantis will be swept away—the entire continent."

Mardu snorted, moving slower and slower as they climbed, breathing harder. "I don't believe you."

Carver let him set the pace, wanting him to take in every word. "Your *belief* doesn't change the fact that Aiela survived Balek's dagger. That Ahna's monster snake killed Montauk before he could kill her. That Ahna and Aiela disconnected power to the dome so that people could evacuate. Nor does your *belief* change the fact that all your technicians are dead in the maze—I killed one myself—and it's impossible to get to the Crystals now."

"Then there's the fact that your own people programmed the Crystals to destroy the Second Moon, then Atlantis. Ahna instructed them the entire time, *while you were there*. They followed her instructions to the letter."

Mardu didn't reply, but his breath came shorter and harsh.

These would be the last moments he would ever spend in the presence of this man who gave him life. This man who'd raised him and contributed more fear and misery than any child should have to survive.

Shocked to realize he didn't feel hatred, Carver examined what he did feel. Relief mostly, that it was almost over. Hope. Definitely, he felt hope. Soon as this task was done, he would join Ahna. Go with her to start a new life someplace else.

Turning so his father would clearly hear him, Carver said, "I want you to know that I forgive you."

"Forgive me?" Mardu's laugh was ugly. "For what? I gave you everything you needed to succeed and you betrayed me! You could have been anything you wanted! You could've ruled the world—but instead you're the biggest weakling of the family! Instead you side with my enemies, you choose *music* and some little *bitch* over power— over all the power and riches a man could ever want. You've been an embarrassment since the day you came sniveling into the world, shoved out of that worthless foreign cunt! Forgive *me*… " Mardu ended with a snarl. "… I don't accept it. You're no son of mine!"

This tirade meant little to Carver. Mardu had said much worse over the years. He couldn't remember when he'd stopped trying to earn his father's approval.

He felt lighter, giddy even. They were nearly at the top. "Well I'm exactly who I want to be." He realized it was true. "And if I'm not your son, then I'm supremely grateful."

Mardu muttered more obscenities under his breath, but Carver ignored it. This man would never terrorize him again—nor anyone else.

It began to rain as they reached the stone needles on top of Holy Mountain.

Every other night somewhere close to midnight, the weather people made it rain. There couldn't be much time left.

Carver hurried as he positioned his father against the smallest stone, which pointed like an accusing finger at the sky. Using the straps around his father's torso, he bound Mardu tightly to the stone.

"Just kill me and get it over with! Avenge your pitiful little wounds." Mardu spewed sarcasm, drawing breath a little at a time.

"Well see, that is *one* thing I've learned from you; that violence solves nothing. I'm done killing. Killing is what ignorant people do. Atlantis was right to give up violence."

Mardu spat blood onto the ground, and laughed harshly. "Atlantis lost all their power when they gave up violence. Those still loyal to the Law of One won't survive its inherent weakness. Violence is the way of the world. Always has been, always will be."

Carver shook his head in wonder. This was the most philosophical conversation he'd ever had with Mardu, right here and now, with both of them bleeding in the rain on top of Atlantis' Holy Mountain. He wanted to laugh at the absurdity.

"Some things are more important than power—more important than survival even. And you're wrong. Violence is not the way of the world—evolution is. Everything moves towards harmony—though change can *seem* violent if you resist it. The Atlanteans taught me that."

Crisscrossing under his crotch and up over his shoulders with the straps, he ensured Mardu would stay on his feet, bolstered by the pillar of stone at his back, even after his legs gave way.

"More important than power..." Mardu mocked. He sounded disgusted, but maybe a little confused too. *"What's* more important?"

"Love." Carver replied. "Wisdom. Peace. Beauty. Grace... there are many things more important than power."

Curiously, Mardu didn't speak again except for muttering, "Wish I had a good plum brandy..." before Carver replaced the gag, tighter than before. He would take no chances that Mardu might make enough noise to get someone's attention. It would be a miracle to be heard so far from the Palace, above the springs that rushed down this mountain and the soft patter of rain. But if they did come looking...

The last thing Carver did was to remove the blindfold.

Mardu's overly large, blunt features were as bloody and swollen as his own, one eye crusted shut. Rain dripped across it. He'd be able to see out of it by the end, Carver had no doubt.

Checking the straps a last time, Carver stepped back. What did one say before leaving his evil, cold-hearted father trussed to a rock on top of a mountain so he could watch death coming for him?

Carver thought about it, but there was simply nothing left to say.

THE EXODUS

"Great heroes need great sorrows and burdens, or half their greatness goes unnoticed. It is all part of the fairy tale."

— PETER S. BEAGLE, THE LAST UNICORN

AIELA

*A*iela wanted to weep when she saw the ruins of the Temple of Healing. Some sections were being rebuilt, but a deep grief welled up at the desolation of this place that was part of her heart.

That's when it hit her. She was soon to lose every place she loved. Before this night was over, the temples, halls, mountains and beaches, the gardens and trees from every memory she had, would be gone. And it was by her own hand.

WHEN THEY WERE THIRTEEN, *the friendly old Eiller tree that was Ahna's sacred place had been invaded.*

Practically a member of the family, all of them had found solace in its branches, enjoyed the serenity of its cooling canopy. No summer would be complete without lazy afternoons in the hammock with Mama reading stories of dragons and faerie folk.

But beetles by the thousands had moved into its bark, were living off its abundant leaves, making the beautiful tree their base from which to breed and multiply.

"They'll move to other trees and kill them one by one, once they've ravished yours." Papa had explained. "It has to be cut down and burned. We can stop them, if we do it now."

Ahna had refused at first, crying at the unfairness of losing what she loved. Finally, she accepted it—even come to see the inherent wisdom. "It's lost to me either way." She mourned, as Papa brought the great green shelter crashing to the ground in the middle of the sunlight dappled forest. "If I tried to keep it, the rest of these would die."

"But you saved them. Which one shall we choose for your new special place?" Aiela had soothed, pulling her twin away to explore new possibilities.

TURNER AND AHNA were warning anyone they encountered as they moved through the main Temple dome. "Get to the outer harbor any way that you can. Go through the north gate. Atlantis is falling. We must all leave right now."

It occurred to Aiela she should help. But first, she'd need to move through this rending grief. *Glad you can feel again.* Ahna sent to her. Then they split up, each taking a wing to spread their message.

Word passed quickly, and by the time Aiela found Healer Lira, she was already preparing her patients.

"Here is water and medicine. Take the blankets too—anything else that you can carry. You'll be alright." Lira was speaking to a middle-aged couple.

The woman was in a bed, both legs wrapped in bandages. "No, my dear." The patient replied kindly. "We won't be going anywhere. Even if I wasn't sick, I'd still choose to be right here."

"Give our seats to the young and the healthy." Her mate added, with a brave smile, settling into the bed beside his wife. "I'm sure there won't be enough anyway. We'd rather see those with many years yet in those seats. Take this to someone who needs it." He handed back the water bottles and medicine. "We'll be alright."

Lira had tears in her eyes when she turned and saw Aiela. "How am I supposed to just leave them?"

Aiela wrapped her arms around Lira. "I don't know."

"Bless you." The couple called as she pulled Lira from the room.

An explosion boomed, and she ran with Lira outside.

"It was at the Palace." Those who'd seen it pointed. "One whole side of it just... blew out." The night hid whatever was happening up there, but the air was filling with smoke and dust.

Together, Aiela and Lira directed those who could walk, in helping those who couldn't. An aero landed on the lawn, then another, and waiting people climbed in. The Temple halls became a slow-moving stream.

Several more patients, too sick or injured, elected to stay behind. Most were older—the oldest ones remaining after the elder cleansing anyway—and echoed what the first couple had said. "Please send the young in our places." Pulling off shawls, cloaks, jewelry, even picking small treasures out of pockets, they offered anything they had, saying "Give this to someone who needs it."

Rizelle nearly ran into them. "There's to be a dedicated healing vessel." She was puffing, out of breath from helping people to the aeros. "Five of our healers are already at the harbor. They're receiving the sick. We can join them when we're done here."

Lira's relief was palpable. "Good. We'd best pack—wisely. Whatever tools and medicines we can't recreate..."

"Just don't leave too late." Aiela reminded, embracing both Lira and Rizelle. It was time to part. She'd done what she came to do. "May you be blessed in the Light of the One."

Fighting back tears, she worked her way to the front of the Temple, finding Ahna and Turner along the way. "Look who's over there, helping!" Ahna pointed to a golden blonde girl, assisting two mothers with tiny babies. Behind them came a tall blonde man loaded down with packs and bags.

"Nanat and Nirka?"

"It is!" Turner beamed. "Ya fall in love in Ireland, it's bound ta last forever."

Stepping back into the night, the three of them began the journey towards the north gate.

Despite such urgency—the dire outcome of this night—families calmly loaded carts with food and water. Aeros landed in parks and lawns, any space large enough, to ferry people and goods to the outer harbor. The canals were filled with loaded down vessels.

Belials hovered at the edges of the action, jesting and laughing about those leaving. "We'll gladly have the city without all you's." "S' goin' t be a real *Belial* city now!" "Go 'head. Get out while you still can! Get, get, get!"

Drinking and shouting, pointing and slinging insults, the large Belial population became ever more mocking, closer to the City wall.

They passed a Belial soldier, watching in dazed confusion.

"Why isn't he stopping it?" Aiela wondered aloud.

"Too many people ta control most like." Turner replied. "I heard most o' the soldiers were up't the Palace. Many o' 'em deid in the blast, the rest buried or wounded."

Jai and his friends were dealing admirably with the congestion at the North gate. Dressed in Belial armor, they waved along boats of every size. "Move along! Keep up, many more coming behind... Hey you there! You can take a few more, pull over right here. We can fit at least four. Anybody have four traveling together?"

Streams of people pulling carts, wearing packs, grouped in couples and families, were passing through on both sides of the canal.

Nadya and Yulio watched, holding weapons ready, alert for Belial soldiers who might come against them.

Aeros landed and took off again from top of the wall overhead, whipping rain-filled air in gusts and circles.

"If the bulk of Belial forces were up at the Palace, Atlanteans must have taken back all the old aeros." Aiela commented.

"Hopefully the other gates too." Ahna replied. "Whatever that blast was at the Palace, it's given us a fighting chance."

"We... *did this*." Aiela stared at the throngs of people escaping into the bleak night, leaving their homes, with no guarantee of a future. "It wasn't a mistake... was it?"

"We'll probably be asking that question for the rest of our lives." Ahna muttered. "However long or short that may be."

Sage

"You will get out of this aero and go home." Sage commanded the Belial pilot.

He snorted, lip curling as he looked her up and down. "And why'd I do that?"

She lifted her right hand, the heavy bulk of Carver's Belial ring gleaming as she shoved it near his face. "Because I told you to."

His expression changed as his eyes went back and forth between her and the ring. Finally, he shrugged, giving in. "Whatever you say. I'm done for t'night anyways."

"Go get the rest of them." Sage addressed a young man waiting outside in the drizzle. "It'll take three trips to get everybody to the harbor. Hurry!"

She and Charis worked, overseeing the loading of every person left in the ruins of OldForest. Thrice packing the aero with every bit of food and herbs, every blanket and even maps, crystals, lights, codices, tools, and jewels—whatever might be useful in a new land. They worked until they were ready to drop.

"Do you want to go with your Forest people or come with me?" Sage asked Charis.

"You are my people." Charis replied. You and the twins are the only family I have left."

Sage squeezed her hand. "Good. There'll be much to do wherever we end up. I'll welcome your help—and companionship."

◉◉

"THE ROWBOAT IS STILL THERE." Sage shouted over the sound of the aero, as she climbed back inside. "Do you see the lights of the ship?" She pointed and the pilot squinted. The glow was barely visible through the rain.

He nodded, lifting off.

Fighting to hover low enough over Nadya's ship, the pilot did his best, trying to hold the aero steady, as increasing gusts of wind slammed against them, churning up the water around them.

Sage and Charis tossed out boxes and barrels, unsure how they were going to get onto the ship without serious injury.

"Maybe we wait for them at the rowboat?" Charis yelled over the fray.

"There won't be enough room for us all!" Sage hollered back.

Below them, two figures waved their arms urging them to hurry. One ran to a pile of rope coils. It took several tries before they tossed it high enough, aiming in the vicinity of the aero door. Together Sage and Charis caught it.

The rope was thick and rough, but at least they wouldn't have to free-drop so far. Still, Sage lost her grip, plummeting the last several yards to the pitching deck, an ankle crunching under her as she landed.

The two dark Banpiro men waved at the pilot, signaling him to go.

Strangely shaped, this ship was well equipped, and outfitted for comfort. She wasn't sure the Banpiro men could speak Atlantean, but they understood it well enough, helping Sage to a berth below decks, with two large bunks, a table, and even upholstered chairs bolted firmly down. Charis labored alongside the Banpiro men, though she limped and left blood traces on the cargo as they lugged it down to stow. Cupboards and shelves fitted clever little spaces, and Sage concentrated on the ingenuity, the beauty and shapes. Anything to keep her mind off of the twins. Where were they? Surely they should have been here by now.

Then the Banpiro brought a basin of scented water and very fine cloth strips. Sage washed the blood from Charis' raw hands and bound her swelling ankle.

Charis grimaced, but followed directions as Sage talked her through setting her own foot, welcoming the mind-numbing focus of pain.

Then Charis fetched fruit from their supplies, and things to make tea.

And they waited.

THE WAGES OF EVIL

9,970 BCE. SUMMIT OF HOLY MOUNTAIN IN HIGH CITY, ATLANTIS

There's a lover in the story but the story's still the same.
There's a lullaby for suffering, and a paradox to blame.
But it's written in the scriptures and it's not some idle claim.
You want it darker, we kill the flame.

— LEONARD COHEN, YOU WANT IT DARKER

MARDU

*M*ardu couldn't see the Second Moon. Hadn't even thought about it as he sagged against the woven straps that traitorous boy had bound him with. But when three blinding beams shot out of the mountainside not fifty feet below where he stood, he did.

The trinity of buzzing rays hit something, far beyond where the clouds and the night blocked his sight. He knew that, because he heard it. Even above the monotonous white noise of water springing from the mountain and gushing down it. Even above the din of rain hitting stone and dirt, trees and bushes. Even above the far off whine and roar of aeros coming and going from the top of the wall, and even within his Capital city—this city he had *taken,* had *earned* by superior power—he heard the impact of the Second Moon being struck.

Struggling once more against his bonds, Mardu wrenched, grunting, muscles bulging with strain, spitting furiously, working his jaw and tongue to at least remove the gag. Pushing up and out with his feet, pulling his arms apart until he thought his wrists might pop out of their joints, he howled his fury at the pain, sounds that came out muffled, and only made his dry throat sorer. But he would not give up. As long as there was breath in his body, he would work to escape.

Then he would find that boy and punish him. He would whip him and pull him limb from limb! Show him what it had felt like, trying to escape for hours!

He stopped when he saw huge burning pieces flung down through parting clouds. Like fiery shards, they came at a speed unnatural to gravity. But where was the rest of it? As though in answer to his question, the clouds cleared. Without rain falling, he stared into the heavens, watched as stars multiplied and grew bright.

But it wasn't the stars that kept his attention.

The Second Moon was split into three massive pieces, each of them scorching red, burning in the atmosphere and hurtling towards earth. The largest ones would impact far far away, somewhere in the western ocean.

Mardu breathed deep and began struggling again. If Carver thought the falling moon would sink Atlantis, he was an even bigger fool. Hope renewed his strength. Someone would eventually find him up here. They would come looking for him. They had to.

Then the beams came again. Again and again they pierced through the earth, this time at widening points, at increasing angles. High City erupted as the beams lasered through, like a fiery needle trying to stitch thread through the earth in some intricate pattern.

Horrified, Mardu watched it happen, entire buildings erupted into the air, a large section of the city burst into flames, another simply melted.

The ground shook violently beneath his feet. The stone at his back swayed and danced, its companions nearly knocking into it.

The deadly beams moved outward, embroidering their destruction as far as his eyes could see. Carver had positioned him facing north.

A gust of hot wind smashed into him and the air began its own thrashing assault.

The entire mountain bucked and fell beneath him now and he looked up, terror coursing through him as another stone tower came crashing towards him. It grazed his side, raking away skin, coming to rest against his legs. Looking down, he realized they were crushed. By the time he thought it odd to feel nothing from so much weight crushing parts of his body, the pain hit.

Screams of agony came uncontrollable, doing more damage behind the gag. Banging his head as hard as he could against the stone, he tried desperately to knock himself unconscious. But it only brought another barrage of unspeakable pain.

Scorching winds pounded against him, fueled by the fires that overtook High City. Cacophonies of distant screaming caught his attention, and he imagined the people trying to escape as the earth split beneath their feet, as entire city blocks lifted up and shattered, as flames claimed everything that was left.

He wondered where the rest of his sons were. Only three left.

Who of his Generals had made it out of the Palace explosion alive? Montauk was dead—if Carver was to be believed.

He thought about the girls he'd enjoyed keeping at his disposal in the Palace. Orja popped into his mind but he pushed her away, feeling once again the shock of her abandonment. Her betrayal. For the first time, he felt the hurt, unable to numb it by forcing someone to do his bidding, or drown it with wine, or distract himself with sexual pleasure.

Memories of his sweet mother, whom Orja had always reminded him of, came next, but even she had betrayed him—cruelly sent him off to a foreign land so she could die in peace.

He saw Jaydee laid out dead on his own bed, not far from his guards.

Mind searching for something, anything to distract him from the terrible terrible pain, he realized there was no one he loved, no moments he cherished. Nothing but a great empty hollow inside that echoed the madness happening around him. How had his life come to this? How had his careful plans ended in such disaster? He'd been patient. He'd had all the power. People feared him, revered him, served him, admired him! He'd won!

Below him, the trees caught fire. Slowly flames began to climb towards him, bush by bush, tree by tree. He felt a moment of relief that death would arrive soon.

But the flames took their time, creeping, as if consuming all the moisture from the recent rain before moving upwards to claim the next meal.

The heat grew intense, scorching his face with steam and smoke. But it seemed more intent on tormenting, than killing.

Rumbling sounded all around, between frequent explosions and echoing booms. Far off in the western mountains he saw a volcano begin to spew fiery light into the air. Then a second peak joined it.

Between the volcano ash and the fire smoke, he could no longer see stars, and the night lit up as if it were day. Gasping for breath, crying out as every movement tortured him anew, time slowed to a crawl. It seemed hours, days, of purest pain.

JERKING back to full consciousness with a whimper, movement to the east caught Mardu's eye.

A wall of water and earth blotted out the horizon. How could a wave possibly stand that high? Gathering earth in front of it, it rushed toward him as if racing the fires coming up from below.

Mardu felt his face start to blister, choked as he inhaled smoke, smelled the sizzling flesh as his clothes caught fire, gagging and panicking as he began to burn alive.

Then the wave dropped on him. Crushing, burying, depriving him of any oxygen at all, earth pummeled him. Then water washed the earth away, but darkness was already descending and Mardu blacked out again.

When he came to again, his entire body was wracked with agonizing sensation and he wept to still be alive. He looked up one last time. Nothing was left of the City below. The ground still shook, jiggling the rock column resting against him. The volcanoes still spewed. Another wave came rushing towards him. All he could see was earth with water pushing it, this time it seemed miles high, blotting out the sky as it came.

"I want to make sure you see all of it." Carver had said. *"Experience the fruits of your violence. Get exactly what's coming to you, set in motion by your own cruel hand. There are wages of love and wages of evil... "*

The words echoed inside his head as the wave loomed over him, closer and closer, sweeping along as if nothing could stop it. *...wages of love and wages of evil... wages of love and wages of evil...*

Indeed the wave swept Holy Mountain and the stone fingers and Mardu along too, and he lost consciousness for the last time, the words of his youngest son still ringing in his head.

WHEN THE EARTH ROSE UP & THE SKY FELL

9,970 BCE. ATLANTIS

"If the world should stop revolving, spinning slowly down to die,
I'd spend the end with you. And when the world was through,
Then one by one the stars would all go out,
Then you and I would simply fly away."

— DAVID GATES

AHNA

From the beach, all five faces were lit and lifted towards the carnage in the heavens, jaws hanging open after the Crystal beams shattered the Second Moon.

"We *must go!*" Nadya's voice held panic as she splashed into rough waves to shove off. Yulio followed her.

"NO!" Ahna refused to get into the little boat. "I'm not leaving Carver! We can wait a little longer."

Aiela put a hand on Nadya's arm. "It's going to be alright. We can afford a bit more time. Please?" She splashed to Ahna's side. "You might prepare yourself... if he doesn't make it. For all we know Mardu has him. Or a guard killed him."

Normally, Aiela would never speak such things aloud. Normally she would support Ahna until proven otherwise. But tonight, normal didn't exist.

"Yes I know." Ahna shriveled inside as she said it. "But we wait until the absolute last second!"

"We can't risk everybody else's lives... " Aiela began, stopping when Ahna took her hand and dragged her toward the boat.

"Get in." Ahna snapped at Turner and Nadya, climbing in herself. "Yulio, you'll push us off when I say?"

The big Banpiro nodded, resting his hands on the row boat edge, waves roaring in and out around his knees as he stood like a rock in the pummeling surf.

All sets of eyes were searching the dark shore when beams ripped up through High City. Again and again they lit up the night, rending sounds like thunder that jerked and shuddered through each cell.

"Let's go." Ahna shouted. Turner and Nadya reached out their hands to Yulio as he shoved the boat and then ran and lunged—

"There he is! There he is! CARVER RUN, get in!" Ahna screamed into the night.

Backlit by blinding flashes, chased by thunderous booms, Carver dashed into the surf, dove into the next huge wave and swam with everything he had in him to survive. To get to her.

Yulio caught Carver and hauled him in, as Aiela and Turner strained with oars against the sea that seemed bent on washing them back to shore.

They fought their way out through the building waves, Yulio and Nadya pulling a second set of oars from the boat bottom. All four rowed, shouting "PULL!" to synchronize each other, words swept away in the rising wind and an ocean suddenly violent.

"Carver." Ahna fell into him with the weight of too many separations and a hope too precarious yet. But for this chaotic moment, she had him and she held on tight.

Swells hid Nadya's ship lights from the little rowboat, until they began to lose all direction. "That way!" Turner shouted again and again, an innate navigation system guiding him true. The blinding flashes of Crystal beams roved ever closer behind them.

Heaving for all they were worth, they pulled away from the land that was breaking apart.

Then waves boomeranged from the land side and Carver took Nadya's oar so she could navigate, shouting and pointing as she caught sight of the ship between foaming crests.

Aiela rowed, Ahna clasping her legs as anchor. Wind and waves spun them, tossing them like a splinter between mountains of water.

Aiela

It was all so familiar to Aiela. Her entire life she had dreamed this again and again.

A small boat made from a dark wood she couldn't nam., Ahna was with her, and a few others. They were fleeing—she hadn't known what, or where they were going. The sea was agitated and wore the navy cloak of pre-dawn.

Aiela gripped an oar in her hands, desperately trying, with Turner using another, to keep the boat from capsizing. Her muscular arms strained. A pale blue linen tunic clung to her body, soaked with frigid ocean spray. Dripping hair slapped against her face in a cyclone, unleashed from her long braid.

Ahna sat across from her on a plank, small hands holding her knees steady. Aiela knew Ahna was connected with Source, co-creating safe passage for them through the storm. Desperate urgency gripped them all as a giant wave towered up from the lee side. All in the boat braced, except for Aiela. Anger overcame her and she stood, brandishing her oar overhead, shouting at the sky "Come on then! Do your best—because we survive! We always survive!" She felt Ahna's hands grip her legs through the rough wool of her pants, trying to pull her down. Then the wave crashed over them, plucking her from the tiny boat. She smashed against something fixed, before sinking down into blessed black.

Turner

It didn't matter that they had found Nadya's ship, had practically run into it. All Turner could see was the place Aiela went into the water. Dropping the oar to dive in after her, Yulio shoved him back roaring "No!" And went in himself.

"Climb onboard! Go! Faster!" Nadya was pushing Ahna up a rope ladder hanging off portside of the rocking, midnight ship.

Carver was lashing the little rowboat to the ladder, only moments before the next wave ripped into them.

"Turner!" Nadya screamed, pulling him. "Get on the ship!"

He shook his head. "Aiela... "

"Yulio will bring her. He does not drown... like you."

It made sense. But what if Yulio didn't find her? Nadya and Carver both grabbed him, shoving him up to the rope ladder, shouting at him to climb. Numb and frantic, he did. Racing to the first rope he saw, he tied it around himself, lashing it to a ring embedded in the ship deck, preparing to dive in.

Carver tackled him, knocking him down and holding him there, both of them rolling around as the ship tilted, and righted, and spun. He was shouting something and finally the words formed into meaning in Turner's brain.

"Yulio has her! Look mate! Yulio has her!"

It was so. Yulio was handing her up and Nadya and the Banpiro made a chain to haul her onboard. "Get below!" Nadya commanded everyone. "Get below before we roll."

It was not easy. The ship seemed about to capsize and Turner didn't take his eyes off of Aiela until they had her below decks.

She muttered and struggled as they laid her down on a narrow bench.

"Shhh. It is good now." Nadya soothed, bundling dry blankets around Aiela, wiping her face with a towel. "It is fine. You are safe, Drey's daughter. You are safe. Turner, come here to her. She needs the familiar..." Nadya waved him to Aiela's side, turning up a light.

Aiela opened golden eyes and stared up at him.

The End

EPILOGUE

ZIEL

I found them in Meihal's wild, magnificent home, and the light of my legacy shone from their eyes.

"I still wonder," Ahna was saying, "if Ziel was wrong about us."

Ah. Here was what had summoned me.

Aiela chewed her porridge in silence, staring at her sister with those deep eyes that had seen too much, and knew more because of it. They sat alone in the warmth of the Irish-manor kitchen. It was early morning and gale force winds still shoved against the solid stone walls, whistling and moaning through window cracks and pipes.

It had taken them half a moon to reach Ireland's shores, even with Nadya's virtually indestructible ship, and some of the world's best sailors aboard. The impact of three main pieces from the Second

Moon had unleashed the equivalent of a planetary cyclone that circled and destroyed in chain reactions. Plus, the Crystal's powerful surges that simply vaporized matter. Earthquakes caused volcanoes, whose heat melted glaciers, which flooded landmasses and joined the tsunami waves already displacing the oceans. Ash blocked the sun in unpredictable patterns of hurricane-force winds, which flash-froze other parts of the continents.

The twins didn't yet know the breadth of the cataclysm. It was a miracle they weren't in the depths of the sea. My miracle. The prophecy wasn't done with them yet.

Aiela's reply came slow. "I still wonder if we'd have done it—sacrificed our home—would he have let us?"

"Of course I wouldn't have let you!"

Ahna's focus was first to fasten sharply on me. "Ziel?!"

Aiela's followed in less than a human heartbeat. "You're really here! Look at you! All golden and shining." Her voice grew thick with emotion and Ahna's eyes were overly bright.

"That wasn't at all what I had in mind for saving Atlantis." I began, "Which is probably why I had to die. I would've hindered you, possibly outright *prevented* you."

"So… you think we did the right thing?" Ahna's voice held so many doubts, it nearly melted my resolve. I was determined not to tell them too much, now that I had an eagle-eye view of earth's timelines.

"Yes. It was the best-case scenario. I just couldn't have seen it—wouldn't have even considered it—from my limited *human* perspective. There was a certain, shall we say, bravado of youth that was required, to stop what was going to rip the planet apart, thereby crippling the solar system, affecting far more universal life than you could even comprehend right now." I chuckled, " What you did put a few dents in earth certainly—but the damage was contained here."

There were quite literally dents in the earth now.

"You still think we're the 'One' of the prophecy then?" Ahna's mind was trying to take in my messages, laden as they were with visuals.

"More than ever." I let them feel the depths of my great affection for them.

Their relief fell like rain-tears as they received it.

AIELA

There were still days Aiela lived inside of a fog. "Will I ever be myself again?" She asked Ahna.

Ahna shook her head. "We all left parts of ourselves behind. But you should be thankful. You're actually *more* than you used to be—just, the new parts are unfamiliar."

"I wish I could be thankful."

Doing healing work helped. She still loved that, and her senses had all heightened and sharpened, both a gift and challenge of the changes in her. At first it served to distract her from the pain of so much loss, but then it brought comfort, peace, and even hope.

There was no shortage of patients. While Ahna, Carver and Turner worked to clear and rebuild, Aiela and Auntie Sage made their rounds, healing, medicating, educating. Gathering supplies where they could.

"Nadya's ship repairs are doon." Turner was undressing for bed, his old quarters now theirs, in the manor house of his father. "Wi' the oceans and winds finally calming, we can sail when'er we're ready."

Aiela watched him closely. "I worry you will give up more of your dreams if you go with me, like you did with Greece. It's not fair to you. You shouldn't have to follow me—"

He took her face in his hands, pressing warm lips firmly against hers, effectively cutting short her worries. "Shhh my loove, ya misunderstand wha' ya did, makin' me 'give up my dreams'." His curls were long, falling into earnest brown eyes. "Sure an' ya likely saved my life! We havena yet heard a word froom Greece. Mam's expectin' the worst... "

"I know." It was sometimes difficult not to blame herself.

"Guess you better say your goodbyes then." She grinned at Turner as they rolled into bed together. "And here I thought the next time I'd arrive on Irish shores would be for a ceremony. Our ceremony. I distinctly remember you *going on* about wanting to have babies with me, and how your parents would 'ne'er forgive ya if ya didn't follow tradition o' wedding here'." Her voice had turned playful, mimicking his accent, though this had been on her mind more seriously the last few days. Should they go ahead and have their ceremony? How long might it be before they passed this way again?

Turner was shaking his head, eyes creased and sparkling with delight. "No' withoot flowers. Ya practically spit... em... indignation when I called ya a lily that night we came here fer the welcome feast. Do ya remember? But I *like* flowers an' I'm no ashamed o' it! I willna wed ya until we can be surrounded wi' them, floating, *drowning* in the verdant green o' my glorious isle again. Yer my moon goddess and I promised ya a fittin' celebration. Still... " he nuzzled her neck, lips nipping lower. "... it's plenty a'right wi' me if the babies come first."

Aiela laughed aloud. "My brawny Irish lover loves flowers. Figures." She relaxed into his arousing touch. There'd been so little time for love making, so little emotional capacity. "Auntie Sage will have to assist with a certain little procedure before babies can happen though." She felt a bulky shoulder shrug under her roaming hand and he lifted his mouth from her nipple.

"We should prob'ly practice though—joost ta be safe. Makin' babies takes practice surely..."

AHNA

Nadya, Yulio and the other two Banpiro embraced their people fiercely. Tears ran. Conversation surged and flowed like the swollen rivers around them.

Though Ahna did not understand much of their language, the emotions were all too familiar. *We'd long ago given you up for dead. Your return brings much-needed joy. I love you. I missed you. With you, we are once again complete.*

Carver, Turner and Aiela stood with her in a clump, trying to stay out of the way, eyes wide as they took in this strange land so unexpectedly full of people.

Leonesse had been situated around a large lake. Now, only the top of towers poked out of the water, far from where the lake's expanded edges lapped at old buildings and ruined flower gardens. Ahna recognized traces of Atlantis here—even after the cataclysm had its violent way—in the old-world shapes of stone architecture, the neat hedgerows and intricate patterns of cobble-laid streets. Statuary were broken and battered, missing heads or limbs. Columns were cracked and pitted. A scatter of fancy metal spires atop their buildings had survived, though most bowed and twisted like filigree jewelry gone awry.

"These are my friends." Nadya was bringing her Banpiro family to meet them. "Here are Ahna and Aiela, the daughters of the great man Drey who saved my life. Here are the men they love. And over there," she pointed to Sage and Charis who were off plucking and sniffing the strange bushes and grasses, "are more of Drey's family."

Each of her family bowed the traditional greeting of Atlantis to the four of them. Then, one by one, the Banpiro stopped in front of Aiela, stared deep into her gold-flecked eyes, then planted a kiss on her forehead. Nothing was said, but Ahna felt the energy of it. They were acknowledging Aiela as part of them.

"Two of these are healers and will help us repair the humans." Nadya continued, "But come, let us go into our home and prepare them food. They are hungry by now." Her family smiled politely at them all, and indicated they should go before them, following Nadya inside of a stone house that would've dwarfed Meihal's.

For all its damage, Leonesse was packed, overflowing with refugees. People fleeing the flooded lowlands of northern England, people whose homes had collapsed from wind and earthquakes, or been washed entirely away, their foundations erased underwater, far from any haphazardly redrawn shorelines. Some of these people were from other continents and had somehow survived the erratic currents and roving tsunami waves, to eventually wash ashore—anywhere there *was* a shore. Many of them had wandered until they found some sort of surviving civilization. Or were found by them.

With their enhanced senses the Banpiro had rescued thousands. Then opened their once-gilded homes, sorting, sheltering and feeding survivors of all colors and kinds. They were a solemn people, intelligent and even aristocratic, but kind.

Banpiro were also beautiful. Every bit as beautiful as Atlanteans.

Tall and healthy, with a radiance that bespoke their zest for life.

"Thank you kindly for the meal, Nadya." Auntie Sage had a hand over her stomach. "I ate too much of it! Shall we get going, making the rounds to see who needs care the most?" They'd brought all the healing crystals, herbs and other accoutrements they could carry from the ship. "Aiela, you take Charis and Turner with you. Ahna, you and Carver come with me. We'll need translators… "

And so they began the long, sweaty, often heartbreaking work of helping those damaged by the fall of Atlantis. At times, it would seem endless to Ahna. But there did in fact, come an end. Both to the healing work, and their time in Leonesse.

"We should probably visit the places we sent evacuees, particularly those who took cargo from the Restricted Archives." Aiela's booted feet dangled off the newly built dock. Night was falling. They watched fish jump at bugs skittering across the lake's surface, a sign of the earth beginning to calm.

"Starting with Alexandria?" Ahna watched the sky turned pastel.

"Starting with Alexandria."

Nadya, Yulio, and a few others went with them as guides, helpers and protection.

It was there in Alexandria, after hiding the most dangerous knowledge and records, installing protective devices to ward off those who'd misuse it, that Sage had her grand idea.

"We must find a way to pass along this knowledge. It shouldn't completely die out. And yet, it must be protected. It is sacred—even more so, with Atlantis gone."

"It is a mystery to the rest of the world." Charis added. "And it will become ever more mysterious as time goes along."

"We'll plant schools." Sage decided. "Small and hidden groups that study the sacred mysteries. This is the perfect place to start." She smiled. "Thoth can help us. It'll begin here and spread out."

SEVEN MOONS PASSED at the speed of light, and then another seven. They'd travelled enough to understand the devastation wrought. And to ensure the safety of their sacred knowledge, hidden and protected by those who had volunteered to serve this purpose.

They had set sail again, this time from Egypt, and been weeks at sea, when Ahna began to crave a home. Having Carver at her side, watching Aiela's joy return in fits and starts, while Turner's solid cheerfulness and natural restlessness buoyed them, was the only home she had left.

Carver mourned his brothers still. "I know the odds are small that they escaped." He leaned on the ship railing beside Ahna, staring at the sandy southern shoreline of Merika. "If they did, I think they'd come here. You can't imagine how much the water is covering! Our Mutazio camps and crystal mines... all underwater now." This grief was unexpected to both of them.

"Do you think it would have changed them?" Ahna asked. He'd told her so many stories of growing up, partly because he didn't have to hide them anymore. It was a healing, a sort of purge.

"I'd hope so." He straightened and pulled her to him.

Her ear lay perfectly over his heart and she listened to the steady beat, reflecting the splash of waves against the ship's hull.

TURNER—LATE SPRING OF 9,968 BCE. ONE AND A HALF YEARS AFTER THE CATACLYSM.

He waited, eyes roaming, restless and impatient. Where was she?

The sky wasn't blue, but neither was it spitting rain. Thankfully. Mist softened the edges of the stone circle that Turner's five times great-grandda had built. It marked the summit of a hill—a rise, more truthfully—marking seasons and ages by the star paths overhead.

The mist turned everything a green that glowed and pulsated, infusing the surrounding trees, bushes and grasses with life itself. A green that looked like velvet, Turner decided, like layers and layers of—

"Shall we start then?" Aiela strode into the stone circle and he forgot to breathe.

She wore a simple gown of purple silk, embroidered with swirling vines and tiny flowers. Her shoulders were bare, tanned by moons of sailing, arms shapely with muscle. Around both biceps she wore flashing silver bands studded with jewels that matched the sparkling diadem around her temple. A single teardrop amethyst dangled on her forehead and her long blackberry braids was arranged in artistic piles above it. He grinned then, realizing there were flowers, tiny white lily of the valley stems, fragrant and sweet, tucked into her hair.

"Ya came." He said wonderingly. "I worried ya may've changed yer mind."

"Do you *know* how long it took to find these?" She pointed at the delicate blossoms. "If I'd known you already had plenty of flowers... " Aiela looked around the stone circle, eyes growing wide at the elaborate garlands, the bouquets taller than Turner himself.

He smiled, proud that he'd kept his promise... in excess—thanks mostly to Mam. He'd mentioned their plans—and his wish to make vows amidst oceans of flowers. She'd had a year and a half to cultivate them.

"But I didna have valley lilies." He reached for her hand. "Our guests're going ta head on back ta the feast wi' oot us if we keep them waiting any loonger. You go first."

Aiela's gaze again travelled the circle, lined with people they both loved.

Auntie Sage already had tears flowing freely, but she was beaming too. Around her were Aiela's childhood teachers Mia and Nate, and the much-loved meditation tutor Zan. Charis stood with other High City guests, among them Frond, Rizelle and Lira.

Turner grinned at Kinny and Colin, grouped with his family, large and sprawling and taking up most of the space. Jai was whispering nonstop to Felicia, Nirka and Nadya.

"Thank you for coming to witness and celebrate our ceremony today." Aiela began simply. All eyes focused on her as she turned to offer him both of her hands. "I've decided to take this one as my life mate. And luckily, he agreed." Laughter flowed around the circle as Ahna stepped up beside them. She too wore purple, to honor her sister.

She handed Aiela a ring and then spoke formally. "Turner, I give my sister into your family, and welcome you into ours. With this joining, we become one family, united in loving you both." She looked at the other Atlanteans and nodded. They all stepped forward and joined hands, forming a smaller circle around Aiela and himself.

"We pledge support of your bond through friendship, honesty, and loyalty." The Atlanteans responded, "So it is." and bowed as one, before stepping back to rejoin the greater circle.

Standing on tiptoe, Ahna kissed his cheek. He embraced her tightly, touched by her words, this new sister of his.

"Turner," Aiela said, once Ahna retreated to stand with Carver. "You've been with me long before we physically met, and no doubt, long before this lifetime. But it was you, in this personhood and this body and this personality, that I began to fall for as soon as we met. Our attraction has been strong and our friendship stronger. But our love is a choice, a bond that we enter into, knowing it will stand when attraction and friendship fails. I *feel* love for you, but I will *choose* to love you even when I don't feel it. That is the vow I make to you now, for this lifetime. And so that neither of us forgets this vow, I give you this ring to remind us." She slid the ring onto the fourth finger of his left hand.

It was silver. Thick and smooth, it had two beautiful engravings of the Celtic double infinity knot that symbolized the interconnectedness of all life in the universe, with the love knot centering them. He wondered where she'd gotten such a finely crafted thing, but then he spied Nadya with her Banpiro, and knew.

"This is your heart finger." Aiela explained. "May I ever attend kindly to your heart, respecting and caring for it as though it were my own."

Turner nodded solemnly, feeling as though he might burst with happiness—and hoping to respond without bursting into tears. "I accept yer vow, and this han'some ring symbol." His voice shook, but he managed to grin into those big gold-flecked eyes.

"Mam? Da? All my family, will ya join us fer a wee bit?" They closed around him and Aiela. "Carver?" He tried to peer between the bodies of his many family members. "Carver? I'd ask ya ta join us too."

"I'm here." Carver's black head stood taller at the backs of the Irish, and they opened their circle to include him.

Satisfied, he turned to his mother. "Mam, I'm takin' a mate! E'en though ya said I'd niver stand still long enough." Laughter rang from the circle, and Diaedra's pretty face split into a wide smile. Meihal slid an arm around her. "I'd ask you and Da ta accept Aiela here, the bonniest girl I could find, as yer new daughter, and my sisters and cousins ta hear me declare; she's one o' us now."

As if on cue, every one of his family members brought forth a white flower, holding it high. There were long calla lilies, bright tiger lilies, and spring lilies as big as a face. One by one, starting with Mam and Da, they offered Aiela a lily and welcomed her to the family. Her eyes brimmed with tears but she was laughing as she returned the bows and hugs.

When they'd returned to their places, she stood with her arms full of lilies, bunched into a bouquet, and he grinned triumphantly at her. "I still think yer pretty as a lily flower. Prettier."

Only Carver remained. He held out a ring, and Turner took it, but grasped Carver's forearm too. "Yer my brother now. So I'd ask ya ta welcome my new mate inta the family as well."

Carver couldn't speak. So he simply nodded and bent to kiss Aiela's cheek. She reached a hand up to touch his jaw, whispering "Thank you brother."

The ring was a solid band of fiery red orichalcum from her home-land, set with a pure white moonstone the size of her thumbnail.

"Ayella." the mist seemed to move into his eyes as he began. "My Moon Goddess. Yeh were a bit daft an' covered wi' blood when we met." He leaned back to look her up and down, regal in her finery. "I'd say I improved ya."

More laughter came and she rolled her eyes, shaking her head. His tone grew serious. "But I was lost back then—an' now I'm found. I've been on the wrong side o' death an' it was you who brought me back. Time an again, ya've proved ya'd fight the de'il himself ta keep me." He paused, solemn. "Some folks might call that desperate..." Aiela narrowed her eyes, "... but I call it, bein' born th' loockiest Irishman there e'er was, ta have ya savin' me, or wantin' me, or lovin' me. Sure an' I'm glad ta give ya my loove for this lifetime—and it seems too little. I'd give it to ya fer many." He slid the ring onto her finger. "This here's a symbol o' my love fer ya. I vow ta cherish ya, provide fer ya, serve ya, and protect ya fer as long as we both shall live."

She kissed him. Long and deep, with the huge bouquet of lilies crushed between their bodies, wafting fragrance and pollen. Turner considered it the scent of heaven.

The feasting and dancing lasted nearly 'til dawn.

CARVER—LATE AUTUMN OF 9,968 BCE.

You'd think the world would've stopped turning, losing so many lives. Carver thought. Entire cities and villages had disappeared.

Where ice ages had frozen portions of the continents, entire civilizations were gone. Of the many places they'd visited—staying and working, rebuilding, teaching, healing, learning—no family had been left whole. Everyone had lost loved ones.

But he'd been lucky. He'd recently found a loved one.

Here in these lonely islands off Scotland's northern coast, he'd found Orja.

"How did you end up here?" Carver held her hand. It felt delicate as a bird wing and Orja seemed frail, so thin and aged, he'd almost passed right by without recognizing her in this seaside town. He supported her as they walked to the little stone cottage she shared with a widowed mother and her three small children.

"It was the last place on earth Mardu would ever look." Orja smiled up at him, stopping to pat his cheek again. She kept touching him, staring at him, barely believing he was really here. He knew exactly how she felt.

"You're smarter than he ever knew." Carver smiled fondly at her. "And the only one I loved in that house."

"I'm sorry about... " he paused, unable to find the right words to finish the thought. How does one possibly apologize for all those unpaid years of servitude?

Orja squeezed his hand. "You're the only son I'll ever have." Her eyes were bright and dark as a bird. "I loved your brothers too, but they're gone. You are what's left to me—the best of them. I'm glad to know you lived."

Turner, Aiela, Carver and Ahna had decided to settle here and make a home, with frequent trips to visit Auntie Sage in Egypt, Nadya in England, and Ireland of course. They'd nearly stayed in Greece. Protected as it was, from the worst of the cataclysm, it quickly became the world's new center. Many surviving Atlanteans had journeyed there to live with extended family. With such an influx, the Grecian cities and islands had flourished. But Ahna struggled with all the energies, and Aiela wanted to be somewhere they could be more of service. Somewhere to forge a new life without being reminded each day of their lost home.

They built simple houses with the help of the natives, and Carver built a special cottage for Orja.

"You have many other things to attend to." She would scold him when he came to see her, bringing food or trinkets, almost every day.

"It is my joy to care for you," he argued gently back, "to give you the peaceful life you deserve. You cared for me all those years."

She accepted with a simple smile. "It is happy, this life you give me."

AHNA FOUND THE BEACH FIRST. "It's very like the one by Benandon-ner's Castle." She was running, dragging him along, breathless with excitement. "Hurry. I'm not sure how high the tide gets.

There were cliffs forming a cove. But this one had fine white sand, and an ocean as clear and blue as gemstones. Arms spread wide, she twirled. "See? Doesn't it remind you of *the night?*"

He laughed. Ahna always referred to their first night of love-making as '*the night*'. It seemed so long ago.

She bent over, studying and then picking up shells. Carver was soon lost in collecting too, and they began building little cairns. "Look." She held out a heart-shaped pebble, tumbled smooth by an eon of currents. "I give you my tiny stone heart."

That's when the idea came to him. He'd been waiting for the perfect time—and a meaningful place.

IT WAS JUST BEFORE SUNSET, three days later when he brought her back. "Wear something pretty." He said. "We're going to have *another night.*"

The gown was cream-colored, thin and soft, hugging her curves. Her hair had lightened to a bright glow over the summer, and she carried a basket of food. Carver brought two large blankets. Everything else he needed was already there.

She whooped with delight when she saw it and raced him to get there. "Even the driftwood is beautiful! Where did you get all this? When did you do it?"

He'd not only made piles of driftwood, he'd set up poles decorated in flowers, with lanterns hanging from them. There was a rolled mattress, stuffed with feathers. They'd lean against it to enjoy the fire, and unroll it later...

Carver had kept pace with her, despite his limp. "I'd hoped to make vows with you." She went very still, staring up at him with those green eyes, staying silent so long he looked away. "If you don't want to... we don't have to... "

"Carver." She laid a hand over his heart. "There's only one way I'll do this."

"Yes, if you want Aiela and Turner here, I can go get them, I had thought it might be nice for it to be private, just you and me, but—"

"That's not the one thing..." She interrupted, drawing out the silence again. "Sing to me. If you had a dulcimer, it'd be even better but I won't ask what you can't give. Just sing to me."

"A lifetime of your love for a song? Deal." Grinning with relief, Carver led her to the line where the water stretched in lacy scallops to wet the sand.

Taking her hands, he kissed her light and quick. "You ready?" The sky was alight with the first colors as he began, "Ahna, you are what love means to me, you are what life means to me, and I vow to be your friend, your lover, and whatever else you need me to be. I vow to love you for as long as you'll let me."

"Very nice." She nodded solemnly. "Pretty words from a pretty man. My turn."

"Carver, I've never seen such beautiful hands as yours. Should you lose your hands, or disfigure them, these vows are null and void." Her smile was jaunty and he laughed, pulling her to him. She spoke the rest of her vows against his heart. "I will love you and care for you, honor and treasure you. Always. Always and forever." They shared a long kiss to seal the deal.

"Now sit." He commanded. "Hurry while the colors are bright. I want this moment to be perfect."

From beside the mattress he removed a pack, and from it pulled a dulcimer. He wished it was battered and black. But he'd searched long and wide for this one and worked hard to get it playable. He was grateful to have it.

Ahna had a hand covering her mouth. "You found one?! I can't... can't believe it!"

He was already strumming. Opening wide to the music of a Scottish beach, under stars just beginning to light up, he sang.

If I were a sculptor, it'd take a lifetime, just to copy your form.
Perfection in your curves, that silky satin skin,
and how would I make it so delicately warm?

If I were a painter, I'd paint a thousand pictures,
trying to tell the story of you.
But there's not enough colors, no there's not enough palettes
And I wouldn't come close to capturing your truth.

I'm just a lonely singer, not a sculptor, nor a painter,
So entranced by your beauty that I want to make it art.
But all I can offer are my words set to music singing
You are forever in my heart.

You are forever in my heart.
And you'll be forever in my heart.

ACKNOWLEDGMENTS

To all our Friends and Family, who've nearly forgotten who we are while we worked like some sort of hermit bees to publish the entire trilogy at once; Bless you. It can't be easy being our people. But we're back—for a little while at least. Until the next series...

We love you each and every one. You've been our encouragers, muses, models, critiquers and inspirations.

Thank You to Readers

Hands together at the heart, we offer a deep and flourishing bow to each one of you, our beloved readers, who've hung on for the ride until the very end. Sorry for the heartless killing of wonderful characters. Let's blame it on Mardu.

Without your uproarious imagination and invested emotions, this story would only be words on a page. Our sincerest gratitude for bringing it all to life.

If you enjoyed this series, please leave us a review wherever you purchased it, and/or on Goodreads. Your rating and words powerfully influence potential readers, and the mysterious algorithms of online marketplaces.

We would love to connect with you. Visit us at www.ddadair.com, and follow us on our Facebook page (ddadair) for future book releases, important announcements, random happenings, and book signing events.

Much Love and Many Blessings.
   Donna and Diana

BIBLIOGRAPHY

Though we read every book and article we could find on Atlantis—or any other ancient advanced civilizations that might relate to Atlantis, the following were the most impactful, with data points that repeated. These are the books or articles we'd most recommend.

Andrews, S 2004, *Lemuria and Atlantis; Studying the Past to Survive the Future,* Llewellyn Publications, Woodbury, MN.

Andrews, S 1997, *Atlantis: Insights from a Lost Civilization,* Llewellyn Publications, St. Paul, MN.

Cannon, D 1992, *Jesus and the Essenes.* Gateway Books, Bath, UK

Cannon, D 2001, *The Convoluted Universe: Book One,* Ozark Mountain Publishing Inc., Huntsville, AR.

Cannon, D 2005, *The Convoluted Universe: Book Two,* Ozark Mountain Publishing Inc., Huntsville, AR.

Cannon, D 2008, *The Convoluted Universe: Book Three*, Ozark Mountain Publishing Inc., Huntsville, AR.

Cannon, D 2011, *The Convoluted Universe: Book Four*, Ozark Mountain Publishing Inc., Huntsville, AR.

Cannon, D 2015, *The Convoluted Universe: Book Five*, Ozark Mountain Publishing Inc., Huntsville, AR.

Cannon, D 2014, *The Search for Sacred Hidden Knowledge*, Ozark Mountain Publishing Inc., Huntsville, AR.

Cannon, D 2012, *Keepers of the Garden*, Ozark Mountain Publishing Inc., Huntsville, AR.

Cayce, E 1968, *On Atlantis*, Hawthorne Books, NY, NY.

Donnelly, I 1882, rev. 1976, *Atlantis: The Antediluvian World*, Dover Publications Inc. NY, NY.

Hancock, G 1995, *Fingerprints of the Gods*, Three Rivers Press, NY, NY.

Hancock, G 2015, *Magicians of the Gods*, St. Martin's Press, NY, NY.

Michell, J 2013, *The New View Over Atlantis*, 3rd Edition, Hampton Roads Publishing Company, Charlottesville, VA.

Santesson, H.S. 1972, *Understanding Mu*, 2nd Edition, Coronet Communications, Inc. NY, NY.

Tyberonn, J 2010, *AA Metatron Channel: 'Revisiting Atlantis: The Crystalline Field of 10-10-10'*, https://atlara.wordpress.com.

Wilson, C and Flem-Ath, R 2008, *The Atlantis Blueprint: Unlocking the Ancient Mysteries of a Long-Lost Civilization*, Delta Trade Paperbacks,

Wilson, S and Prentis, J 2011 *Atlantis and the New Consciousness,* Ozark Mountain Publishing Inc. Huntsville, AR

ABOUT THE AUTHOR

Author Bio

Sisters Donna (Adair) McMurtry and Diana Adair, were trekking up Colorado mountains or soaking in hot mineral springs while they plotted the Golden Age Series. Atlantis, and other periods of history, have been a long-time obsession and over 10 years of research went into their first series. Luckily, being Quantum Healers who specialize in past life regression hypnotherapy, they can access history first-hand" so there's many more stories to come!

They both live in the wild west. Diana has built her own tiny home in the mountains with her partner and two big hairy dogs. She loves trail-running and climbing fourteeners. Donna writes, hikes, and plays in her own mountain paradise with husband, two nearly grown sons, and two dogs.

Together they're known for hugging trees, constantly plotting future stories, and occasionally podcasting. (thespiralpath.podbean.com)

facebook.com/ddadair

amazon.com/author/ddadair

ALSO BY DD ADAIR

Golden Age Series Book 1; Colors of Atlantis

Golden Age Series Book 2; Shadows of Atlantis

Golden Age Series Book 3; Atlantis Moirai

www.ingramcontent.com/pod-product-compliance
Lightning Source LLC
Chambersburg PA
CBHW030927260626
47169CB00002B/396